TRAILER TRAMP

Her mind and her body were co
know what she was doing. She sh
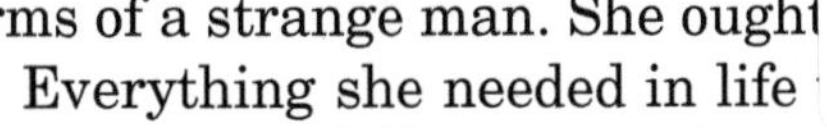
arms of a strange man. She ought

Everything she needed in life
very moment. Life was music and this man and her body—its desires. Life was now, this instant!

TRAILER CAMP WOMAN

Hank wanted this smooth, sophisticated woman, wanted her badly. He wanted to kiss her, make vicious, violent love to her, taste the passion she obviously held locked beneath the veneer of high class manners. He wanted to make her bow to his every whim and command. And finally, he wanted to possess her.

That was Hank Mitchell. Any woman, once his, became nothing but a thing to him, a body he'd enjoyed. And he was determined to enjoy this woman, so different from anyone he'd known . . .

LOVE CAMP ON WHEELS

She had no reason to think Stan would want a permanent attachment to grow out of having shared a motel room with her for a couple of hours. She knew that men came fully equipped with a built-in double standard.

A good woman simply did not go to bed with a man because that was the thing she wanted to do. Not in the good old U.S.A. American women were supposed to come antiseptically sealed in cellophane and mounted on a wholesome split-level pedestal. Then, as if inhibitions were turned on and off at the flick of a switch, they were expected to bring their husbands all the know-how of a street walker . . .

TRAILER TRAMPS

A Beacon Books Trio

Trailer Tramp

by Orrie Hitt

Trailer Camp Woman

by Doug Duperrault

Love Camp On Wheels

by Tom Harland

Introduction

by

Jeff Vorzimmer

Stark House Press • Eureka California

TRAILER TRAMPS: A BEACON BOOKS TRIO
Published by Stark House Press
1315 H Street
Eureka, CA 95501
griffinskye3@sbcglobal.net
www.starkhousepress.com

ISBN: 979-8-88601-057-2

Cover & text design by Jeff Vorzimmer, ¡caliente!design, Austin, Texas

First Stark House Press Edition: May 2023

LOVE . . . ON WHEELS

From the perspective of the twenty-first century, some of the sub-genres of 1950s sleaze fiction, often referred to as "mid-century erotica" in recent years, might seem odd. One of these is the trailer park novel, which, like another sub-genre from the same time period, the swamp novel, shares the common theme of loose women from the lower strata of society.

In the context of post-World War II life, though, it isn't all that surprising. Although mobile homes had been around for decades by the 1950s, it wasn't until GI's returned from the war and faced a housing shortage—brought on by the slowdown in home building during the war—that the demand was fueled for quickly-manufactured, low-income housing.

For veterans whose college education had been interrupted by the war and who were now taking advantage of the GI Bill, the mobile home provided less expensive housing than a house with a mortgage.

The atmosphere of trailer parks was more transitory in nature, quite literally, and less staid than traditional neighborhoods. The residents of trailer parks often tended to be young married, still childless, couples that so often leads to a swinging, more sexually-charged atmosphere.

Like the new subdivisions that were also proliferating at a rapid rate in the late 1940s and 50s, the trailer parks developed a reputation as havens of iniquity. There were rumors of rampant extramarital affairs and wife-swapping in the form of the notorious "key parties," all of which were enthusiastically chronicled in the pages of the men's magazines that also began to proliferate in the mid-1950s.

The gradual loosening of sexual mores of the decade also lead to the rise of risqué paperbacks for sale at newsstands, drugstores and bus stations. Previously taboo subjects and otherwise uncomfortable topics were the subject of these salacious paperbacks with their lurid covers.

They tackled subjects like juvenile delinquency, adultery, homosexuality, incest, organized crime, and drugs, often under the guise of providing a service by bringing it to the attention of the American public, presumably to shock them into writing to their congressman or taking the matter up with their local school board. But, of course, the publishers were just interested in selling books.

These paperbacks definitely supplied the goods. Whether or not the story lines had any basis in reality is another matter. Generally the books about trailer parks, and the women of questionable morals therein, could easily identified by the obvious use of "trailer" in the title or ". . . on wheels" and "woman," "girl," "tramp" or "trollop."

Two novels, though, that featured "wheels" in the title, *Wantons on Wheels* and *Women on Wheels* were about women in the roller derby. Another novel with the title *Sin on Wheels* was about a driving school that apparently also taught sex education on the side. Interestingly, another book with the same title *was* about life in a trailer park *and* written by the same author, Robert Silverberg, employing two different pseudonyms—Don Elliott, for the former, Loren Beauchamp for the latter.

Women were almost always the focus of the trailer park novel, and more often than not, these women were lesbians or bisexual, touching on two sub-genres of the time. They definitely could be considered primarily lesbian novels . . . on wheels.

Occasionally there are exceptions to be found, the title likely changed by a publisher trying to cash on the trailer park novel craze. A good example is Glen Canary's *The Trailer Park Girls*, which is essentially a heist novel with the characters, the three men planning it and the three women they involve, living in a trailer park.

The three novels contained herein, all published by Beacon, are fairly representative of the sub-genre and all have lesbian themes and all of them portray lesbians in a somewhat positive light, which wasn't always the case with 1950s and 60s paperbacks.

Jeff Vorzimmer
Austin, Texas
Valentine's Day 2023

TRAILER TRAMP

Orrie Hitt

Part One

Hell On Wheels

1

The long house trailer was mired in the mud all the way up to the wheel hubs.

"Well, there's no sense fooling around with it any more," Joan Baker told Mr. Perkins. As she looked up at the black sky, the cold, slanting rain struck her in the face. "You jack up one side and the other just goes down again."

"So what do you want me to do with it?" Mr. Perkins demanded. "Dig another hole and bury it?"

"No. I thought I'd call a wrecker from town."

"At this time of the night?"

"I think Jim Birdsell would come."

Mr. Perkins straightened with an effort. He was quite fat and rather short. His face, revealed in the glare from the flashlight in Joan's hand, was covered with streaks of brown and yellow clay.

"Probably charge me twenty bucks, wouldn't he?"

Joan sighed. She hadn't even ought to bother with Mr. Perkins; it was his own stupid fault that his trailer was stuck in the mud. The sign at the mouth of the cut-off was very plain: no trailers. Mr. Perkins was the second one within two weeks who had ignored the sign. Some day, Joan supposed, she ought to put a fence across the road.

"It's all right," Joan said. "I'll pay for it, Mr. Perkins."

"You will! Well, why didn't you say so before?"

She laughed. "I wasn't quite so wet before, I guess. And I was a little provoked at you. I didn't have that sign put up for the heck of it."

"Sorry."

They started walking toward the highway. "Just remember the Beachlake Trailer Camp the next time you're passing through," Joan said. "And tell your friends about us."

"Why, sure."

Lightning crept across the sky and thunder boomed through the hills. The rain began to descend in torrents.

They reached the highway and swung left, in the direction of the big red-and-white trailer Joan used for an office and living quarters. Her dark hair, she knew, was matted to her head in angry, natural curls. She could feel the water running down off her face and dripping into the cleft between her breasts. Her brassiere was soaked and very tight; she wished she could take the thing off and throw it away. And down below that she was soaked, too. The next time, she thought, when she got panties she would get a larger size. Lord, the way she sat around these days she must be all of thirty-eight across the beam.

"You think this fellow will come out, Miss Baker?"

"He will if he's in."

The man glanced back over his shoulder at her.

His face appeared both weary and desperate.

"I sure hope he is." He stepped into a mud puddle and stumbled. "Damn magazine business, anyway! Always getting transferred."

Joan circled the puddle and said nothing. Perkins had been at the camp only two weeks—or had it been longer than that—and had kept pretty much to himself. She had seen him a couple of times, when he'd stopped by to leave his rent, but she had paid very little attention to him. With more than four hundred trailers at the camp she seldom indulged in the luxury of being curious about one person. As it was, there were too many things for her to do. Luke, she supposed, was right—she ought to have a full-time assistant to help out. She smiled and felt the rain strike her parted lips. Luke, of course, had been speaking for himself. But this, she reflected bitterly, had been before Nora. After Nora everything had changed. Nora Justin had walked into Luke's life and Joan had walked right out.

"Looks like you've got business," Perkins said to her as they approached the floodlights. "And on a night like this!"

Joan's own trailer was dwarfed by the huge double-decker parked alongside it. A double-decker, Joan thought, usually meant a large family. Generally, the family would be loaded with money and the husband and wife would insist on a plot with lake frontage. Actually, Joan hated double-decker trailers. A double-decker always reminded her of the Curtis family and of Joe Curtis in particular. Joe had caused a near riot when he had, one moonlit night, crept into her bedroom. Joe, she remembered, had mistaken her professional smile of friendliness for a smile of invitation. After that, she hadn't smiled at the male population of the camp quite so frequently or so warmly. Also, she had stopped wearing shorts and halters, even though they were much more comfortable than dresses. She had decided, after the Curtis episode, that she should be more subtle in her dealings with the men.

"You'd better come in," she said to Mr. Perkins as she opened the door of the trailer. "You can wait in here out of the rain and watch television if you want."

Mr. Perkins waved for her to enter first and she stepped inside. He grunted as she stopped suddenly and he slammed into her.

"Sorry," he mumbled.

The man standing in the center of the office was gigantic. Joan thought, looking up at him, that she had seldom seen a man so huge. His young freckled face, beneath a shock of unruly red hair, smiled down at her.

"Hi," he said. "Know where I can find the boss?"

"I'm the boss," Joan said.

He nodded approvingly as his glance drifted down over the wet lines of her dress. She began to wish that she hadn't given up wearing shorts and halters. The way the thin dress clung to her made her feel like an obscene picture.

The big man grinned. "In another couple of minutes you'd have needed a life preserver." He paused, listening to the rain on the top of the trailer. "You figure it to stop?"

"I suppose so. It always does."

His grin widened. "I guess I asked for that," he said. Then, "What are your rates here?"

"Twenty-five a month, or ten a week. There's no extra charge for sewer, power or water hook-ups. Swimming and fishing are permitted in the lake."

"Sounds okay. Have you got any room?"

She crossed to the location map which hung on the farther wall. Her small finger pointed out several areas.

"Nothing right on the lake," she told him. "Perhaps, later, if your family should like to be near the beach we could—"

"I don't have a family. Just myself."

Surprised, Joan turned and faced him. "My apology," she said. "I just thought, when I saw that double-decker, that you wouldn't be traveling alone."

The redhead shrugged. "It isn't a double any more. I ripped out the upper rooms to give myself more head space." He laughed. "I use it for my headquarters—I'm the engineer with the new pipe line coming through—and I walk around a lot. You've got no idea the complex a fellow can develop if he thinks he's going to crack his head against the ceiling at any moment."

"Oh. I see."

She got a card from the desk and watched while he registered.

"Mike Summers," he said. "Some people call me Big Mike."

"Do you plan to stay long?"

"Several weeks. Or until we have this part of the line in. There'll be more of the gang coming tomorrow and later in the week. I hope you'll have room for them."

"I hope so, too."

"They're a good bunch, Mrs.—"

"Baker. Joan Baker. And it's Miss."

"Yes." His eyes lingered upon her face for a moment. "One other thing," he said, "have you checked in a family by the name of Collins?"

"No."

He nodded and laid two tens and a five on the desk.

"Do me a favor, please? When they arrive, place them on the opposite side of the camp, will you? The man's name is Gerald and his wife—she's very small and dark and pretty—is named Sally. They—" Mike Summers hesitated and lit a cigarette. "It would be a lot better," he added, "all the way around."

Joan assured him that she would do the best she could. Evidently tension existed between Mike Summers and the Collins family. She hoped that it wouldn't develop into another Wilkins-Channing feud. Sid Wilkins had fooled around with Channing's wife and it had required the services of the police to escort them from the camp.

"Do you have any cleaning services, Miss Baker?"

"Oh, yes! But that's five dollars a week extra."

He placed another five on the desk.

"Fine," Mike Summers said. "I'll take that, too."

"The girl's name is Millie."

"I'll try to remember that."

Mr. Perkins, who had been watching the proceedings, now came forward.

"I hate to rouse you, Miss," he said, "but that trailer of mine is still in the mud. And I should have been on the road an hour ago."

"Mud?" Mike wanted to know. "You got a swale patch here, Miss Baker?"

"Not at all. Mr. Perkins tried to take a short cut and mired himself down in a spring run-off."

The redhead frowned. "You in deep? You got any traction with your truck?"

Perkins wet his lips with his tongue. "She's down to the hubs, in back. And I'm not using a truck. I've got a new Buick."

"Crazy," the big man said. "There ought to be a law against using cars to pull trailers."

"There is, in some states," Perkins acknowledged. "But on the highway, once you get rolling, you never have any trouble. It's only times like now when you get—"

"The trailer got duals in back?"

"Why, yes."

"Hell," Mike Summers said, "we'll get you out in five minutes."

But it required somewhat longer than that, almost an hour. The redhead unhooked his International pickup from the double-decker and drove them down to the site. Then, while Joan held the flashlight for him, he cut two long dry chestnut poles with an axe, tapering an end of each so that they could be placed on the ground between the dual tires of the trailer.

"We jack up one side and shove the pole in," Mike Summers said. "Then we jack up the other and do the same thing. After that, Perkins, you get in your car and give her everything she's got. If the Buick won't haul it, the truck will."

The Buick didn't have it. All it did was roar and spin its wheels in the mud.

"Damn fancy cars," Mike Summers said.

They unhooked the Buick from the trailer but still Perkins couldn't coax the car up onto the road.

"Here," Mike said to Joan, "let's give the poor slob a shove."

She got behind the Buick and put her hands upon one of the fenders. Perkins threw his foot to the floor and the snarl of spinning tires and burning rubber filled the air.

"Impatient fool," Mike said and grasped the bumper in either hand.

Joan felt the car lift, drop, lift and drop again. Suddenly, as the tires found a solid grip, the car shot forward. With a gasp she stumbled and fell to the ground. Her breath left her in a rush as her body collided with the cold, wet mud. Some of the dirt got into her mouth and grated against her teeth.

"You all right, Miss Baker?"

Strong, gentle hands lifted her. For a moment the hands lingered, then he took them away.

"Oh, I'm just great," she stated, staring at Perkins as he came toward them through the rain. "What's a broken rib, more or less?"

Mike Summers chuckled. "I like you," he said. "You've got guts."

It took their combined efforts to get the truck hooked onto the trailer but after this was completed it was only a matter of moments before Mike hauled the trailer up onto the highway and parked it behind the Buick.

"Let that be a lesson to you," Mike told Perkins. "Buy yourself a truck and live modern."

Perkins spat at the trailer. "I'll buy me a house," he said.

A few minutes later Perkins pulled off down the road. The red and green night lights of the trailer disappeared from sight.

"Well, thank you," Joan said as they got into the truck.

"Forget it."

They drove back to the office. A new Ford stood in the parking area.

"Another bite," the redhead observed.

"No. A friend."

Or was Luke a friend? Joan wondered. How should she class a man who had made love to her and to whom she had, until recently, been engaged? Was he still a friend?

"Your block is number forty-two," she told Mike Summers, opening the door. "Drive to the right, then left at the second corner." She stepped out into the rain. "And thanks again, very much."

"Sure. You can make it up to me by doing what I asked about the Collins family. Remember, on the other side of the camp."

"I'll do my best, Mr. Summers."

"Call me Mike."

"Yes, Mike."

"Good night."

"Good night, Mike."

She opened the screen door and stepped into the trailer. Luke Miles, who had been lying upon the red leather settee, sat up. She noticed that his blue eyes were dull, his blond hair disheveled.

"Luke," she said derisively, "you're drunk."

"Naw. Not drunk. Looped."

She sighed and picked at her dress, trying to pull it loose from her skin. She wished Luke hadn't driven out tonight—she hated him when he was like this.

"Well, whatever." Her voice was mildly concerned. "Luke, why do you do it?"

"Do what?"

"Drink so much?"

His right shoulder lifted and fell. "What else is there to do?"

Joan sighed again. When Luke was like this, confused and defeated, she was almost glad that Nora Justin had come between them. Though it still hurt to remember how they had looked that night in the car.

"All right," she said, wearily. "What is it you want, Luke?"

Last week Luke had wanted money and the week before that he had wanted her. Luke, she decided as she sat down at the desk, was getting to be a problem.

"You know, Nora took that massage course. You remember me telling you about it?"

"Yes."

"Well, she's been teaching me how to do the work."

"I'll bet."

"Aw, baby, you've got a dirty mind."

She couldn't imagine why Luke was taking this tack. Nora had a massage parlor on Fulton Street, in town, and she'd been operating it for more than a year now.

"You still got that five-room Husky for rent?" Luke asked.

"I have." Joan's parents, when they left for the West, had purchased a new Rover. "Why?"

Luke stood up. He was about four inches taller than Joan and very slim.

"I hear you've got a lot of construction workers moving in. On the pipe line."

"The first one checked in tonight."

"Yeah. Well, Nora and I figured it out that these guys might be good prospects. You know, they get sore muscles and like that. We got to talking it over and we thought we'd like to rent that trailer and open up a salon out here. Sort of a branch, like. I told Nora I'd ask you how much you want."

"Sixty a month."

"Ain't that high?"

"Not when I don't think I'll get it, anyway."

Luke leered at her. "You can get it," he said. "I'll give it to you."

"Luke! You keep your hands off me!"

He laughed at her, patted her once on the shoulder and went on outside. After she heard the car start up and drive away she got up and walked back to the bedroom. She was trembling.

Damn him, she thought and threw herself flat upon the bed. Damn him, damn him! Painfully, miserably, she began to cry. She was, she knew, still a little bit in love with Luke Miles. And it wasn't good.

It was pretty much all bad.

2

The hot rays of an early morning sun splashed into the trailer. Joan came awake, felt the warmth probing her flesh and stretched languidly. What a wonderful day, she thought. What a wonderful gorgeous, beautiful day!

She heard cars leaving the camp as the men went to work in the factories and offices in town. Someone walked past the trailer, whistling. That would be Millie, she thought. Millie always whistled in the morning. Millie, Joan decided, made a habit of being happy.

Unable to go back to sleep, she rolled over on the bed and sat up. Her reflection stared back at her from the mirror.

"Everybody likes you," her father had told her once. "You can run this camp better than any of us."

Some of the men, Joan reflected, had liked her too much. There had been that retired banker, the gray-haired man with the trailer that resembled a rustic cabin, who had offered her twenty-five dollars to spend the night with him. She had acted and—really had been—shocked. The next day when he had learned she was the operator of the camp, the banker had departed in haste.

There had been others who had wanted her, too. When she was fifteen, a farmer had accosted her at the edge of his fields, on her way home from swimming in the lake. She had run from him in terror. A boy had tried to ravish her after a school dance ... and there had been plenty of others afterwards who had pressed her pretty hard ...

Luke, she thought now, had been little different, except that she had been in love with him. She had met him during college—she had wanted to be a teacher then and Luke had worked in a local gasoline station. He had followed her to the trailer camp. They had talked about marriage, even planned on it, but he had ruined it all when he had insisted that he couldn't wait.

"What's the odds?" he had demanded. "We're going to be married, aren't we? So why do we have to wait?"

He had acted so hurt by her constant refusals that she had, in desperation, promised to let him have his way. They had driven up into the hills, parked near a secluded stream, and crept into each other's arms. But at the last minute his face had not seemed Luke's. It had seemed the twisted face of the boy at the high school dance.

"I'll show you!" Luke had raged when she made him stop. "I'll show you! If I can't get it from you, I'll get it from somebody else."

She hadn't believed him, not until that night when they'd gone to the carnival and, when he was supposed to be at the dancing girl show, she had gone out to the car for a pack of Kleenex and found him on the back seat with Nora Justin.

"Just playing," he'd assured Joan on the way home. "Just playing for kicks."

"Well, play for keeps," she'd told him. "I'm through!"

For several days after that she had been completely lost and alone. When her parents had announced their intention of taking an extended vacation trip she had been grateful. She had thought the responsibility of running the camp, the pressing hours would help make up her mind about Luke. They had helped, but she hadn't yet made up her mind entirely. There was still something about him that she wanted to own. She wished, feeling the hollowness in her stomach, that she knew what it was.

Her body came fully alive in the mirror as she stood up. Slowly, critically she took an inventory of what she saw.

Her hair was dark, almost black, cut short, and even after sleep the tight curls were attractive. Her eyes were laughing, the high delicate arch of the brows lent her a look of amusement no matter how she felt. Her nose was small, straight; her lips were full and red. She smiled and her eyes laughed louder. A lot of people told her that whenever she smiled she smiled all over. She supposed this was a minor advantage.

Her glance traveled downward, across the smooth, flowing lines of her throat to the high, jutting points of her breasts. They were, she thought, bountiful breasts, full of life's promise. Not the way some men thought, though—unaccountably, she remembered big Mike.

There was a strength and ruthless competence about him that both impressed her and gave her an uneasy feeling. He'd seemed decent and civilized enough, but a man like that could kick up a storm if things weren't run to suit him or his crew. And his crew was probably a pretty roughnecked bunch, bound by their own loyalties and conflicts. Mike had already given her a hint of conflict when he'd asked her to locate the Collins family—whoever they were—on the other side of the camp.

A favor for a favor, his tone had suggested. Would he be demanding more favors and paying them back when his mood and convenience suggested? Joan shook her head thoughtfully. Some people tried to run whatever place they happened to be in—she'd just have to be firm with this gang. Never let them forget that this was her camp.

But it was at times like this that she wished she had a man to depend on—someone to handle things that might get out of hand. Someone like Mike? The thought startled her—why, she hardly knew him! But certainly he knew how to handle people; he had handled both Mr. Perkins and herself with ease last night—solved their problem too. In fact, the problem had practically ceased to exist once Mike had arrived on scene, and there might be her solution to the immediate future. Keep Mike on her side—let him police his crew for her. If she could do it.

Why couldn't Luke have been a little more like Mike?

She picked up a pair of panties and stepped into them. Her legs were smooth, brown and straight. Not long, but about right for a girl five feet five. Nice legs, she thought, flaring to full, wide hips, the kind doctors said made child-bearing easy. Some day—the thought ended there. She'd better learn to get over Luke first. Then her mind flirted on. Would she love her baby's father? Or would she hate him, the way some girls hated their men?

She slipped on a yellow dress, scuffed her feet into white sandals and went into the kitchen. While the coffee perked she read the morning paper. But this morning she was not interested in Ed Sullivan's column or anything else. She was, she was forced to admit, more interested in herself.

How, she asked herself, did a girl know when she was in love with a man? Could she kiss him, the way she had often kissed Luke, and tell herself that this was love, that this was all that mattered? If this were so, and this were all that mattered, why hadn't she let Luke go further? Surely Luke had been right—they had been on the verge of marriage. The wedding night, Luke had said, was only a formality—love came first. No man, Luke had said, wanted a virgin on his wedding night. A man wanted a woman experienced in the art of passionate sex; a woman who no longer had to be taught but a woman who knew what love could mean.

"I won't hurt you," he'd told her. "You'll be glad later."

But she had denied him, then and later, and he had turned to Nora Justin for satisfaction. Again she berated herself for brooding on the past, but she couldn't help speculating about whether Nora had encouraged Luke—had she wanted Luke Miles so badly that she would do anything to get him?

The door opened and Millie came in. Millie was a small, delicate blonde with huge blue eyes and a small, compact shape.

"Good morning, Miss Joan."

"Good morning, Millie."

Millie had been in the employ of the Baker family ever since her graduation from high school in Unionville. She lived with her parents on a farm about three miles away. Even in the winter Millie walked to work. She said it was good for her figure.

"I've got another customer for you," Joan said to the girl. "A man. In block forty-two."

"That means I've got forty-four trailers now?"

"I don't know. I've lost count." Joan poured the coffee. "And sweep out the Husky, will you? Luke Miles rented it last night."

"On what?" Millie wanted to know.

"His nerve, I think."

"They say he quit his job in town."

"So I heard."

Luke had worked for a while at one of the garages, selling cars, but he hadn't been very successful, seldom taking home much more than his weekly drawing account.

"It beats me," Millie said as she went out. "That Nora must be nuts, fooling around with him."

Old Andy Carlton, who had charge of the half a dozen handymen employed at the camp, arrived a few minutes later. Andy was angered by the fact that one of his men had failed to report for work.

"He's drunk," Andy said. "I know the kind—one pay and a bottle of booze and it's all over."

Joan smiled and went over the day's work with Andy. She wanted the grass mowed and the papers picked up from the roadways. Also, there was a float at the beach that needed fixing.

"I hooked my suit on a nail and almost ripped it off yesterday," she told Andy. "And I think one of the barrels may have a leak."

Once she had hired a lifeguard from town but he had become involved with one of the wives at the camp and the two had run off together. Joan had not tried to hire another man, preferring to pull the beach duty herself. It gave her a good opportunity to get out in the sun, to get to know the people and to make note of the various things that required attention around the place.

"I wish you'd do something about number two-ten," Andy reminded her. "Every morning it's littered with beer cans down there."

"All right. I will."

It was funny, she thought, as she watched Andy go—a trailer camp was a world of its own. Some of the people were good while others were unbelievably and horribly bad. Many found a home and security within the huge metal monsters, while a few discovered only pain and heartbreak. Most were family people, but there was the other kind, too—the drifters, both men and women, who would scrounge the camp for every loose dollar.

At eleven, just as she was changing into her bathing suit, a black and gold trailer stopped in the roadway. Moments later she heard the screen door slam.

"I'll be with you in a second," Joan called.

The girl was small and dark, a sort of pixie type, and wore a tight-fitting black dress.

"My name is Collins—Sally Collins. My husband is with the pipe line. We would like to have you put us up."

Joan's glance wandered to the wall chart and then back to the girl's face.

"Do you have any children?"

"No."

"Then, you wouldn't care to be near the lake. I mean—"

"Did someone check in here last night? A man by the name of Big Mike Summers?"

"Why, yes, I believe he did."

Sally Collins looked relieved. "Could you place us near Big Mike's trailer?"

No, Joan thought as she recalled her impression of the night before, there wasn't any tension here. The girl acted as though she wanted to be near Big Mike.

"I'm sorry," she said, "but we don't have anything in that immediate area. Maybe later on—"

"You could let us know?" Sally Collins inquired, anxiously.

"Certainly."

The girl registered, paid a month in advance, declined the use of the cleaning services, and returned to the car.

"Big Mike's here," she told her husband. The husband, a brown-haired man with a tanned face, said nothing. "Didn't you hear me? I said, Big Mike's here."

"I heard you," the husband said, savagely.

Sally Collins got into the car and they drove off. As the big trailer slid from view, again came that feeling of possible tension. Why had Big Mike been so much in earnest about not being near the Collins family? And why had Sally Collins wanted to be near him, while her husband acted as though he wished Big Mike were in another county?

Joan shook her head and adjusted the strap on her bathing suit. It took all kinds to make the world—or a trailer camp. Some of the people who lived in the tin wagons enjoyed happiness, some suffered tragedies. She wondered, idly, which it would be for the Collins family and Big Mike Summers. Presently, as she walked toward the beach, she began wondering about something else, too.

Which, in the end, would it be for her?

3

The afternoon was hot, humid. The sun glistened from the sands on the beach, the pale blue water—overhead an occasional white cloud drifted across the sky. It was, Joan thought, a perfect afternoon. But, then, every afternoon was perfect at the Beachlake Trailer Camp, the circulars said—every day was wonderful.

She had been born and brought up in the shadows of Berry Picker's Mountain. Just why it was called Berry Picker's Mountain, she didn't know. A person could climb for miles along its craggy crest and not find so much as one berry among the thick oak and towering pine trees. Perhaps, following some forgotten fire, there had been berries there, when the sun could get at the hillside, but it would have been long before she could remember. All she could remember now, as she lay on the sand with her eyes closed, were the tumbling mountain streams, the cool, clean shade and the pine-scented coolness that rose from the ground.

She had been fortunate, she thought, luckier than most girls. Her father was an enterprising man and had been quick to recognize the undependability of dirt farming and the financial rewards that could come from a modern trailer camp. He had purchased adjoining land wisely, during a drought, and had paid cash for it. Later, after the land was graded and the shale roads were in, he had borrowed enough money to install a sewer line. He had worked long, hard hours and his family had helped him. Joan's mother rode the scrapper during more than one emergency and Joan herself had picked up thousands of rocks and placed them on the old stone boat. Their combined efforts had paid well. Her parents were now in the West, traveling without a care in the world, and she was where she liked to be, earning more than enough money to support three or four families.

She sat up quickly as a child screamed, blinking her eyes against the glare of the sand and sun—then smiled as she recognized the offender. The Adams boy was always screaming. He was ten and made every effort to draw attention to himself. Sometimes he even swam out toward the raft and, floundering, shouted for help. Joan had gone in after him once, only to have him laugh in her face. She had not gone in for him again, although each time he pulled this prank she felt her heart lift into her throat. You could never be sure with a kid like that. Well, just for now, let his mother worry.

There were about forty or fifty women on the beach and about twice as many children which was, except for week-ends, a normal turnout. While some of the residents of the camp were retired people, most were young couples with young families. A few were permanent residents of the area, but many were migratory workers who followed the seasons of the year from coast to coast. A large percentage were saddled with debts, either for monthly payments on a car or a trailer or a combination of both, and only a small handful could issue a check that would be worth the paper it was written on. But whatever other differences they may have had, they did have one thing in common—they were all restless, eager to be on the move, confirmed members of the new and modern gypsy movement that found adventure in the smell of burning gasoline and the sounds of singing tires on distant highways. None were strangers. All were friends. The ownership of a trailer, no matter what its size, was more potent than a handshake. The problems of one became the problems of all. They discussed best routes, state laws, jacks, dolly wheels, tires, insulation, camps and new trailer models. The men wrote letters, found new jobs, said goodbye and "put the show on the road." The women compared closet space, kitchen fans, laundry problems and hated every school in a radius of fifty miles. Together, the men' and the women drank and sang, fought and loved and, infrequently, died in a trailer explosion or a fire. None of these many problems appeared to discourage them. These were simply the disadvantages and the hazards of life under tin.

"Miss Baker?"

"Yes, Mrs. Whitney?"

"My sewer line is plugged up again."

"All right. I'll have somebody look at it."

"My boy, he lost his toy duck down the thing."

"All right, Mrs. Whitney."

Careless, stupid, juvenile parents who had even less sense than their children.

"Thank you for the birthday cake, Miss Baker. It was most thoughtful of you."

"You're welcome, Mrs. Sampson."

Kind, wonderful, sensible people who placed a value on themselves and on others.

"We'll be late with our rent this month, Miss Baker. Tommy was sick and the doctor charged us twenty dollars to come out from town."

Humble people with a burning passion for honesty—little people ripped by the claws of life.

"Miss Baker, can I borrow ten from you? We'll pay you thirty-five next month."

Crafty people, trading tomorrow for today but trading with the other man's dollar.

All kinds of people.

Good, bad. Honest and dishonest, truth-tellers and cheats—four hundred mobile homes harboring hate and love, misery and happiness. Four hundred homes where women borrowed sugar and where men, if they had the opportunity, might borrow wives. Four hundred homes that were hardly different from any other four hundred homes, except that they were on wheels. Their inmates loved and hated and feared, but did so on a basis unlike a street dweller's. They might not have to face their neighbors the next morning. They could always hitch up the trailer, pull out the jacks and drive away.

Joan stood up and walked across the beach. To the north and the west were the glistening roofs of hundreds of trailers, each with its own private plot, each its own private world. The roadways were white gravel and the grass was green and thick. It was, Joan thought, a most modern camp. Outdoor pay telephones were scattered throughout the park and coin-operated milk machines were on every other corner. A first-aid kit had been placed in each telephone booth and to the right of the lake, beyond the hill, was a small red building which housed a fairly complete fire apparatus. Modem, Joan thought again—

a modern trailer camp and, together, she and her parents had built it with their hands. No longer did they have to worry about last month's bills; the money was always there. No longer did they have to do without the things they wanted; they could buy a Cadillac and pay for it in cash.

"Hey, Joan!"

She turned. It was Luke.

"Hi," she said.

Again that strange feeling of weakness assailed her. What did she see in him, anyway? Did she love him—or pity him? Was she jealous because she had lost him to Nora Justin?

"Nora's coming out with the truck," he said. "We've got a table to move in, a couple of curtains to put up and that's about all."

"And pay the rent," Joan reminded him.

Luke grinned and when he grinned, Joan thought, he was quite handsome. His face was nicely tanned, smooth, and the crinkles went all the way up to his gray eyes.

"You care if we hang up some signs?" he wanted to know.

"I don't care."

"Or knock on doors?"

"I'd rather you didn't do that."

"But what's the harm?" he protested.

She shook her head. "You know the rules of the camp, Luke. No soliciting. Why, we don't even allow the bread trucks in here."

"Okay, okay." He kicked a clump of sand out of the way. "I was only asking." He put a cigarette in his mouth and lit it. "Thanks for renting us the trailer, Joan," he said. "You're pretty regular. I guess I'm just beginning to find out how regular you are."

Something hard came into her throat. "Let's not go into that again," she pleaded. "If you came out here just to—"

"No, I didn't. We've got a good trade in town during the day and we thought we could operate this branch at night. That's all. There's no other reason."

The Adams boy raced by, kicking up sand and screaming. He jumped across a couple of women who were sunbathing, continued down the beach and plunged into the water.

"Little devil," Joan said.

She watched the boy as he swam out toward the red and white raft. He used long, overhand strokes and his feet churned the water. About a hundred feet from shore he suddenly stopped swimming, went down once and came up shouting.

"Help! Help!"

Luke glanced at Joan in alarm. "Jeeze," he said, "you're not just going to stand there!"

"He's all right. He does that almost every day."

"How do you know?"

"Don't worry. I know."

The boy's arms thrashed the water. He continued to call for help. Luke looked first at Joan and then back at the boy. His face was white, strained.

"To hell with it," he said, kicking off his shoes. "I'm going out there."

Before Joan could stop him Luke was speeding to the water's edge. Several women, noting Luke's concern, began to laugh.

"Cut it out!" Mrs. Adams shouted to her son. "Come on in and dry your ears."

But the boy continued to shout for help. Luke hit the water with a terrific splash and came up, his long arms knifing the surface of the lake. The boy, as Luke neared him, floundered and went down again. With a tremendous burst of power Luke shot down into the depths after him.

"Silly man," somebody said.

The boy's head appeared and then Luke was beside him. Silence fell over the spectators as they waited for the boy to laugh. Only he didn't laugh. His youthful voice rose to a scream as he continued to shout for help and his hands were gripped into Luke's hair, forcing Luke's head under the water.

"Luke!" Joan cried, running forward.

She saw Luke come up again, saw the ball of Luke's fist, saw the smashing fist strike the boy on the point of the chin. Instantly, the screams stopped and the boy lay still. Carefully, Luke turned the youth over on his back and began swimming to shore with him.

Trembling, Joan sank to the warmth of the sand. She felt cold and numb all over. The boy had been in trouble, real trouble, and she had done nothing about it. Thank God for Luke, she thought—thank God that he was here and that he had the presence of mind to act.

The Adams woman was mad. She cradled her son in her arms and accused Luke of having struck the boy needlessly. Patiently, Luke attempted to explain that he had done the only thing possible, that the boy would have drowned him, too, if he had not used his fist. Disgusted, Luke finally walked over to Joan and sat down.

"Damned idiot," he complained.

"Luke." Joan's eyes were wet as she looked into his face. "Luke, thank you so much! What happened to him?"

"Cramp. It's okay."

"No, it isn't. I would have let that boy drown!"

"It wouldn't have been your fault. Nobody's got any right to horse around like that."

In that moment, thinking about the Adams boy, she realized that the operation of the camp was beyond her. She needed help. Someone she could trust. Luke had told her several times that she needed a man to help here, and once she had planned on Luke's being that man, on Luke's being her husband. Well, she had lost him—more accurately, they had lost each other—but that didn't mean he couldn't be partly right. Luke knew and liked the trailer life. He could do a good job for her.

"Luke, how much do you make working with Nora?"

"More than I made selling cars," he replied, evasively.

"No. I mean, honestly?"

"Well, seventy a week. Last week it was a little more."

Her heart thudded. "Luke, would you work for me—for a hundred?"

He yawned and stared at her. "Are you serious?"

"Of course I'm serious."

"I thought you hated me."

"Why should I hate you?"

"Because of—"

"Nora?" Joan smiled and pushed her hands deep into the sand. "No, I couldn't hate you because of Nora. A little bit of it may have been my fault too, you know."

"Do you mean that?" he inquired anxiously.

"I wish I didn't—but I do."

The Adams woman led her son across the beach and everybody followed them. Presently, Joan and Luke were alone. He stretched out beside her and looked up at the blue sky.

"I can't let Nora down," he said. "This new table cost her seven hundred bucks and she wouldn't have gone into it out here if it hadn't been for me."

"Well, you could help her, too. I'd have no objection to that."

"You wouldn't?"

Her eyes found his face and held.

"No," she replied. Her voice was tight. "This would be a business arrangement with us, Luke."

His glance moved over her in a way she remembered, appreciating all she had and more.

"That's a lousy piece of luck," he said.

Her face colored. "I wish you wouldn't talk that way."

"What way?"

"You know, the way you used to talk to me. Like—well, funny."

"Straight," he corrected her, smiling. "I told you what you needed to make you a woman and you didn't believe me."

"Please, Luke!"

"You live in a shell," he went on. "A shell of frustration. Your body tells you to do one thing and your mind tells you to do something else, or do nothing at all. How can you ever be happy unless the two of you get together?"

"You're beyond me," Joan said. "Believe me, you really are."

"No. You're beyond yourself. You're mixed up. You want to do the things that every woman wants to do but you're afraid. Isn't that so?"

"Not exactly. I'm afraid of being wrong, yes. I don't ever want to be wrong—in that. Life means a lot to me—life and what I do with it. But there's no sense of talking about it, Luke. What you and I have to say is over and done. You've got your life and I've got mine. I—Luke, if you want to work for me, fine. But if you don't want to, that's all right, too."

"Oh, I'll take the job."

"You will?" Somehow, she was relieved. "Thank you, Luke."

Before she could move away from him he took her in his arms and placed his lips firmly on her mouth. Almost before she knew it she had kissed him back.

"And I'll take the girl, too," he whispered. "I'll take the girl when the time is right."

She strained against him, pushing herself free.

"The time isn't right," she told him huskily. "And you know it."

"I know it," he said. "But do you?"

Later, as she walked toward the office, she had a feeling of a great superiority over Luke Miles. Luke, for all his masculine experience and knowledge, had been dead wrong.

She had been ready.

More than ready.

4

The Saturday-night party turned out to be a real blockbuster. Generally Saturday nights at the camp were quiet affairs—people lounged around on the lawns, talking or dancing to music from the juke box. But this Saturday night the pipe line workers were fresh off their first pay and raring to bust the silence wide open.

"Listen to them," Luke said to Joan. "They just about shake Berry Picker's Mountain, don't they?"

They were sitting in lawn chairs beside Joan's trailer.

"We'll be lucky if somebody doesn't complain," she said.

"So what?" Luke wanted to know. "You can't be in church every day, can you?"

"No, I suppose not."

"You ought to have a drink yourself."

It was hot and the night was young. She felt relaxed, now that she had Luke to share some of her burden.

"Maybe I will," she said. Then, as Luke rose, "Make mine rye with a lot of ginger."

"Sure."

He went into the trailer and she slid down in her chair and thought about Luke. The last few days had been better, a lot easier for her; Luke had done his work well. The handymen, she knew, liked him and would do anything he asked them to do. Not only that, but Luke had been working himself, cutting grass, opening sewers, or anything else that needed to be done. In addition to this, he was helping Nora at her massage parlor which, surprisingly enough, was doing well. Luke said if business kept up Nora might put on another operator. Perhaps, Joan decided, there was something to that body pounding business after all. Some evening, if she ever got the time, she might go in and find out what it was all about.

Luke returned with the drinks. Her drink, when she sipped it, tasted strange, but then liquor always had an odd taste for her. She drank only rarely, when things were good with her, and she drank moderately.

"Feel like dancing?" Luke wanted to know.

"No, not right now."

He stretched out in the chair and unbuttoned his shirt. It was always a source of amazement to Joan that a man as skinny as Luke could have so much hair on his chest. It was like a brown bear blanket, matted and thick and the ends of the hairs were sharp.

"There's something I've got to talk to you about," Luke said. "About Millie."

"What about Millie?" She swallowed some more of her drink and it still tasted strange. "What's Millie done now?"

Luke looked at her through a cloud of cigarette smoke. "Millie's been peddling it," he said. "All over the camp."

"Peddling what?"

"Herself."

Joan sat up. "I don't believe it!"

"Well, it's true. She told me I could have all I wanted for five bucks."

"Luke, you're lying!"

"Why would I lie? Ask the man in ninety-six. The old guy with the sore leg. He gets his every morning while his wife is out for the mail. And there are others, a lot of them. I was surprised myself, but it's so. She'll throw herself down on a mattress faster than she can change sheets."

The liquor reeled through Joan's body and slammed into her brain. No wonder Millie had never asked for more money. No wonder Millie whistled on her way to work.

"The little idiot!" Joan said, angrily.

"Sure."

Joan finished her drink and placed her glass on the ground.

"Luke?" she wanted to know. "Luke—did you?"

"Are you crazy?"

"I just wondered. She's—nice."

"Yeah, but I like five bucks better."

That drink, she thought, had been strong, very strong. A warm glow filled her whole body, threatened to spill over, drowning every reasonable emotion in its wake.

"Do you, Luke?"

He laughed and patted her on the knee. "I like something else better," he said, quietly. He laughed again. "Another drink?"

She shouldn't, not really, but the news about Millie had upset her. If her mother and father ever found out about it they'd be furious. And if the word ever got around that flesh could be purchased at wholesale prices at the Beachlake Trailer Camp it would drive many respectable people away. In the morning she would have to fire Millie—she would have to give the girl her time and find somebody else.

"A small one," she told Luke. "And not too much rye."

Luke nodded and picked up the glass.

"We'll drink to Millie," he said.

Joan nodded. Drink to Millie. That was a scream, that was. The poor dumb kid—what could she expect to get out of selling herself? Fame? Fortune? A howling baby, who might look like any number of men, to remind her of what she had done?

"To Millie," Luke said, placing the glass in her hand.

"I won't drink to that."

"To us, then."

"All right. To us. Whatever that means."

To me—because it's the one thing I want just now—and it's the one thing I'm afraid to take ...

Ever since that day on the beach she had wanted Luke. She had wanted him to make her alive, to make her a woman, but she had been scared, too. Actually, she supposed, she had been more frightened of the consequences than the act. The eventual commission of the act was, she now felt, a forgone conclusion. If she had to do something like that to insure her happiness—well, she simply had to do it. She had starved herself so long, so painfully, that it hardly seemed worthwhile to continue depriving herself.

"Luke," she said, "you made this drink awfully strong." Her words sounded hesitant, slurred together. "You must have made it almost all whiskey."

"No," he said. "Not all whiskey."

But the drinks had been strong. Never before had a couple of drinks bothered her so much. Her mind felt fuzzy, incapable of thought, her whole body filled with a wild yearning.

"What's the matter with you, Joan?" he inquired, softly.

"I—I don't know."

His arms were around her, lifting her, carrying her into the trailer.

His lips found her mouth—hungry, searching, demanding.

"Joan! Joan darling!"

She pressed her lips to his. She felt his hand at the top of her blouse, fumbling with the buttons.

"No! No, Luke!"

"What's wrong?"

Insanely, she started to cry.

"I'm—afraid."

"You don't have to be. You don't have to be afraid at all."

She clung to him, crying and trembling. In the distance a night owl screeched and from the direction of the highway came the sounds of rolling tires. Gravel crunched nearby and she sat up quickly.

"Luke," she said. "No, Luke!"

He cursed bitterly and released her. A huge figure loomed in the open doorway.

"Miss Baker?"

"Yes?"

"Mike Summers." The man peered into the trailer. "Hi, Luke," he greeted. "How's it going?"

"Not bad," Luke said, without conviction.

"Good." Big Mike hesitated for a moment. "I wondered if you might care to join me in a dance, Miss Baker? I can't seem to find myself a partner, and the joint's kicking up."

"Why, I—"

She looked at Luke. If she stayed here with Luke she knew what would happen. She wouldn't be able to help herself now, the tortuous ache in her body told her. She had lost the battle with Luke longer ago than he knew. Yet Mike's coming brought relief.

"Why, yes," she said, standing up. "I'd like to. Thanks for remembering me."

She didn't look at Luke's face. She knew what she would find there—displeasure and hurt. But she couldn't help that. They had been over this before, and once again she was glad of being out of it. Tomorrow the drinks would be gone and things would be different. Tomorrow she would be glad that she had refused Luke. Or would she? That was the maddening thing—would she?

Big Mike took her arm as they walked down the road.

"I didn't want to say anything in front of your friend," Big Mike told Joan, "but the fact is I've had a little difficulty with that Collins family again."

"Mr. Collins?"

"No. His wife. Sally. She—can I be frank with you, Miss Baker?"

"I don't know why not."

"And—can I call you Joan?"

"If I can call you Mike."

He squeezed her arm, gently. As they drew near the pavilion the sounds of the music grew louder. The gay, excited laughter of men and woman filled the air.

"I hope you won't run off and leave me after I tell you this but I feel you ought to know. There's been trouble before. Mrs. Collins—well, a long while ago, before she married, I was quite friendly with Sally. After her marriage I naturally assumed that our friendship was finished. But, for some reason, it hasn't been quite that way with her. She keeps—bothering me. What I wanted to ask you for was a kind of special dance."

"You want me to let her know you're not on the open market?" A little to her surprise, Joan found her voice cool, collected.

"Something of the sort, I guess." He looked down at her and smiled. "It seemed like a good idea when I thought of it. But, now—well, now, I'm not so sure."

"It's all right," Joan said. "I'll do what I can."

And she did. In fact, she thought, she ought to be grateful to Mike for having arrived at the trailer when he did. She felt bitter, disgusted and shameless. She might as well act it—what difference did it make if this was just a sham to mislead Sally Collins? Didn't that, really, give them something in common? Weren't they both trying to fool somebody?

They arrived at the pavilion and Big Mike turned to take her in his arms. The music was soft, sensual, a modified beat of some jungle rhythm from South America. She threw back her head, laughing up into his face, and crept close to him. His arms were huge, strong and when he pressed her in against the hard muscles of his chest and stomach she had the sensation of being crushed ...

"You're doing fine," he said, lowering his head.

"You're pretty good yourself, Mike."

For a big man, he was light on his feet. When they reached the corner and he spun her she had the giddy feeling of being lifted clear from the floor. The movement brought them closer together and she felt crushed against his chest. She closed her eyes, knowing an abandoned, glorious feeling.

"Am I overplaying it, Joan?" His arm relaxed.

"I don't mind."

His arm tightened again and she did not attempt to move away.

The beat of the jungle music became wilder, more intense. The couples around them moved faster and faster. When Big Mike spun her first to the right and next to the left she felt the cool night air caress her legs as her skirt rode high. Then, with a rush, she was back into his embrace again, her arms clinging to his waist and holding him tight.

Run, run, run, she told herself. Run, you little fool! Run! Don't stay here in his arms like this—he isn't the man you wanted. Run! Run till the liquor is gone, till the frantic need is gone. Run, run, run!

"I'm glad I came with you," she told him, laughing, breathless. "Glad!"

It was the liquor talking, she thought miserably a moment later. Why had Luke made the drinks so strong? Her mind and her body were confused, tormented. She didn't know what she was doing. She shouldn't be here like this, in the arms of a strange man. And she shouldn't be glad—not the way she was. She ought to loathe Mike, as in that instant she loathed Luke. Luke had made her glad to escape. She ought to run, but she couldn't.

Everything she needed in life was here. Life, itself, was this very moment. Life was music and this man and her body, its desires. Life was now, this instant!

The music stopped but she was hardly aware of it. Breathlessly, she pressed herself against him.

"Mike!"

"What's the matter?" His voice was unsteady.

"I don't know—am I all right?" She hung on his answer.

"Would you care for a drink?"

"No, thanks."

"Maybe if we took a walk—"

She lifted her face, smiling. She shouldn't go with him. She knew that. If she went off into the darkness with him, feeling as she felt, something was bound to happen. Something big and wonderful was bound to happen. Also something terrible and shameful.

"Yes," she murmured, huskily. "Please, let's take a walk."

They crossed the pavilion and as they passed the beer tub Joan saw Sally Collins watching them. Sally's eyes were filled with hurt and something else. Longing? Or contempt? It was difficult to say which.

"Mike," she said, softly, as they walked into the shadows. "Mike, we don't have to go far."

His arms went around her and he crushed her against him. His mouth on hers was eager and warm.

"Farther than you think, baby," he said.

Her lips moved against his mouth. "All right, Mike—but tell me."

"I've never met anybody quite like you."

"That's the beginning—where's the end?"

He laughed. He lifted her, holding her tight, and carried her down to the beach.

Mike! Mike!

He placed her gently upon the beach and got down beside her. The moon was behind a cloud and it was very dark. She could not see him but she could hear his heavy breathing and thrilled to the sure touch of his huge hands.

Then, almost as a plea, "Mike, should I? Should I!"

His mouth lingered upon her lips.

"If you like me as much as I like you, yes."

She kissed him passionately. It was better now. It was good!

"Mike—" She whispered it, almost soundlessly.

She closed her eyes, drinking in the fury of his kiss. She knew that he would not ask her and she knew that she would not have to tell him. This was an awakening she had to know.

His body was like a giant flame and when he brought her to him, molding her to his will, she felt fear and pain and panic and happiness.

"Mike! Mike!" She cried his name softly.

The fear and the pain and the panic disappeared into a blazing light that swung upward through the night; a powerful, giant light that exploded with a shattering roar and showered her agonized body and heart with a series of strange new wonders that left her weak and sobbing.

Later, as she turned to face him, she knew that she wasn't the only one who had cried. Big Mike was crying, still.

"You should have told me," he said. "I didn't know."

She patted his hand, affectionately.

"I'm glad it was you," she told him.

"Are you?"

"Yes, Mike."

It was a good thing she was. It was a little late to change matters.

5

Joan awoke with a frightful headache. She opened her eyes once, shuddered, and closed them tight. How could she look at herself in the mirror? How could she ever face anyone again?

The events of the night came back to her, flooding her with misery. She remembered talking with Luke, drinking with him—she remembered Luke's carrying her into the trailer. But mostly she remembered Mike, who had succeeded where Luke had failed. She remembered Mike's violent kisses, his savage, lustful need. She lay on the bed, trembling.

What if she were pregnant! What a horrible thought! But what if she were? What could she do? Was she any better than Millie? Was she any better than the common whore who walked the streets and sold herself to the first man who was interested? She cradled her head in her arms and tried to shut out the light.

No, that wasn't the question. That wasn't the question at all. The question was ugly in its simplicity. Was she worse—she had given herself away.

She tried to remember when she had first been kissed and held by a man. It had been during her last year in high school, at the prom, and the boy's lips had been soft and cool, hesitant—not at all like the lips of the boy who had tried to rape her after the dance. She had kissed the first boy back carefully, like a sister, because she had read somewhere that a boy expected something in return for a nice evening. But the movement of her lips had done something to the boy and his hand had slid to her breast, hurting her. She'd cried out in pain and he had stopped and, after that, neither one of them had had a very good time.

Then there'd been Luke, when she was going to college. Luke had never gotten fresh until he'd returned from service. Then he'd been after her, like a hound dog cut loose from a leash, and it had been the only thing they'd ever really fought about—sex. It had been a dirty word to Joan, a word not to be spoken, but to Luke it had not been just a part of life. He had coaxed her, pleaded with her and, finally, he had become insistent. She had meant him to be the first man in her life, but at the last moment she had become petrified with alarm. And now—had it been Luke she had wanted last night ... or just a man?

"Luke," she cried. "Luke!" But Luke had become a dream.

She threw her arms wide and buried her face in the pillow. Hot tears stung her eyes. Reality was Mike.

"Mike!" she sobbed. "Oh, Mike!" She felt defeated.

It could have been any man, she thought—any man strong enough or adept enough to take her from Luke. With Luke she'd been safe. She hadn't been safe away from him—any more than the Adams boy had been, left to her care. Luke had saved the Adams boy—would he have saved her as well?

The eroticism, now gone, which had seized her the night before had been unconquerable. No women, she felt, could have survived its assault, could have defended herself against the overwhelming urge that had driven her into Big Mike's arms. That, in itself, was bad enough—but the realization that it could have been any one of a number of men was the most awesome of all.

"Please," she whispered. "Oh, please!"

Would it happen to her again? Would it, like a thunderous storm, rise up to hurl her once more into a wild inferno of passion? Or was this simply a woman's natural craving?

Oh, God, she thought twisting on the bed, make it this! Make it right and natural and fine. Don't make it wrong and shameful. Don't make it something that will scream for the comfort of a man I might loathe for the rest of my days. Don't make it something dirty that can be found in the streets and the gutters. Make it beautiful, the way it was, and keep it beautiful always.

But it wasn't beautiful. She knew that. It couldn't be beautiful. It was degrading. She had thrown herself at Mike. What did he think of her now? With the night gone and only the memory of her body to hold, what could he think? If he had drunk enough, would he even remember?

A whore, she told herself—Mike would think her a whore. He would think of her as a round-heeled one; a pushover. An untamed bitch—she remembered his shock when it was all over and he realized she'd been a virgin. He'd been disgusted at himself—what would he think of her?

Slowly, she arose from the bed. She didn't look at herself in the mirror. She didn't want to see herself. She might never want to see herself again.

She dressed conservatively in a pink and white polished cotton dress that had a low, squared front and was sashed with bow-tied streamers. She put on white, high-heeled shoes and went out to the kitchen to make coffee.

Luke came in as she was getting the cream out of the refrigerator.

"Nice day," Luke said.

Joan placed another cup on the table and glanced out into the brilliant sunlight. "Nice," she agreed.

He sat down and stretched his legs.

"You have fun last night, Joan?"

"So-so."

"Nothing exciting."

She thought her face flamed. "No, nothing exciting."

Joan poured the coffee and Luke dumped a liberal helping of sugar into his cup.

"The redhead want you to run interference for him with that Collins dame?" Luke inquired, grinning.

"Not exactly."

"What do you mean, not exactly? She's been chasing that poor guy all over the camp." Luke's grin broadened. "Not to be disrespectful to my charming hostess, but she wouldn't have to chase me very far." Luke stirred his coffee thoughtfully. "In fact, on second thought, she wouldn't have to chase me at all. I'd run her right into the damn ground."

"Luke!"

"Well, I would. Some of the men say that she's hot after having a kid and that her old man can't give her another one. I guess that must be why she cruises around after Big Mike."

"Must you be so crude?" Joan demanded.

"Crude? I'm only saying."

"I don't care." Joan lit a cigarette. "I think it's a lot of gossip. There must be something deeper to it than that."

Luke leered. "Maybe there is." He stretched his arms and yawned. "Anyway, to hell with it. I've got my own problems with Nora. She's so snowed under that she doesn't know what to do. You'd hardly believe it."

"That's true."

Luke stood up.

"You going to do anything about Millie?"

She thought, briefly, about Millie's pale gray eyes, her blonde hair, the compact little shape. So Millie sold herself, did she? So Millie took a man's money, went to bed with him and gave him his fun. Did that make Millie bad? Did it, really? Hadn't she, Joan, done the same thing with Big Mike Summers—for nothing? Hadn't she done it purely out of need? Didn't Millie, honestly, have a little more to show for her actions—didn't Millie have something left, other, than disgust, that she could count on?

"I'm going to let Millie go," she heard herself saying. "I don't want to, because I don't want to hurt her, but I can't let her go on with what she's been doing."

Luke nodded. "Well, I've been thinking about it," Luke said. "You let her go, just like that, and she may kick up a fuss. You never know what a girl like Millie might do."

"I hadn't thought of that, Luke."

"No. But I have. You can't walk up to her and tell her that she's got to hit the road. Hell, I couldn't prove she is if I had to, not unless I told about how she came up to me. So here's what I thought—Nora's got a lot more to do than she can take care of and I don't see why we can't fit Millie into our picture. That way, she'll be making a living and she won't be able to work the trailers. A deal like that would help Nora and it ought to help you."

"Luke," Joan said, hesitantly, "you're a charm!"

"Ain't I though?"

"No. I mean, you can think when you really have to."

"Sure." When he reached the door he swung and faced her. His stare fingered at the top of her dress. "And I can think of more than one thing at a time." He opened the door. "I'll send Nora up to talk to you about it."

"Thank you, Luke."

She found the Sunday papers on the outside steps and sat down in the sun, waiting for Nora. But she didn't read the papers. She thought about Luke.

He's changed, she thought, much for the better, but it was too late now to make the change count for them. It was one thing for a man to take on a strange woman but it was quite another for a woman to do the parallel thing. She couldn't, for instance, go to Luke and say that she was sorry and that what happened last night would never happen again. She could say she was sorry, of course, and Luke might believe her but she couldn't be sure that it wouldn't happen again and again and again. She hadn't even remembered Luke when she'd been with Mike. Luke could never trust her—not until she saw Big Mike again. And she couldn't bear the thought of facing Big Mike. Suppose it was just the same—that she wanted his arms just as much, that she needed every bit of him just as badly? What would she be able to think then?

"Hello, Joan."

She looked up as Nora turned from the roadway and came up the walk.

"Hello, Nora."

Nora was a small girl, auburn haired and very pretty. She wore a high-necked, baby-size black and white check dress. The dress was sleeveless, very tight and full across the bodice. The stalk-slim lines of the skirt made her full contours prominent.

"Luke said you wanted to see me about Millie."

"Yes. I have to let Millie go."

"So I heard. Do you suppose I can do anything with her?"

"I don't know. Luke said you might be able to use her. If you could, it would make everything easier."

Nora shrugged. "Well, I don't know what I'll do, but I owe you a favor for letting me have the trailer. Send her down after you see her and I'll work something out."

"Thanks, Nora."

Nora laughed. "I should thank you. You've been very understanding." Her face grew serious. "I've wanted to talk to you before, but I didn't have the nerve. That night—well, that night was my fault, Joan. Not Luke's. I want you to know that. And you might like to know that it didn't do me any good. Luke, you see, is very much in love with you."

"Oh?" She was surprised to find her voice steady.

"Yes. What did you think?" Joan would never know if Nora's smile was really mocking.

A few minutes after Nora had left, Millie came down the road, whistling.

"Good morning, Miss Joan."

"Good morning, Millie."

Millie accepted her new assignment graciously. She made no protest. "It's all right—I'm getting a little tired hopping those beds, anyway."

As soon as the girl was gone Joan went inside and made a list of names of the trailer owners who would have to be notified that the cleaning service would be temporarily discontinued. She smiled when she thought of the term. Some cleaning service they'd been having at the Beachlake Trailer Camp!

She started on the far end of the camp, at the highest plot numbers, and began working down the roadways.

"I'm sorry," the woman in three-forty said. "What am I going to do with my broken arm?"

"It's a good thing," another woman said. "I go out in the morning and when I get back there's nothing done. What did she do with all her time? Talk to the men?"

"I don't know," Joan said, honestly. All she really had was rumor.

The man in two-fourteen was quite upset. He said he lived alone and he needed somebody to come in and do his cleaning.

"You know how it is when a man's alone," he said.

"I can guess," Joan answered, smiling.

The woman in one-thirty was glad to hear that Millie would never again darken her doorway.

"I think she's been making up to my husband," she said.

"Now, Mrs. Masterson!"

"Well, I really do!" The woman lowered her voice. "And I don't mean she's been giving it away. Why, last month my checking account was short almost fifty dollars that my husband couldn't explain. Fifty dollars! That's a lot of money, Miss Baker."

"Maybe he spent it for cigars."

"Sure," Mrs. Masterson acknowledged. "Only he doesn't smoke or drink."

"I see."

"He just likes to get next to a young and pretty girl. Why, even now he's talking about going down to that massage trailer. Can you imagine that? An old bull like my husband getting his kicks out of a rub down! What are they going to think of next?"

Sex, Joan thought as she walked down the road; the whole world thought of it, worried about it. How many people could you speak to, who wouldn't mention it? As to herself—last night she had kicked the secret world apart, walked the forbidden pasture, soared the full flight in one sudden leap. Why, then, didn't the early morning feeling of dirt and shame persist? How could she look back upon it, now, and feel nothing except a reverence for the body that belonged to her?

She walked up to the door of the trailer and knocked.

"Come in!"

She opened the door and stepped inside. The giant redhead seated at the kitchen table looked up at her.

"Oh," he said. He stood up, his shoulders hunched. "Hi."

"Hi," she said in a weak voice.

For a long moment he looked at her. His eyes were soft and warm.

"About last night," he began. "I—"

Suddenly, she had to find out, she had to know.

"Mike," she said. "Mike!"

He took her in his arms, just the way she had known he would. She could feel the heat of his body and the pound of his heart against her own.

"I couldn't sleep," he told her huskily. "I haven't done a damned thing since I left you."

She lifted her lips to him. "Kiss me, Mike." She told him.

In the instant he obeyed, she thought she knew everything. The knowledge was blinding, in a way—but at last she had all the answers.

6

For a long time neither of them said much that made any sense. Joan found herself crying a little—something she never did—and holding on to Mike. Gradually her tensions eased and she relaxed in his arms, feeling a certainty she had never before known. For the first time she realized just how frightened she had been.

"I love you, Big Mike," she whispered, unashamedly. "I love you very much."

"Do you, Joan?"

"I do."

It was a funny sort of a room. The upper floor of the trailer had been ripped out and this made the ceiling high. It was a man's room, with heavy leather boots in one corner and plaid shirts hanging around on several nails. The scents of shaving lotion and pipe tobacco hung in the air.

"I was afraid to come here," Joan confided. "I was so afraid after—last night. I thought you might feel that I was—well, you know, loose. And it was the first time for me, Mike."

"I knew." His voice was very soft.

"You don't think I'm terrible, Mike?"

"No."

"I was afraid you would. I acted shamelessly last night."

Mike laughed. "Well, I was no gentleman."

She sat up, her body suddenly rigid. "Mike—suppose we made a baby, Mike? Wouldn't that be something?"

She saw Mike stiffen. "It'd be something all right," he agreed. "Let's not talk about it."

"But we could have."

"I know that."

"We could have made a baby, Mike—what would happen if we did?"

"We'd have to get married, I guess."

She felt better. Mike would marry her. Mike wouldn't let her give birth to a child all alone. Mike would be there with her. Mike would never run away.

"Would you marry me, Mike?"

He returned to the bed and sat down. He put his arm around her and kissed her on the cheek. A husbandly kiss, she thought vaguely.

"Let's not worry about it," he said.

"But, Mike—"

"Let's not worry about it."

Suddenly, she was frightened. "You could have given me a baby," she insisted. "Neither one of us knows right now whether you did or not." And that would change things. Plenty.

He turned his head and kissed her. "I said not to worry, didn't I?"

"I don't mean to be this way."

"Well, I know how you must feel. I guess every good girl must feel the same way."

She took his hand between her own and squeezed it very tight.

"Oh, Mike," she sighed.

She kissed him, but nothing was as it had been last night. She felt nothing of what she'd known then. Her reactions frightened her.

She was driven, not impassioned …

"Mike," she wanted to know later. "Mike, is it always nice for you?"

He laughed. "If it weren't, I wouldn't work so hard at it."

"No. I mean, is it always the same with everybody?"

"You ask a lot of questions, Joan."

"Well, this is new to me."

"No, it's not the same," he said, finally. "It's not the same at all." His lips brushed her cheek. "You're different."

"In what way?"

"You're clean. You're honest. Besides, I want to marry you."

"Oh, Mike!"

"Short notice?"

"Not to me."

"Well, I'm thirty years old and I've been banging around quite a while. I never thought it would happen to me so fast."

She was curious about Mike and she had to know more about him.

"I was born in New York," he told her. "East Side. We were poor but not the kind of poor that you read about in the papers. My father was a house painter and my mother worked in a factory for a while. They're both dead now. My mother died first and my father died the last year I was in college. I've never been back there. There never seemed to be any reason why I should go."

"Didn't you have a girl?"

"I didn't have a girl in New York."

"Rut afterward?"

"Yes, there was one afterward. She's here at the camp now."

"Sally Collins?"

"How did you guess?"

"It wasn't much of a guess. I knew there was some reason why you didn't want to be near them."

And maybe I'm jealous, she thought.

Mike puffed thoughtfully on his cigarette. "That girl has me stumped," he said. "She really does. Hell, I only went with her a couple of months before she met Gerald. In fact, I'm the one who introduced them. But shortly after they were married, maybe a month or so, she started chasing after me. It's the damnedest feeling to have a woman chasing you around."

"But you know what it's all about, Mike."

Mike grinned. "Yeah, I guess I do, at that. She claims Gerald won't give her a family. But why pick on me? Even if she got rid of her husband I wouldn't marry her."

Joan was glad to hear that.

"It's a crazy world," Joan said. She didn't know whether to take Mike seriously.

He kissed her for a long moment. "Will you marry me, Joan?"

"You know I will."

"When?"

"Whenever you say."

"What about the trailer camp?" he asked.

"It belongs to my folks. I'll write to them. They'll have to come home, that's all."

"We could stay on here, if you'd like."

"But you've got your job. This couldn't be as good."

"No, I suppose not."

"And I won't mind, Mike. I really won't. You travel a lot and I'd like that. It would be a change, something different." Her lips melted against his mouth. "Oh, I'm so happy, Mike. So happy!"

Mike stubbed the cigarette out in an ashtray. "I'm going in to the home office the end of the week," he said, "to see about a transfer. We'll keep it quiet until after I get back, huh?"

"Why, Mike?"

"That Collins family. The less they know the better I'll like it."

She nodded. "All right, Mike. Whatever you say."

"But you can write to your folks."

She sat up beside him. She took his arm and pressed it to her bosom. "Oh, Mike," she breathed, "it's so wonderful! So wonderful!"

His mouth sought her again. "You're beautiful," he murmured. "Beautiful!"

Laughingly, she pushed his head away.

"My man," she announced with mock sternness, "I have work to do. In fact, I came here to tell you that you had lost your cleaning girl."

"I won't need one much longer, anyway. There's a girl I know who's going to do it for the rest of her life for free."

He was so handsome, so nice, that she had to kiss him again.

"Really, Mike, I've got to go. There's work to do."

"I don't know of any better work."

"I don't either—but let's make it later."

"Tonight?"

"Tonight," she promised.

As soon as she left the trailer, a new emotion hit her, something she never had known in all the years of her life. It was aloneness. These familiar surroundings seemed suddenly to possess a kind of sentience. In the absence of her parents, the camp itself seemed a kind of guardian ... a guardian that had trusted Joan no less than her parents did.

Had she betrayed that trust? As though she were a criminal, she had a terrified impulse to go back to Mike's side, not only because she loved him, but because he was someone whom she had been good to, not someone she'd betrayed.

She fought the crippling sense of guilt. We love each other, she reminded herself. We're married in all but name. When people love, it's right ...

Yes, but did she love him? Or was she just soothing herself with that idea?

She faced it—last night's madness had had that much justification ... that she hadn't been able to fight it, that she'd wanted to give herself.

But this morning—hadn't she submitted merely because she'd submitted once before? To justify last night, plead before the fates that she was possessed by love?

The answer—face it, she told herself, this is the honest sunlight; if you lie to yourself now, you may go too deep to find the way back again—the answer was simply: Guilty.

She had not felt revulsion at his touch. His physical attraction for her was powerful. She approved of him. And the act of love—she would not have believed it, she had implicitly believed that love between man and woman, carried to its ultimate expression, must be either horror or glory—the act of love itself had for Joan been merely mechanical, no more exciting than a chore, less mental than a clasping of hands in a moment of understanding.

If we were married, she thought—if the world knew it, if his trailer were my house—I think I'd go to a doctor. I'd have a right to ask if something is wrong with me. This way—where do I turn?

In college, and before, she had lived by a certain creed ... that creed, she realized now, was belief in the individual dignity of any human being. A forgiving, innocent creed ... she could have forgiven herself a seeming lapse of morals if only she could believe in what she felt for Mike.

It should have been cleansing as fire, it should have been a path to the moon ...

It shouldn't have been—common. Easy. Nothing.

She knew instinctively that work, the necessary everyday operation of the camp, was her salvation. It was her lingering thread between now and tomorrow, and she ought to be grateful for it. It would give her back her sense of her own decency, and her own importance, as nothing else could.

Tonight, she'd promised Mike.

Maybe that was it.

Of course that was it—her mind this morning had gone out of sheer custom into its working habits. Even while she'd been with Mike, part of her mind had nagged her below the surface, reminding her of routine things that had to be done on time ... tonight, when her mind was free, everything would be different. Joan forgave herself. She had to forgive herself.

She left the trailer and continued along the shaled roadway. The sky was clear overhead, the sun hot on her back. When she reached the corner, someone hailed her. It was Luke.

"Cripes," he said, coming up. "You make a speech to Summers, or something?"

She hoped that the guilt didn't show on her face.

"I wanted to tell him about Millie not being around any more," she said. "We got to talking."

Luke nodded. "I saw you go in there and I didn't know whether or not I should disturb you. That Ludlow kid wants to put his motor boat on the lake, but I told him I'd have to ask you about it first."

Joan's father had been opposed to motor boats. He claimed that the Lake of Tears was a good fishing lake and that motors destroyed the fishing. He had lost several good customers because of this rule.

"It's all right," Joan said. "But tell him to stay away from the beach."

The Ludlow youth was in his late teens and plenty wild with the family car. It was fair to suppose he would be the same with a boat. But the Ludlows were good, year around residents—they occupied a double plot and they always paid their rent in advance. It seemed only fair that the boy should be allowed to place his boat on the lake.

"Another thing," Luke said. "We've got a pot-and-pan salesman down in two-forty who's been knocking on doors. What do you want me to do about him?"

"Have there been any complaints?"

"No—no complaints."

"Then let him alone."

Luke was surprised. "Cripes, but you're charitable today," he said. "Maybe I should ask for a raise."

Joan smiled. "All right. From now on it's a hundred and a quarter a week."

"You mean that?"

"Why, certainly."

"What's come over you?"

"Nothing," she said, moving off. "It must be the weather."

Or love, she thought gaily. Yes, that was it—love. Love made a person think and feel differently. Love made the sky bluer, the sun hotter and the world better. And love did something else, too—it made a girl live inside, brought her body alive.

She entered the trailer and walked back to the bedroom, removing her dress as she did so. In the mirror she looked no different, though she felt different. There were no marks upon her, no visible evidence that she had been possessed by a man. She still looked more girl than woman—she wondered how she knew the difference.

She switched on the electric fan and lay down upon the bed. She lay there for a long time, her eyes wide open, staring up at the ceiling. Finally she closed her eyes and tried to fight down the helpless sensation that assailed her.

It was not true, she thought; it would never be true. She hadn't been looking for just any man the night before—she had been looking for Mike. But was this really so? Hadn't she considered going to bed with Luke? If Mike hadn't come along and asked her to the dance, wouldn't she have taken Luke into her bed?

There was no use fighting against it any longer; she might as well admit it. Telling herself that she was in love with Mike was a purely defensive measure. If she could make herself believe that she was in love with Mike she wouldn't have to acknowledge that the man of the night before could have been any man.

She had been abandoned that first time, wildly eager—she had felt pain and enjoyed it. Today, with Mike, she had felt dirty because of what she had done. Why was that? Why couldn't it be always the same? Where was the yearning she had experienced the night before, the tremendous urge that had seized her? If she were in love with Mike, really and truly in love with him, why couldn't she have felt the same way again?

I'm no better than Millie, she thought miserably; not a bit better. She had let him take her, use her body, and it hadn't meant nearly as much to either of them as it should have. Why would Mike be different from her?

She turned over, face down, and began to sob. Somehow, this had to be right and decent—this had to be the way love happened. To believe less was to believe that there was something wrong with her, something terrible hidden where she couldn't reach it. Maybe she was frigid. She didn't know. She wished she did.

Still crying, she went to sleep.

7

Luke entered the trailer about ten the next morning. He was whistling.

"Started earning my raise," he said, reaching into his pocket. "Look at this."

Joan, seated at the table, drank her coffee and examined the paper Luke placed in front of her.

"It's a lease," she observed. "A year's lease on the Husky at a hundred dollars a month."

Luke nodded. "That's right. Any objection?" he wanted to know.

"Why, no. I don't think so. We can always use an extra forty dollars a month."

"That's what I thought."

Joan smiled. "I thought you were working for Nora, too. This doesn't look much like it."

Luke pulled out a chair and sat down opposite.

"I am," he said. "I work for her in the evenings and I work for you during the day. This happens to be during the day."

"Luke!"

"I mean it. Besides, it's protection for her, too. She's got a nice business started down there. The way things are, there'd be nothing to stop you from raising her rent and making her get out. With the lease, you know what you're getting and she knows how long she can stay and what she has to pay."

Joan looked at him. "You seem to be doing a good job working for two people," she said. "It isn't everybody who can do that."

Luke grinned. "Well, I'm trying. I've got my nose so far down on the grindstone that I can't see it for sparks."

Joan laughed and reached for a pen. The lease, she thought, was a good deal, both ways. Luke had certainly used his head.

"There's something else I wanted to talk to you about," he continued. "You know that old shed, the one down near the bathing beach? The only things in the shed right now are some oars and stuff like that. Know the one I mean?"

"Yes."

"Well, I was thinking—we've got a lot of people on the grounds. The kids drink soda pop and eat candy and ice cream and the older folks use cigarettes. Right now, they're getting those things in town. I don't know why we can't fix up that old shed, put in a few counters and some supplies and make a little money on it. We could get a school kid or somebody retired to run it for us."

Joan returned the signed lease to Luke and reached for a cigarette. Luke's idea had merit—in fact a great deal of merit.

"I don't care," she said. "But it just seems to me that you're putting more work on yourself. You can get paid just as much and not break our back."

Luke helped himself to coffee. Then he sat down again and lit a cigarette.

"Let's not kid ourselves," he said, blowing smoke toward the ceiling. "I never had a job as good as this one and we both know it. When I was trying to sell cars, I made fifty or sixty a week, tops. And you know what I made in the army. Before that I never did much better, just a buck here and there. This is a good job for me. I make a dollar and I can save a little. If you have no objection, I mean to do everything I can to keep this job."

Joan was thoughtfully silent. This was a new Luke talking, a Luke whom she had never met before. He was older, more serious, determined. It was a good change. Before this he had always taken a to-hell-with-it attitude, putting today before tomorrow, living up his money as fast as he could earn it. Yes, it was a good change, and it fitted in with her plans perfectly.

"How would you like to earn even more money?" she asked him.

He was doubtful. "I don't know how I could," he said, "unless you turned the camp over to me free and clear."

"Oh, be serious, Luke!"

"I am serious. There isn't another job around this part of the country that pays as much money as I get right now. Why, last night I was talking to the engineer of the plastics factory in Unionville and he only gets a hundred a week. It made me feel pretty good, knowing that I'm earning more than a college graduate. Not only that, but I pick up a little from Nora. Not much, but a little. I don't need any more than I've got, Joan. And I wouldn't want you paying out extra bucks to me just because we—"

Joan waved his suspicion aside. Somehow, without dragging Mike into it, she had to get her point across. A tiny lie, she supposed, would do no harm.

"You know that mother and dad are touring the West," she began. "They wanted me to go with them, but I couldn't because somebody had to stay here. Now that you're working for me, and doing so well, I don't see why you couldn't take over the entire operation. There isn't much more to it. You just assign plots and collect the rents and see that the money is put in the bank. Other than that most of the things you would have to do you're doing already. It wouldn't be much more work on your part, but you could earn more money, Luke."

He shook his head. "I would do it for you, Joan, but I wouldn't want any more money. You don't have to pay me more money to get me to do something like that for you."

"This isn't charity," she said. "This is business."

He reached across the table and took her hand. His gray eyes were very sober.

"I had hoped it was something else," he said.

"Luke!"

He wouldn't let go of her hand. "Give me a chance to show you that I'm a better guy than you think I am," he pleaded. "You've been generous to me but let me be generous, too. Don't make this all business between us, Joan. Give me the chance to show I'm not as bad as you think."

"I never thought you were bad, Luke."

"You did the night you caught me with Nora."

"Well, that's different."

He pushed the coffee cup aside and leaned across the table. His mouth was only inches away from her lips.

"It isn't different," he said. "It's the same. We're the same two people, aren't we?"

"I don't want to talk about it, Luke."

"I do. I felt lousy about it the next day and I've felt worse about it since. I was wrong that night, Joan. Wrong! And I was wrong before that. I had no right—well, you know, insisting. You're a nice girl. You've got a code that you live by. No one can make you change that code and no one should try to get you to change it. I shouldn't have tried. I should have gotten a good job, settled down. We should have got married. But I didn't have sense enough for that. I had to go and be a fool. And I wanted to tell you, now, that I know I've been a fool."

For some strange reason Joan felt like crying. She was pretty sure that she wasn't in love with Luke, not any more, but in some way she felt she had betrayed him. She wondered what Luke would say, what he'd think, if he knew that she had gone to bed with Big Mike Summers three times in less than twelve hours. Would he still think her pure and innocent, or would he laugh at his own stupidity? And what would he say if he knew that, except for Mike's having asked her to the dance, he could have been the very first?

"It's all right," she said. Her voice sounded far away, weak. "Let's forget about it."

"Can you, Joan?"

"Yes." She hoped she was telling the truth.

He squeezed her hand gently. "You're a good kid," he said.

This time she wanted to laugh at him. A good kid. She had gone to bed with a man she hardly knew and she was a good kid. She wondered, if she had taken Luke into her bed, what he would have said about her then. A good kid? A good kid for what?

Luke stood up and walked to the door. He turned and faced her. He was smiling.

"We start fresh?"

She nodded. "Yes. We start fresh."

"Good! How about going dancing with me to the Lakeside Casino tonight?"

"I can't, Luke."

"You can't? But I picked up the tickets in town. They're having a big orchestra up from the city and it's going to be a real ball."

"I'm sorry, Luke. But I can't."

He reached into his pocket, found the tickets and dropped them carelessly onto a chair.

"Maybe you'll want to use them," he said.

"No."

His lips parted in a thin smile. "For you and the redhead," he said.

"Now, Luke!"

"You going to fire me if I say something?" he wanted to know.

"You know I wouldn't do that."

"Well, we'll see. You were in his trailer an awful long time yesterday. An awful long time, Joan."

She hoped her face wasn't as red as it felt. "I had to tell him about Millie," she said. "I told you that."

"Sure. A whole half an hour. What were you doing, making his bed for him?"

"Luke, I'm going to get mad in a minute!"

"I don't care if you do. The guy is nobody for you to mess around with. Believe me. One of these days Collins and Summers are going to tangle and it won't be so healthy for anybody caught in the middle."

She was furious with Luke, not because what he said wasn't true but because it was none of his business. She had a right to go around with Mike or anybody else she felt like taking up with. It was none of Luke's business. Maybe it had been once, but he had canceled that out. He had canceled it out with Nora Justin.

"Take your tickets," she told him. "Maybe Nora would like to go."

"Now, there's an idea."

"I said, take them!"

He scooped up the tickets. "You don't have to get sore," he complained. "I was only trying to be helpful."

"I'll just bet you were!"

"And that about Nora going isn't a bad thought at all. She's got a yen for dancing."

She's got a yen for something else, too, Joan thought. Luke could take Nora to the dance and he could get from her almost anything he wanted. He could get from Nora the same thing that she, Joan, had been giving to Big Mike. The comparison, she found, was a little shocking.

"You'd better get back to work," Joan said.

Luke returned the tickets to his pocket. "I wasn't sure I still had a job."

"You won't have it for long if you keep on talking about the same thing."

"Don't worry. I've had my say."

"That's good."

"I won't say another word about it. From now on it's just business between us."

"That's even better."

He pushed the door open and stood there holding it.

"There is just one thing more," he said, quietly. "Is it all over between us, Joan?"

"Yes," she replied, looking straight at him. "It's all over."

"That's what I wanted to know."

He turned and left.

All over, she thought after he had gone—at last it was all over. She had thought so the night she had discovered him in the car with Nora, but now she felt sure. Luke would not bother her on a personal basis again. He was an employee and their relationship would stay that way.

She supposed she should feel good about it having been settled, but she didn't. She felt oddly empty inside; it was almost as though someone close to her had died after a long illness. You expected the death, you knew that it was coming, but when it happened there was a shock to it, still.

She arose and walked around the trailer. There were a dozen and one things she ought to do but she didn't feel like doing any of them. Luke had upset her with his talk about the Collins family and Mike. There was something there that she didn't understand, an undercurrent both deep and dangerous. She had to know more about it.

There was one way in which she could come to know Sally Collins better—she could visit the Collins trailer. As the owner of the camp, this was a perfectly natural thing for her to do. It was the rule, rather than the exception, for a trailer camp owner to become friendly with the guests. It made for better understanding all around and it was an accepted part of the world in which all trailer people lived.

If she could come to know Sally Collins better it was possible that she would be able to understand the girl's problem better and be able to help Mike. One thing she didn't want was an emotional explosion in the camp—the Mike-Collins situation was one that could erupt in violence.

Did Sally really want a man other than her husband to give her a baby? Mike must have been kidding.

Joan returned to the kitchen and poured another cup of coffee. Slowly she evolved a plan, a devilish, ruthless plan, but if it worked it would help Big Mike. If it worked, Sally Collins could have her baby.

Luke Miles would be most happy to give her one.

The words, bad and bald, leaping across her brain, gave her a moment of shock. It was as though her father who had built this camp, had momentarily returned and read her mind.

Joan, what has become of you? her image of him seemed to be asking. Uncomprehendingly.

Her father would not have soiled his hands with any of this sordid mess. He wouldn't have hired Luke, perhaps. If Joan's father had sensed incipient trouble from the Collins' domestic situation, he would have found a way of getting rid of the Collinses—or of getting rid of Mike.

That's just it, she explained to her absent father. You said it once yourself—up to a certain point, you have to accept people as they are. You can't be preachy and holier-than-thou, and expect to stay in business or even have a right to stay in business. It's easy to criticize people. People have troubles, make their own trouble, poor devils, and as long as they keep it private, it's not our place to judge.

It's just, she explained to her father, that I want to be rid of Sally and Luke, want them shunted away out of Mike's life and mine, and I know what they are, and what will keep them away from us. I could try to reform them both. I tried it once with Luke. I could try it for a million years, and I know enough about people to know that it wouldn't work.

There's ugliness in the offing, and I know it mustn't touch Mike ... nothing must damage Mike and me ... if something happens to us ... to our love ... I cannot even measure how much I have to lose.

She feared heartache. She feared the loss of her own self-esteem. If she threw Luke and Sally together, the rest was up to them.

She wondered if she hated them. She wasn't sure. A woman, she thought, has an enemy, built into her at birth, and that enemy is herself.

It seemed to put her mind in order to putter with seeming purpose about her trailer kitchen. She invented things to do ... she scrubbed a microscopic spot off a coffee pot, she waxed a counter surface that had been clean before. She found an old folder of recipes of her mother's. The recipes had been torn from newspapers and magazines in the course of fifteen years. With kitchen shears, she trimmed the ragged edges of all the clippings, arranged them in cook-book order, beginning with main dishes, finishing with desserts.

She knew what she was doing. She was trying to reach back to a time of goodness and little responsibility, before the dormant woman-thing awoke in her girl's heart. She was being good little Joan, minding Daddy's business for him, cleaning Mother's kitchen.

It was no better than other escapes. You were what you were, she thought, you were like a series of letters posted from no one knew where, all addressed to yourself and mailed at different times. You learned from one day to the next just who you had become.

She had been a fifteen-year-old, running in stark panic from a clumsy eager boy ...

She had been Luke's troubled sweetheart, reluctant, in the end ungiving ...

She had been Mike's woman.

She wanted no one else to be his woman too.

8

The Collins trailer, a huge black and gold affair, was neat inside. Nothing was out of place.

"You have a nice home," Joan observed. "One of the nicest I've visited."

"Thank you."

Sally Collins had seemed surprised when she opened the door and found Joan standing there. But she had been friendly, smiling, as she invited Joan inside.

"I meant to get here sooner, to outline the services of the camp, but I just didn't get around to it."

"I guess you're pretty busy," Sally Collins said.

"Yes."

She was the pixie type all right, Joan thought, dark and vivacious.

"I haven't seen you on the beach. That's free, you know."

"Yes, I know. I'll get down there one of these days."

"And there's a movie in town, or did you know about that? Movie, bowling alley and once in a while the dramatic club puts on a fairly well-acted play."

"So I heard."

Joan laughed. "Other than that I'm afraid we're pretty dull. Once in a while there's a dance at one of the casinos—"

"There's one at Pinehurst tonight. We're going to that."

"Oh, are you?"

"Yes, I love to dance."

Joan smiled and relaxed. Maybe Mike would like to run out there. Luke was a wonderful dancer and it was just possible that she might be able to get Luke and Sally together.

"One thing you might be interested in is our trailer-care service."

"Trailer-care service?"

"Yes. The paint on a trailer, you know, is something like the paint on a car. If you don't take care of it, it fades and rusts. It's important to wax the exterior of a trailer, though very few people do it. Unless you have the right equipment it's quite a job. We have a power polisher and can do it in about a day."

Sally's eyes expressed interest. "How much does it cost?"

"Twenty-five dollars and we guarantee the work."

"That isn't so bad."

"Not when you consider that it helps preserve a six or seven thousand dollar investment."

They discussed the polishing job at length. Originally, Joan's father had introduced the plan but it had been abandoned when not enough people subscribed to it. The equipment was now stored in the old shed by the beach with other seldom-used things.

"I guess Gerald would think it all right," Sally agreed, finally. "You can go ahead and have it done."

"I know you'll be pleased with the job."

"I hope so."

A few minutes later Joan said good-bye and left the trailer. Now that she had found a way to put her plan into operation the project filled her with doubt. There was no guarantee that Luke would become involved with the Collins woman or, if he did, that anything would happen as the result of it. The problem seemed more remote than ever.

She found Luke at the old shed. He was stripped down to the waist and was busy sorting out junk in the back room.

"Some of this stuff must have come over on the ark," he said, grinning. "I haven't seen an ox yoke since the old man sold the farm."

Luke's face was dirty and he was perspiring freely.

"I've got a job for you, Luke."

Sure.

"Sally Collins wants the outside of her trailer waxed."

Luke paused. "I'd like to wax the inside of her trailer," Re said.

"Now, Luke!"

"She's a cute trick. Some of the fellows say she wants to get herself knocked up."

"I wish you wouldn't talk that way, Luke."

"That's what they say," he protested.

"I don't care if they do. It isn't nice."

He's going for it, Joan thought happily—he's going for it big.

"So she wants her trailer waxed," Luke said. "I'll put a man on it in the morning." He indicated the buffer. "Is this the thing we use?"

"Yes. I thought you might want to do it, Luke."

"Me, work so hard? Like I said, if she wanted the inside of her trailer waxed, why—"

"She's paying twenty-five dollars. I don't want her money. You can have it, Luke."

There were two things, she thought, that Luke liked—women and money. She often wondered which he liked most.

"Now, then," Luke said, "that's different. For twenty-five bucks I'd wax the gravel in the road, stone by stone."

It was hot in the shed. She wished that she had worn shorts and halter. She hated to feel the dress sticking to her skin.

"Maybe you could do it tomorrow," Joan suggested.

"First thing in the morning."

"Thank you, Luke."

"Don't mention it."

She went out and walked down the roadway. It was an innocent pitch, she decided, and there could be no harm in it. After all, her plan required the unwitting cooperation of the principals. Sally was old enough to know her own mind, and so was Luke. If they found something in common it would take some of the pressure away from Mike. And if they didn't, she had only wasted a half hour of her time.

Nora was in front of the Husky, stretched out on a lawn chair in the sun. She wore an abbreviated costume that looked more like a bra and pantie outfit. She had a ripe, fully developed figure and most of it showed through the pale pink material.

"I got my lease," she said. "Thanks."

"That's okay."

"We both know where we stand. I can't walk off without paying you and you can't kick me off."

"I never thought of doing such a thing."

"No?" Nora smiled. "You never can tell. Times change, you know."

"Which reminds me," Joan said, "I haven't seen any money as yet."

Nora arose from the chair. "I'll get it for you," she said. When she reached the door she turned. "Would you care to see my salon?"

"Why, yes, I'd like to."

Joan followed Nora into the trailer.

"We're seldom busy during the day," Nora explained. "Only on Saturday, when the men don't work. Almost all of our business, both here and in town, is from six until midnight."

The living room, with the exception of a health-row machine in one corner, was normally furnished. A sofa ran the full length of one end and there was an easy chair by the wrought iron separator that cut off the kitchenette.

"I had Luke store the bedroom furniture in the bunk-bed section. I hope you don't mind."

"Oh, no."

The bedroom contained a large table similar to that used by chiropractors. Nora demonstrated how it could be adjusted up and down and from side to side.

"And this is a vitalizer," she said, lifting a small hand machine. "These four little rollers bring muscle tone to the body. It's a great little gadget and all the men love it."

There was a set of barbells beneath the window but Nora said they were seldom used.

"The men on the pipeline get enough lifting," she laughed. "They don't need those things to prove their strength. What they care about is relaxing and getting the aches out. It's wonderful how this thing has caught on. I didn't get out of here until one this morning."

"Does Millie help you?"

"Yes, both here and in town. She's very good. I hardly had to teach her anything."

Nora opened her pocketbook and extracted two hundred-dollar bills.

"For this month and next," she said.

"But the first month was only sixty."

"That's all right—keep the change."

"I've got a feeling that I'm in the wrong business," Joan said, laughing.

Nora smiled. "You are. You could do very well in my line. Believe me, honey, you could."

She was glad to get away from Nora.

She spent the afternoon on the beach, under a huge red and white umbrella. The Adams boy, now thoroughly chastised by his narrow brush with death, sat on the sand nearby, playing with a three-wheeled truck.

"I gotta apologize to Luke," Mrs. Adams stated. "I shouldn't've been so sore at him when he pulled sonny out of the water."

That night, when Mike stopped by the trailer, Joan suggested that they drive out to the dance at Pinehurst.

"Sounds good," Mike said. "Let's go."

They rode out to Crystal Lake in Joan's Caddy convertible. The top was down, the air warm, and Mike drove with one hand.

"I've been thinking about you all day," Mike said.

"Have you?"

"Yes." He slowed the car and kissed her.

Her lips moved against his mouth. "And I about you," she whispered, "the whole day long."

"Tell me about it."

She snuggled against him. "Well, first I wanted to get on top of the nearest trailer and shout out that I was going to marry Big Mike Summers."

"But you didn't?"

"No, you told me not to."

He kissed her again, this time on the neck.

"I ought to explain that," he said. "First off, there's enough bad blood between me and Jerry Collins right now. He doesn't just blame his wife but he blames me, too. He's wrong there. All I want her to do is leave me alone, but for some damned reason she won't do it. In the meantime, I need Collins on my gang. He's one of the best line foremen in the business and I couldn't keep up my quota without him. Frankly, it's been a ticklish business all the way through. I try not to insult Sally because I know that she could cause real trouble between us. And I try to keep Gerald happy because I need him. That's why I'm trying to make arrangements to go in to the home office—if I can get transferred to another crew, and I see no reason why I can't, I can say to hell with the whole mess. The way it stands now, I just have to be careful. That's why I told you to keep quiet about us until after I've made other connections. You wouldn't want a husband who didn't have a job, would you?"

"I'm not worried about that, Mike."

"No, but I am."

He's good, she thought; good and straight. He would make a wonderful husband. She would be able to depend upon him. Physical love, if it were important, would come later. Sometime he'd be able to awaken her again and she would recapture her first thrill.

He steered the Caddy off onto a side road. She didn't want to stop, but she wouldn't tell him so. He would be offended. He parked the car in the mouth of an old wood road, beside a stone wall. The moonlight filtered down through the trees, washing over them. There was the smell of wild roses in the air. It was a perfect night.

"Joan."

He turned to her, taking her in his arms. Anxiously his lips sought hers. She responded to his kiss a little desperately, seeking the spark that might ignite the flame in her.

"I love you," she whispered. "I love you so much."

She wanted it to be true.

And Mike almost made it come true. He was gentle with her—he made no demands. They talked. He told her a little more about himself, about his youthful struggles, and she felt she began to understand him a little better. He hadn't had her sheltered life. He had earned his own way with heart and muscle and physical labor; he had put himself through school. He had done some things that weren't nice—on these he refused to elaborate. But she understood him; she had been no paragon herself these last few days. It gave them something in common.

She told him about her plans for Luke and Sally. She was fighting for her man, she said. Mike laughed, then sobered.

"Wish you hadn't told me," he said. "Keep me out of it—after all, Collins is one of my men. I'm responsible for his actions."

"Then, why don't you fire him?"

Mike looked a little shocked. "I can't do that—he does his job. I can't fire a man just because his wife goes crazy. You've never had to worry about making a living, have you?"

In a sense he was right—she had never had to worry. Her father had done all the worrying for the family, and by the time she had been old enough, the financial problems had been settled. Still she had worked, was working now. If anything in her personal life made her unfit for the job of running the trailer camp, she would have to bear the consequences.

But nothing she ever did with Mike would accomplish that. Even Mike's attitude toward Collins suggested a sense of responsibility. That was the kind of man she wanted, that any woman wanted.

"Mike," she whispered. "Kiss me once more. Then I think we'd better get to the dance."

9

The Lakeside Casino was a large resort hotel on the North End of Crystal Lake. The buildings were old, poorly painted and the shaled driveway was marked with numerous deep holes. The dancing pavilion was the main feature of the place. It ran along the lake shore and was ringed by dozens of multi-colored Japanese lanterns. The dance music was always good, sometimes hot, sometimes sweet, and the breeze from the lake was usually cool.

"Table for two," the headwaiter said.

They followed the headwaiter along the edge of the dance floor. At the moment the music was hot, plenty hot, and the floor was crowded. A couple near the bandstand was really dancing up a storm. The girl wore hardly anything under her dress and every time she was spun by her partner bare flesh showed. Several men stood on the sidelines, watching.

Joan and Mike passed a long table which was unoccupied except for an elderly appearing couple.

"Hey, Mike," the man said. "Why not join us?"

Mike turned toward the table. "Is there room?"

"Aw, there's always room for two more." The man stood up. "Good evening, Miss Baker."

"Good evening, Mr. Parsons."

"It's Pearsons." The man smiled, forgiving her. "My wife, Ellen. Ellen, Miss Baker. Miss Baker owns the trailer camp, dear."

"Oh, yes," the gray haired woman said, smiling. "I remember you now. I saw you when we came in."

Mike held a chair for Joan and she sat down.

"Todd and his wife are with us," Pearsons said. "And the Shipleys. Also the young fellow from the camp—what's his name?"

"Luke?" Joan suggested.

"Yes. Luke. And Collins and his wife."

Mike hesitated before sitting down. "It's going to be mighty crowded here," he said. "We can find another table, Alex."

But Pearsons was insistent. "Since when," he wanted to know, "did the high brass of Davis Construction refuse to drink with the peasantry?"

Mike grinned at that. “You put it that way, Alex, and a guy can’t very well refuse you.” He sat down. “But just to teach you a lesson, you can buy the first round.”

“Sure. What’ll it be?”

“Scotch.”

“Ouch, that hurt. Say, Mike, when are we getting that raise?”

“I don’t know,” Mike replied. “The union’s working on it.”

Joan ordered rye and soda. “Make it tall on the soda,” she told the waiter.

Mike and Alex Pearsons discussed trenches, welding and pipes. In self-defense, Joan found herself engaged in a most uninteresting conversation with Ellen Pearsons.

“That’s the only thing I hate about trailer life,” the woman said for the fourth time. “I miss my canning. Oh, I can put up tomatoes and fruits and the like, but after I get them put up where can they be stored?”

“I don’t know.”

“Yes. Well, that’s what I say to Alex. I say, now why would I go to all that work when—”

“Mike,” Joan said. “Mike, why don’t we dance?”

Mike, who was on his second drink, looked at her as though she had just arrived.

“Yeah, sure.”

Mike was a good dancer. He was light on his feet and had a way of holding Joan that was just right.

“Damn luck,” he complained. “I would have to sit down at the same table with the Collinses.”

“They seem to be dancing.”

“They won’t be after he gets a snootful.”

“Does he drink much?”

“They all do. Show me a pipeline man and I’ll show you a guy who’s two-handed with a glass.”

“But not you, Mike.”

“I have my moments,” he said.

It must have been Mike’s night to drink. When they returned to the table he ordered a double scotch for himself and a double rye for Joan. She didn’t want the double rye but Mike seemed to be enjoying himself and she didn’t want to spoil his fun. Besides, now that the band had taken an intermission, everybody was back at the table and they were all drinking heavily.

The Todds were elderly people but the Shipleys were young and so much in love with each other that they were hardly aware of anyone else being present.

"They've only been married three weeks," Mike said. "Every week is an anniversary for them."

The Collins couple, seated opposite Joan and Mike, paid little attention to each other. Gerald Collins was talking to Todd about a new ditch through a swamp and Sally, her eyes very bright, was listening to Luke recite something about himself.

"It must have been fabulous," Sally said. "I can't imagine anybody having so much fun."

"Yeah," Luke said, nodding his head. "The army was okay."

Luke was getting drunk, Joan thought—each time he got drunk he fell in love with the army all over again. The truth was that Luke had hated the army. He'd gone over the hill twice and served time in the stockade twice. He'd gone into the army a private and come out as a private. Luke's enlistment had been a stalemate—he had done nothing for the army and the army had done nothing for him.

"I put vinegar in with my beets," Ellen Pearsons was saying. "Alex, you know, likes them better that way. But, as I say, you do all that work and then where do you store—"

My God, Joan thought again, won't that woman ever stop? Beets, beans, pickles—she should have stayed back on the farm. In despair she looked for some other topic.

"I like your dress," Joan said to Sally Collins. "It's pretty."

"Thank you!"

The dress was an off-the-shoulder affair, dark as midnight.

"Luke is going to wax the trailer for us. Aren't you, Luke?"

"Sure," Luke replied. "I'm going to put it on with a broom and rub it in with a dirty mop."

Sally laughed. "Honest, if you aren't the one!"

Joan smiled and sipped her drink. Things were working out better than she had hoped. Luke wasn't wasting any time with Sally.

"I thought Nora was coming along," Joan said to Luke.

"She had to work."

"That's too bad."

"You cry for her," Luke suggested. "Make the tears big."

"If you aren't the one," Sally Collins said again.

But Sally, Joan saw, wasn't looking at Luke. She hardly ever looked at Luke. Most of the time she was looking at Mike.

"I put soda in with my beans," Ellen Pearsons said. "Baking soda. It keeps them greener. Do you ever do that with your beans, Miss Baker?"

"Not any more."

Why didn't the orchestra play again, or why didn't the woman just pass out? Why didn't something happen?

"We're going to have a hell of a time boring through that swamp," Collins said, addressing Mike. "You'd better come out and take a look."

"I will." Mike's tone was guarded and forceful.

"There's a puddle in there all of fifteen feet deep."

Mike nodded. "I'll look at it," he said. "As soon as I can."

"Well, don't put it off. We'll be up to it day after tomorrow."

"Okay."

"Make it tomorrow," Collins said. His voice lacked any warmth. "It's your baby. I only follow your stakes."

Alex Pearsons leaned upon the table, upsetting his drink.

"We didn't follow them on Big Knobby," he said. "We shot right across the lower part."

"That was to save time," Collins said.

"And a good job it was," Mike stated. "It put us into Andersonville two days early."

"I hope you noted it in your report," Collins said.

Mike frowned. "Of course I did."

There was tension here, Joan thought—big tension. The two men hated each other at work. And Sally stood between them. It was a situation which could explode at any moment.

The waiter hopped back and forth, between the table and the bar, lugging empty glasses and fresh drinks. Big Mike's face was red and when he held up a match he had difficulty locating the end of his cigarette. Gerald Collins lapsed into silence. His wife, still talking to Luke, kept watching Big Mike. Luke, who had switched to beer, seemed to be holding his liquor very well.

"Why don't they have draft beer?" Luke wanted to know. "I hate bottle beer—it tastes just like a skunk smells." The complaint was perfectly cheerful.

"Honest, Luke, if you aren't the one!"

The Todds had gotten into an argument about Todd's group insurance with the company.

"It ain't right," Mrs. Todd told her husband. "Sybil's way out in California. I ought to be the beneficiary."

"You could die before me," Todd pointed out. "And if you don't stop drinkin' so much gin, you got a good chance of doing it."

His wife began to cry. "Well, I don't care. It ain't right."

The Shipleys excused themselves, saying that it was time to go to bed. Somebody laughed. A bed was the place for a couple like the Shipleys. They could stop teasing themselves and get down to the business at hand.

"I don't know why Alex doesn't pick some berries," Ellen Pearsons said. "I could put up a few quarts."

Her husband overheard her. "Give me a bucket," he said, "and I'll go out and get some right now." He looked around the table for sympathy. "Damn woman," he continued, "always steamin' up the trailer—"

Ellen Pearsons' face darkened. "You've had enough," she announced, rising. "You always get nasty when you drink."

Pearsons shrugged and stood up. "You drive me to drink," he stated. "You and your damn canning."

They departed, still arguing.

"Hell of a thing," Mike said. "People fighting over stuff like that."

Gerald Collins nodded. "Ridiculous," he observed, thickly. "The whole world is ridiculous."

"I'll buy that," Luke said. He lifted his glass. "To a screwy world."

Collins glared at him. "I hope you didn't mean that the way it sounded, fellow."

Luke grinned. "Screwy means nuts," he said.

"Well, that's different."

The waiter brought another round.

"I'm getting drunk," Mike confided to Joan. "Either that or I've grown four hands."

Joan laughed. "I don't mind," she said. "I'll drive home."

"That reminds me of something," Luke said. "I came out with the Shipleys and they've gone. Can I bum a ride down to the camp with anybody?" He was looking at Sally Collins. "I didn't bring my car. It had a flat."

"Ride with us," Mike said.

Luke looked disappointed, but he accepted the offer.

The orchestra returned to the bandstand. Music drifted over the pavilion. Chairs scraped as couples got to their feet.

"Dance with me?" Luke asked Joan. "Once around the floor and then out?"

Joan glanced at Mike and Mike nodded.

"I've got a full load," he said. "I couldn't crawl over the notes."

Joan patted him affectionately on the cheek. "You're a bad boy," she told him. "A bad boy."

Luke was a much better dancer than Mike. He seemed to float over the floor and he was easy to follow.

"I never saw people drink so much," Luke said.

"You didn't do so bad yourself."

"No, but I still know what I'm doing."

His arm, circling her, drew her in close. She glanced toward the table they'd left—there was no one there.

"Collins went to the men's room," Luke said, following her glance. "I don't know where the other two went."

Perhaps, Joan thought, Mike had gone up to the bar to talk to someone he knew. There were a lot of pipeliners present and he couldn't refuse a drink without being offensive. She wished Mike and the others didn't drink so much, but she supposed their work had something to do with it. It was tough, brutal work and it demanded rough, careless lives.

"That Sally Collins is quite a girl," Luke said.

"Yes, isn't she?"

"I think she hates her husband."

"Or the other way around."

"Did you see how she was watching your friend?"

"Let's not talk about it."

"You got a crush on him or something?"

"I think he's nice."

"You used to think I was nice, too."

"Let's not get into that again."

He bent and kissed her on the cheek. "I never did," he said. "And you know it."

She supposed she should be angry with him, but she wasn't… Luke had been drinking. They had all been drinking. He couldn't hurt her with words. He couldn't ever hurt her again.

"I think Sally Collins likes you," Joan said.

"Do you?"

"Well, she seemed to think that you were pretty cute."

"That doesn't mean anything. No one at the table, including her husband, had much to say to her. I couldn't just sit there and let her stare off into space."

"I still think she likes you, Luke."

"She's married."

"I didn't know that would bother you any."

"Say, what is this—you trying to build something?"

"No. I'm just talking."

"Well, stop it. Sally likes your redhead."

She tried to draw away from him. "I don't like that, Luke."

"I didn't think you would. And I don't think you'll like it any better when I tell you where the two of them went just now."

"What!" She froze inside. "What are you saying, Luke?"

He guided her toward the sidelines.

"I'm saying that as soon as her husband staggered away from the table the two of them were digging for the woods."

"Luke!"

"I'm saying it and I'll prove it."

She didn't want to go with him. She tried to get away from him but he wouldn't let her go. His fingers were steel on her wrist.

"You might as well know it now," he said, gently. "It's better to find it out now than later."

They walked off the pavilion and into the night. The shadows hung low beneath the trees. A fine dew covered the parked cars. Beyond the ring of darkness the lights of the hotel filled the night. A couple stood near a new Mercury. They were locked in tight embrace.

"Do you see what I mean?" Luke asked. "Do you believe me now?"

It was Mike and Sally.

Sobbing, Joan turned and fled.

Her world had come to a sudden halt.

Part Two

Trailer Travail

10

The big Cad devoured the highway in the night. Luke was driving.

"I didn't know that guy meant so much to you," Luke said. "If I had, I wouldn't have done what I did."

"It—it's all right, Luke."

The initial shock had been terrific. She had run to the car, crying—she had almost driven off without Luke. All she had wanted to do was get out of there, away from Mike, away from that girl. All she had been able to think about was that she had given herself to Mike and that he had betrayed her. Now that she was away from the casino she could look at it a little more objectively. Mike didn't love her—he had simply used her. She had been a little fool and was gathering a fool's reward. It hurt to know this but, as Luke said, it was better to know it now than later. To have found it out later, after they were married, would have been even more terrible.

"Let's stop somewhere and have a drink," Luke said.

"I've had enough." And she meant it.

"Just one. Do you good. And I sure as hell can use it. It isn't every night that I have a girl cry on my shoulder."

Luke had been fine. He hadn't complained. And he had said nothing as she'd clung to him, sobbing. He had merely held her close, comforting her with his nearness.

"All right," she agreed. "Just one."

They stopped at Timmy's Rest, a little place south of Button Ridge.

"Let's sit at a table," Luke said. "Those bar stools are terrible."

She walked back to a table while Luke stood at the bar, waiting for the drinks.

I hate Mike, she thought, and I hate Sally. I hope Luke can do something with Sally. I don't care what he does as long as he does it.

The thought startled her. Maybe Mike had already taken care of Sally.

"Here," Luke said, handing her the drink. "This will make you feel better."

"Thanks, Luke."

She didn't want the drink. She didn't want anything. All she wanted to do was go home and lie down in the dark. She wanted to think. She had to think! Was there any point of going to a doctor so soon? Could a doctor tell? And if he could tell, would he be willing to do anything for her? Would a doctor help her?

"Jeeze," Luke said, sitting down, "your face is white."

"Is it?"

"Just like you'd seen a ghost."

Not a ghost, she thought.

"Here's to it," Luke said, lifting his glass. "Here's to the ghost—may it soon be forgotten."

The drink tasted funny, like old wood and sand. It was a small glass and she guessed the liquor was too strong for the soda. She made a face and put the glass down.

"Thank you again, Luke," she said. "For showing me."

"You don't mean that, really."

"Maybe I don't exactly, but it is better this way."

"I guess you thought quite a lot of the guy."

"I guess I did."

"Well, he's good looking."

"Yes."

"And he has a certain amount of charm."

"Yes."

"He'll get himself into plenty of trouble with that dame. You see if he doesn't."

"I think so, too."

Luke reached across the table and lifted her hand.

"Know what?" he demanded. "I think the guy's a chump. If I had my choice, between the two of you, I know who it'd be."

"You're nice, Luke."

"Do you mean that?"

"For saying such a thing, yes."

"Well, you've always been my girl. You know that, don't you? No matter what troubles we had, you've always been my girl."

And you were my guy, she thought, until you spoiled it. Oh, Luke, why did you have to ruin it?

Aloud she said, "We'd better be getting back to the camp."

"Finish your drink."

"All right, but it's awfully strong."

"When you feel weak you need something strong."

"I suppose so."

The liquor burned her throat and warmed her stomach. She could feel the warmth of it, spreading. Luke had been right. She had needed that drink.

"I'll drive," she said when they got outside.

"You want the top up?"

"No, leave it down."

It was a nice night for driving. The moonlight lay flat on the highway and the mountain breezes were cool.

"Let's take a ride," she said, suddenly.

The suggestion surprised her. She didn't want to take a ride. All she wanted to do was to lie down in some dark corner and forget.

"All right," Luke said.

The Caddy rolled down the highway. When they reached the intersection she turned left, in the direction of Wellsboro.

"Luke, did you put anything in my drink?"

"Me? Why, no. What makes you ask that?"

"I feel—strange."

Luke laughed. "Hell," he said. "I feel strange, too. It's the booze."

Turn around, she cautioned herself; turn around before it's too late.

"What are you doing now?" Luke inquired.

"Turning around."

"But I thought you wanted to go for a ride."

"I changed my mind." Did that surprise him?

She drove steadily toward the camp. Occasionally she glanced at Luke. He sat in the middle of the seat. His left arm was near her shoulder.

"Luke," she said. "Luke, don't touch me,"

"I'm not."

"Well, don't."

There's something wrong with me, she thought—something very wrong. The need for a man was all through her, boiling over. She could hardly stand it. It was as bad as the first time. Her whole body throbbed. She closed her eyes, briefly, and tried to think about something else. She couldn't. All she could think about was a man. Any man.

She drove faster. She had to get Luke back to the camp and say good night to him. To do what she wanted to do was insanity.

"I hope you stay on the road," Luke said. "You're going like hell."

"I'm in a—hurry."

"You can stop."

Her face flamed. "It isn't that, silly."

She pulled in at the trailer camp and brought the car to a halt alongside the red and white trailer.

Somehow, she had to get away from him. Somehow, she had to leave him alone. Somehow ...

Clutching the dress to her body she got out of the car. She stood there for a long moment, undecided, desperately trying to fight down the torrent of emotions which seized her.

"Come with me," she said, finally, walking toward the trailer.

Silently he followed her.

11

She awoke with a start to the ringing of her telephone.

"Hello," she said.

"Mike Summers. New York calling."

"He's not here."

"Could you call him to the phone, please? This is important."

She didn't want to see Mike; she didn't ever want to see him again. But he was a resident of the camp and as such he deserved the same courtesy as anyone else.

"It'll take a few minutes," Joan said. "I have to get him."

"Very well. Have him call operator five-three, in New York."

The operator broke the connection and Joan replaced the receiver.

"Damn!" she exclaimed.

She dressed hurriedly in slacks and halter. As she started out of the doorway she stopped long enough to scuff her feet into a pair of white sandals.

Luke's coat lay on the living room floor. She picked it up and placed it upon the davenport. Thinking about Luke made her sick—but thinking about herself made her feel even more ill.

She was no better than Millie had been. She might just as well admit it to herself. Admitting it wouldn't make the crime worse; it might help her to understand her problem. Suddenly, at the age of twenty-two, she had been claimed by not one but two men. There was no use denying it. Denying it would only make it worse. She could go to a doctor, of course, but a doctor couldn't help, not unless she could help herself. In some way, she had to guard against another similar attack, destroy the fierce yearning that had seized her the night before.

She had enjoyed Luke but, then, she supposed she would have enjoyed any man. Her body had been a mass of hot need, her mind a tortured thing. Yes, she would have given herself to any man. Luke, she remembered wryly, had been pleased with her, his ego inflated.

Mike was not at home. She knocked several times but received no response. Just as she was getting ready to leave the woman next door came out and called to her.

"Are you looking for Mr. Summers, miss?"

"Yes, I am."

"Well, he said to tell anybody who came around that he's out at Panther Swamp, if you know where that is."

"Yes, I do."

"He'll be there all day long."

"Thank you."

Panther Swamp was on the east side of Berry Picker's Mountain. It bordered the New York-Montreal highway and extended deep into the guts of the woods. Hunters claimed it to be the roughest swamp in the state.

Joan walked back to the trailer and got into the Caddy. The least she could do was to drive out there and give him the message. Perhaps it was merely a confirmation of his planned visit to the company's home office. And it might be a transfer. She hoped it was a transfer. The sooner Mike left the camp the better she would like it.

Halfway out to Panther Swamp she began to cry. There was something else that she couldn't deny, either—something that was more important than anything else. She was still in love with Mike. And she wasn't good enough for him. No matter what he had done, she wouldn't ever be good enough for Mike. She had traded all of that away with Luke. She had traded it blindly and thoughtlessly.

I don't feel that way this morning, she thought; I don't feel I need a man for the pure sake of having him. I just feel as though I want somebody near me, someone I can trust, someone I can confide in. And I haven't got anybody, nobody at all. And I've ruined all of that.

She had played the part of the little fool the night before. She shouldn't have run when she saw Mike kissing Sally. She should have confronted them, both of them, and she should have had it out right then and there. Her mistake had been in running. She had attempted to run from Mike, from herself, and she had gotten into something far worse. Now she was in it—deep. The jungle she had made of her life was far more complex than the jungle of Panther Swamp.

She parked the Caddy behind Mike's pick-up truck. A laborer stood near-by, axe in hand, watching her as she got out of the car.

"I'm looking for Big Mike," she said.

The man stared at her bare midriff. "He's up on the knoll."

She followed a wood road toward the knoll. At one point she had to get out of the way of a horse pulling a long length of pipe. The pipe rattled and scraped over the stones.

"Hello," she said when she found Mike.

He looked at her with interest. "Hello," he said, his tone cold.

"There was a phone call for you. You're to call operator five-three in New York."

"Okay. Thanks."

"You're welcome," she said, turning away.

"Just a minute," Mike said. "I think I have an apology coming."

"Do you? For what?"

"I had to walk home last night."

Joan laughed. "That's the funniest thing I've heard today."

"I'm glad you're amused. As far as I'm concerned, walking eight miles isn't funny."

She swung around, her eyes mocking him.

"What did you want me to do after I saw you kissing Sally? Send you a letter of congratulations?"

Mike frowned. "You saw that?"

"I know what I saw."

"Well, I did kiss her," Mike admitted. "I kissed her for the last time. I kissed her because she wanted me to."

"I'll bet!"

"I decided to tell her that we were going to get married. It was sort of a goodbye—for us."

"You can't expect me to believe that?"

Mike shrugged. "It's the truth," he said. "She wasn't mad at all. In fact, she seemed happy for me. I was a little surprised."

"So was I," Joan retorted. "I didn't think that of you, Mike."

"But I just told you how it happened!"

"I know what you told me."

"And you don't believe it?"

"No."

Mike's face darkened. "I don't give a damn what you believe! That's how it was."

"You don't have to swear at me."

"No? Well, somebody better swear at you. Somebody had better swear at you good before you get yourself in a lot of trouble."

"Mike! What are you talking about?"

"You know what I'm talking about."

"But I don't, Mike. I don't!"

Mike's eyes were hard. "And I thought you were the fine one," he said. "I should have known it was too good to be true. Mike Summers never had that kind of luck. Let me ask you a question. You know that Husky trailer you rented out to that girl—Nora?"

"Yes."

"Well, what goes on in there?"

"It's a massage parlor."

Mike guffawed. "A massage parlor? That's a new name for it. Or maybe it isn't so new."

"If it isn't a massage parlor, then what is it?"

Mike looked at her incredulously. "Why, it's a fancy house," he said. "Now don't tell me you didn't know that."

"I—"

She was speechless.

"You don't have to put on an innocent act with me," Mike said. "I know how it is. You have to pick up a buck one way or another."

"Damn you," she said. "Damn you."

"Look who's swearing at who." He laughed. "How dumb do you think I am, anyway? I've known about it for days. I even thought I'd talk to you about it, but I didn't have the guts. It's made trouble for me, the kind of place you run."

"If it's true," she said. "I didn't know. Honest!"

He shook his head. "Maybe before last night I'd have thought so, but not now. The way you took off with your boy friend last night—"

"Boy friend!"

"And left me, makes me think that you're not near the kind of a girl I thought you were. It makes me think that you just might let a whorehouse operate in your backyard and not even give a hell about it."

Before she had been upset, hurt, but now she was angry.

"I don't care what you think!" she screamed at him. "I don't care, Mike Summers. To hell with you!"

"To hell with you, too," Mike said, flatly.

She wheeled and left him. Hot tears of anger and shame filled her eyes. Just who did he think he was, saying terrible things like that? If he was provoked with her about the night before, and she supposed he was—and rightfully so, perhaps—he could come right out and say so. He didn't have to hurt her this way, didn't have to say things that weren't true. He didn't have to hurt the whole camp—the thing her father had built.

She drove homeward. She was no longer crying. Her eyes were wide open, bright, and her mind was alert. Perhaps there was something to what Mike had told her, after all. She had wondered, several times, how a massage parlor could do so well, but men were strange creatures and she hadn't thought too much about it. In a way the operation had made sense—in another way it hadn't.

Cold fear twisted her insides. She had fired Millie because Millie had been going to bed with the men in the trailers, and Nora had hired Millie without any hesitation. In fact, Nora had wanted to hire Millie. Or had that been Luke's idea? Hadn't Luke suggested it?

She thought about Luke. Luke was a lot that he shouldn't be, he'd done a lot of things that he shouldn't have done, but this, Joan was sure, was one time Luke wouldn't be on the wrong side.

Every man had to have some standards he wouldn't violate. Luke was no different. Luke must have some of those standards, too. No, Luke wouldn't be a part of such a thing, not knowingly.

Maybe, Joan thought further, there isn't any truth to it at all. Nora Justin liked most men, she was friendly with them, and her attitude might have led to gossip. It would be easy enough for one man to get a story like this started. Mike could have heard it and Mike could have believed it. Joan couldn't blame him for that. She knew it wasn't so and, she was almost willing to believe it.

There was one way in which she could end the whole thing, she decided—she would refund the rent Nora had paid her and would tell her to pack up and leave. Perhaps it was an unfair thing to do but it was a lot better than doing nothing at all. If Nora had a legitimate business she could set up somewhere else and her customers would follow her. There would be no harm done. And it would demonstrate to Mike that she, Joan, was doing the right thing. It was important to her that he know this.

Then she wondered how she could ever convince him, when she no longer could convince herself. Last night had made all the difference. Mike's defection couldn't explain Luke—what had happened last night had to do with herself and no one else. There was something wrong with her, something terrible and unnamable—she wondered if she hadn't been with Luke last night, whom would she have invited into her trailer.

The thought was unbearable and she began to cry. There was some relief in crying, but not much. She had spoiled whatever she had had with Mike by her actions last night—even if Mike didn't know just what she had done, she herself knew. Last night had left her not only with a sense of shame; it had given birth to a feeling of personal disgust. She could no longer trust herself, her own thoughts, her instincts. She could ask no one else to trust her. Her body was a law unto itself and would have its way. There was nothing she could do about it—except, perhaps, destroy it. In the end, she supposed, it would destroy her.

After a while she stopped crying. What was the good of tears? Tears wouldn't solve anything. Tears would not bring back the thing she had shared with Mike, unsullied and complete. Tears would not turn back the hours, the days, the years, and put her back to where she could have a fresh start.

Tears were for those who had something left to cry about.

When she arrived back at the camp she drove directly to the Collins trailer. There was a ladder lying on the ground and a couple of buckets nearby. Luke was nowhere in sight.

He's inside, she thought, getting out of the car—he's inside making love to Sally Collins. The thought amused her. She had made such careful plans and they had blown up in her face. Mike had been driven into Sally's arms. Joan guessed it served her right.

Sally Collins answered the door immediately. Obviously, she was alone.

"It's noontime," she said in reply to Joan's question. "Luke went to lunch."

"Oh. Well, thank you."

Sally's eyes were mischievous. "You left early last night, didn't you?"

"Yes."

"Mike was so mad that he walked home."

"So I understand."

"He told me you were going to be married."

Joan felt ill. Mike had been telling the truth and she hadn't believed him.

"Yes?" Somehow, she had to go on with the conversation.

"Mike and I are old friends," Sally Collins said. "Very good friends. He's a good man, Miss Baker."

"Yes, he is."

Sally Collins stepped aside. "Won't you come in?"

"No, thank you. I'm in a—hurry."

"I see."

"I have to find Luke."

"That's too bad. I had hoped I could talk to you about Mike."

But Joan didn't want to talk about Mike just then. She wanted to see Luke and get this thing about Nora Justin settled. After that she could take the time to talk about Mike or anything else.

"I'm sorry, but I am in a hurry."

"You must have a minute."

"All right. A minute."

"I'm not going to say very much, Miss Baker. Only this—Mike is very much in love with you. I can tell. I've known Mike a long time. I've never seen Mike in love before. Be good to him, Miss Baker." Sally's voice became husky. "Be good to him or you'll be sorry!"

"I don't know what you mean."

Sally didn't smile. "You don't have to know what I mean. Just remember it, that's all."

"I—will."

She drove to her own trailer. Sally's remarks annoyed her. It was none of the girl's business what happened.

Luke was waiting for her in the office.

"Twenty-five bucks," he said. "The next time you take on a trailer wax job, make it thirty-five. I'm busting my hump on that thing."

Joan nodded and sat down opposite Luke. He was covered with sweat and she could smell the heat from his body.

"Luke," she said, "we've got to do something about Nora Justin."

He frowned. "What about Nora?" he wanted to know.

"I want her out of here."

"Out of here?"

"Yes, Luke."

"But, why?"

"I just do, that's all."

Luke shook his head. "It isn't that easy," he said. "She's got a lease. A year's lease. You signed the lease and she says she paid you two months rent. Did she?"

"Yes."

"Well, how can you break it? That's the reason for leases—both parties are protected. Ask a lawyer. You know what you're to be paid each month and she knows how long she can stay. It was a fair deal all the way around. You and I both know that the Husky was worth only about fifty a month. You charged her sixty and she was willing to pay a hundred. That's why I suggested the lease. You get more money and she gets some security for the extra."

"I don't care, Luke. I want her out of here."

Luke sighed. "You don't understand," he said. "You can't do things that way. I don't know what this is all about, or why you've suddenly decided that you don't want her any more, but I do know that she has some rights. And it's all in writing."

"Rights!" Joan stormed. "She's got no right to do what she's doing."

"All right. So what's she doing?"

"She's running a brothel."

"Who told you that?"

"It doesn't matter."

Luke grinned. "Come on, you can tell me."

"No."

"Was it the redhead?"

"It doesn't matter," she said again. "What difference does it make?"

"A lot of difference. The redhead tried to date Nora a couple of times and she wouldn't have anything to do with him. He was sore about it."

"I don't believe that!"

"Suit yourself."

"When was that?" she inquired, lamely. "When did he try to date her?"

Luke thought about that for a moment. "I don't know when the first time was," he said, "but I know when he tried to date her the last time. It was yesterday. He came over there in the morning and hung around for quite a while. She told him she wasn't interested."

"But—why?"

Luke laughed. "That's a hell of a question. I don't even know what you mean. Maybe he liked her looks, and she didn't like his. Ask him. He ought to know."

But she wouldn't ask Mike—she'd never ask Mike another thing. All the while Mike had been making love to her he had been chasing after both Sally and Nora Justin. The knowledge made her feel even worse.

"What do you know about Nora?" Joan asked.

"I know she runs a massage parlor."

"But you don't know anything else?"

"No."

"You're not lying to me, Luke?"

"Hell, why would I lie to you? I've got a good job here, working for you. How much do you think I make from Nora? Nickels. She doesn't need anybody to sell for her any more. She's got more business than she can handle. Last week I didn't earn a dime from her. I don't care. I'm set here with you—or it would seem as though I am—and that's more than enough for me. Last night—well, if you think you made a mistake, I guess you did. Girls do these things—I know."

Joan passed over his allusion to last night. "I don't want to discuss us, Luke. Are you sure Nora's running just a massage parlor?"

"I'm sure."

"Nothing goes on down there that shouldn't?"

"No."

"What about Millie? Millie doesn't know very much about massage."

"Maybe not. But she learns fast and there isn't a great deal to know. Nora says she's doing all right and Nora pays her. That's all I can tell you about it."

Joan felt relieved. Not because of Mike—nothing could make her feel differently about him—but because Nora was all right and no scandal would touch the Beachlake Trailer Camp. A scandal could very well ruin the future of the business and the Bakers had worked too hard to gain what they had to throw it away like that.

"Thank you, Luke," she said. "I feel better."

"Just don't believe every blabbermouth you hear."

"No."

"Nora's clean, believe me."

"I believe you."

"I wouldn't tell you that if I didn't think so."

"I don't imagine you would, Luke."

He got up and came over to her. He tilted her head with his hand, bent down and kissed her on the mouth.

"There's another reason I wouldn't lie to you," he said. "I'm in love with you."

"Please, Luke."

"After last night, how could I help it? You gave me the world last night, honey—"

"I'll—I'll see you tonight," she told him huskily.

She had to find out what had gone wrong with her—she had to find out!

12

That night, Luke could do nothing to please her.

"I don't get it," he said. "You were willing enough before."

She wanted to tell him that she was testing herself, trying to fathom her own depths—but she knew he wouldn't understand.

"I want something left," she told him. "Just a little bit of something left that I can call my own."

He grinned. "Don't worry. You've got plenty left."

"Now, is that a nice way to talk, Luke?"

A little later he left.

The next morning, just before nine, Mike showed up at the trailer. He was dressed in a blue suit. She admitted to herself, somewhat reluctantly, that he looked very good in blue; it made him seem even bigger, broader.

"In case anybody comes looking for me," he said, "I'm going to New York for a day or so."

"All right." Her tone was cold, disinterested. "I'll tell them."

"I notice you didn't take what I said about the massage parlor seriously, did you?"

"No."

"I told you that you can get in a lot of trouble. Remember that, Joan."

"There's nothing wrong down there."

"Is that what you say?"

"That's what I say!"

"Okay."

There's one way to prove it, she thought; there's one way to prove he accused Nora because he was vindictive.

"I understand you asked Nora for a date."

"Who told you that?"

"Never mind. Did you or didn't you?"

"Sure," he said. "I asked her twice and she turned me down both times."

"Well, if she's that kind of a girl, why did you ask her?"

"Maybe that's why I asked her," he replied. "Because she is that kind."

"I'm glad I found out."

Mike's look was stony. "I'm glad you did, too."

A few minutes later, while she was outside watering the flowers alongside the trailer, she saw Sally Collins and Mike drive out in the new Mercury. In that moment, she hated both of them.

Or is it myself I hate? she asked of the tormented person she had become.

Our bodies, she thought. Mysterious and finite, beautiful or ugly, old, young, sick or well, they can be prisons to us. Whatever they do, we pay for. There seemed no corner of human spirit that could serve as refuge from follies of the body. All that her spirit felt—longing, jealousy, panic, loneliness, self-loathing—was part of her body's self-betrayal.

For once, she wanted the day to herself. The bread-and-butter routine of taking care of the camp had no solace in it. Even her working hands seemed part of that physical prison. She knew she had changed subtly in the last few days ... that at last even her appearance was not quite a girl's appearance. She looked like a woman—the difference was indefinable, almost mental. Her face in the mirror showed thoughtfulness, the mere shadow of sorrow.

Passion had not been cruel. It had not left in her a look of ravishment.

She was beautiful, she knew. She had been a pretty girl. Cute, some people said. Cute figure, they said. She had become a beautiful woman.

It had not made her happy. She sensed a division of herself that had not been there before—the body of Joan, the soul of Joan—and the soul hungered now for innocence and peace.

How good it would have been, she thought, to be back one day in school. She pictured the library at college, the books written by men and women dead a hundred years. They too had struggled and sorrowed ... in the end they had escaped. Nothing was left of them but thought.

Was that what she really wanted? She knew it wasn't true. The books in the library spoke to you ... you sat in the shadow and opened the book and the book gave you its thought ... but the speaker could not listen. No matter how full your heart was, no matter how you longed to answer and be heard, the wise free dead were cut off from your anguish. Their thoughts were a one-way road.

She thought of the clean boys, students she had known either well or slightly, and the girls in her own dorm, and the bull-sessions at midnight. Topic A, they'd called it. Men.

We didn't know, she thought. None of us knew. We thought you could learn it all from one of those one-way roads ... that it all had happened before, and if you studied enough, were sane and straight enough, you could profit by mistakes in other peoples' pasts.

Go tell the flowers in front of the cabins that some day winter will come. Tell them to save themselves. How can they? They are trapped, rooted not only in earth but in time's ruthlessness. They will stand there when the frost comes—stand there and lose their bloom. Just as Joan had done. Not only the obvious bloom, the birthright of virginity, but that subtler thing of the spirit—freshness. Expectation.

I could learn, she thought, to loathe this body of mine, to blame it for what it has done to me, how it has wracked my emotions. I could turn on it in quiet fury, not overtly, as do the tortured people who hurl themselves from bridges, but savagely nevertheless. I could stop caring what happened ...

The day was uneventful. A few new trailers arrived and several old guests departed. A man reported a stolen watch. A woman insisted that her garbage be removed every day. A little girl fell down, cutting her lips, and Joan called a doctor from town. But nothing unusual happened until five o'clock. Then Gerald Collins slammed into the trailer. Collins was angry. It showed in his face and the way he walked. He banged the door as he entered.

"Where's my wife?" he wanted to know.

Joan was surprised. "Why, I don't know," she said. "She's not here."

"She left a note on the kitchen table that you'd know where she is."

"Well, I don't. She hasn't been here all day."

"Didn't you see her?"

"I saw her this morning, but not to talk to. She drove out in the car."

"What time was that?"

"It must have been about ten."

"Was she alone?"

"No. Mike Summers was with her."

Collins' brown face whitened. "The bastards," he said, softly. "I should have known that his trip was a phoney."

"He said he was going to New York. He didn't say what for."

"He's going with her!"

"Well, I don't know."

"I think you do."

"Now, see here—"

Collins grabbed Joan by the shoulders and shoved her up against the wall. His face was hard, his eyes deadly.

"I ought to kill you," he said.

Terror gripped her. The man was wild, out of his mind. She tried to jerk free, but he twisted his fingers into her halter, hurting her.

"Mr. Collins—"

"Shut up!" He slapped her once across the face, hard. "Shut up, you sleazy bitch!"

"You'd better stop this," she told him, "or I'll call the police."

The mention of the police seemed to pacify him only momentarily. He relaxed his grip and then tightened it again.

"What did you do?" he demanded. "Fix it up for them?"

"You must be crazy," she gasped. "Crazy!"

"I'm crazy mad, that's what I am."

"Yes, but why are you mad at me? I didn't do anything."

"Don't act innocent with me," he grated. "I know what you're running here. A whorehouse, that's what you're running—"

"Whatever gave you that idea?"

"My wife told me."

"Your wife?"

"Yes. She told me, just last night, the kind of a place you're running." Collins shook Joan violently. "Why did you do it? Why did you have to go and do it? Just when we were getting along so—"

Again Joan tried to get away from him. She was unable to do so. "Believe me, Mr. Collins, I don't know what you're talking about."

"Don't lie to me!"

"I'm not lying. I'm telling you the truth. So help me, I'm telling you the truth!"

She kept talking, talking, talking. She didn't know anything about his wife. She didn't know where Sally had gone. How could she know; she hardly even knew the girl. And as for Nora, she had heard this before but she hadn't believed it then. She didn't believe it now. No one believes all rumors.

"I don't care what you do," she told him. "If you don't let go of me I'll get you into trouble, Mr. Collins. I know nothing about your wife. I am not a madam. I have never been a madam. You can think what you want, but you can't ever change any of that."

She saw that she was getting through to him. His face was not quite so tense, the pressure of his hands not quite so hard. She continued to talk.

"I don't know where your wife went," Joan said. "I haven't the faintest idea. Maybe she had trouble with the car and Mike offered her a lift. Maybe she went with him for some reason. How would I know? But I'll do this for you if you'll let me go. I'll try and help you find her. I don't know where she is, but it's the least I can do. And I won't go to the police about your manhandling me, not if you cut it out now. I can't be more fair than that, can I? I could have you put in jail, Mr. Collins. Do you know that? I could have you put in jail!"

Slowly, he released her. She noticed that his hands shook. He wet his lips.

"Forgive me," he said. He was almost crying. "I didn't know what I was doing."

She rearranged her halter and stepped away from the wall. She was breathing heavily.

"That's better," she said. "Maybe we can talk sensibly."

Her shoulders still ached but she was no longer frightened. He looked like a little boy who had been caught in the wrong room.

"I'm sorry," Collins said. "I must be crazy."

"Would you care for some coffee?"

"No, thank you."

"A drink?"

"I could use a drink."

"Then, why don't you sit down?"

He sat down on the settee. He looked uncomfortable. In a moment of compassion, she felt terribly sorry for him.

Joan got glasses from the kitchenette and crossed to the liquor cabinet.

"Rye or scotch?"

"I'd prefer scotch, please."

Luke liked scotch but Joan couldn't stand the stuff. In fact, she didn't care much for liquor at all. She hadn't had a drink since the night at the casino.

"I want to apologize," Collins said, as she handed him the glass. "You've got every right to be pretty sore at me."

She sat down on the settee beside him.

"Let's not talk about that now," she said. "Let's talk about your wife."

Collins nodded. "We don't get along very well, you know."

"I had heard that."

"From Mike Summers?"

"I didn't say so."

"No, but I can guess. He's always caused trouble between us."

Joan said nothing. She lifted her glass and drank. The liquor tasted terrible. She decided to give up drinking—whatever taste she had for it, seemed to have vanished.

"You don't believe that, Miss Baker?"

"I'm in no position to judge."

"No. But I am. I've been married to Sally for more than a year now and I know what it's like. I go to work in the morning and I worry about her being there when I get back at night. You don't know what it's been like."

"No."

"You're going to think I'm cruel saying these things about Sally, Miss Baker. You're going to think that a man doesn't talk this way about his wife. And I wouldn't, not unless I was sure she had left me for good. And I wouldn't, even then, not unless I was sure she wasn't any good."

"No good? Then why would you want her back?"

"Can I tell you a few things?" His eyes, looking at Joan, were filled with tears. "In confidence?"

"If you trust me."

"I think I can."

"You didn't act that way a few minutes ago."

"I thought we weren't going to talk about that."

"No—I'm sorry."

"It's all right. I believe you, Miss Baker. I think her telling me about you was just one of Sally's—tricks. I don't believe you really know what is going on here at your camp."

"I don't think anything is going on," Joan said firmly.

He shook his head. His drink remained untouched.

"You're wrong," he said. "And you're a little bit of a fool. That woman isn't running a massage parlor, she's operating a house of prostitution. Every man on the job knows it. How can they help but know it? That Millie comes right out in the woods and solicits. And that's more than a rumor."

"Can you prove that?"

"I can prove it," Gerald Collins said. "You can ask any man on the job. Naturally, they don't discuss it all over the place because many of them have gone down there and they don't want their wives to know. But some of the wives do know. I heard that Birch's wife had threatened to leave him over it."

Birch was a welder. His wife, a tiny blonde with pale blue eyes, seemed to be a good homemaker.

"I'll get to the bottom of this," Joan vowed.

Luke, she thought, would be plenty sore when he heard about this; he had been so sure that everything was all right.

"You'd be doing yourself a favor if you did, Miss Baker. If somebody put in a complaint and there was a raid you'd find yourself in lots of hot water."

"I can see that," Joan admitted.

"I'm afraid my wife may be mixed up in it, too."

"But you said you thought she'd gone away with Mike."

"I know. Thinking it over, though, I've changed my mind. That's the obvious thing. That's what she wants me to think. She wants me to get in a fight with Mike. She wants to get me fired."

"But, why?"

"Because she hates me."

"And you love her?"

"I can't help it. Sometimes I wish I didn't. Sometimes I wish I'd never met her."

"You don't mean that."

"I'm afraid I do. You see—well, when I met her she was Mike's girl. She wanted to marry Mike but Mike knew what she was. I didn't. When the job moved on and I asked her to marry me she agreed just to be near Mike. But it didn't do her much good. Mike still knew what she was. He does yet. She hasn't changed. She never will. That's why I think she may be mixed up in this thing. She's been wild, just because she couldn't have a child. She may have gone back to it for spite."

The implications of what Collins said shocked Joan. His wife, before marriage, had been a prostitute.

"Every woman wants children," Joan said.

"Yes, but you can't have two or three abortions and expect nature to be kind."

Joan looked at her empty glass. She wished she hadn't taken that drink. Something was happening to her. She closed her eyes, took a deep breath, and tried to ignore the sensation within her. But it was there and she couldn't help herself. Her mind was distorted, confused.

"Are you all right, Miss Baker?"

She smiled. "Yes. I'm fine."

Collins stood up. "I think I'd better go," he said.

When Collins had left, Joan ran to her bedroom. Sobbing, she flung herself down on the bed. Unaccountably, she felt again as she had that night with Luke. The whole bed shook as her body twisted and rolled. She wanted Luke here. She reached for the head of the bed and gripped her fingers around it. She squeezed down tight, forcing the numbness up into her arms. The numbness felt good, peaceful. It spread down into her legs, her thighs. Finally, it spread all through her and she fell asleep.

13

It was almost midnight. She sat in the office, waiting for Luke. Why didn't he come? What was keeping him?

He arrived at twelve-thirty. Joan was glad to note that he seemed to be entirely sober.

"I ran into some friends," he explained. "Sorry."

"Luke," she began, "we've got to talk about Nora again."

"I thought that was all settled."

"Well, it isn't."

He walked to the liquor cabinet.

"Drink, Joan?"

"No."

"Aw, come on! Just one."

"No!"

Luke shrugged and poured a shot of scotch. "You don't have to get sore about it," he said. He took a drink from the glass and made a face. "That's horrible!" he complained. "What did you put in with it?"

"Nothing. Why would I put anything in it?"

"No reason. I guess it's just lousy stuff."

"It must be."

He sat down on the settee. "About Nora," he said. "There's nothing wrong there."

"There is, Luke," she said. "There is. Mr. Collins was here this evening. He was—upset. He didn't say so directly, but I gathered that he thought his wife had gone somewhere for Nora."

"Why would Sally Collins do that?"

"Because of what Nora does."

Luke returned to the liquor cabinet and took another drink.

"This is way over my head," he said. "I don't know what you're talking about. Come to the point, will you?"

"Mr. Collins said that Millie had been coming out to the woods to see the men."

Luke didn't sit down again.

"I don't believe it," he said. "Maybe she went out there all right but there wouldn't have been any harm in it. You know how a girl like Millie can get. She may have taken a liking to one of the guys and just followed him out there."

"Luke, you're lying!"

"Lying? I don't get it. Why would I lie?"

Tears filled her voice. "I've been thinking about it, Luke. I've been thinking about it all evening. I—I can't help it, but I think you've been lying to me. I think you've known, all along, what Nora has been doing at the trailer."

He came over to her. His eyes were very intense.

"Do you believe that of me?"

She felt helpless. "Luke, I want to believe you—that things are all right—but what can I do? First Mike told me and then Collins. I haven't asked anybody else. I'm ashamed to ask anybody else."

Luke bent down. "Listen to me, Joan," he said. "I love you and everything I've done has been because I love you. Can't I get you to see that?"

"I want to, Luke."

"All right. I know that things aren't quite as they seem, but I didn't want to worry you about them. I feel guilty about this—I honestly do. I'm the one who got Nora to come out here in the first place. I did it because I was working for her at the time and it seemed like a logical spot. After she got out here and I started working for you, I got you involved in that lease. I thought it was more money for you and that it was the right thing to do. As it turns out, it's the worst thing I could have done. She sits down there in that trailer and there's no legal way of getting her out."

"Then it's true about what she's doing?"

Luke nodded. "Yes, it's true."

"Oh, Luke, what are we going to do?"

"I don't know." Luke frowned and took one of her hands in his. "There's something else that I ought to tell you, too. Maybe you won't think I'm so smart after I tell it to you, but I have to just the same. It wasn't me who suggested the lease to Nora—it was Nora who suggested it to me. I was stupid enough to fall for it, and I brought the thing to you. I wish I hadn't, Joan. I wish I'd been just half as cute as she was."

It wasn't his fault, Joan thought—in the final analysis, the blame belonged to her. She had signed the lease. She should have given it more thought.

"I'll see a lawyer," she said. "I'll see one the first thing in the morning."

"It won't do you any good, honey. The lease is legal. You can't just toss her out. The only thing you could do would be to go to the police and that would mean a raid. A raid would bring you plenty of bad publicity. There is also the possibility that you might get caught in it, too. The police are funny that way. Nora might say that you knew about it all along, that you were one of her partners, and there's at least a chance that they'd believe her."

"Luke," she asked for the second time, "what are we going to do?"

"Well, I've been working on it," Luke replied. "Millie is her girl out here, but she has that place in town, too. The parlor in town seems to be legit—I think dates are made there and that the men go somewhere else. That makes me think, too, that she has a partner, somebody she takes orders from. Those two nights when I was away, and tonight, I've been trying to get a lead from cabbies and people like that. I haven't had much luck."

"Why didn't you tell me this before, Luke?"

"I said I didn't want to worry you. I thought I could solve this whole thing before you got excited. And I didn't want you running off to the cops with it and getting yourself in a great big jam. That's the last thing that you ought to do."

"Maybe you're right."

Luke stood up and walked back to the liquor cabinet. Generally, she asked him not to drink so much but tonight she didn't. Tonight she wanted him to drink. She had her reasons.

"Luke," she said, "you've been working for Nora. Why didn't you know about this before?"

"I work for you, too," he said. "Do I know about everything you do?"

"No."

"There's no difference. She paid me regularly and I didn't ask any questions. Why should I? There didn't seem to be anything wrong until after we got out here."

"No wonder she wanted to hire Millie. Millie was just what she needed."

Luke took another drink. His face was beginning to get red.

"Sure. And Millie was competition. Millie, like a fool, propositioned me and I got her fired for it. The whole thing fell right into Nora's hands."

Yes, Joan thought, everything had gone well for the girl. Even Mike had chased after her. That hurt the most.

"You sure you don't want a drink, honey?"

"No, I don't care for any."

"Not even one?"

"Not even one."

"You don't mind if I do, do you?"

"Of course not."

"This thing has had me upset. I feel better now that you know about it, though. I was afraid you'd blame me for the whole mess. And I didn't want that to happen, not after the other night." He grinned, crookedly. "The other night was pretty perfect, honey. You know that, don't you?"

"Yes," she replied.

He placed his glass on the liquor cabinet and came toward her across the room. He staggered slightly.

"Give me a kiss," he said. "We'll forget about this whole thing while you give Luke a little old kiss."

She lifted her lips to his mouth. He tasted of rye and scotch. She wondered how he could drink the mixture.

"I love you," he said.

He came down upon the settee beside her. Again his lips sought hers.

"Luke," she said. "Please don't."

"Don't stop me," he mumbled. "Don't stop me." Nausea filled her.

"Luke!" Suddenly she knew blind terror—was it of herself or Luke?

Desperately she looked past him. Without hesitating she reached for the lamp on the end table. She picked it up. She lifted it high in the air, as high as she could.

She struck him flush on the top of the head with the lamp. The bulb shattered, showering her with glass, plunging the room into darkness. A long cry escaped Luke and she felt him slip away from her. His body made a thud as he struck the floor. Trembling, she stood up.

"Damn you!" she sobbed. "Damn you!"

She knew now what had been wrong with her before. That first night when she had let Mike take her she had been drinking with Luke. The feeling of needing a man had been there inside of her long before she had seen Mike that night. Luke had fixed the drinks and she had thought hers tasted peculiar. The night of the dance at Lakeside, when she had later gone into Luke's arms, they had stopped at a bar on the way home. He had gotten the drinks from the bar and he had had plenty of opportunity to add something to her drink. Something that had made her furious with desire.

Joan stepped across Luke's prostrate body. Well, he would know now what it was like to suffer and yearn. He would know when he woke up. She had mixed the rye and the scotch. And she had been right about the rye. It had been doctored. Luke, a moment ago had been a man possessed.

She hated him, hated everything about him. She stood looking down at his prone shape. I could kill him, she thought; I could kill him and not feel any remorse or regret. I could kill him for what he's done to me.

She turned and walked to the door.

Outside, the night was dark and cool. The loose gravel crunched under her feet as she walked down the roadway. When she reached the second lane she swung left and stopped beneath a large maple tree. There was no one in front of the Husky; a light burned inside.

She went up to the door and knocked.

"Hello," Millie said, answering the door. "What do you want?"

"Where's Nora?"

"She ain't here. She left just a few minutes ago."

"Then I want to talk to you, Millie."

"I don't know why. I don't work for you no more. Ever since you fired me, I've been working for Nora. I got no call to talk to you none."

Joan jerked the screen door open and stepped into the trailer. She wasn't backing down now.

"You're nothing but a whore," Joan said. "A cheap, stupid little whore."

Millie backed away from her. The girl's eyes were filled with fright.

"You got no call to talk to me that way."

Joan followed the girl.

"I'll talk to you any way I want to, Millie. This is my property and I don't like some of the things that have been going on."

"Don't tell me about it," Millie sulked. "I've got nothing to do about nothing."

"You're a fool, Millie," Joan said. "A fool."

A car drove up and stopped outside. The screen door squealed as Nora came in.

"What are you doing here?" she demanded of Joan.

"Talking to Millie. But I really wanted to talk to you."

"What about?"

"I want you off my property. I want you off by tomorrow night."

Nora smiled. "Isn't that a little drastic?"

"No. You've been making a fool of me and everybody here at the camp. A massage parlor! Whom are you kidding?"

Nora was still smiling. "We kidded you for a while," she said. She laughed. "But we haven't fooled the men. The men like us pretty well."

"I don't want to hear about it."

"Don't worry—you won't. And we're not getting out, that much I can tell you."

"I'll go to the police," Joan threatened.

"I wouldn't do that if I were you," Nora said. "If you do, I'll throw the whole thing right in your lap."

"How do you mean?"

"How much am I paying a month for this trailer?"

"A hundred."

"That's right. And anybody in his right mind would know that it isn't worth more than sixty. All I have to do is tell them that the extra forty is part of your cut and there isn't a person in Union County who would doubt me. I could even say that I was giving you a rake-off on the rest of it and you couldn't prove otherwise. It's one time my word would be just as good as yours, Joan Baker."

Nora was right and Joan knew it. Going to the police was not the answer. She had to think of something else.

"I'll see a lawyer about the lease," Joan said.

Nora shrugged.

"Go ahead."

"I'll see him in the morning."

"Suit yourself. You'll only be wasting your time. The lease is valid."

Unhappily, Joan turned away. She had been foolish coming here in the first place.

"Why don't you smarten up?" Nora demanded. "Throw in with us. We're using your camp anyway—why not be cooperative? You could make a nice piece of change if you would."

"I wouldn't touch that kind of money."

"Oh, no? Well, already you have. Don't forget that."

Joan left the trailer. Slowly, she walked up the roadway. Everything had gone wrong in her life the past few days. There was only one good feature about her office when she returned to it—Luke was gone.

She hoped she would never see him again.

Part Three

Road Block

14

The lawyer in Unionville read the copy of the lease and then rendered his verdict.

"Only a nonpayment of rent could invalidate this contract," he said. "If she pays her rent on time, there isn't anything you can do."

"Even though she may be violating the law?" Joan inquired.

"Well, if you feel that she is violating the law in any way you can place the matter in the hands of the police. You can't place yourself in the position of deciding whether or not she is a law-violator. You have to let the proper public officials determine that."

Disappointed, she left the lawyer's office. She had hoped to find some solution there. Now it seemed she had nowhere to turn.

She drove back to the camp. Luke, at the time of her departure, had not reported for work and she hoped that he wouldn't. An unpleasant scene with Luke could not make matters better; it could make them worse.

He was waiting for her in the office.

"You gave me a hell of a time last night," Luke said. "I thought I'd go out of my mind." He rubbed his head. "Say, what did you hit me with?"

"The lamp."

"Well, that's a nice romance."

She shrugged. "I did the same thing to you that you did to me. Now you know what it's like to have something put in your drinks."

Luke grinned sheepishly. "I thought that stuff tasted funny." He sobered, then said slowly, "If you think I fixed your drinks, I guess it sort of finishes things for us."

"You should have known that without coming back here."

"I did, but I wanted you to know something, too. I'm going into town and I'm going to get to the bottom of this business with Nora. You see if I don't."

She said nothing, and after staring at her for a moment, Luke left.

She was glad when he was gone. A few minutes later, while she was making coffee, Mike arrived in a taxi. He was alone.

"Any calls for me?" he inquired.

"No."

"Well, I didn't think there would be."

"Didn't Sally come back with you?"

"No. What makes you think she should be with me?"

"You left with her."

Mike smiled. "You've got a suspicious mind," he said. "She only drove me to the train."

"Her husband was looking for her."

Mike seemed unconcerned. "He's always looking for her. What am I supposed to do—keep her on the end of a string?"

"Hardly—but you can't keep him from wondering. She did go away with you, or she was with you when you went away. And she hasn't returned."

Mike hunched his shoulders. "Come off it, will you?" he said. "I haven't the least idea where she might be."

Joan stepped forward as he started for the door.

"Mike," she said, "I'm in a awful lot of trouble."

He was unsympathetic. "I told you you would be, but you didn't believe me."

"Because you thought I was part of it."

"And you aren't?"

"Oh, no, Mike. No!"

His eyes softened. "What do you want me to do?"

"I want you to help me. I want you to talk to the men and tell them not to go there. They'll listen to you. If you just talk to them—"

Mike shook his head. "It wouldn't do any good. It's the one thing that men don't understand. If a woman is selling herself and the man has the money he's a good prospect. Believe me, Joan, I know."

"Can't you think of something I can do?"

"I don't know. I'll try. But it'll have to be before next week."

"Then you got your transfer?"

"Yes. To Lancaster. Bigger gang, bigger job."

After Mike was gone, Joan went into her bedroom and sat down on the edge of the bed. Somehow she had to find Sally

Collins. If she didn't, Collins would go to the police and everything would fall apart.

She waited until after five and then she walked down to the Collins trailer. Collins was alone, fixing his supper. The odor of canned spaghetti filled the room.

"I wanted to talk to you," Joan said.

"Yes?"

"Mike came back and your wife wasn't with him."

"I know that."

"Do you still intend to go to the police?"

"I'm going to find her, if that's what you mean."

"Would you do me a favor?"

"It depends on what it is."

"Wait two days," Joan said. "Don't do anything until then. If I haven't found her by that time, I'll go to the police with you."

Collins toyed with the idea. "In the meantime, I don't know where she is or what's happening to her."

"You wouldn't know, anyway," Joan told him. "Going to the police won't bring her back automatically. They'll have to find her, too. It's just possible that I'll be able to do it sooner than they will."

"How do you plan on doing it?"

"I won't tell you that."

"The houses would be the most likely places," Collins said. "I know that. I could go from one to the other and I might find her. But I wouldn't go into a house even for Sally."

He seemed like a straight man, she thought; straight and to the point in what he thought. And weak. He was so weak that he didn't have the strength of his own convictions. Maybe he wouldn't go to the police. Perhaps, at the last moment, he would back out. Rut she couldn't risk it. If he was in love with Sally, he might do anything.

"Promise me you'll wait," she said.

"Okay."

"Two days?"

He nodded. "But not a bit longer."

"That's fair enough," Joan said. "Either I'll be able to do something by then or I won't."

She returned to her trailer, locked it and climbed into the Caddy. She drove out to the highway and turned in the direction of Unionville. In town, she left the car in an all-night parking lot, then hailed a cab.

"Where to, lady?" the driver wanted to know.

She smiled and slammed the door. She handed the driver a twenty dollar bill.

"I'm a prostitute," she told him. "I want to find a house."

The cab moved forward and changed gears.

"That's a hot one," the driver said. "I get a lot of guys asking for a dame, but this is the first time I ever picked up a woman like you."

"Well, it takes all kinds, mister."

"I guess it does."

They rode a couple of blocks in silence.

"Where are we going?"

"You wanted a house," he replied. "I'm taking you to a house."

She sat back, her heart beating rapidly. She was frightened. She hoped Luke had told her the truth about Nora's having a partner she took orders from. If she could find him she could go to the police. She could trade them his name for the reputation of her camp—or at least she could try.

"I know of two places," the driver said, slowing the cab. "One is on Second Avenue, near the bridge. It's a high class place and the girls get anywhere from twenty to fifty bucks. You want to go there?"

Joan thought about it. It seemed to her that Nora's clients would go somewhere less expensive.

"What about the other place?"

"That's on York Avenue, maybe three or four blocks from here. A guy pays three bucks for the room, five for the girl. You want to go there?"

"I just want you to show me where it is."

The driver scratched his head. "You sure you're not a cop?"

"No, I'm not a cop."

"If you was a cop you'd ruin a good thing for me. I pick up a nice buck running guys out here."

"I'm not. I told you what I am."

"That's the place," the driver said, halting the cab.

The building was a large brick house near the corner. A factory stood on one side of it, a gin mill on the other.

"Ask for Midge," the driver said. "She's the boss."

"Yes. Thank you."

The cab slid forward through the night. She turned her head and looked back at the house. In a few hours she would be walking up to that door.

It was a fearful thought.

15

Two police cruisers were parked alongside the office trailer. Joan's first thought was that Collins had broken his word and had gone to the police. She didn't know whether to stop or to keep right on going.

She pulled up next to one of the cruisers.

There was no point in trying to run away. If they had raided Nora, she, Joan, had to face the consequences.

As she was unlocking the door of the trailer a police officer got out of one of the cars and came forward.

"Are you Miss Baker?"

Her hands shook as she turned to face him.

"Yes, I'm Miss Baker."

The trooper smiled. He was tall, bronze-faced and he had a pleasant smile.

"Little trouble," he said. "But it's all taken care of now."

"Wh-at happened?"

"Two of your guests got into a hassle. We sent one into the hospital. The other is okay. The doc's with him now."

Joan felt relieved. There had merely been a fight. Pipeline workers often fought—it was a part of their lives.

"Who?" she wanted to know.

"Fellow by the name of Collins tried to knife a guy named Summers. Summers got cut up a little but he got the knife away from Collins. We don't know, but we think he may have busted Collins' jaw. One of his neighbors took him in to the hospital."

"Took Mr. Summers to the hospital?"

"No—Collins. Summers is okay but he won't be able to use his right arm for a while."

"Where is Mr. Summers now?"

"He's at his trailer with the doc."

"Could I go down there?"

"Why, sure," the officer replied. "No reason why you can't."

"Thank you. Is there anything else?"

"No. We just wanted you to know what happened, that's all."

"I'll see the doctor," she said. "Perhaps I can help."

The trooper nodded. "You've got a nice place here," he said. "First time we've ever been called out for you. We don't like it any better than you do."

Nice, she thought. She wondered what the officer would say if he knew about Nora. She guessed he wouldn't be very happy.

Two other troopers came up the roadway, talking. They got into one of the police cruisers.

"You coming, Harry?" one of them wanted to know.

The trooper who had been talking to Joan nodded. "Sure," he said, "there's nothing more here." He turned to Joan. "You give us a ring if anything else comes up, won't you?"

"Of course."

The trooper named Harry got into the second car and started the motor. She waited until they had driven away. After that she walked down the road.

Big Mike sat in a lawn chair in front of his trailer. Several people stood nearby and a small man with gray hair leaned over Mike.

"Hello," Joan said.

Mike grinned at her. "That Collins is a real cut-up. Or have you heard?"

"I heard."

Mike introduced Joan to Doctor Pawling.

"Got a nasty cut here," the doctor said, indicating Mike's bandaged right arm. "Extends all the way from the wrist to the elbow. Not deep, but painful. He won't be able to do much with it for a few days. I'm trying to convince him that he ought to go into the hospital for a few days."

"I'll see he gets care," Joan said.

"You will?"

"Yes."

"Well, all right." The doctor picked up his bag. "You call me if you have any trouble with that, young fellow. I cleaned it out but you can't tell what was on that knife."

"Sure," Mike said. He smiled up at Joan. "I'll be all right. I've got a good nurse."

"You've got a lot of luck," the doctor said. "That could have been your throat."

The doctor left a few minutes later. He said he would look in the next day to see how Mike's arm was doing.

"Never saw a guy worry so much," Mike said after the doctor was gone. "You'd have thought I lost a leg, or something."

"Well, you have to be careful."

"I should have been careful before."

One of the women came over and wanted to know if there was anything she could do. Mike told her there wasn't.

"I'm in the next trailer," she said. "Just holler if there is."

Young Shipley, his wife hanging on his arm, came over to speak to Mike.

"I'm not surprised," he said. "Collins has been real off these last couple of days. It's been almost impossible to get along with him."

"It isn't his fault," Mike said. "That wife of his drove him out of his mind."

Shipley glanced fondly at the girl beside him. "If he loves her enough, I can see why she did," he said.

One of the men asked Mike what they should do about the swamp crossing and Mike said they'd have to wait until he could get out to the site.

"Collins had a plan," the man said. "But I don't know what it was."

"Collins always had a plan," Mike said.

When they were finally alone Mike sighed and put his head back against the canvas chair.

"I'll let you in on a secret," he said. "I've never been so scared in my life."

Joan sat down on the grass.

"What happened?" she asked him gently.

"Well, I was getting supper. It was late, because after I left you I walked around thinking about things. I came back to the trailer and peeled some potatoes. The knife was lying on the kitchen sink. Just as I was putting the potatoes in the pan Collins came in. He wanted to know about his wife."

"And he stabbed you?"

"Not right away. He asked where Sally was and I told him I didn't know. He seemed to think I should and he got sore. Finally he grabbed up the knife. He made one swipe with it and cut me on the arm before I could get it away from him. After that I smashed him on the jaw and that was the end of it. But somebody outside heard the fight and called the cops. I'm sorry they did. There was no need for it."

"He's better off locked up," Joan said. "A man like that is dangerous."

"You may be right."

"I didn't tell you but he slapped me around the other day. He thought I knew where Sally was."

Mike shook his head. "He's nuts over that woman," Mike said. "And she's no good. She never was any good. I don't know why he bothers with her."

"Love," Joan explained. "It does funny things."

Mike glanced at her. "Such as offering to nurse a man?"

"Mike!"

"Or don't you think it's the time to talk about it?"

"You know what I mean," she said. "Everything is so mixed up."

"Are we mixed up?" he insisted. "Are we, Joan?" When she didn't answer, he went on, "That's what I was thinking about tonight when I was walking around—about—how foolish we've been. We've let a cheap woman come between us, and it isn't right. We're in love or, at least, I think we're in love. I know I'm in love with you. I hope you're in love with me."

"I am, Mike. Or at least, I was."

"I want you to be again. I want you to be so much in love with me that you'll never let me go. I've thought about us a lot. You wouldn't be happy traveling around the way I do. This is your life, here. This is where you want to live. I know that. And I'm willing to accept that. Frankly, I'm getting a little tired of moving around, too. I told you I was going to move to another job—well to hell with that."

"Mike—you'd stay here—for me?"

He laughed. "Surprised?"

On an impulse she leaned over and kissed him.

"Mike I have to tell you something."

"You don't have to unless you want to."

"But I do. That first night, Mike—that first night I wasn't responsible."

"I know. I was."

"No, not you. Neither of us. Luke had put something in my drink."

Mike's face hardened and tears filled her eyes. Perhaps it would never be right for them again, no matter what they did. The memory of that night with Luke was again with her, haunting her. How could she come to Mike, bringing him love, when there was that to remember?

"You're trembling," Mike said.

"I'd better go now." Suddenly she wanted to be away. "I'll bet the doctor would want you to get some rest."

"I could do with something to eat," Mike said. "I lost out on my supper."

"It's too late."

"Now, there's a fine cook for you!"

She laughed and kissed him. "In the morning," she said. "I'll fix you bacon and eggs and a great big breakfast. Then I'll see the woman next door and see if she won't come over and fix lunch and supper for you. She said to let her know if you needed anything."

"Where will you be?"

"I have to go away for the day."

"Business?"

"Yes," she said, "business."

Some business, she thought, looking down into his eyes. She wondered what she really would do in town tomorrow. And whether she would have any control over what happened to her.

16

She arrived at the hairdresser's a little before eleven. Three women sat in the waiting room, reading magazines.

"I don't think I could do anything for you this morning," the operator said.

Joan squeezed a bill into the girl's hand.

"I'm sure you could."

The girl examined the bill. "Come this way, miss."

Joan entered a tiny booth and sat down. She had only been in there a few minutes when another girl arrived.

"Wave?"

"No. Bleach."

The girl looked at Joan's lustrous dark hair.

"You must be out of your mind," she said.

"Maybe. But my boy friend wants me to be blonde."

"Then your boy friend is out of his mind."

The operation required the better part of two hours.

Joan took a room in a hotel and spent more than an hour on her face and eyes. She applied several layers of powder and just a touch of rouge. The results, following the application of eye shadow and lipstick, were more than satisfactory. She looked, at least, cheap enough.

Outside, she hailed a cab and directed the driver to take her to the downtown address. Outwardly she was calm but inwardly she was tense. She had no idea of what she was getting into. It was like a treasure hunt without a prize.

"You a model?" the driver wanted to know.

"No."

"Well, you look like a model." He leered at her.

"Thank you."

She got off at the corner, in front of the factory building, and paid the driver.

"I bring a lot of models down here," he said grinning. "I thought you was one."

"I'm not."

The cab pulled away and she walked down the street. She was conscious of the men at the factory entrance who stopped to stare at her as she passed. She was aware of the trucks in the streets and the people around her and wondered if she was as conspicuous as she felt.

She went up to the front door of the brick house and rang the bell. For a long time no one answered. Finally the door opened.

"I'm looking for Midge," Joan said.

"Who are you?"

"I'm a—girl."

"Oh? Well, who sent you? Marty?"

"No. A cab driver."

The woman laughed. "That's a hot one," she said. "Come on in."

The hall was dark and smelled of disinfectant.

"Come with me."

She followed the woman down the hall and into a big room with several easy chairs scattered about. There was a portable bar in one corner, several dirty glasses on it.

"You just sit down and wait," the woman said. "I'll see if I can find Midge."

Joan sat. The room smelled of stale tobacco smoke and sweat. She noticed for the first time, that the room had no windows, that it was lighted by an overhead neon light.

"Hello, dearie. I'm Midge."

Midge was a washed-out blonde, apparently in her middle forties.

"Hello," Joan said, rising.

"What's on your mind?"

She swallowed. "I wondered if you might have a place for me."

"Doing what?"

"You know what."

Midge smiled and looked at Joan carefully.

"You're pretty," she said after a while.

"Don't you want your girls to be pretty?"

"Oh, I have no objection to it. Some of them are and some of them aren't. Most of them aren't. You know the kind of a house I run here?"

"I know it's low rate."

Midge nodded. "The girls cost five and the room three. I get the money from the room and I split the five with the girl, if you get twenty customers a night you come out with fifty bucks. It may not be the world but it isn't bad. You can depend on making a living."

Joan shuddered. "That sounds all right to me," she said.

"Sit down, dearie."

Joan sat down.

"Now tell me about yourself."

"There isn't much to tell."

Midge crossed to the portable bar and fixed a drink.

"A man?"

"Yes."

"What did he do to you?"

"He left me."

Midge nodded. "They always do. Tell me, dearie, are you pregnant?"

No.

"Are you from town?"

"I'm from Westford."

"That's on the other end of the state?"

"Yes."

"Did you work alone, before, or in a house?"

"Alone."

"How much did you get?"

Joan tried to remember some of the things she had read.

"Sometimes twenty dollars," she said. "Sometimes more."

"If you can make that kind of money by yourself, why do you want to go into a house?"

"The protection is worth it."

"You're right. The protection is everything."

"Yes." She was passing muster, Joan thought.

"Have you ever been arrested?"

"No."

"How did you find me?"

"I asked a cab driver."

Midge poured another drink. "That's right—Esther told me. And that was smart. That's the way to do it. Cabbies know everything."

"That's the way I had it figured."

Midge carried the glass across the room and sat down. She walked with a slight limp. One leg seemed to be smaller than the other.

"Do you have any specialties, dearie?"

Joan felt her face flame. "No."

Midge looked at her critically. "The boys will like you," she announced. "I've got an idea that we could ask ten dollars for you and get it, easy. That would mean more money for you. You'd get half, just the same."

"Thank you."

"When could you start?"

Joan tensed. "Right—away."

"Tonight?"

"Yes."

Midge stood up. "That's fine. Now all I need to know is your name."

"Joan. Joan—Adams."

Midge smiled. "Of course that isn't your real name."

"No, it isn't."

"Well, don't let it bother you none. As long as the rest of you is for real, the name doesn't matter none." Midge laughed. She finished her drink. "There's a couple of rules that we have, though."

"What are they?"

"All girls have to live in the house. You don't live in the same room where you work. We've got some nice rooms on the third floor where the girls share. You'd be in with Carol. Carol's a nice kid—a little droopy and dumb, but nice. You work on the second floor."

"Yes."

"The other rule is that the boss always has first crack at any new girl. You wouldn't object to that none, would you, dearie?"

This, Joan thought, was better than she had hoped for. The boss would be the man who was also Nora's partner. Once she knew his name, she would have what she came for. She could go to the police then.

"I wouldn't mind," Joan said.

"That's a sensible girl." Midge moved toward the doorway. "Don't you have any luggage with you?"

"No."

Midge led Joan up a flight of stairs. The second floor hall smelled pretty much like the first, damp and musty, but the third story was better. The third story smelled of perfume and bath salts.

"Number fourteen," Midge said, halting before an open door. "You'll like it here."

Joan followed Midge into the room. It was fairly large and airy and attractively furnished with a blonde birch dresser, vanity and matching double bed. A pale brunette was seated at the vanity, brushing out her hair.

"Joan, this is Carol," Midge said. "Carol, Joan Adams."

Carol scrutinized Joan carefully. "We're going up in the world," she said. "Where'd you get her—out of some chorus line?"

"Never mind," Midge said, crossly. "You be nice to her."

The girl continued to brush her hair. "Oh, sure. You know I will."

"Don't mind Carol," Midge said. "She is a good kid. You can ask her anything you want to know."

"Thank you."

Midge walked to the door. She turned and looked back.

"Seven o'clock is curfew. You can go out but be sure and be back by that time."

"Yes."

"As long as we understand each other, we'll get along fine."

"Old bitch," Carol said after Midge had gone. "Never lets you forget that she's boss."

Joan sat down on the edge of the bed.

"I didn't think she was," Joan said. "I thought there was somebody else. A man."

"There is. But I've never seen him."

"I thought she said that he—had every girl first."

"Not every girl," Carol replied. "Just the pretty ones, the ones like you. I don't know why." Carol laughed. "Maybe the old bitch is looking for a promotion."

"She seems tough."

"She is. You cross her and you might just as well open up your head with an axe."

Carol got up from the dressing table and walked across the room. "There's one thing I like about this place," she said. "You don't have to parade yourself in the parlor. Midge has a guy come up and take your picture and they put it in a book. You get your business from that. It's better than having every guy in the joint try to handle you."

"But no one took my picture."

"They will. This afternoon, probably. You don't have to worry about him none. He's an old guy. He couldn't make a pass at you if his life depended on it."

About an hour later the photographer arrived. He was an elderly man with stooped shoulders and he seemed to be in a hurry.

"Bra and pantie shot," he said to Joan. "Get out of your clothes."

"You've got the shape and a face to go with it," Carol said after the photographer departed. "You should do well here. You're even better than the new girl."

"New girl?"

"Yes, she just came a day or so ago. But I don't think she'll last. Thinks too much of herself. Our trade isn't big stuff but the guys are all right. Most of them work in the factories or are from the pipeline crew."

"Do you get many from the pipeline?"

"Quite a few. They're rough but they're good spenders."

"How long have you been with Midge?"

"You ask a lot of questions, honey."

"Oh. Well, you don't have to answer unless you want to."

"I know that. I've been with Midge about two weeks. Ever since she opened."

"Opened? I thought she'd been here a long time."

"Oh, no. She took over the building right after the massage parlor moved out downstairs. I don't know where Midge came from. I guess from out of town. But she's been around and she knows her business."

The afternoon wore on. Joan lay down on the bed and tried to take a nap. It was impossible for her to sleep.

17

The room was small, about eight by ten feet. It contained a cot, washstand, dresser, a straight-back wooden chair and an electric fan. The electric fan made a great deal of noise and once in a while, when the blades slowed, it began to squeal.

Joan sat on the chair near the window. The window faced the street, overlooking the intersection next to the factory. A dirty-faced kid played in the gutter. A policeman wearing a short-sleeved shirt stood at the intersection, talking to an elderly woman. It was a typical summer night—hot, humid.

She wondered what she would do when the man arrived. She had been wondering about it all afternoon. Now that she was here in this room, she knew she should never have left the trailer camp. She should have stayed up there and minded her own business—and taken her chances on Nora.

She watched the cop at the intersection—she had been studying him for a long time. She wondered if he was at this corner all the time. She hoped so.

If things got really out of hand for her, maybe she could attract his attention. Then, again, maybe she couldn't. He probably knew the kind of place this was.

The cop was now talking to a man in a blue shirt. The man in the blue shirt seemed to be upset; he was waving his arms and making gestures. The cop nodded a few times and looked up the street. Obviously, he was disinterested in the man's problem.

Someone knocked on the door. Startled, Joan got up from the chair and moved across the room. Her legs felt wooden.

"Yes?"

"Unlock your door. It's Midge."

Joan unlocked and opened the door.

"You only lock your door when you have a friend," Midge said. "Remember that, will you?"

"Yes."

Midge wore a full-length red dress which did little for her.

"You're going to be a sensation," Midge said. "Some of the men have seen your photo and they have just about gone nuts over you."

"That's—nice."

"The boss ought to be along in a little while."

"All right."

"I just thought you'd like to know."

"Yes."

Midge opened the door. "Oh, one other thing. The girl who used to use this room may show up here after a while. Tell her to take the second one on the right, down the hall."

"I will."

Midge smiled. "I want you near the top of the stairs. I think the traffic will be heavy."

Joan managed a smile. "I hope so."

"Need anything?"

"No."

"Remember," Midge said, "what I told you. I collect the fee downstairs. Don't let any man in the room who doesn't have a pink slip. You take the pink slip from him and turn it in after work. I pay you five bucks for every slip you have. On the other things you charge a dollar but I get the take from that. They're for your—protection."

"Yes, I understand."

"Another thing—don't argue with the girl who had this room before. Just tell her what I said. Her name is Millie."

"I won't."

Midge left the room, closing the door behind her. The woman's footsteps beat out a rhythm as she descended the stairs.

Joan returned to the chair and sat down again. The cop was now talking to a pretty girl. He was smiling. His badge shone brightly in the late evening sun.

She looked at the fan. It was the only heavy object in the room. It would make a great deal of noise when it went through the window. It would make enough noise to draw the cop's attention.

The door opened and a man entered. She gasped. It was Luke.

"Hello," Joan said. Her voice was low.

She hoped he wouldn't recognize her. She wished, now, that she hadn't left the light burning by the side of the bed.

"Hello," Joan said.

"Hot in here," Luke said. He looked at the fan on the dresser. "That thing doesn't do much good."

"No."

Luke laughed. "Look at me so I can see your face." She looked straight at him.

"The photo downstairs was right," he said. "You have got a pretty face. Stand up."

She stood up.

"I can't say I care for that thing you're wearing."

"Well, it isn't mine."

"Then, take it off."

She looked out of the window again. The cop was still on the corner. He stood alone, swinging his nightstick.

Get Luke over to the side of the room, she thought. Get him near the dresser. Once he started to kiss her she could pick up the fan and smash him over the head with it. Then she would hurl the fan through the window. After that it would be up to the cop in the street below.

"I can tell you're new," Luke said. "You act scared."

"Yes."

"You don't have to be afraid of me. I won't hurt you."

He was several feet away from the dresser. Joan walked to the dresser and stood with her back against it. The fan, swinging from side to side, bathed her body with cool air.

"You're the one who wants it," she said, trying to make her voice sound harsh. "Come and get it."

Luke grinned. "All right. I will."

He came toward her. Her right hand moved up to the top of the dresser and came to rest on the base of the fan. His long arms came out, reaching for her. For an instant she was tempted to grasp the fan and bash it against his head, but she hesitated. And then it was too late.

Luke's arms crushed her—he was kissing her and this was a different Luke from the man she'd known before. She'd always been able to stop him before; she couldn't now.

She tried to fight him, but knew she would fail.

For the first time in her life, Joan fainted.

18

The long shadows of night filtered into the room. The fan on the dresser slowed, squealed and then resumed its speed. It was hot in the room, suffocating, and the darkness only made it worse.

Joan got up from the bed and walked to the window. The cop was no longer on the corner. The street was vacant.

She had no recollection of Luke's leaving—but he hadn't completed his violence. That much she knew, and she was oddly grateful to him.

She sat down on the chair and waited. She didn't know, any longer, just what she was waiting for. He had come and she had failed. But he might come back.

She found a cigarette and lit it. Her hands shook. Her whole body shook.

Somebody came up the stairs, walking steadily, and she froze inside. The steps approached her door, then passed. She began to breathe easier.

Again footsteps sounded on the stairs. They came to her door. The door opened and a girl came in.

"Say, what the hell are you doin' here?"

"I'm new—are you Millie?" Millie evidently didn't recognize Joan.

"I'm Millie. And this is my room."

Joan kept her head averted. "Midge moved me in here. She said for you to take the second one down, on the right."

"Well, that's some nerve!"

"She told me to tell you."

"Old bitch," Millie fumed. "Who does she think she is?"

"I'm sorry," Joan said.

"Sorry?" Millie turned at the door. "What have any of us got to be sorry about? Ain't it a little late to be sorry?"

The door closed behind Millie and the fan began to squeal again. Joan got up and walked over to the dresser. She hit the fan once and the squeal stopped. Then she returned to the window. The street was dark and deserted.

She crossed to the closet and found her dress. The thing for her to do was to get out of the house and go to the police. She would tell them all she knew. Everything. She could leave it up to them.

She dressed hurriedly.

There was no one in the hall. She closed the door and started down the stairs. She could hear the sounds of music from below, the voices of men. She reached the second landing.

"Joan!"

It was Midge. She was coming down the hall, walking rapidly. The red dress swirled around her legs.

"Where are you going?" she asked.

"I felt ill," Joan said. "I was going out to the drug store."

Midge stopped in front of Joan. The woman's face was livid.

"Nobody leaves this house," she said. "Nobody!"

"But I said I was—"

"If you're sick, I'll see you get something for it."

"But I'd rather go myself."

Midge shook her head. "You don't understand, dearie. I said you're not going."

A wave of panic seized Joan. She had to get out of here!

"I changed my mind," she said. "I'm leaving."

"No girl changes her mind."

Desperately Joan sought an explanation. "I'd rather work by myself," she said. "I just decided that I don't want to be in a house. I—"

"Shut up! And take off your dress."

"What?"

"I said, take off your dress." Midge smiled and held out her hand. "You can't go very far without a dress. If I have your dress, I'll know where you are."

"I—I won't!"

"Suit yourself," Midge said. "I'll take it, anyway."

Midge grasped the front of Joan's dress and yanked. The material split all the way down the front.

"Go back to your room," Midge commanded. "And stay there."

There was nothing else she could do. She couldn't get past Midge and even if she could she couldn't go out on the street this way. She turned around and returned to the third floor room.

She walked over to the window and looked down at the street again. It was still deserted. It would do her no good to scream. There was nobody. Nobody. The factory building on the left was closed for the night and there was so much noise coming from the gin mill that nobody would be able to hear her.

Once again footsteps sounded on the stairs. These were slow, plodding, the heavy steps of a man. In terror she stared at the closed door. The footsteps stopped outside. The knob turned. The door swung open.

"Hello," the man said.

It was Big Mike Summers.

"Oh, Mike!" she whispered. "Mike!"

He was startled. "Who are you?"

"Joan. I'm Joan." She came forward, touching her hair. "Don't you recognize me? Oh, Mike!"

He came into the room and slowly closed the door.

"I didn't recognize you," he said. "What are you doing here?"

But she couldn't talk. All she could do was go into his arms and cling to him. He felt so good, so strong. Surely he would be able to help her.

"I'm a silly girl," she said after a while. "A very silly girl."

He stroked her hair. "This is a funny place to find you, Joan."

"I thought I'd die here! Oh, Mike!"

Gently he removed her arms, pushed her away from him and looked down into her eyes.

"Tell me about it," he said.

"There isn't much to tell. I thought I could break up that thing out at camp by breaking it up in town. I—I went in over my head. It just isn't that easy."

"Let's sit down," he said. "This has been quite a shock to me."

He led her over to the cot and they sat down. The old springs sagged dangerously.

"You've bleached your hair," he said.

"I did that so nobody would recognize me."

"And you've done a good job of it. I saw your picture in the book downstairs but I didn't know who you were. I honestly didn't."

"But why are you here, Mike?"

He grinned. "You might say it has something to do with the same reason you're here."

"Oh, Mike!"

His tone became serious. "Have you seen anybody you know?"

"Yes, I saw Millie."

"Did she know you?"

"No, I'm sure she didn't."

"Good. Anybody else?"

"Luke."

"The fellow from the camp?"

"Yes."

"Did he know you?"

"I don't think so."

"Where did he see you?"

"He came—here."

Mike's face hardened. "What did you do?"

She told him. "I don't know when he left—but he left without—hurting me."

Mike put his left arm around her. It made her feel secure, safe.

"I have to get out of here, Mike. You can help me." She looked up at him. Her eyes were filled with tears. "Mike, will you help me?"

"I will, if I can."

She began to feel better. "There's a cop on the corner," she said. "He was there a little while ago. I don't think he could be very far away."

"What could a cop do?"

"He could raid the place."

"I don't see how that will solve your problem."

"Well, if we break it up here we'll break it up at the camp, too."

Mike shifted his arm. "You think this Luke is at the head of things?"

"I know he is. I'll testify so in court."

"Testify that you were in a house of prostitution?" He shook his head. "There's got to be another way."

"What can I do?" she pleaded.

"We're back to the problem of getting you out of here. When we do, go back to the camp and forget about the whole thing. In a few weeks the pipeline crew will move on and Nora's massage parlor will fold by itself. In six months you'll hardly know that anything like this ever happened."

Six months or a year later she would still remember.

"I don't know," she said.

"The important thing is to get you out of here," Mike said. "I'll find you a dress. There aren't any stores open at this time of the night but almost anybody will sell a dress for enough money. It doesn't have to be the right size, as long as it covers you."

"She'll never let me out of here," Joan said.

Mike laughed. "She will if I'm in front of you. I've bulled my way out of worse places than this."

It made sense. If he could find a dress for her to wear Mike could fight her way out—even with one arm. With only one arm Mike Summers was stronger than most men.

He walked over to the window and stood looking down at the street.

"You said there was a cop there a while ago?"

"Yes."

"He isn't there now."

"No. I told you he left."

Mike turned his back to the window.

"You have to promise me one thing," he said. "You have to promise that you won't run to the cops as soon as you get out of here. At least, think it over. Cops won't do you any good and they can do you a lot of harm."

"All right."

He left the window and walked to the door.

"I'll get the dress," he said. "It may take me an hour or so, but I'll get it."

"What will I do if somebody else comes?"

"Just keep the door locked."

He opened the door and started out.

"Mike?"

He paused. "What, Joan?"

"You'd better leave me the pink slip," she said. "In case Midge comes around."

"Pink slip?"

"Yes. You know, the one you got downstairs."

Mike stood motionless. "I haven't got a pink slip," he said.

"But everybody gets one!"

"I didn't."

"Mike, you must have!"

"I'm telling you, I didn't."

"Mike—"

Suddenly it was clear, strangely, terribly, awfully clear. She hadn't asked Luke for the pink slip because she had assumed that he didn't have one. She had thought Luke to be the boss. Only the boss would not have a pink slip.

"Mike!"

He closed the door and came across the room. His shoulders were hunched slightly forward and he looked huge.

"So what's wrong with not having a pink slip?" he wanted to know.

"Mike, stay away from me!"

He laughed and looked down to where she cowered on the cot.

"You don't have to be afraid of me," he said. "I'm not going to hurt you."

"Mike!"

He bent over her.

"Tell me about the pink slip," he said.

"You should have one."

"And if I don't?"

"It means you didn't pay."

"And if I didn't pay that means I'm—"

She nodded. "It means—you run this place." Her throat felt as though it were filled with sand. "Oh, Mike!"

"Did you ask Luke for his ticket?"

"No."

"Why not?"

"I thought he—I told you that."

Mike waved her reply aside. "Never mind," he said. "You know now. What else is there to say?" He sat down on the edge of the bed. "Of course, the whole problem is different now. I can't let you louse me up—any more than I could let Sally do it."

"What—happened to Sally?"

He shrugged. "Let's say she's gone, lost—permanently."

"You killed her!" Joan gasped. "You killed her, Mike!"

Mike said, "Whatever happened to Sally doesn't have to happen to you. I'll give you a choice."

"What choice?"

"Let me tell you about it. I run a few girls for the boys—send 'em from town to town as we move. Midge makes the local arrangements—she's good at it. You can come along as one of the girls. I had that in mind at the start, when I got Millie to doctor up your booze." He grinned at her. "You thought it was Luke did that."

She couldn't speak—she could only stare at him.

At last he moved impatiently. "Sally would have jumped at your chances—what do you say?"

She managed at last: "You'll have to do with me—whatever you did with Sally."

His laugh was mirthless. "You don't mean that."

"I do!"

She got to her feet. Mike moved toward her. Behind Mike, slowly, steadily, the door was being pushed open. Someone would share her fate.

"No!" she screamed. "No!"

Luke stepped into the room. His face was white, impassive. His hands were at his sides. He lifted one of them.

"Here's your pink slip," he said. "It cost me a hundred bucks."

Mike whirled. Luke set his weight on his heels and threw a long punch. It landed soddenly on Mike's face.

Mike laughed and shook his head.

"I'll kill you both," he said evenly.

He smashed Luke in the face with his left hand. Joan screamed as blood poured from Luke's mouth. Luke staggered backward and struck the wall.

"I'll kill you!" Mike roared.

He drove in, hammering at Luke with his left. His right arm was useless but he didn't need it. He was big and strong and one hand was enough. Blood streamed from a cut on Luke's forehead.

"Run!" Luke shouted to Joan. "Run while you've got the chance."

Joan rushed to the dresser. She grabbed up the electric fan and jerked the cord loose from the outlet in the wall. The blade of the fan began to squeal. She turned, lifting the fan high in the air, and came up behind Mike.

"Damn you!" she screamed. "Damn you!"

She struck him on the head, the shoulders, anywhere she could hit him.

Mike tried to swing around. His giant arms pawed the air. Blood gushed from a deep wound in his scalp. The blood spattered as Joan drove the fan downward onto the same spot. Mike grunted and put his hands to his head. The blood seeped between his fingers and dripped to the rug.

He tried to say something.

She hit him again and again and again. Her arms became weary from the blows. Blood covered her hands, her face. He was on his knees now. He looked up, once, his eyes blank, and she smashed him squarely in the face. The expression in his eyes did not change. He opened his mouth again to say something and then fell forward.

Mike Summers was through.

19

Joan watched the big, gray-haired man as he got out of the mud-spattered Lincoln. He came forward, walking with a slight limp. When he got to the beach umbrella under which Joan was sitting, he turned and looked back at the car and trailer.

Both were dusty from travel.

"Hell of a trip," he said. "All the way from Nebraska."

"Long haul," Joan agreed.

"Pounded her all the way through. Hardly ever stopped." He stared down at Joan and grinned. "My name is Parker. George Parker. I'm the new pipeline boss."

Joan nodded. “I got your letter,” she said. “You’re in block sixty-four. That’s near the lake.”

“Lake? Is the fishing any good?”

“Some bass. And bullheads.”

“I like bass,” Parker said. “More fun than trout.” He reached into his pocket. “What’s your rate?”

“Forty a month.”

“That’s not bad. Last place I stopped, I paid fifty.” Joan got up and entered the trailer. She was tired. It was the eighteenth check-in that day. She wrote out a receipt for the money, placed the bills in a tin box and returned to Parker.

“Read about your rumpus here in the papers,” Parker said. “You must have had a rough time of it.”

She’d be glad to let that cover it.

“Yes.”

“Too bad about Collins losing his wife. I met them once and I had an idea that he was pretty much in love with her. How’s he taking it?”

“Well, he’s back to work.”

“That’s good. Collins is one of the best field men we have.”

It had taken the police more than a day to break Mike Summers down but after his confession they’d had no difficulty locating the Mercury or Sally Collins’ body. Both had been buried in Panther Swamp, in one of the deep water holes. A wrecker from town had pulled the car up onto dry land and they had found Sally inside. They had also found the hammer with which Mike had killed her.

“It was a lousy thing to happen,” Parker said, “but you must have gotten a million dollars’ worth of publicity out of it. Bet there isn’t a person in the country who doesn’t know about the Beachlake Trailer Camp.”

She winced a little.

“I guess you’re right.”

She had Luke to thank that the stories hadn’t been worse—he had invented a fantasy about Mike’s having kidnapped her and brought her to his house. Mike had denied it, of course—but Mike’s denials were no longer very effective.

Parker asked, “What are they going to do with Big Mike?”

“He’s in jail. They’re holding him pending trial for murder.”

Parker pocketed his receipt. “I hope they swing him high,” he said. “A guy like that deserves it.”

Joan sat down again. She felt weak. She always felt weak when she thought about Mike. He had wanted to kill her. He had said so. She still had nightmares about him. And people wouldn’t let her forget.

But she still had work. It helped.

“We have a cleaning service,” Joan told Parker. “Once a week. It costs five dollars.”

“I’ll buy that,” Parker said, reaching into his pocket again. “I track in mud all over the place.”

He returned to his car, got in, started the motor and drove off down the roadway. A fine screen of dust rolled up behind the trailer.

Thoughtfully, Joan followed the trail of dust toward the lake. It was time for her to relieve Luke at the refreshment stand so that he could go to supper. Maybe it wasn’t right for a wife to let her husband cook his own supper but it was the only way they could get anything done any more. The camp was booming, busting with visitors, some morbidly curious-all of them demanding service. And there were a thousand things to be done, permanent matters that would outlast the curious.

The refreshment stand, which was making money, was supposed to remain open till nine. The boats at the dock had to be hosed out and made ready for the next day. Not only that, but the day’s receipts had to be tallied and a deposit slip made out for the bank. Yes, it was much better that they didn’t try to eat supper together.

Supper was the least of the evening.

They could always keep the best of it for last.

The End

TRAILER CAMP WOMAN

Doug Duperrault

Chapter One

"Hot," someone said.
"Not bad," Buddy answered.
"Humidity's 92."
"I've seen it worse."
"Down in Texas, I thought Virginia'd be *north.* But hell, it's *worse'n* Texas."

Buddy yawned and the man shrugged, then walked away. Arlene looked at her husband, wishing he'd make more of an effort to be sociable with the people who lived in the trailer park. He was away all the time, on the road selling, but she had to stay there, cooped up, bored—and these were the people she had to be friendly with.

"You certainly didn't encourage him any."

"So it's hot," Buddy told her, frowning. "Hell, everyone I meet talks about the damned weather."

"He was just trying to be friendly."

"Who needs him? Now shut up, will ya?"

Arlene realized he was ready for a family fight. At thirty-nine, he was twelve years older than she was, and the added age showed, not only in his balding head, the slight paunch of his stomach, but in his manner. Often he was like an old man with a bunch of kids, even if the 'kids' were adults in their thirties.

"Look at that," Buddy said, pointing.

Arlene, wanting to see the evening go by pleasantly, looked in the direction he indicated.

There were over one hundred people in the grassy area behind the trailer park. The park management gave a barbeque dinner once a month for the trailerites. Thick woods surrounded the place, and most of the people, once their plates were full, sat around the edges, leaning against trees, watching any activity that took place in the center. Arlene and Buddy had finished their meal, and now he was pointing to Agnes and Francie. The two women lived in the lot next to theirs, Agnes thirty-four and masculine, Francie 25 and a beauty, her hair platinum blonde, her body voluptuous. They were walking away from the serving table, their plates heaping, laughing together at something Agnes had said.

"Something strange about those two," Buddy said.

"Why?"

"I dunno. Two women living together like that."

"Maybe no one ever asked them to get married."

"You know what I mean," he said, impatiently.

"But you don't *know.*"

"If I ever saw two women in love, I know."

"So?" she said, wishing he'd change the subject. He was continually making reference to them, hinting, making sarcastic remarks. Arlene didn't know if his suspicions were true or not . . . and what's more, she didn't care.

"Oh, get off your high horse!"

"I just don't think it's any of our business, what they do, what they like, as long as they leave *us* alone."

"I know, I know," Buddy said wearily. "Forget it."

"I will."

"Person'd think you were one too, the way you stand up for 'em."

"You know better than that," she said, snuggling against him kittenishly.

It had never failed to work before, and this time was no exception. Buddy hugged her, his hand pinching one full breast. Arlene pushed the hand away.

"Someone'll see, Buddy."

"We're married. Hell, after five years a guy oughta be able to pinch a little in public." He was grinning, and she knew his good mood was restored.

"I'd prefer a *lot*—in private."

"Now?"

"I can wait."

"Okay. We'll stay a little while. Here comes Hoskins and his tribe. What'd we do to deserve this?" Buddy stood up, extending his hand. "Hi, Henry, how the hell are ya? Good to see ya. Hi, Gladys, kids. Come join us."

Arlene marveled inwardly at her husband. Typical salesman. Think one way, act another. She knew Hoskins bored him, yet Henry would surely never guess it from the greeting. Buddy made eight thousand a year, selling office supplies for Barnhart Company in Norfolk, and that took a lot of handshaking. But sales had been his life, as long as she'd known him . . . and he was good at it. There were disadvantages. Like tomorrow.

Sundays should be for the togetherness everyone talked about. Yet Buddy would be off bright and early to Richmond for a three-day sales trip.

It was swell . . .

. . . for him.

She nodded to Gladys Hoskins. She never failed to feel better when near Gladys. The two were about the same age, but four children and near-poverty had driven Gladys to a continual sloppiness. She was fat, too, and always tired. Arlene knew it was bitchy for her to feel as she did, but she couldn't help comparing herself favorably with the woman. Her sleek, creamy body, her high, jutting breasts, her blonde hair smartly kept, her long slender legs . . .

"How's everything, Gladys?"

"Ohhh . . ." the woman eased herself down beside Arlene. "Same old rat race. Found another leak in the trailer when it rained last night."

"How old *is* yours?"

"Six years."

"Have you thought about a new one?"

"Sure," Gladys said, laughing bitterly. "A million times. Thought about mink coats and steak dinners every night too, for all the good it does."

"You could probably get a better one . . . it wouldn't have to be new, would it?"

"Honey, until the Post Office pays Henry about twice as much as they pay him now, it's all blue sky. Besides, I think I might be pregnant again."

"Good Lord, I hope not."

"Me, too. But ol' Henry, he's an impatient man. He doesn't look it, but . . ."

"Well, I hope you're wrong. For your sake."

"Oh, I guess I wouldn't mind too much. Might as well have 'em young, get it over with." Gladys huffed herself to her feet again. "Hey kids," she bellowed. "Gotta get 'em home to bed," she told Arlene. "See ya around."

"Good night."

She watched Gladys leave, then moved closer to Buddy, listening to his conversation with Henry.

". . . it's not a trick. Lotsa people say it is, but it ain't. I *know.*" Henry was a skinny, intense man, and he talked at a rapid pace. "I've done it too many times not to know something about it."

Buddy included her in the talk. "Henry's an amateur hypnotist, honey. You know that?"

"No. How long has this been going on, Henry?"

"'Bout two years. I got a book, figured I'd try it out, and damned if it didn't work. Everyone can't do it, of course, but I can."

"Is it true that some people can't be hypnotized?"

"Yeah. But not many. Most of 'em can as wants to."

"I'll bet it's fun to see," she said, not meaning it.

"Sure is. I'm thinkin' I might try a little later, once some of the kids go on home. Too noisy around here right now."

"Maybe you could do Arlene," Buddy said.

"Probably."

"No, thanks," Arlene said emphatically.

"It doesn't hurt," Henry said, staring at her with unblinking eyes. "Nothing to it, really."

"Still not interested."

"Think it over, Arlene," Buddy said. From years of marriage, she knew this meant, I want you to, so change your mind, but I'll give you a few minutes.

Agnes and Francie walked by, heading back to their trailer.

"You ever do them?" Buddy asked.

"Nope."

"Bet you'd find out some interesting stuff, you get one of them talkin' under a spell."

"You think so?" Henry asked with interest, his eyes following the two women.

"Never can tell."

"'Scuse me," he said, and walked after the women. Arlene watched as he caught up with them, talking agitatedly, then finally shrugging and starting back. As Agnes and Francie walked past Arlene's trailer to their own, she found herself wondering if Buddy was right . . . and a tingling curiosity danced in her mind.

"No deal," Hoskins said, rejoining them. "They say they gotta get to work early in the morning."

"Well, maybe some other time, Henry," Buddy said.

The crowd was thinning out. A cool breeze appeared miraculously and Arlene heard audible sighs of relief. Most of the youngest children had gone off to bed in their trailer homes, and a few adults had gathered around the dying embers of the barbeque pit and were singing. Hoskins left to join them.

"Gladys thinks she's pregnant again," Arlene said.

"Oh?"

"You'd think Henry would hypnotize *her,* or himself, Many more kids and they'd never find a trailer *big* enough, even if they could afford it."

"Is that supposed to be a crack at me?"

"No, of course not."

"You sure?"

"Yes."

"Well, I'm just waitin' for you to start. Just because we don't have any kids after five years, that doesn't prove it's *my* fault."

"I never said it did, Buddy," she told him, startled, wondering what had brought this on. Maybe his age, she thought. He's almost forty. They say men get sensitive about their abilities, when they get that old.

There hadn't seemed to be such a gulf in ages when they got married. He'd been thirty-four, she twenty-two. Coupla young kids. Or so it had seemed. But in this last year or so, his age had become more apparent, and it was as though every hair he lost on his head exposed another area of sensitivity about his male prowess.

"Henry's working on someone," Buddy said, changing the subject.

"Who is it?"

"Don't know 'em. Some gal. Come on, let's go watch."

They pressed into the clustered group about Henry and his subject. Arlene had seen the woman occasionally, and thought she lived somewhere near the grocery store at the entrance. She was in her thirties, rather plain. She was lying full length in a rattan lawn chair, her eyes closed as Henry talked to her in a low monotonous voice. The crowd was hushed, watching. Buddy peered avidly at the experiment, nudging Arlene as the woman began answering Henry's questions in a monotone.

Henry told her that she was itchy, and the woman scratched herself fiercely while the assembled people giggled and laughed. Then Henry told her she was cold, and she huddled herself together in a tight ball, her skirt falling above her knees, exposing large areas of smooth white flesh. No one made any effort to help, and she remained exposed while Henry told her she was happy, then sad, then angry, finally giving her a post-hypnotic suggestion and awakening her.

The woman opened her eyes slowly, frowning, then smiled shyly at the gaping throng, who burst into applause for Henry's performance.

Henry started talking to someone else, casually using the key words of the post-suggestion. The woman, hearing the words, looked about in confusion for a moment, then walked up to Henry, slammed her soft belly against him, and kissed his mouth. Abruptly, she stopped, blushed, and ran toward the darkened rows of trailers. Henry started after her, but some men grabbed him.

"Don't go. Do another one, Hank."

"Yeah. Do my wife."

"Do her, do her," several of them said, pushing forward a young girl. When she consented, the crowd was deathly still as Henry began the same routine with her.

Arlene found herself wondering about the first woman. Where had her husband been, to allow such a thing? Maybe out to sea somewhere. Over half the trailer park population was Navy men and their families. There were a lot of lonely women there, and all over Norfolk.

Buddy bumped her with his shoulder. "I'm gonna have him give you one of those suggestions."

"Oh?"

"Yeah. Everytime I say a word, you're gonna take your clothes off and drag me to the bed." He laughed at her reaction, and Arlene wondered if he was kidding.

"I don't think I need any help, do you?"

"Well, it wouldn't hurt. There's some things I like to do that you won't let me."

Arlene shrugged, wishing he'd change the subject. "Each person has their own standards."

"I just want you a little wilder, that's all."

"Let's not talk about it here."

"Why?"

"Someone might hear."

Henry was having no luck with the second girl. Finally, he gave up, and she went thankfully back to the anonymity of the crowd. "Who's next?" he asked.

"You go," Buddy said.

"No thanks."

"Go *on.*"

"I told you I wouldn't, Buddy. Now let's forget it."

"Look, Arlene, I want you to, understand."

His face was reddening with anger and frustration at her refusal, but she didn't care. She wasn't going to let any amateur hypnotist fool around with her. There was too much danger, too many hazards. There'd been a TV show about that very thing, not long ago. She remembered it vividly.

"I'm sorry, Buddy. I'm going home. You let him hypnotize *you* if you're so anxious."

She turned abruptly and walked away from him, not waiting for his reaction, knowing he'd be furious. When she approached her trailer, she saw he hadn't followed her, and relaxed consciously. Maybe when he came home later, he'd have decided it wasn't important after all.

Walking into the patio, Arlene felt a surge of pride. The lawn was neat, ample. A huge aluminum awning covered over thirty feet of the fifty-five foot trailer, and underneath it they had their barbeque grill, lawn implements, lounging chairs . . . everything that bespoke comfort and relaxation outdoors.

Inside it was the same. She never entered it but that she didn't feel just a bit overwhelmed by the beauty and smartness of it. On the right as she came in was the kitchen, complete with all the appliances she'd ever wanted, including the utility and breakfast bar. The living room was large and adequate, and in the rear were two large, enclosed bedrooms, and a roomy bath.

The walls were beautifully paneled, the floors carpeted, and Arlene loved it. It was that simple. They'd had the trailer over a year now, and she knew she'd have no desire to exchange it for any other way of life.

There were a lot of them, of course, who didn't feel as she did. How many times had she heard a woman say, Lord, it's all right I guess, but I can't wait to get a house. Maybe it made a difference too, if there were children. But for her and Buddy it was perfect. And a house? Too much trouble, too many taxes, too much upkeep, too much money.

Amen to that.

This way, they could save, and did, regularly.

Of course, the main reason they'd bought it had been mobility. Want to move? Tape the cupboards shut, wrap the dishes in towels, and away we go.

The move they'd expected hadn't materialized, but still, they were ready if and when the time came.

Arlene undressed slowly, listening tensely for the sound of Buddy coming in, as she hung her dress in the closet, laid her slip on the chair, and sat on the bed to remove her stockings.

Please don't be mad, she thought. Durn it, a girl's gotta have some rights, some opportunities to make up her own mind. Let's just let sleeping dogs lie, huh?

She sat for a moment, wondering what she should say if he mentioned it. She didn't want to fight with him. There was too much of that lately. Just go to bed, and sleep, and peace and quiet.

Was that too much to ask?

She heard him come into the living room, and her entire body tensed. "Buddy?"

"Yeah."

"Just wanted to make sure it was you." He came into the bedroom, staring at her scantily clothed body wordlessly. "You can see I'm not dressed for company," she finished, trying to make it a joke.

"There's something I want to get straight with you," he said, leaning against the wall.

Oh God, she thought, here we go!

"Buddy, I'm awfully tired."

"You're my wife," he began, "and when I tell you I want you to do something, dammit, you're supposed to do it."

"Only if I want to."

"That's a helluvan attitude."

"Anything else is old-fashioned. A wife's got *some* rights nowadays."

"Not to cross her husband and make him look like a damned fool in front of his friends."

"Friends?"

"The hell with what the word is, smarty. You still made me look like a jackass, for those who were looking."

His face was flushed and she knew he was working himself up to a good temper.

"Buddy, I was afraid *I'd* look like a fool, if he made me do something like that first woman. I just don't trust him, I don't think he knows enough about it, that's all. It's dangerous to play around with things like that."

"You say?"

"Everyone says. It's a medical fact. There was a TV show . . ."

"Damn the TV show! All I know is I wanted you to do something and you didn't. You were my daughter, I'd beat the bejeezus outa you."

"Well, I'm obviously not your daughter."

"Meaning what?"

"Nothing. Just what I said. Why do you have to put hidden meanings into everything I say?" She got up, tried to walk past him to the bathroom, but he shoved her back, pushing her down on the bed.

"You just sit tight 'til I'm through with ya. I know what you meant. It was a crack at my age, wasn't it? Wasn't it?"

"No."

"You're lying."

"*No*, I said."

"Bitch," Buddy yelled and slapped her face.

"You'd better settle down before you have another attack," she warned, trying to make her voice calm.

"I'm all right. I've told you a thousand times, that wasn't any heart attack."

"The doctor said it was."

"Just over-exhaustion, is all. And don't try to change the subject. You're gonna start doing what I tell you around here, by God. I've had enough of your sassy lip to last me a lifetime. There's gonna be some changes, and *fast*. You sit around here all day on your behind and then give me lip when I get home, huh? Well, the honeymoon's over, Arlene."

She started to sit up on the bed, but he pushed her shoulders and she fell back again.

"Don't you move. Settle down and don't move." He watched her for a moment to see if she would obey. She did, her lips tight with restrained fury. There was nothing to gain by bucking him now. And despite her present hatred of him, she was also concerned about his heart. No matter what *he* chose to call it, it had been a minor heart attack that time, following an afternoon of heavy physical work.

She knew he associated heart attacks with old age, and for that reason remained blind to a physical problem. But if she did nothing to anger him further, perhaps he would settle down.

Buddy grinned slowly. "That's better."

"Is it?"

"I don't like to push you around, Arlene. But sometimes, a man's got to."

Oh sure, she thought. A man's got to. Back to the old bull, a woman likes a man who dominates her, treats her casually, tells her what to do and when to do it like she didn't have a brain of her own.

Like hell, she thought. Maybe some women do, spineless, stupid women. But no one with any guts or intelligence does, and no one's going to convince me otherwise.

"Am I submissive enough now, Buddy?"

"Yeah." He sat on the bed beside her. "You stay like that, remember what I told you, and things'll be all right."

"Will they?"

"You gettin' smart again?" he asked intently.

"No," she said with perfect innocence.

"Well, you better not. I meant every word I said, Arlene. And one thing I don't like is a wise guy."

"I know, Buddy." Next he'll want me to bow when he comes into a room, she thought bitterly.

His hand rested on her full breast. Arlene knew from the change in his expression where his thoughts were.

"It's hot, Buddy."

"I'll turn on the fan," he said, easing off the bed and walking the length of the trailer to the kitchen. In a moment, the whirring blades were pulling a delicious breeze through the bedroom window. Well, there goes that excuse, she thought.

But not tonight, I don't want to tonight. Everytime we have an argument, we end in bed, as though that made everything all right . . . or as though the stimulation of arguing aroused the passions in her husband, titillated him.

Buddy came back to the bedroom, flicked the light out. In the moonlight that streamed through the window, she saw him undress.

"Cool enough now?" he asked.

"I don't feel well, Buddy."

"Bull."

"Buddy . . ."

"Take off your things."

Slowly, Arlene sat up in bed, arching her back to unfasten her brassiere. The action pushed her breasts out magnificently, and Buddy grabbed them, his hands rough, insistent. He fumbled the bra off, his hands clasping the naked globes.

His mouth found hers, his lips and teeth rough and bruising on her softness.

"Be gentle," she urged, whispering.

"Don't tell me how," he said, shortly, clipping his words as his passion increased.

"It's not that . . ."

His hands fumbled at her last garment, tugging it impatiently.

"Slow, honey, please."

"Hurry."

"I'll try."

"Now!" he ordered.

Damn him, why couldn't he *wait,* why couldn't he realize it took longer with a woman?

At first, it had been different. But lately . . .

"Please," she begged.

If Buddy heard her, he gave no indication of it.

"Hurry," he ordered, and Arlene tried to accommodate him, tried to forget her own body, her own unreadiness.

"NOW," he said, then, the tension gone, collapsed on her.

After a moment, he got up without a word and left the room. When he came back, ready for bed, Arlene went into the kitchen, a housecoat thrown hastily over her shoulders.

She put coffee water on, leaning against the drainboard while she waited for it to boil.

"Arlene?" he called.

"What?"

"You coming to bed?"

"In a little while."

"Don't be long."

She grimaced, then stuck out her tongue in his general direction. Immediately, she chastised herself for a childish action . . . when what she felt wasn't in the least bit childish.

Damn! At least tonight, she hadn't become too worked up. Sometimes, her mood was more conducive, Buddy was slower, and in the end he left her even higher . . . dryer.

And there *were* the rare occasions when he didn't. Rare and getting rarer.

She fixed her coffee and carried the cup to the dark living room, sitting on the couch, her feet on the coffee table. Across the room through the picture window, she could see the barbeque place, the dark brooding trees and woods that surrounded it. Through the window beside her, she could see the trailer where Agnes and Francie lived. There was a light in the living room, and she found herself watching. She knew she couldn't be seen from her dark vantage point, but still felt a finger of guilt stabbing at her.

The two women were sitting on their couch, watching television. Occasionally they would laugh at something they saw, grinning at each other in the sharing.

Once Agnes got up and brought back two beers.

And once Francie patted Agnes' knee.

Arlene sat up alertly, but nothing else happened, and after awhile she tired of the game.

She finished her coffee, rinsed the cup in the sink, and turned out the kitchen light.

There was a brief flare of light from the direction of the woods, like a match being struck, and Arlene peered out, wondering who it could be. Probably some of the teen-age kids in the park, out necking.

She saw the faint glow of a cigarette as someone inhaled . . . and felt her knees weaken.

It couldn't be, she told herself, fighting the panic that started in her breast. But in the instant reflection, she'd thought of John Edwards. Old crazy John. Ex-fiancé.

Arlene told herself she was seeing things. Gosh, at that distance, and such a weak glow . . . ridiculous. Funny how I'd forgotten him, though. All these years, then something like that reminding me of him.

She breathed a sigh of relief, knowing her mind was playing tricks.

The lights in the trailer next door went out, and Arlene wondered what the two women were doing. She'd read books about . . . about things like that. Not to say that Buddy's suspicions were true, but if he was right . . .

The books hadn't ever been too explicit. Her imagination had to fill in too much, and she was sure some of the ideas she had were pure fantasy.

Again, she felt the faintest tingle of curiosity.

"Arlene?"

"I'm coming."

She crawled into the bed beside him.

"Took you long enough."

"I had some coffee."

"I didn't hear you ask if *I* wanted any."

"Sorry. Do you?"

"Nope. But it never hurts to ask."

"I said I'm sorry."

Oh, shut up, she thought. Just leave me alone, let me like you, let me turn to you for comfort and say, Buddy, I just got a shock, remember John Edwards . . . you remember, I told you about him, before we met, I just thought I saw him, and it almost scared me to death. Let me cuddle against you and feel safe and please, for crying out loud, shut up so I can do it . . .

"You oughta remember things like that. Hell, you don't have much to do all day, least you could do is make things a little more comfortable for me when I'm home. That's not askin' too much is it?"

"No, Buddy."

"Okay. Heck, honey, it's for your own good."

Thanks, she thought, turning her back on him, knowing she would get no comfort from him, not that night, and possibly no other.

Thanks a *lot.*

Chapter Two

Arlene awoke Sunday morning with the realization that it was late. The morning sun streamed through her window with a stifling heat. Already the humidity was high.

Another uncomfortable day.

She checked her watch. Ten-thirty.

"Buddy?"

When there was no answer, she eased out of bed, her body stiff and unresponsive from too much rest. She padded into the kitchen in her bare feet, saw the dirty dishes stacked in the sink, the note attached to the refrigerator by scotch tape.

Have gone on to Richmond. Back Thursday. Be good.
You can reach me at the same place. Buddy.

Pardon my haste, she thought. He'd be in Richmond for lunch. Then what? Arlene began fixing her own breakfast. Lucky thing for him I'm not the jealous type. Could look awfully suspicious, all that extra time in Richmond.

Not that Richmond was a wide-open town or anything. But she guessed a man on the make could find what he was looking for there . . . or anywhere else, for that matter, if he looked hard enough. Not that Buddy would.

Necessarily.

She knew she wasn't being fair. She'd never had reason to suspect him of infidelity. But a hard core of anger remained from last night, and she used that to justify her thoughts.

It was almost noon when she finished her last cup of coffee. Sweating delicately, she sat on the couch with the Sunday paper, next to an open window on the shady side, letting the window fan pull the humid air with all its power.

Francie and Agnes came out of their trailer and Arlene pulled back from the window without thinking. Her curiosity about the two had been whetted by Buddy's remarks, and she wanted to observe them without their knowledge.

If someone had accused her of 'peeping', she would have been furiously angry. It wasn't that at all. Just curiosity.

The two women wore halters and shorts. They spread a huge beach towel on the grassy patio of their yard, lying full length in the sun.

Arlene studied them objectively. Agnes wasn't really thin, but she hadn't blossomed as most women's bodies do. Her breasts, at least as far as Arlene could see, were small, her hips slim and narrow, her legs muscular.

But Francie? Like day and night. The girl's bosom spilled from the confining edges of her abbreviated halter. Her hips and thighs swelled like luscious fruit.

Almost obscenely, Arlene thought from her vantage spot.

A curious dryness came to her throat as she watched the women. She tried to recall things she had read about girls who loved other girls. What they did . . . and how.

She told herself that she wasn't missing anything by *not* knowing, but she remained unconvinced.

For a long time, Agnes and Francie simply lay there on the beach towel. When they spoke it was in whispers, and Arlene couldn't hear what they said.

Once, Agnes reached over and walked her fingers on Francie's stomach. Francie smiled, her eyes closed. Agnes' fingers walked on up to the edge of the girl's breast, and Francie quickly pushed the hand away.

"Agnes! Someone might see."

"I doubt it," the woman's masculine voice said.

"Well, they might," Francie said hesitantly.

"Let's go inside for awhile."

"Right now?"

"Right now."

"All right."

They got up and went into their trailer. Arlene watched them through their screened entrance door. As they closed the door Agnes hugged the blonde girl to her fiercely, bending her back until Arlene thought they would fall down. Agnes' hand started fumbling with Francie's halter . . .

. . . and they went out of sight, back toward the rear of the trailer.

Arlene took a deep breath, her heart pounding with the excitement of her body.

She crossed to the refrigerator and opened a beer, drinking the icy cold beverage deeply.

What's wrong with me, she thought? Watching them like that, then getting so tense and trembly. It must be last night and what *didn't* happen. I've felt funny all day.

Whatever the two women did, it obviously pleased them, for they were both grinning when they came back outside some thirty minutes later.

Arlene watched them for a while longer, but they just lay in the sun, and soon she got bored.

What to do? Television was out. The summer was so full of repeats it was hardly worthwhile. And in Norfolk, you could only get two stations. The third station was UHF, and the Ford's set didn't have a converter.

Typical, she thought. Typical of Norfolk. They talked about three-quarters of a million people and progress and redevelopment and building and all . . . but in many ways it was still a small town, with small town ideas.

A sailor town, Buddy said. And he was right. Over thirty percent of the people were Navy. Not that that was so bad, but it made you wonder where the devil Norfolk would be without the Fleet.

The answer seemed obvious.

Well, it's not like we'll be here forever, she told herself. And added a 'thank goodness' audibly.

She wasted time through the afternoon, then dressed to go into town. She seldom went anywhere without Buddy, but the days without him stretched intolerably ahead of her and she was determined to do something besides sit around the trailer park, wearing a low-cut, flowing peasant blouse and full skirt, she locked the trailer and walked toward Military Highway and the busses.

Henry Hoskins was cutting his lawn, and she smiled and nodded as she walked by.

"You missed all the fun last night," he called.

Arlene shrugged and kept walking. Maybe *he* thought it was fun.

At the end of the row of trailers, a small grocery store sat on her right, the trailer office on her left. She waved to some people she knew, then walked across the highway, waiting at the bus stop across the street from the park, in front of the seafood restaurant where she and Buddy usually ate when she prevailed upon him to take her out in the evening.

The bus came soon, and she settled back for the ride into town and the movie she'd decided to see.

She hoped Buddy would call her for some reason and find her not home. It would serve him right.

As she was walking into the movie house, stuffing her change back into her purse, she dropped it, its contents spilling out in all directions. A young sailor who was following her inside helped her retrieve everything, grinning in such a friendly way at her discomfort and embarrassment that Arlene returned the grin as she thanked him.

"No thanks necessary, ma'am."

She entered the lobby, then stopped at the candy counter. The sailor stopped beside her.

"Are you alone?" he asked, and Arlene felt a shiver.

"Yes."

"Would you mind if I sat with you?"

Before she could answer, he added: "I'm not trying to pick you up, honest."

Maybe I should be insulted, Arlene thought. Yet the boy was young, younger than she by several years. She started to tell him no politely, but something stopped her. He's probably lonely, she thought. So why shouldn't he sit beside me? What harm is there in that?

"I have no objection, if you plan to behave," she told him.

His relief delighted her.

"Thanks. Let me buy the calories."

They sat in the balcony as intermission began. Arlene always tried to see a movie from the beginning and timed her attendance accordingly.

"My name's Corey," the boy said. "Corey Donovan."

"Arlene," she told him, figuring that was enough.

"I appreciate this, Arlene. There's just something nice about sitting with someone in the movies, even if you're not with 'em. I hate to sit alone."

"I know how you feel."

"I don't know anyone in this lousy . . . in this town. Just—got in yesterday."

"Have you been in the Navy long?"

He shook his head. "Not long, too long."

"Oh."

The movie began and they said no more. After an hour, Corey had worked his arm around the back of her chair„ but except for an occasional slight contact with her shoulders, he didn't touch her.

Arlene figured him to be about twenty-one, wanting to act like the sailors you read about but not knowing how to go about it. She would have been amazed at the correctness of her diagnosis.

When the picture concluded, he turned to her anxiously.

"Would you like some pie . . . or anything?"

"I really shouldn't."

"Please." He was so intense she laughed.

"Okay."

They went to a downtown restaurant that served beer. "I just about live in here," he told her.

The place was filled with sailors in their summer whites, most of them with girls, although several booths were occupied by six sailors or more. The place was alive with loud chatter and occasional laughter, the air smoky.

Corey waved to a couple of sailors he knew as they waited for a booth.

"Nice guys," he said.

"Mmm." What am I doing here, Arlene thought? If Buddy could only see me now!

They ordered beer and hamburgers finally, and Arlene ate hers ravenously, remembering she hadn't had any supper. When Corey offered her a second, she accepted, knowing she shouldn't.

But the more she remembered last night, and Buddy's hasty departure that morning, the more she knew it was all right to be where she was, letting Corey treat her.

Afterward, they stood on the street outside.

"Thanks, Corey. I've enjoyed your company."

"You're not going yet?"

"I'd better."

"I . . . I noticed your ring."

"Well, it's not that . . ." she stopped, not wanting to say 'my husband is out of town, so that's no problem.' It didn't sound right, not right at all.

"Look, Arlene, I . . . I don't want to sound . . . fresh or anything, but I have a car, and . . ."

"And?"

"I'd like to drive you home . . . if you'll let me."

She felt like a high-school girl on her first date. "I don't see what's wrong with that?"

"Then you will?" Corey's elation was infectious.

"Yes."

He took her arm as they walked to the parking lot. He had a '54 Mercury convertible, red and cream-stripped. Corey held the door for her, and she wondered how long it had been since Buddy had done that.

Why do I keep thinking of Buddy? Everything that happens, he pops up in my mind. Habit, I guess. Five years of habit.

They drove slowly out Tidewater Drive.

"You mind if we go the long way?" he asked, talking above the dance music that came from the radio.

"How long?" She was relaxed against the seat, enjoying the wind whipping her hair, the cool sensation of the night air.

"Just a little. Go out through Ocean View, then back."

"All right."

It was only a few miles out of the way, and she was relishing the ride too much to argue. Neither of them talked all the way out to Ocean View, through the amusement Center . . .

A short distance later, Corey executed a sharp left hand turn and pulled into a dark parking area overlooking the sandy beach.

Arlene sat up abruptly. "What's this?"

"I . . . just thought we might stop for awhile."

"You said you wouldn't get fresh."

"I won't." His voice sounded hurt, and she wondered if he really *hadn't* thought of making a pass at her. Maybe she was too old, maybe he wasn't attracted to her except as a mother-image in whom to confide and talk and be a friend.

Arlene began to feel insulted, then laughed at her own thoughts. Worried he'll make a pass at me, and worried that he won't . . . how's that for utter confusion?

"What's funny?"

"Nothing. Just a thought."

They sat silently, listening to the radio. There were other cars parked there, and dimly Arlene could make out couples kissing, moving around in the cars. On the beach, too, when a new car would pull in, its headlights beaming, she could see dark shapes on the sand.

After awhile she realized Corey wasn't going to make any advances. At least not soon. She started him talking about the aircraft carrier on which he was stationed, prodding him with questions about the 'city on the sea.'

Finally, he began asking her questions about herself.

"That's not important, Corey. I'm just a gal you met in the movie. We'll never see each other again."

"Why?"

"Because I'm married."

"Service?"

Arlene shook her head, and Corey seemed to be visibly relieved. "No, just a guy. But I don't cheat on him."

"I'm not asking that. Just . . . to talk to you, go to a movie, anything!"

"That could only lead to trouble, Corey. And that I don't want."

"It wouldn't have to be," he pleaded.

"You need to find a younger girl, someone your own age, who's single, unattached." She smiled gently at him, sympathizing with his loneliness, flattered by his stated need of seeing her again. But it wouldn't make sense, no sense at all.

Arlene realized he had shifted in the seat and was sitting very close to her. His arm was around her shoulders, his face coming nearer. She turned to tell him not to spoil it . . . and his mouth found hers with a warm, searching eagerness.

Her first startled impulse was to push him away, but she found herself liking his kiss, the urgency of his young mouth, the difference between his kisses and Buddy's.

With Buddy it was almost perfunctory, a duty. But Corey put his heart and soul into it, and the difference was startling. In a moment, Arlene responded with her own lips, and Corey pulled her body against his.

At length she stopped him. "Whew! That surprised me, Corey." She straightened herself in the cramped front seat of the car.

"Me, too," he admitted, sheepishly. "I . . . I meant it when I said I wouldn't get fresh. But you're so pretty . . ."

"C'mon now, let's keep it honest. Don't start being a sailor with a line at this stage of the game."

"I mean it, Arlene. You're beautiful. All of you. I . . ." He substituted action for words, kissing her again with the same result. Arlene knew she should insist he take her home, but she tasted his kisses avidly, knowing it had been years since she'd been desired in this way, with this eagerness, this frightened fumbling way, and it made her feel younger again to experience it.

Corey's hand touched her breast tentatively, brushing against it and withdrawing quickly so that she couldn't tell him to stop. When she made no attempt to move further away from him, he touched her again, his palm resting gently against her blouse, his fingers cupping the shape of it.

His mouth found her again, and as his kiss gained in passion, his hand grew bolder, squeezing her, outlining the shape of her with deliberation.

Arlene pulled his head down, mashing his mouth against hers, raising her hips until they pressed against his. She knew she was letting this go too far, but it felt too good to stop. Then a car pulled in, its headlights sweeping over them, and she broke away from him hastily.

They faced each other like two racers who had almost rushed over a precipice, breathing heavily from their close call.

She decided they'd better talk, and asked him about his family, his home, why he joined up, wanting him to get his mind off her. Then she lit a cigarette and listened.

He started, faltering, obviously wanting only to hold her, touch her, kiss . . . but gradually he saw she was adamant, and took pleasure in talking about himself, as most people will. Arlene had started it simply to get his mind off her body, but she found herself liking him, and enjoying hearing him talk.

Corey Donovan had been born in Michigan, the third boy in the family and also the last. His father had been a salesman all his life, and when Corey was four, had moved the family to South Dakota where he sold building materials in Rapid City. Life had been good. His father had been 4-F, and during the war years, had prospered when so many others had been away.

But the money he made so easily had gone to his head, and when Corey was ten, his father had hung himself in the garage, after being discovered in an affair with a waitress at a local hotel. It developed later that she was only one of many girls he had been keeping for years, and he had seen the handwriting on the wall with the first discovery.

Corey's mother, always a shy, retiring person, had never worked, but now, with three boys, 15, 13, and 10, she used the insurance money from her husband's death to open a small gift and book store. It had never been tremendously prosperous, but provided enough money to see all the boys through high school. Corey's oldest brother had joined the Air Force upon graduation, his other brother the Army. Corey had chosen the Navy for the same reason that most boys from the Midwest do . . . they know little or nothing about the sea, and want to learn.

"So all your family's in service?"

"Paul . . . he's the oldest . . . he got out and went to college. He's a senior this year. But me and Roger, we're still in."

"You're going to college when you get out?"

Corey shrugged. "I don't know yet. I'm still trying to decide what I'll do in the Navy, let alone afterwards."

Arlene laughed. "Do you have much choice?"

"Some."

He moved closer to her again. Arlene shifted but found herself against the door. His lips sought hers. She turned her head, felt his kiss on her cheek, then her neck. The warmth was coming back, the warmth that had frightened her, caused her to lead him into conversation.

But she compared his attempts at lovemaking with Buddy's. Buddy was always so sure of himself, so rough and hurried. Maybe that was normal after five years of marriage, but she still didn't think so . . . at least not for me, she thought. I want respect, I want to be asked sometimes.

She turned until her mouth met his. The hell with it. It's just harmless petting. And it serves Buddy right.

Corey's hand found her breast again, caressing it through the blouse and bra. In a moment, he needed more and pushed her blouse down off her shoulders, baring them to his kisses. Then he slipped halfway behind her, his hand over her shoulder, the fingers sliding into her bra, touching the naked flesh of her.

"Don't, Corey," she whispered.

"I love you."

"Don't say that." No seriousness, she thought. Just a few minutes to pretend things are different, to pretend I'm not married, that I'm young and desirable again.

He knew enough not to labor the point, and kissed her again as his other hand duplicated the movements of the first, until both her breasts were bunched in his warm fingers.

After a moment, he tried to unfasten her bra, but she pushed him away, trembling with the desire she felt, but knowing it wasn't right, not at all.

Not just the car seat.

The other cars around.

It just wasn't to be. She was married. Good or bad, it was a fact she had to live with.

"I'd better go home."

"Please, honey!"

"Really, Corey. Will you take me?"

He watched her face, saw that she meant it, and nodded. "Will I see you again?"

"No."

Arlene had him let her out a block from the park entrance. "Thanks, Corey. I enjoyed your company."

"Arlene . . . won't you meet me again? I'll promise not to touch you, anything. But meet me."

"I can't Corey. If my husband even hears about tonight, he'll kill me. Besides, that's not the way I like to play the game. If I gave you another impression, you'll have to forgive me. I might have gotten carried away a bit, but usually I play it pretty straight." She paused and took a deep breath, hoping she was getting through to him. "So you can see . . . there's no future in me. Not for a nice young guy like you. Good luck."

She waited until he drove away, slowly at first, then faster when he realized she wasn't going to go into her trailer while he was in sight.

Arlene's body tingled from his touch as she walked. She almost wished she'd gone some place else with him, some place where they could have relieved the tension that surged in her.

Petting, she thought. For kids. All it does is build you up and leave you there, no release, no nothing.

She shook her head as she entered the park. Looking at her last few hours objectively, she was ashamed of herself. Yet there had been a definite pleasure in being desired, being wanted, being treated politely as though she were somebody.

It was nice.

She looked into the other trailers as she walked back to hers. Couples watching television. Kids watching, or playing in the living room. Women washing dishes.

Gladys Hoskins was sitting outside under her awning, fanning herself.

"Hey!" she said to Arlene.

"Hi. Hot?"

"Always. Carry too much weight around is what it is. Wanna sit?"

"Better get home, I guess. I went to a movie and I'm pretty tired. Thanks anyway."

Henry came out of the trailer. "Got plenty of cold beer, if you want."

"No thanks. I'll take a rain check."

"Sure. Anytime."

Arlene unlocked her trailer door. Now that she was home, she knew any after-thoughts she might have had about going anywhere with Corey were silly. Her body's excitement was calming, and she slipped into a housecoat preparatory to taking a cold shower.

That'll get the sex out of ya, gal, she told herself. Freeze your tail and then maybe you'll think of something else.

There was a knocking at the door, and she paused a moment before answering it, wondering who it could be.

She opened the door to Agnes Raymond.

"Hi. Sorry to bother you, but there was someone here looking for you."

"Oh? Won't you come in?"

"Just for a minute."

Arlene felt something powerful in the woman as she stepped past her into the living room.

"How about some coffee or something?"

"Oh, that's not necessary . . ."

"I know, but I'd like the company. Buddy's away in Richmond until Thursday."

"Okay, don't mind if I do. This guy, he didn't give his name, just said he'd be back."

"What did he look like?"

"Oh, about my size. Kinda heavy-set."

"How old was he?"

"Maybe thirty, thirty-five."

It couldn't be, Arlene thought. Yet last night, in that frightful moment when she thought she saw John . . .

"Did he wear glasses?" she asked, holding onto the kitchen table with the fear that flooded her. Oh God, don't let him wear glasses, maybe it was just a salesman, selling magazines or brushes, or . . .

"Yes, he did," Agnes said, her deep voice almost too loud in the stillness of the room. "Horn-rims, I thinks. I just saw him for a minute. He wanted to know where you were, and when you'd be . . . what is it?"

Agnes crossed to her, steadying her.

"Just got a little faint."

"Here, lie down on the couch . . ."

"I'm all right," Arlene protested, but knew she wasn't all right, nothing was all right. It was John Edwards, it *had* to be he. She'd never really been afraid of him before, not until the night when IT happened, but now there was something spooky about it . . . if it was truly him, and she was almost convinced it was.

"Did . . . this man . . . say what he wanted?"

"No. Just that he'd come again."

"You didn't tell him Buddy was out of town, did you?"

Agnes laughed. "Gosh, honey, how could I tell him that? I didn't even know it myself until you just said it."

"Of course. I'm sorry."

"Are you feeling any better? You got white as a sheet just before I hopped over there and grabbed you." Agnes studied her face with concern.

"Must have been something I had for supper. Happens sometimes when I have fish," Arlene lied. "I can't imagine who that man was. Did he have a car?"

"I didn't see one. That doesn't prove anything, though. He could have parked it up front."

"Yeah."

"Let me fix that coffee. That might make you feel better. Unless you'd like a drink or something. We've got some stuff at our place."

"Coffee's fine, but I hate to put you to any trouble . . ."

"Hush now, no trouble at all, baby."

Agnes ran her hand through her short, straight hair. It was brushed straight back, and Arlene envied her the ease of caring for it. She watched the woman preparing the coffee, and felt a surge of warmth for her. In a lot of ways, it was like the feeling she'd had for her mother, on occasions when she realized how hard her mother worked to make her comfortable.

They drank their coffee, smoking slowly, and Arlene began to feel better. Even if it *was* John, there was nothing he could do to her, not with all the people who lived around, not when Buddy was home, not when she could simply pick up a phone and call the police. It was even possible he only wanted to apologize for what he did, that night when she broke their engagement, that night when he wanted to sleep with her and she turned him down.

Arlene shuddered just thinking about it, and Agnes touched her shoulder quickly. "You all right?"

"Yes. Just thinking about something I shouldn't have, I guess. Gives me the willies everytime I do."

"You want to tell me about it?"

"No, thanks. It's just something in the past I'd as soon forget."

"And this guy coming today reminded you of it?" Agnes asked off-handedly.

"Yes."

"You'll make me sorry I told you."

"Don't be. I don't mean that at all."

Agnes' hand remained on her shoulder, resting lightly on it, then stroking soothingly.

"Arlene?"

"Yes?"

"If a backrub would make you feel any better, I'm pretty good at it. Or at least that's what Francie tells me." She said the words tentatively, but Arlene sensed the strong magnetism of the woman beneath them.

The prospect was appealing. Her mind left John Edwards, and returned to the present. This woman with her was the one she had wondered about. And they were together, alone.

"Sounds good."

"Why don't you lie down on your bed? Then when I'm through you can just go to sleep. I'll lock the door when I leave."

"All right."

Arlene preceded Agnes down the hall to the rear bedroom. She turned on the bed lamp, fixing the blinds so that the fan would pull air into the room, but no one could look in.

Boldly, nervously, Arlene dropped her housecoat to the floor. Agnes studied her body with an equal boldness.

"You're a lovely woman, Arlene."

"Merci. Maybe I should put on a nightgown."

"Suit yourself."

"Maybe just panties then."

"Fine."

"I mean . . . I don't want to offend you." She watched Agnes carefully, sensing something new in the woman.

"You won't," Agnes told her quietly.

Arlene found a pair of thin briefs and put them on, then lay on her stomach on the bed. Agnes sat astride her legs, hiking up her shorts until she was comfortable, then slowly began kneading Arlene's back muscles with practiced hands.

"I appreciate this," Arlene said.

"Don't talk. Just enjoy it."

"Maybe I can return the favor sometime?"

"I wouldn't be surprised."

Agnes' fingers slowly wove a spell as they relaxed Arlene's tensions expertly. Down her back they moved, then up to her shoulders, then hammering her spine rapidly, then switching again to the slow, steady kneading, down her back, down further, the fingers resting on her hips as the thumbs worked on the base of her spine.

Arlene felt herself growing groggy, almost hypnotized. She wondered if Hoskins' experiment made a person feel as good as this, and doubted it.

"This is the greatest," she murmured.

"Thank you. I *am* pretty good at it, even if I do say so myself."

"You could go in business."

"I might some day. Never can tell."

Her voice sounded far away, faint and soft, and Arlene knew she was almost asleep. Funny, really. A few minutes ago, so wide awake, nervous, frightened.

Now there was just the sensual pleasure of Agnes' touch, the delight in the manipulations of her fingers and hands.

Vaguely, she was aware of the fingers traveling up and down, up and down. The touch started her body tingling again, but in a way different from any she'd ever known.

She wanted to say something to Agnes about it, but it was too much work to say a word. Her eyelids grew heavier, and she knew she couldn't open them, wouldn't open them for anything.

Her head started spinning and she knew sleep was just around the corner.

Only dimly was she aware of Agnes getting up, turning out the light and leaving the trailer.

A great feeling of peace and happiness flooded her, and she embraced the nothingness of sleep with a smile on her face.

Chapter Three

Monday dawned with overcast skies, making the humidity seem even more oppressive.

Arlene awoke with a smile, her first thought the relaxation that Agnes had managed to give her.

Then she remembered Corey, and knew she'd made a mistake right from the beginning. She should never have allowed him to sit beside her, much less take the liberties that he did. Well, that was over and done with. He didn't know where to find her, so finis, and thank goodness she didn't get caught.

When she thought about it, it seemed impossible that anyone married could get away with an affair for very long. When you lived with a person, you generally understood them, and any change from the norm became apparent.

She was sure that was why you heard so many times of people being found out in an infidelity. She had no doubt that some got away with it . . . but not many.

Corey had been fun. But she sensed a danger in trying for a continuation, and told herself he would be a memory, and nothing more.

After lunch, a steady drizzle began falling, bringing with it a slightly cooler breeze. She fought the boredom of the long, lonely day with magazines and television, envying Agnes and Francie their jobs at the TV station. She wasn't sure exactly what they did . . . Francie a secretary, Agnes a writer or something . . . but they were occupied with their work, and she wondered if they realized how lucky they were.

Arlene had worked the first two years of their marriage, while Buddy complained constantly.

'I'm capable of supporting you,' he would say. 'People see you working, they think I'm not makin' any kind of dough. What do you need to work for, anyway? Isn't it enough to keep a house and have meals ready on time, lay around all day, and take it easy? I don't understand you.'

She'd suffered with it for two years before quitting, unable to make him understand that the days were endless, without any children to occupy them.

Of course, the first few weeks had been fine, giving her a chance to catch up on much reading, a chance to sample all the daytime television fare, a chance to meet her neighbors for the first time. But soon the reading was up to date, the daytime entertainment palled, and the neighbors talked too much about their kids.

Since then she'd fought a losing battle against boredom, and had all but stopped trying to make Buddy understand.

Before her marriage, people had warned her that he was too old for her, that his ways, after all those years, were set, and she would have to adjust to them, not vice versa.

But Arlene hadn't listened, knowing only that he had proposed and she'd accepted, anxious to get married and get away from the home town, get away from John Edwards.

But that wasn't something you could tell people, in trying to explain her rush to marry Buddy.

She felt herself growing nervous just thinking about it. Walking to the big picture window on the side of the trailer living room, she looked across the road to the woods. The rain had dampened everything, making it soggy and sodden and gray.

Suddenly, she saw a movement in the trees, and her heart stopped beating for an instant.

It was in the same area where she'd thought she'd seen John . . . and as she peered intently through the gloomy day, she could make out a man's figure, leaning against a tree, standing out in the rain.

Arlene shook her head and blinked her eyes, trying to make the scene go away, but it remained.

There was a man standing in the woods.

She pulled the blinds almost shut, then sat behind them, watching the spot avidly. For a long time, there was no movement, then she could see the figure move, changing position, lighting a cigarette.

John Edwards, she thought, panic rising in her breast.

No. It can't be. It's just my mind playing tricks. Oh, there's a man out there all right. And he must be a little touched to stay out there in the rain like that, but it *can't* be John. Not after all these years.

Besides, he wasn't serious when he threatened her.

It was just the heat of argument, disappointment.

The man moved again, his head peering slowly from behind the tree.

Arlene gasped.

Even through the rain-stained window, the dull day, she knew she was looking into John Edwards' face.

And he was watching her trailer!

Arlene put her hand on her heart as its pounding seemed to grow to a point where it would burst.

Her first thought was to call the police . . . but what could she tell them? That a former fiancé was standing in the woods getting wet.

They certainly couldn't do anything. Could they?

Edwards moved away from the tree, started walking slowly toward the trailer, looking about furtively as though not wanting to be observed.

Arlene watched him approaching. He hadn't changed much in five years. He didn't stand much taller than she herself did, and his chubbiness had increased until now he was corpulent. His thick horn-rimmed glasses were steamed, and he wiped them off with a handkerchief, standing outside the gate to her patio, looking about carefully.

Arlene was frozen, watching him come closer and unable to move. She felt a desire to scream, but fought it desperately.

Edwards walked to the door of her trailer, grasping the handle and pulling it. Arlene watched it turn, knowing it was locked, yet frightened that somehow it wasn't.

He turned it again, harder, and when it still didn't yield, Edwards knocked on the door heavily, a slow, deliberate knocking.

Arlene pulled her skirt up and covered her mouth with it as she watched him through the narrow slit in the blinds, her eyes wide with terror. Edwards hesitated, then pounded on the door again with the same rhythmical beat.

Finally, he looked the trailer over, his eyes meetings hers in a frightening moment, but he apparently didn't see her watching, for he turned and went back to the woods, disappearing into them, not stopping to watch again as far as she could tell.

When he was out of sight, Arlene went from one door and window to another, checking them all, making sure they were closed and locked.

The trailer soon was stifling hot and uncomfortable but she didn't care, just so she was secure within and he couldn't get at her unexpectedly.

Once that was done, she relaxed, slumping on the floor, tears flooding her eyes and her body shaking with her sobs, the aftermath of the alarming ordeal, the frightening knowledge that Edwards was there and obviously intent on carrying out his threat.

The time until Agnes and Francie came home from work dragged intolerably, each minute taking an eternity, each second one of vigil and fear.

But finally they were back, and Arlene went immediately to their trailer.

"May I come in?" she asked Francie, who answered the door with a puzzled expression.

"Sure," the blonde said, opening the door for her.

Agnes had started their supper, and turned from the kitchen. "Hi."

"Hi. Listen, I know this is an imposition, but could I stay here with y'all for awhile?"

"Sure," Agnes said, coming into the living room, wiping her hands on her apron. "Anything wrong?"

"Well . . . when Buddy's away, like now, sometimes I get frightened all by myself."

"I'm not surprised."

"There was . . . a magazine salesman there today, he seemed a little bit crazy. I wouldn't want to be alone if he came at night."

"Of course not. How about having supper with us?"

"No, look, I don't want to be any trouble . . ."

"Don't be silly. We're not having anything special, so we'll just set another plate."

Gratefully, Arlene helped set the table. She was sure Edwards had gone away for awhile, but still it was comforting to be with people, talking with them, sharing with them, feeling sure he would never bother her unless she was alone.

After supper, Francie pleaded a headache and went into the bedroom, shutting the door. Agnes looked after her curiously, a tight expression on her lips.

But she said nothing, and was her usual self as Arlene helped her with the dishes.

"I'd better see if Francie's all right. Be right back," Agnes said after the last dish was washed and dried.

Arlene sat on the couch, pulling the window drapes shut so that no one could stand in the dark wet night and look in. She heard Agnes and Francie whispering in the other room, heard Agnes say 'Don't be silly, it's not like that at all.'

She wondered what the problem was. But then everyone who lived together in any degree of proximity argued occasionally. Arlene didn't think anyone could truthfully say that someone didn't get on their nerves sometime.

Even if it was a minor thing. It was just part of living.

Agnes came back smiling. “She’s feeling a little better. Had a rough day at the station.”

“Must be fun, working there.”

“Well, there’s no glamour, if that’s what you mean. But it’s exciting sometimes.”

“I’d like to go back to work, but Buddy’s ‘agin’ it.”

“Men!”

“He can’t understand how dull it is at home every day with no one to talk to, nothing to stimulate you mentally.”

“That’s right. Hell, you get in that kinda rut, and you can get pretty dull as a person if you don’t watch out. I know there was a period where Francie didn’t work . . . for various reasons . . . and pretty soon we didn’t have too much to talk about. But when she went back to work, everything was different. How about a drink?”

“Sounds good.”

Agnes mixed them a bourbon and soda, splashing the liquor into the glasses with a practiced measurement.

“Agnes?”

“Yes, kiddo.”

“Would you mind if I slept here tonight? On the couch?” Arlene was afraid that she would be denied for some reason, but the woman’s answer relieved her instantly.

“Sure thing. No trouble at all.”

“Thanks. I . . . I don’t know why I got spooky all of a sudden, but I sure did.”

“Shoot, we all do I guess, one time or another. Don’t think about it. I just hope you’ll be comfortable on the couch. If that bed back there was a little wider, we could all sleep on it, but I’m afraid that would be a little crowded.”

“The couch’ll be fine.”

“How long have you been married?”

“Five years.”

“Like it?”

Arlene shrugged, thinking the question was a strange one, wondering why Agnes was watching her so intently. “It has its good points . . . and bad ones, I guess. Like almost anything.”

“I don’t mean to be personal.”

“Oh, I don’t mind, really.”

"I was just . . . well, I guess you'd say curious. I've never been married, of course, and I wonder about it sometimes, wonder if I'm missing anything." Agnes ran her fingers through her hair briefly.

Arlene wanted to say that she'd wondered too, wondered about women like Agnes, wondered if *she* was missing anything. But she didn't know her well enough to risk offending her, "It'd be hard to say. Men are a form of companionship, protection . . . in addition to any sexual benefits."

"Companionship, of course, can be obtained from a number of sources."

"I'd have to agree."

"As far as the sex is concerned . . . this doesn't embarrass you does it?"

"No. I've always felt I was broadminded."

"Good. If I do get too personal, just tell me to stop, honey. But this sex business. I just wonder if it's all it's cracked up to be."

"Well . . ."

"Not having experienced it, I can't say personally. Francie's a virgin too. So there's nothing we can tell each other when we get to thinking about it."

"I imagine."

"It's not that we don't know what happens. At least, clinically. God knows there are enough books that describe all the organs and the functions, the methods and positions and all that. But still all we know about the exact feeling is what we get from love and romance novels, and that's not enough to answer all the questions."

Arlene was beginning to feel slightly embarrassed, not from what they were saying, but from the intense glances that Agnes was giving her. The woman's eyes were on her face, her body, almost as though she were undressing her, watching her experience the male-female sex of which they talked.

"Well, it's . . . it's hard to describe. It's sort of intangible, if you know what I mean."

"I see. Well, I'm probably being rude to you, but sometimes you just feel a person won't mind?" Agnes fixed them another drink. When she sat back down, Arlene had decided to use a little boldness herself.

"There's something I've wondered."

"What's that?"

"I'm in the dark about . . . what women do . . . when they don't have a man?" She felt herself flushing, and looked down at the floor.

"That's kind of hard to describe, too," Agnes said, smiling thinly. "You're back in the realm of the intangibles again."

"I thought maybe."

"I think it's pretty damned closely associated. The only variation would be the methods used to arrive at the common goal. And those depend to a large extent on the individual."

Arlene nodded as though she understood. In a vague way, she did, yet there were so many questions she had, so many little specifics that had never been answered. She sensed that Agnes had deftly bounced her question into limbo, without really saying anything.

The phone rang, and Agnes answered it, talking with someone from the station about a problem with a commercial. When she was through, the mood of intimacy they'd shared had evaporated, and Arlene wasn't able to ask anything else.

In a little while, they decided it was time for bed. Agnes fixed the couch, finding sheets and a light blanket underneath it, making the bed swiftly and deftly.

Arlene sat on the edge of it, unbuttoning her blouse. "I can't thank you enough for letting me stay here tonight."

"Happy to do it. I want you to feel that we're your friends, Arlene. All the time."

"Good." She removed her blouse, laying it carefully across the back of the couch, then stood to remove her skirt. Agnes made no move to go into the bedroom, and Arlene caught her watching the movements of undressing with frank desire. It sent a strange sensation racing through Arlene's body, and she felt her breasts firming, her thighs tingling inexplicably.

She stepped out of her skirt, hanging it also over the back of the couch.

Agnes put out her cigarette and walked close to Arlene. "How about another massage?"

"Would you mind?"

Agnes shook her head slowly, then pointed to the couch. "After you."

Arlene stretched on her stomach. Agnes unfastened her bra, her fingers instilling in Arlene a sense of power and purpose as they worked on her back and shoulders. It had the same relaxing effect as the previous night, and when Agnes patted her buttock to indicate she was through, Arlene whispered 'thanks' gratefully.

But sleep didn't come immediately. She was in a strange bed, with unusual sensations coursing through her body. Agnes' hands had been almost like a man's hands . . . like Corey's . . . and they had awakened dormant needs in Arlene.

She rolled over, lighting a cigarette, listening to Agnes and Francie in the bedroom.

They whispered about something. Francie sounded mad, then suddenly she giggled, and there was more whispering.

Arlene wondered what they were doing.

Exactly what.

A temptation seized her to go in there, join them, see what they were doing, and maybe . . . the thought was shocking, yet she played with it . . . participate!

In what, she asked herself?

And only knew vaguely. And knew also that they'd resent her bursting in on their privacy. It would be the same if some relative were staying with her and Buddy, and the relative decided to come into their bedroom when he heard the bedsprings rattle, wanting to see what was going on.

She realized there wasn't much difference in what she had thought of doing, and cast the idea from her mind.

Much later, she was still awake. The sounds from the bedroom had ceased long before, and it was still in the trailer but for the slight buzzing of the electric clock in the kitchen.

She heard a rhythmic pounding and sat up in bed instantly.

It was coming from the direction of her trailer, a steady, monotonous, heavy sound, and she knew with a certainty that Edwards was back!

Her first thought was to awaken Agnes and Francie . . . but that wasn't necessary. He wouldn't come there, not to someone else's trailer, not when he couldn't be sure where she was.

There was a long pause, and Arlene crept to the window, peering out into the night, across the patio to her trailer.

A dim, bulky shape was moving around her trailer, stopping at the windows, peering in.

If I had a gun right now, I'd kill you, she thought, hating him, hating herself for her fright.

The man turned around, and Arlene knew he was looking toward Agnes' trailer. Then he walked back around front, knocked at the door once more.

After that, the night was quiet again. Arlene was fully awake.

What can I do, she asked herself?

I could call Buddy, tell him to come home . . . only he'd probably laugh at me, tell me I was imagining things.

Or, when John comes next time, I could talk to him, ask him what he wanted.

Maybe it was something logical.

How *could* it be, she asked herself? At this time of night. Standing in the rain.

But maybe . . .

She lit another cigarette and lay back on the couch, remembering how the whole mess had started . . .

Arlene had dated John Edwards for a year. Not steadily, but with enough frequency so that people often talked of them as a 'pair.' During that time, she'd found him fairly pleasant, not particularly aggressive, and generally good company.

When they were on dates, they talked about the town, his father's grocery store, her job, his job . . . nothing special, although occasionally he talked about his time in the Army, and the discharge they gave him, never talking too specifically about the reasons for it, but making it clear that they had 'done me dirty.'

The way he told it, there was a sergeant who was jealous of Pfc. Edwards, and this sergeant picked Pfc. Edwards for all the unpleasant, rotten, filthy jobs that came along.

Finally John had enough, and one night he waited for the sergeant on the dark street, falling upon the slightly drunken man with a knife and wounding him seriously.

At the court-martial, the psychiatrist was also picking on Edwards, according to Edwards, and told a lot of lies about his mental stability.

The result had been a dishonorable discharge after a year at hard labor.

When John Edwards came back home, there was no sign of his present fat. But for the first year he was back, he spent all his time drinking beer, eating, and lying around his house all day.

He improved somewhat after that, working in his father's store, but the endless bottles of beer and his laziness added to the weight he carried, until he was often referred to as 'Fat John' to differentiate him from his father, 'Old John.'

If this name bothered him, he seldom let it be known, and seemed quite content to work for his father, date girls once in awhile, and drink beer.

Arlene had been twenty-one when she had her first date with John Edwards. She had known him for years, had heard vague tales about his Army service, most of which she discounted as rumor, and was working as a clerk at a downtown women's store at the time, having finished Junior College and now wondering what would happen next.

She knew a girl should want to be married, and was pleased when Edwards proposed after a year of off-and-on courtship. She knew she didn't love him, but he seemed innocuous, his father was old and he would soon inherit the business, which would provide a tidy income and good standard-of-living in the town, and she could see no better prospects.

Their engagement was announced, and she was complimented by all her friends. Things went along well for over a month.

Then IT happened.

During all their dating, John had never asked for more than a kiss, a brief bosom-caress. Therefore on this particular night, she had no qualms whatever when he took her far into the woods away from town, high up on a bluff overlooking the river that wound through the town. They were alone in a quiet, darkened world, and Arlene was enjoying it.

John spread the blanket he always carried in his car, and they lay on it, looking up at the stars, not speaking, their hands clenched tightly, first one pressing, then the other.

Arlene knew that soon he would roll over and kiss her, and if she responded adequately, he would be encouraged to squeeze her breast, which would feel good because she could enjoy it without worrying about him wanting anything more.

There were many advantages in their relationship that she cherished.

It took him so long to kiss her that she was almost ready to initiate the action herself. But sure enough, he rolled over on his stomach, his mouth pressing against hers with a steady, proper pressure.

"Mmmm," she said, not enjoying it any more than usual, but wanting her fiancé to feel proud that he could please her.

John's hand went immediately to Arlene's breast, which was ahead of the usual script, but she thought nothing of it. The sensation of his hand resting on the resilient flesh was good, and she closed her eyes, savoring it, anxious for the day when they would be married and there'd be more . . . much more.

"We should set a date soon, John."

"Huh?"

Arlene repeated her words.

"What's the rush?"

"I'm just anxious to have you all to myself," she said, and in part it was the truth.

"It'll be soon enough."

His fingers fumbled with the buttons of her blouse, which was definitely a departure from anything that had gone before, but she made no move to stop him. Rather, her body sensed a new experience coming, and pressed forward to meet it.

When her blouse was open, he laid his head on her bra, his lips nibbling at her neck. Arlene held his head close with her hands, stroking his hair, waiting for his next move.

It was a long time coming, but finally he raised up until he was sitting beside her.

Then, with a savage motion, he grabbed the edge of her brassiere and pulled it up and off her breasts, the band of it cutting into her back, hurting her.

Arlene started to protest, but he had fallen on her bared flesh with rough hands, pulling at her with a sudden fury, then leaning over and kissing her.

Arlene tried to push him away, frightened of him for the first time in her life, but he clung to her like an enraged animal.

"John, dammit, stop!" she said, yelling at him, but he paid her no heed. Arlene struck him with all her strength.

John stopped, looking at her dumbly, his eyes puzzled. Then as abruptly as he'd begun, he stopped and threw himself on the blanket, weeping bitterly.

Arlene felt little compassion for him. Her breasts and thighs hurt achingly from his roughness.

Yet she knew he was sick, knew there was something wrong, and patted his shoulders as he cried. She didn't know what to say to him, torn between hating him, and wanting to understand him.

"I'm sorry," he said at length, when his tears were under control.

"What happened?"

"I want you. That's all."

"Gosh, do you have to be so rough?"

John shook his head wearily. "I don't know what made me do that. I was afraid you wouldn't let me, I guess."

"Well, I won't. Not until after we're married. But that's no reason to be so cruel. You hurt me, John . . . you . . ."

"You won't?" he asked, as though he couldn't believe it.

"That's right."

"Why?"

"I'm not that kind of girl."

"We're engaged."

"That doesn't make any difference, John. If you want to love my body *gently,* I'll let you. But that's all. Nothing else until we're married," she told him firmly, always before finding it the perfect way to deal with him; but this time was to be different.

He chuckled meanly. "You savin' it, like a little treasure, like a dowry, huh?"

"No. But don't you want to marry a virgin?"

He shrugged. "After the first time, it's all the same anyway, isn't it?"

"I wouldn't know."

"Meaning what? That you're a virgin?"

"Naturally."

"Ha!"

"Johnny!" Arlene was truly shocked. She *was* virginal, a status that had given her some anxious moments and required some clever strategy in the clinches, but virgin she was.

"What about all those fellas in high school? Don't think I didn't hear you were a pretty hot necker."

"Necking's a little different."

"You say."

"Johnny, I don't like this at all. I think we'd better go home."

Arlene started to stand, but he pushed her back down. "Not yet, baby. I'm gonna find out what I'm gettin' when I marry you. If I do."

"That's just what *I* was thinking, Johnny boy."

"What?"

"If. If we get married. I'm beginning to have my doubts about you."

He was looking at her strangely, and she should have known enough to keep her mouth shut, but she went on: "I'm beginning to think the Army was right about you. You are crazy."

As soon as the words left her mouth, she would have given anything to call them back. He gave an anguished cry of pain, his eyes glazed, and punched her in the stomach with a hard, driving fist. Arlene fell back on the blanket, gasping for air, as he stood up and kicked her sharply in the ribs several times.

She screamed at him to stop, but he only laughed.

"Crazy, am I? Crazy, maybe, to get tangled up with a bitch like you? Crazy to be nice and gentle with ya, when you're layin' everything around here that wears pants? You dirty, lousy, stinkin' . . . . ." he rambled off unintelligibly, mouthing foul words at her while her shocked mind tried to decide what to do.

He was beyond placating, and there was no help near. She tried to run, but he knocked her down again before she even had her balance, then began ripping her clothes off, tearing the fabric easily in his fury.

"Please, Johnny, I'm sorry for what I said. But don't spoil it, don't." Knowing she would never marry him, never go out with him again, anywhere. But she had to get away from him, and soon.

Her words fell on deaf ears as he came nearer. With a sudden movement he dumped her to the ground where the rocks and sticks scraped her back, falling beside her, half on her, wrestling and fighting. When she saw he was determined, that nothing would make him stop, she waited for her chance, then rammed her knee between his legs as hard as she could. He screamed in pain, then fell down, writhing on the ground in agony.

Arlene waited to see what would happen. She debated running to the car, trying to get away, but doubted he would let her. He continued rolling and yelling for many minutes, finally kneeling up, holding himself there, screaming filthy words at her.

Then a serene smile crossed his face and his hands searched along the ground until they found what he wanted. He picked up a stick and came slowly toward her.

Instinctively, she backed away from him, but she stumbled over a rock and fell, with John leaping on top of her immediately, laughing as he jabbed at her with the stick.

As she yelled with the pain, her knees retracted instinctively and caught him again between his legs.

This time, he gave no further thought to her, but ran to his car, throwing his clothes in back, and drove crazily away, back toward town, leaving her there on the bluff, her clothes torn, her body battered and bloody.

Arlene made her painful way home just before daybreak, destroying her shreds of clothes. She refused to comment on what had happened, denying stoically her mother's pleas that she tell.

Her family thought they knew what had transpired when John didn't call the following week, but Arlene never admitted anything.

When she heard from John again, it was the day he received her note that the engagement was off, over, the end, period.

He made little sense, except to threaten her if she didn't marry him. "I don't care where you go, bitch. I'll find you, and I'll get you, and I'll rape you until you die. And you know I can do it." Then he began rambling again, and she hung up on him.

Within a few weeks, Arlene had met Buddy Ford, and shortly thereafter married him and left home.

Now, after five years, John Edwards had found her . . . and Arlene was sure he meant to carry out his threat.

She tried to get comfortable, tried to sleep, but rest wouldn't come.

Thinking about it again, after all this time, had reawakened all her fears to their fullest, had brought back all the pain and humiliation.

There had been so many times in five years . . . especially at first . . . when she'd been able to forget him completely, and his face wouldn't cross her mind for months at a time.

But now all that was over.

She wondered fearfully what the outcome would be.

Chapter Four

The minutes flew by the next morning as Francie and Agnes prepared for work. Arlene tried to think of something she might do to postpone the inevitable . . . but an honest confession of her fear was out of the question. They'd probably think she was crazy or something.

After breakfast the women left, Arlene staying on to wash the breakfast dishes.

She stalled the chore for over an hour, then knew with a sudden determination that she couldn't remain there at the park all day, all by herself.

It would just be asking for trouble.

She went home to her trailer to change, her eyes watching the woods with dread fascination, as though Edwards would pop out from behind a tree and come running at her.

Inside, she locked the door securely while dressing, stopping every few moments to look again toward the trees across the road. When she was ready, wearing a simple, body-hugging afternoon dress, she re-checked the woods, her heart almost stopping as she saw a blurred movement amongst the trees, gasping for air when she recognized it as the O'Neil boys playing Indians.

I'm really spooked, she thought. And with cause. There's no telling where I might run into him, or when.

It was almost noon when she arrived in Norfolk, hastily finding a fairly decent movie and losing herself in the theatre's darkness for two hours.

Coming out, she wandered aimlessly, window-shopping, standing on a corner for a few minutes, just watching the people who passed. She found herself in front of the restaurant where

Corey had taken her, and wondered on a sudden impulse if he might be inside.

Despite her promises to herself, the thought of having a man with her for awhile was appealing, and she walked in, her eyes searching the interior booths and tables anxiously.

Corey was sitting toward the back with another sailor. Arlene started walking toward him when he saw her, leaping to his feet and meeting her midway.

"Hi. I was afraid I wasn't ever going to see you again, honey."

"Well . . . you never know."

"Got a little while?"

"Sure."

"Great. Here's an empty booth."

They sat together, facing the door, and ordered coffee.

"How ya been?" he asked, nervous and eager.

"Pretty good."

"How'd ya know I'd be here?"

"Well, you said you hung out here, remember?"

"Oh, yeah. Gee . . ." he shook his head, smiling, "Here I was, just wondering what the devil I'd do to kill a day's liberty. We can . . . ah, stay together awhile, can't we?"

"Yes, Corey. All day if you want."

"Oh, baby. Now you're talkin' my language."

Arlene ate a sandwich, then they got Corey's car from the parking lot.

"How about the beach?" he asked, drumming his fingers on the wheel.

"I don't have a suit."

"Can't we buy you one?"

"No," she protested. "Not just for the day."

"I don't mind."

"I don't really feel like swimming, Corey. Couldn't we just go out there and watch the others?"

"Crazy."

They drove out Virginia Beach Boulevard. Arlene was able to relax almost completely as they drove. The day was sunny, the humidity not too bad, and it was possible to forget John Edwards for minutes at a time. Corey rented a gigantic beach towel at the resort, and they found a sandy spot under a fishing pier on which to rest. Corey took off his shoes and socks, stretching full length on the towel, smiling up at her happily.

"It's a great life."

"Sometimes," she answered, smiling back at his obvious pleasure. "I guess it's the high spots that make the low spots tolerable."

"You don't have any low spots, do ya? Pretty gal like you?"

Arlene almost told him, but reminded herself it wouldn't do any good. Corey was good for diversion, for company on a day like this, but she didn't want him getting involved. He was too young to be dependable when the chips were down . . . and that could happen anytime.

"Not many," she said, looking across the broad expanse of pure sand. There were hundreds of people there, mostly vacationers who crowded the Virginia Beach area every summer, enjoying the beaches and ocean and sunshine. A Navy jet roared overhead, and far out in the water she could see the car ferry plying its tedious way from Kiptopeke to Eastern Shore.

Arlene stretched out beside Corey, letting him hold her hand innocently.

Holding hands used to be almost everything, she thought dreamily, her mind going back to her high school days. It was the touch, the understanding, the togetherness. Nowadays, as a person got older, it was never enough for long. It was too pure, too sterile.

The afternoon passed rapidly, the tide washing in steadily until the breakers were splashing the sand only ten feet from their area. Then the tide turned, and the water level slowly backed away, so gradually that you didn't notice it except after fifteen or twenty minutes thinking about something else. Then you'd look where the water used to be, and find it several feet further down the beach.

As the sun lowered, the bathers started leaving. By six-thirty, she and Corey were alone in their immediate area. She knew she should probably be going home, but the thought of the park, the trailer, the woods, frightened her. And with Buddy out of town, there certainly would be no harm in staying out awhile, letting dusk and evening come and returning home after dark.

"Hungry?" he asked.

"A little bit."

"You don't have to go?"

"Not yet."

"I know a place. The Jolly Pirate. Good pizza and pretty good jazz."

"Sounds fine. I've heard of it."

"I'm starved myself, if you're ready."

They returned the beach towel, then made their way slowly across the beach to the parking area, their feet sinking and sliding in the deep sand.

At the Jolly Pirate, the night air was filled with a bouncy jazz combo that pierced the dark sky, the sounds reaching them even as they turned on off the highway and entered the parking lot. Inside they found the place only half-full, it being a week-night, and easily obtained a table near the bandstand. Five men performed there . . . piano, drums, sax, guitar and trumpet . . . and the sounds they made went through Arlene's body rhythmically, awakening something that had been lying dormant. She tapped her feet to the music, knowing the combo was good, knowing that the others there had to be jazz aficionados from their rapt attention.

After the next number, a slight, dark-haired girl took the mike, belting out a classic number with a voice that approached Christy's.

Arlene turned to Corey with sparkling eyes. "I've been missing something."

"You a jazz bug?"

"Not really. But I enjoy this kind of music. I keep forgetting how much."

"The girl's good. She doesn't have the discipline yet, but she'll get there."

They ordered a large pizza with mushrooms, anchovies and Italian sausage, served with a schooner of beer that was cold enough to frost its container. This they topped off with spumoni, had more beer, and found it was only eight-thirty when they returned to the car.

"You don't want to go home yet, Arlene," he said, pleading for a negative answer.

"Not really."

"You name it."

"Oh, anyplace, really."

A car pulled into the lot, its light blinding them for a moment. Arlene's eyes followed it as she wondered where she could have him take her, postponing the eventual need to return home.

Two women got out of the car, glancing her way, and with a shock she recognized Agnes and Francie. Instantly, Arlene turned her head, hoping they hadn't seen and recognized her with the sailor.

If they saw her, they gave no sign, and Arlene could believe it had been only a close call, and nothing more. But she had to get out of there, that was for sure.

"Let's go back to the beach," Corey said, moving close to her. "Nice moon out, and there won't be many people."

"Any place," she said, wanting only to leave the Jolly Pirate before they came out again, or . . . something.

Corey whipped the Merc onto the highway, heading back to the beach. Arlene wondered if it was wise to return to the place after dark, but decided it wasn't important. She could control him, that much she'd discovered the other day. And it might be nice and peaceful.

Corey parked, then unlocked the trunk and pulled forth a blanket.

"We should have used that this afternoon and saved the quarter," she said, beginning to feel nervous.

"It's got a hole in it. Looks tacky in the daytime, but s'all right at night, I think."

They walked back across the sand, finding their spot of the afternoon waiting for them, with no one else in sight up or down the beach. Corey spread the blanket and they sat on it, watching the glistening reflection of the moon on the swelling ocean, hearing faintly the raucous, infectious noise of the amusement park a mile away. A cool breeze came from the sea and Arlene was glad she'd come.

The memory of the music at the Jolly Pirate haunted her, filling her body with a pulsating tempo that seemed to match the dancing moonbeams on the ocean.

"Arlene?"

She turned to him. "Yes, Corey?"

"Are you going to tell me any more about yourself?"

"For instance."

"Like your last name . . . where you live . . ."

"Is it important?"

"It is to me. When you just get to know a girl's first name, it's not really as if you know her at all. It all seems like a dream kinda."

"I told you last time, there's no future for us."

"I know it. And I don't intend bothering you. But I just want to know."

"My last name is Ford."

"Thanks."

Arlene was surprised. Corey seemed to actually be grateful that she told him, and she found it hard to believe that a person's last name was that important. But apparently it was to him.

"You must live near where I dropped you off."

"That's right." She wasn't going to tell him anymore, fearful that he might get a little tight some night and decide to come see her . . . and bump into Buddy. She flinched at the thought. God, that would really be the end!

"Where?"

"Uh uh. Because that's not really important, Corey."

"It is to me." His young face was sober, serious, and she leaned forward and kissed his mouth softly.

"I think you ought to get your mind on something else," she told him, patting his cheek gently as she drew back.

Corey caught her soft body, pulling it against his as his lips mashed hers hungrily. Together, they toppled down until they lay on the blanket, their arms embracing each other with an urgent need.

When their mouths were tender from bruising kisses, they released each other for a moment, inhaling the fresh sea air keenly, holding hands as they stared at the sky, sprinkled with thousands of pinhole stars.

"I love you, Arlene."

"Now, Corey . . ."

"Well, I do. I don't care if there isn't any future for us. I love you, and we have tonight. And I just want you to know how I feel."

"Thanks," she whispered, leaning over him and kissing his neck with little nibbles.

"Is it wrong for me to love you?"

"No. I'm glad you do, really. I just don't want you to get emotionally involved where you might be hurt."

"I can take care of myself," he said, almost defiantly.

"I know, I know."

Funny, she thought, sometimes he was like a man, other times a young boy. Which was all he was, really. So much younger than she. I should be ashamed, she told herself. But I'm not. I needed someone with me today and I knew where to find him. So what in the world is wrong with that?

She kissed him again, knowing what was wrong, knowing that all the excuses in the world didn't make it right, but not caring.

Like he said, they might not have anything else, but they had tonight . . . and suddenly she knew she wanted to make it a night he would long remember.

Her hand stroked him slowly, carefully, moving down his body until he jumped from the unexpected contact of her fingers.

"Arlene?"

"Kiss me, darling, and don't talk."

Corey kissed her feverishly, his hands bunching her full breasts, then dropping down to her legs, caressing the firm smooth flesh of them, moving up to her knees, then pausing as he kissed her again, his lips inquiring.

She gave him the answer he needed, for his hand moved on the warm flesh of her thighs, the fingers trembling against her.

Again he paused, and Arlene waited patiently, sensing his unfamiliarity with what he was doing.

"I love you," he said again, as though the words would give him time to find out what he could do without objection.

"I want you," he whispered, and his face mirrored the wonder he felt.

"I know."

"I . . . I love you."

"Shhhh."

"I've thought about you every minute from the first time. I drove out Military Highway for hours, hoping I might catch sight of you. There're a couple of trailer parks out there, and I even drove through them. Oh, Arlene."

"You're sweet."

His hand moved out from under her skirt, the fingers tackling the buttons of her dress.

"Do you think someone might come?" she asked, suddenly practical in the midst of her own whirling desire.

Corey looked up and down the beach carefully. "I don't see a soul. I don't think so. Too early."

Arlene helped him with the buttons, opening her dress.

"Take it off," she told him, raising up to help him.

His fingers fumbled with the clasp of her bra, finally opening it. Her breasts tumbled freely into his waiting hands, the warm palms holding their quivering fullness.

"Do you want to take off your dress?"

"I'd better not. If someone comes . . ."

"Okay."

Arlene wondered how many years it had been since a combination of haste, necessity and impromptu beds had occasioned physical contact while dressed . . . or partially anyway.

In a way, it made her feel younger again.

Corey made love to her, caressing, kissing, teasing, going from playful to an almost savage seriousness.

Arlene held him tightly, enjoying his manipulations, the slow ascent that she had missed with Buddy.

But it reached a point where she was ready for the delay to end, and still he waited, even when she squirmed against him, her every pore oozing sex and want.

When she reached for him urgently, and Corey made no further move, an anger flooded her, and she pushed him off, sitting up to light a cigarette.

"What's the matter?" he asked.

"You don't know?"

"No."

"Come on, Corey."

"I *mean* it."

"I don't like to be played with." She could see what was going to happen right now. Probably reach a screaming point like this, where every nerve in her body cried for release, then get left high and dry, when he finally got ready to do something.

"But . . . I wasn't. I . . ."

"I was ready, Corey. Why didn't you do something?"

"Arlene . . ."

"Were you afraid? You suddenly wondered what would happen if you took me and my husband found out?"

"No," he protested. "I want you, honey. God, I can't tell you how much I want you . . ."

"Then what the hell did you wait for?" she said, almost crying with her frustration. Hell, she thought, make a decision (that wasn't easy) that this was going to be a big night, and what happens?

"I . . . I didn't know," he said, mumbling, turning his face away.

"Didn't know what?"

"That you were ready."

Arlene wanted to laugh, but something in his voice, in his expression told her he might be telling the truth. "Corey dear, what does a girl have to do to convince you she's ready?"

"I . . . I never had one that was, before," he told her, still mumbling.

It can't be, Arlene thought. Don't tell me he's never had a girl! But why not? There had to be a first time for everyone, and it wasn't as though he were an old man or anything. She met his eyes, forcing his head around until he faced her. "You aren't kidding me, are you?"

"No." Even in the pale moonlight she could tell that he was blushing.

"You've never had a girl?" She was having trouble assimilating this bit of information.

"No."

"I'm sorry. It never occurred to me that . . . well, that you'd be a virgin." She laughed lightly, and he turned on her violently.

"Don't laugh at me!"

"I'm not, I'm not. Myself really. I was so mad because I was ready and you didn't take this gift I was offering. I'm just laughing at myself for never thinking that . . . well, you know what I mean."

"Yeah."

"Let's try again," she said softly.

"Will you help me, Arlene?"

"Of course, darling."

In a few moments, they had regained the swelling passion that had enveloped them so completely before. Arlene whispered to him. His breath was quick on her neck, his hands hugged her feverishly.

"Now," she whispered hoarsely.

Corey moved, first fearfully, then with greater freedom as he fell into the age-old rhythm of love.

Amazed, Arlene found that his eagerness was under control. They built the bonfire of love, after that one false start, built it to a high, consuming flame that licked at them as it grew, warming them with its darting tongues of fire.

When the fire was at its greatest height, they quenched it with their surging love, until only the smoldering ashes remained, and soon even those cooled in the pleasant chill of the breeze that blew across them.

"I don't know what to say, Arlene honey."

"You don't have to say anything."

"But I'm stunned."

"It can do that," she said, smiling.

"I never knew."

"I'm glad I was first," she told him, meaning it, knowing she'd repaid the favor of his company, his stated love.

"Me, too. God, it's wonderful."

"Yes." It had been like a new experience for Arlene, too, so long had it been since she'd thoroughly enjoyed lovemaking.

"I *do* love you, Arlene. And don't tell me to hush. Even if you don't love me back, that doesn't change a thing."

"I *can't* love you back, Corey. Not the way you mean."

"I guess you're right."

"I've got to go home."

"So soon?"

"I shouldn't have stayed this long."

"But . . ."

"Please. Right now. I really do."

Corey knew her well enough to realize she meant it. Within a half-hour he let her out near the park.

"When will I see you again?"

"I'll find you."

"Is that the way it has to be?"

"That's right."

"Couldn't I call you? During the day?"

"I'd rather you didn't." She remembered that he knew her last name now, and probably could find her number easily enough, simply locating the Ford nearest the area where he left her. "Please don't, Corey."

"Okay, baby, I sure enjoyed today."

"I did, too. That's a nice memory we'll have."

After he drove off, she walked rapidly toward her trailer, stopping abruptly when she saw a light on inside.

Her first thought was that John Edwards had forced the lock, letting himself in, but as she started to turn in panic, she saw Buddy's car parked beside their lot.

A new fear clutched at her breast. She wondered how long he'd been home. To her right was a community washhouse, with a men's room and women's restroom for those whose trailers weren't equipped with lavatories. There weren't many of them so lacking, especially the modern ones, but every park had its few small trailers, old trailers usually occupied by single men, that needed the availability of such a building.

Inside, she calmed herself, repairing her appearance as much as possible. Thanks to the blanket, there was no sand in her hair. Her dress was rumpled from being pushed up around her waist, but it could have been spending a day in the heat that did it. With fresh makeup on, she went home.

Opening the door, she braced herself, forcing a smile of surprise as she saw Buddy sitting on the couch, watching television.

"Well," she said. "What's the occasion?"

He looked at her narrowly. "Have to be an occasion for a husband to come home?"

"Oh, Buddy, you know what I mean. You weren't due back tonight, were you?"

"Nope. Looks like I surprised ya, too."

"You sure did."

"Figured. You probably would've been right here, if you'd known I was comin', huh."

"Sure."

"But you thought I was safe in Richmond."

"I wouldn't put it just that way."

"Prob'ly not."

"I don't know what you're thinking, Buddy . . ."

"Don't you?"

"Maybe I do. And I don't like it!"

"I don't like it either, when I come home an' find my wife out God knows where . . . and with who," he added, snarling at her.

"I was at a movie."

"What one?" he asked quickly, and she named the movie she'd seen that noon. In rapid succession, he asked her the stars of it, the plot. Finishing, he looked at her with disgust: "That don't prove a damned thing."

"Then why did you ask?"

"Don't get smart."

"Look, I was glad to see you home early, dammit, but you start this suspicious business, and I don't know." She turned and went into the bedroom, Buddy close on her heels.

"Who were you out with?"

"No one. Who the hell do I know to go out with anyway?"

He grabbed her arm with his fingers roughly, hurting her with a vise-like grip. "I warned you to watch yourself when you talk to me."

"All *right.*" Her defiance was based on her fear that she might have overlooked something, that he'd see something that meant 'beach' and that would really be the end. "Please let go."

"When I get ready."

"You like to hurt me."

"No."

"Well . . ."

Buddy released her unwillingly. "I just want you to talk nice to me."

"I'll try. But don't push me so hard, Buddy. If you had any cause to be suspicious it would be different."

"Maybe you're right."

"I know I am. This time anyway."

"So I'm sorry," he said, making it obvious that he wasn't, was just saying words to appease her.

"Thank you." She wanted to add, 'you're forgiven', knowing that the words would drive him to livid anger by their inference that he'd done anything that *needed* to be forgiven. But she knew better.

After Arlene showered, Buddy was engrossed in the late movie on TV. She went to bed quickly, glad that he was occupied, glad that he wouldn't want his husbandly due that night.

She closed her eyes in the darkened bedroom and thought back over the day and evening, relishing again the shuddering impact of their bodies at the beach.

She remembered John Edwards too, and started to go into the living room to tell Buddy, but decided against it. His first thought would be that she'd given Edwards some reason to come looking for her again.

Maybe it would work out. Some way, she thought.

Good night, Corey. Sleep tight, lover.

Arlene smiled with pleasure as she turned over and went to sleep.

Chapter Five

Arlene awakened to feel a masculine hand on her shoulder, shaking her rather roughly, and in her dream-drenched mind she at first thought that John Edwards had managed somehow to gain entry to the trailer.

She suppressed a scream, sitting up in bed, and saw with relief it was only Buddy.

"You startled me."

"Oh? How 'bout crawlin' outa the sack and fixin' my breakfast?"

"Sure. What time is it? I didn't hear the alarm."

"Seven. I woke up and turned it off. Hurry it up, huh? I've got an early appointment."

Arlene drew on a thin housecoat. Already the Norfolk day was warm and humid. She fixed Buddy's meal to the accompaniment of his electric shaver buzzing in the bathroom, sipping at a cup of coffee in an effort to fully awaken.

Another day, she thought. Another long, dull day. At least I *hope* it's dull. *And* uneventful.

Agnes and Francie were stirring next door. Lucky, Arlene thought. Lucky to be going to work, to have some dough of your own to spend as you like.

"Those eggs ready yet?"

"Almost."

"What are you gonna do today?" he asked with apparent unconcern, leaning against the work surface of the sink, staring out the wide windows at the trailer park.

"I don't know."

"Going anyplace?"

"Not that I know of."

"I'm working in town today."

"I know."

"I'll probably call home sometime."

Arlene was taking the eggs from the frying pan. She stopped, turning to face him. "Why?"

Buddy shrugged innocently. "Why not?"

"No reason. Except I don't remember you doing it before."

"Well, I've decided I haven't been . . . close enough to ya. It'd help break up your day, to talk to me on the phone. Don't you think?"

"I think that's a fine idea Buddy. I just hope it isn't because you might be worried about my fidelity." She said the words with cold-chiseled brightness, understanding his reasoning and resenting it.

"Now why on earth would I feel *that* way?" he asked with an equally brilliant smile. "Eggs ready?"

Arlene served his breakfast, pouring a large glass of cold prune juice at his reminder, then joining him at the table with her second cup of coffee. They seldom spoke during breakfast, even when their relationship was on a smoother plane. Buddy opened the morning paper and buried his attention in it, and it annoyed him to be interrupted while concentrating on the American League results or standings, or on the latest adventures of Peanuts.

Arlene heard the murmur of voices from Agnes' trailer and wondered if the two women were getting dressed for work, wondered if they ever did IT in the mornings, or just later in the day. Thinking about IT made her body tingle, and she got up from the table quickly, going into the bedroom to make the beds, before Buddy, in his currently suspicious mood, sensed anything of what was running through her mind.

She knew how he would label her curiosity, knew the ugly words he would use to describe two women together . . . and the even uglier words that would describe his opinion of her inquisitiveness.

He came into the bedroom before she was through, patting her buttocks as he walked past her to get his coat from the closet.

"What's for dinner tonight?"

"I don't know. I haven't thought that far ahead."

"Well, I'm gone. I'll give ya a call later."

"Okay."

He made no attempt to kiss her. *That* little business had been ended years before . . . almost three.

At first she'd been hurt, but never enough to ask him about it. Her pride had recovered within a month or so, and since then, the only times they kissed came when Buddy wanted her.

"Kissin' just for the helluvit is for kids," he'd said once, unasked.

She heard him drive away, and went back into the kitchen, her mind relaxed by her aloneness. In a little while, Agnes and Francie came out and drove off to work.

The sun was bright. It was eight-thirty and hot.

She wondered when Buddy would call, asking herself if she had the guts to just let the phone ring, let him imagine she was out some place, with someone.

Probably not, she decided. She recalled the last time she'd deliberately aggravated him, remembered the belt whipping against her flesh. That was an experience she didn't care to repeat.

She put a load of clothes in the washer, then picked up the residue of the evening and morning. The filled ashtrays, empty beer bottle, dirty dishes, ashes on the floor.

She took the clothes from the washer, carrying them outside to the rear of the trailer, where a small clothesline saved her from using the community lines, a couple of blocks away.

As she hung out the clothes, she glanced toward the woods . . .

. . . and saw John Edwards walking toward her slowly, a slight grin on his face.

Terror seized her and she dropped everything and ran frantically back inside, slamming and locking the door. She waited, panting with fright, peeking out through the Venetian blinds of the picture window, waiting for him to come.

Moments passed, and when he still didn't appear, her courage returned minutely.

Arlene tiptoed to the rear of the trailer, crawling on the bed and peering out the small window there.

Edwards was standing at the clothesline, holding a pair of her thin panties, staring at them with fascination. Arlene's mouth trembled with her desire to scream, but she put her thumb between her teeth and bit on it hard.

Edwards pressed the garment against his cheek, still smiling vaguely, then suddenly tore it, ripping it apart with a burst of energy. His eyes swept over the trailer, angry eyes.

Arlene summoned all her nerve.

"What do you want?" she asked, knowing her voice trembled, knowing he could hear it.

Edwards smiled again, finding her in the small window, walking closer until he looked up directly at her face.

"Hi, Arlene."

"What do you want, John?"

"Talk to you."

"There's nothing to talk about."

He shook his head slowly. "You're wrong."

"It's all over between us. I told you that five years ago."

"But I told you I'd find you, didn't I?" he said, grinning even more broadly, his voice patient as though talking to a little child.

"It's no good."

"We'll see."

"John, I'm telling you. I want you to go away and leave me alone."

"After."

"After what?"

"I rape you."

"That's no way to talk."

"I promised. I keep my promises, Arlene. I'm going to rape you."

The smile never left his face, and Arlene wondered just how seriously she was threatened, knowing he meant what he said, realizing he was unbalanced, but unsure how far he would go to achieve his end.

"John, it was never meant to be. You've got to realize that, and forget me, go away."

He shook his head. "You earned what you've got coming."

"How do you figure that?"

"I spent a lot of money on you. Now I want payment, that's all. Simple."

"You're sick, John."

The smile left his face, and it clouded with anger. He struck at the trailer with his fist, and she felt the vibration of it.

"Let me in," he said furiously.

"No. Now go away or I'll call the police."

He stared at her a moment, as though wondering if she really would do it.

"I mean it."

"I haven't done anything." There was the beginning of a pout on his mouth.

"You talk like you mean to."

"I do."

"I'll call them if I have to, John. They'll lock you up for a long time."

He grinned again. "For what?"

"For threatening me. For using filthy language. Now, please go away and I'll just forget about it."

"Arlene, why don't you just let me in, and we'll get it over with? Just take a few minutes."

The thought of exposing her body to him made her shudder.

"Never."

Edwards stared back at her, then quickly ran around the side of the trailer to the front door. Arlene ran there too, hearing him pull at it mightily, but the lock was firm. She opened the blinds, rolled the window open a crack.

"If you don't leave right now, I'll call the police, John. I'm not fooling."

"I'll leave," he said. "But I'll come back. And I'll kill you, you bitch."

Without another word, he turned and walked back to the woods. Arlene started shaking with relief, knowing she would have to tell Buddy, have to tell the police. Edwards was obviously sick, and she knew he meant his threats. If he wasn't put away, he'd catch her some day, alone. And she knew what would happen when he did.

She poured herself a stiff drink, promising herself she wouldn't leave the trailer all day. There was nothing to go out for, and as long as John Edwards was free, she knew she would have to be extra careful.

It wasn't the prospect of the attack that frightened her, as much as his threats against her life. If she thought she could give him her body once, and end all this, she would. But if he started to strangle her, there would be little she could do.

Buddy called at two.

"Didn't know if you'd be home or not," he said.

"I am. Listen, can you come home early?"

"Why?"

"I have something I need to tell you."

"Tell me now."

"No. I can't."

"What is it?"

"Later. But please come home early, Buddy."

"I dunno if I can get away or not. Is it important?"

"Yes. Very."

"Well, I'll try. But this better not be a gag."

"It's not a gag."

"I'll see what I can do."

He arrived at five, rather than five-thirty or six, which was his usual time. He came into the trailer, accepted the drink she had fixed him.

"Now what the hell is the problem?"

"Sit down. It'll take a while to explain."

"I'm always leery of things that take a lot of explaining," he said, but he sat on the couch and waited.

"You remember my mentioning John Edwards, back before I married you."

"Yeah, vaguely. You were engaged to him, weren't you?"

"Yes. He . . . he was very angry when I broke off with him, and . . . when I married you, he swore he'd find me later, and . . ."

"And what?"

"And rape me."

"What?!"

Arlene nodded.

"You never gave him any when you were going with him?"

"No! I was a virgin for you. You know that."

"Well, that's what you said. I don't have any way of knowin' for sure."

Arlene fought down her anger. "Anyway, that's beside the point."

"What *is* the point? I'm hungry."

"He's here."

"Who's here?"

"John Edwards. I thought I saw him hanging around in the woods the last few days. But today I talked to him."

"Why didn't you say anything, if you've been seeing him?"

"I wasn't sure."

"What'd he say?"

"He said he was going to rape me, and kill me." She began trembling again thinking about it.

"I'd imagine anyone who talks like that is pretty harmless. It's usually the quiet ones you gotta be careful about."

"He's *insane*."

"That's pretty strong. If he was insane, he wouldn't be out walkin' the streets, would he?"

"There are different kinds of insanity."

"Well, I don't know about that. How'd he find you?"

"I don't know."

"You didn't write to him, did you?"

"No," she said, shocked at the thought.

"Well, *I* don't know. You get the mail everyday. I don't know what the hell might come in without my knowing it." He got up and walked into the kitchen, mixing another drink.

"What are we going to *do,* Buddy?"

He shrugged. "What do you *want* to do?"

"Have him arrested."

"You really worried about this guy?"

"YES."

"You don't have to shout."

"You . . . you seem so unconcerned. I'm scared to death all day, Buddy, wondering if he's around, if he'll come to the trailer, if he'll break in, if he'll . . ." She stopped, unable to continue, and slumped into a chair, giving vent to the tears of frustration that begged for release.

"Don't cry, dammit!"

Arlene said nothing, unable to reply even had she desired.

"All *right,* we'll go to the cops," Buddy said angrily.

"Now stop that cryin' and fix supper."

"When will we go?"

"After we eat."

"You promise?" She dabbed at her eyes with her handkerchief, gulping air as she tried to control herself.

"Yes, I promise."

"Thank you."

During the meal, Buddy brought it up again.

"This guy never had you, huh?"

"Never."

"He try, or is he a fruit?"

"He tried. That's why I broke off with him. He was a little crazy then."

"You sure about all this, Arlene? I don't want to go to the cops, and have you make a fool of me. You sure you weren't out with this guy yesterday? You sure you're not givin' me a song 'n dance to cover up something?"

"How can you think that?"

Buddy shrugged, saying no more, as Arlene continued to stare at him. Sometimes this man was a stranger, and not a very nice one. Their marriage wasn't exactly winter and summer, but it wasn't far from it, and every year it came closer to that comparison. He ate with apparent unconcern now that he had questioned her virginity at marriage, questioned her whereabouts yesterday without cause, regardless of suspicion, had questioned her motives in wanting police aid.

Buddy glanced up and found her watching him.

"Eat," he said.

"I'm not hungry."

"Mad, huh?"

"Yes."

"Big deal."

"Sometimes I wonder if you ever loved me."

"Here we go."

"Or if you just saw a chance for an old man to get a young girl . . ."

"That's enough!" The reference to age had destroyed his composure. "You're being silly. If you were a better piece, it might've been for a reason like that. But seeing as how you *are,* it *hadda* be love."

"I guess I asked for that."

"Damn right you did. You ready?"

"Yes."

They drove wordlessly to the police station, once there being shown into a small cluttered office where a sergeant joined them.

"What seems to be the trouble?"

Briefly, Arlene told him of her former fiancé, his threats at the time she broke off with him, his reappearance, and the words he'd spoken that were still etched in her mind from that morning.

"And?" the sergeant said when she was through.

"I want him arrested."

"For what?"

Bewildered, Arlene answered. "For threatening me."

The sergeant shrugged with his hands. "But he hasn't done anything illegal, Mrs. Ford. Not yet."

"That's what I told her," Buddy said, starting to rise.

"But wait," Arlene said, a cold ball of fear hardening in her stomach. "There must be something you can do."

"Tell you what, Mrs. Ford. If this man comes around again, you give us a call, and we'll come out and talk to him. Maybe we can convince him he should go away somewhere and leave you alone."

"Is that *all?"* Arlene couldn't believe it, wouldn't believe what her ears were relaying to her shocked brain.

"I don't what else we can do," the sergeant said. "The laws here are designed to protect people from being arrested wrongfully. We could put him away for sixty days, if a close relative signed the papers. Or, if he commits an act of violence, or acts in an irrational manner in public, we can lock him up on the basis of the police officer's testimony who sees him do it. I don't know of any other way, Mrs. Ford."

"So I've got to wait for him to do something violent . . . to me . . . before I can have him arrested."

The sergeant smiled wanly. Buddy got up.

"Let's go, Arlene."

"But that's not *enough,"* she protested.

"It's all he can do, Arlene. You can't just have people arrested for nothing. Right, sergeant?"

"That's right, Mr. Ford. Look, ma'am, this guy shows up again, you give us a call, we'll come out and talk to him. But we just can't do anything right now."

Arlene looked at the florid-faced policeman. "I suppose if I kill him while he's attacking me, you'll put *me* away."

"You call us. We'll come right out."

"Thanks," she said bitterly.

The police, who were to have been the entire answer, now provided not even a small part of it. She understood well enough what the sergeant had told her. But there *had* to be a law about people like John. There *had* to.

Yet he didn't act irrationally. Really. He talked very well. It was just the action that his words promised that was irrational.

"What am I going to do?"

"Like he said. This Edwards shows up again, call the cops. They'll get rid of him."

Arlene shook her head. "It won't be that easy."

"Sure it will. They have ways of talkin' to people, scare 'em to death."

"Not John."

"You'll see."

The subject was reopened only once more that evening. After watching a few television programs, on which Arlene found it impossible to concentrate, they went to bed.

Buddy was all over her as soon as they lay down, pulling her pajamas open, handling her roughly.

"Don't worry about that Edwards," he said, as he rolled over on her. "I'll take care of him, if he bothers you."

Arlene suffered his desire without answering. She realized that Edwards was her problem, and hers alone.

Chapter Six

Buddy was late leaving for work Thursday morning. His departure coincided with that of Francie. Looking out, Arlene wondered where Agnes was, and after the cars had driven off, she walked over to the woman's trailer.

"Agnes?" she called, knocking lightly on the door.

"Just a minute." The voice came from the bedroom, and in a moment, Agnes opened the door for her. "Hi."

"You're not working?"

"No. Felt a little under the weather, so I'm staying home and resting. C'mon in."

"Okay." She welcomed the chance for company, someone to talk to, someone to be with during at least a part of the long day.

"Excuse the looks of the place. I haven't got around to picking up yet."

"Let me help."

"You don't have to."

"Please. I don't mind a bit."

"Well . . . all right. Let me get a dress on and I'll help."

"Not if you don't feel well."

But Agnes changed into a skirt and severe blouse, and pitched in with Arlene to clean up the trailer. In less than an hour they were done, and rewarded themselves with a leisurely cup of coffee.

"Kind of nice, staying home," Agnes said.

"I imagine. For you. It sure gets dull, though."

"It would. Unless you had something to occupy your mind."

"Like kids?"

"No, I wasn't thinking of that especially. Maybe a hobby, or even something you could make money at. Writing, or painting, or something like that."

"Oh. I wish *I* could do something like that."

"You ever try?"

"No."

"Maybe you can."

"My husband told me right after we were married that I have two talents. Cooking is one. I'm inclined to agree with him."

Agnes shook her head, running her long fingers through her hair. "You shouldn't let a man dominate you like that."

"It's a little hard to avoid."

"I guess so." Agnes smiled at her gently. "But surely you must do something to occupy your time?"

"Nothing unusual."

Agnes continued to smile, and Arlene wondered what was on her mind. But the woman said nothing more about it.

"Think the mail's ready at the office?"

"Might be. It's after nine."

"Let's take a walk and see."

The two women walked slowly to the park office, where the daily mail was distributed. There was nothing for Arlene. Agnes got a bill from a dentist and a notification that a magazine subscription was expiring with the next issue.

"Nothing like mail," Agnes said, as they walked back.

"So they say," Arlene laughed. She was in a good mood, enjoying the company, as they approached their trailers again. Arlene was smiling at something Agnes said, when, out of the corner of her eye, she saw a hint of motion in the woods.

Edwards again. She knew it as surely as if she'd seen him plainly, as if he stood in the open and waved a flag.

"Agnes?"

"Yes, dear."

"May I stay with you today? I can help out and . . . well, I'm just so lonely I could bust."

"Sure. Glad to have you." The woman's arm rested on Arlene's shoulder, the fingers clenching her arm with a gentle strength. "Let's have some more coffee."

Arlene was relieved. John would get tired of his little game, she hoped, when she stayed away from her trailer. Maybe he would get tired of the whole thing, his whole scheme, and just go away soon. God, if praying would make it so, she was ready to drop to her knees then and there and get started.

But prayer wouldn't help. Nothing would, except his getting weary, or achieving fruition of his warped dreams. Arlene wondered which would come first.

After lunch, the women went into the bedroom.

"I've got to take a nap," Agnes said. "Not worth staying home from work if I don't. How about you?"

"I seldom do. But today I feel like it too."

"Good. Maybe I can prevail on you for a back rub?"

"I don't know how good I'll be . . . but I'll try."

"Good."

Agnes took off her blouse and skirt, lying on the bed in her underwear. Arlene followed her example, laying her dress across a chair.

Agnes watched her intently, and Arlene felt a little nervous as though it were a strange man there in the bedroom with her.

She had undressed with girls before, undressed to the nude for any number of reasons, showers after sports, pajama parties, swimming . . . but never had she felt as she did then.

Agnes turned on her stomach. "Undo my bra," she said.

Arlene obeyed.

"Let me just take it off."

"All right."

Agnes sat up in the bed, pulling the garment off, stretching with obvious satisfaction. Her breasts were small, but perfectly formed, her nipples small and pinkish brown.

"Feels good."

Arlene nodded, returning the woman's smile.

"Take off yours, honey."

Arlene complied, duplicating Agnes' stretching motion, knowing her own breasts were standing out nobly, the quivering flesh close to Agnes, whose eyes were glued to the sight of Arlene's body in such proximity.

"It *does* feel good."

Agnes lay back slowly. "Just sit astride my legs when I turn over."

"Okay."

Agnes instructed Arlene in a back rub, telling her when she pounded too hard, when she should bear down more. Arlene knew she wasn't nearly as proficient as Agnes had been, but the woman seemed to be satisfied.

"Let me return the favor."

They switched positions, and soon Agnes' hands had soothed Arlene into that now-familiar state of drowsiness.

"Mmmmm," Arlene said.

"Saw you the other night," Agnes said, and for a moment the words didn't register.

"Oh?"

"At the Jolly Pirate."

Arlene's body jumped with the implication, and Agnes, sensing it, worked harder at her massage.

"The Jolly Pirate?"

"Yes. With some sailor."

Arlene said nothing. What comes next? she asked herself. Would the woman tell Buddy? Why was she mentioning it, unless she hoped to gain something by so doing?

"Mmm," she murmured, letting Agnes decide what it meant, waiting for the woman to say more.

"You don't sound too concerned."

"Should I be?" Arlene asked cautiously.

"No. Not really. I won't tell anyone."

"It could have been someone else."

"No. I'm sure of that. But you needn't worry. You'll find your secrets are safe with me."

Arlene didn't know what to say. She could tell the woman, oh, that was my cousin, or that was really quite innocent. My husband knows all about it. But there was no need really. Agnes apparently just mentioned it for the heck of it, having no intention to use the information.

"Just sitting in a car."

"Oh."

Agnes' hands lulled Arlene again, the strong, practiced fingers playing a melody of relaxation on Arlene's back and shoulders, her arms and along the sides of her full breasts.

"There," Agnes said finally, and lay down beside Arlene, her hand rubbing Arlene's shoulder gently, idly.

"Thank you."

"Nothing. You have a nice body. It's a pleasure to work on you, believe me."

"Maybe you can teach Buddy how to do that. It would sure be nice, every night. Not that he'd do it."

"Why wouldn't he?"

"I'm not sure he wouldn't, understand. Just ninety-nine percent sure. He's just . . . not the kind of a guy who would. He'd figure it was beneath his masculine dignity, or something." Arlene wondered why she was able to talk so freely with Agnes, unabashedly admitting things that she seldom acknowledged even to herself. But there was something about the woman that inspired confidence.

And added to it was the intimacy of the moment, both women lying together naked except for their briefs, their shoulders brushing against each other frequently.

"Now, if *I* were your husband," Agnes said, "I'd want to work on you every night . . . and a backrub wouldn't be *all* I'd have in mind, either." She propped herself up on one elbow, looking down into Arlene's face, her eyes narrow and bright.

Arlene felt herself blushing slightly. “Funny. I used to imagine when I got married it might be to someone insatiable. I used to wonder what it would be like.”

“Your husband’s not?”

“No. Frequent, but not too often. It would be almost too much, every night.”

“I’ve heard of some where it’s more than that.”

“You mean twice a night?” Arlene asked. She’d heard of that too, but it seemed unlikely it happened after the first few weeks.

“That, or in the mornings, afternoons, any time’s the right time, and all that. I imagine it works out all right where both people are oversexed. It would sure be rough, though, if one was and the other wasn’t.”

“God, I guess so. Woman’d feel like hiding after a couple of days . . . at least *this* one would.”

Agnes laughed. “Mental picture. The husband comes home from work, ready and anxious, and the wife runs into another room, locks the door, bolts on the chastity belt . . . can you see it?”

Arlene laughed too, amused by the image. “If it were me, I think I’d go mad.”

“Are you cool enough?” Agnes asked.

“Yes, Just right.”

Suddenly, Agnes bent her lips to Arlene’s skin, kissing her tenderly.

Arlene went rigid at the first touch, then slowly relaxed. It felt good, this woman’s touch, her lips pressing gently. She watched Agnes with fascination as the woman’s eyes met hers, the desire in them obvious.

“Did you mind that?” Agnes asked, frowning.

“No.”

“I guess you think I’m pretty awful.”

“No, really.”

“Are you sure?”

“Yes.”

“I want to kiss you, Arlene.”

Their eyes met again. Arlene trembled slightly. She was going to find out, finally. The curiosity, the thirst to *know,* was to be answered, and it frightened her. She closed her eyes, waiting.

She sensed Agnes' face coming closer, felt the delicate breath before their lips met in a gentle kiss. The woman's mouth was soft as it pressed lightly against hers, the breath sweet.

Gradually, she returned the continual pressure, until their mouths mashed together with growing desire. Finally, gasping for air, she ended the kiss. Agnes' face was alight with a new quality, and her eyes were misty.

"You don't know how much I've wanted to do that," the woman said, biting her lip.

"I . . . I think I did, too. I've been awfully curious."

"About . . . me?"

Arlene nodded. "I wanted to know what it would be like."

"Did you like it?"

"Yes. A lot," she added, and turned her face away. What am I doing, she asked herself? What am I letting myself in for? I shouldn't be here, it's the same as being with Corey.

Isn't it?

Or is it? She didn't know, only that she was going to stay and see what happened.

Then she would know. And not before.

Agnes kissed her cheek, then her throat. It was loveplay, similar to what a man and woman would do, and surprisingly, the reactions were the same.

"I want you, Arlene."

The intensity frightened Arlene. Again she questioned what she was doing, what unknown journey she would embark upon. But she had to *know;* there would never be a better chance than this, ever.

And it wasn't as though it was hurting or anything. So far, it had been wonderful, the best lovemaking ever, and what was there to fear?

"I don't know what to do," she whispered.

"Don't worry, darling. You don't have to do anything but relax and enjoy it."

"Are you sure?"

"Yes. Just close your eyes. I wouldn't hurt you for the world. I just want to love you . . . like you've never been loved before."

Agnes' lips met hers again, this time firmer, more demanding, and Arlene answered with demands of her own, expressed in the kiss as she'd never been able to before, never been as uninhibited as she felt in that moment.

She was helpless in the grip of the desire that swelled within her, helpless to think of anything but this fantastically overpowering sensation.

Finally, she felt a release so sudden, it swept her from that fractional moment of unbearable tingling to shuddering relief as though in a misty dream.

As though it was happening to someone else, and she was merely watching.

But it happened to her, and she knew it, felt it in every living pore of her body.

Shuddered again, draining herself of the immense tightness, until she could only lie limply, savoring the memory, knowing nothing like this had ever happened to her before, nothing even came close.

She opened her eyes and saw Agnes watching her, a slight smile playing on her face.

"Wow," she said.

Agnes chuckled. "I hope I made you happy."

"I had no idea," Arlene told her, shaking her head slowly in wonderment.

"It had to be great, you being the way you are. You were built for love, made for caresses."

"What about you, though?"

"Don't worry about that now."

"But I do. I'm a strong believer in mutuality."

"Don't think about it. Just relax and enjoy it."

"I am. But . . . I mean, what would happen, if I knew what to do? Tell me, Agnes. Please."

"Same thing, honey. With variations. There are a million variations."

"I can imagine."

"Maybe we'll try some . . . soon."

"I think I'd like that."

"It's a date."

When they were dressed, it was almost time for Buddy to come home. Arlene awaited him in their trailer, resting on the couch, her mind wrapped in the events of the day.

She knew she should probably feel badly, feel ashamed, feel *something* other than the immense peace and satisfaction that shut out everything else.

But she didn't.

She caught herself wondering if she looked any different, just like the day after her virginity had been taken, and had to laugh at herself.

When the phone rang, it took her a moment to answer it, so engrossed was she in her thoughts. It rang as though in a dream, and finally she realized with a start that it was real, and rushed to answer it.

"It's Corey," the voice said, and it took her an instant to remember who Corey was. Then a shock of fear thudded through her as she looked out the trailer window and saw Buddy's car heading down the row.

"I thought I asked you not to call me, Corey."

"Couldn't help it, baby. Missed ya." She heard the slur in his voice, knew he'd been drinking. Buddy's car was almost there.

"Corey, I can't talk to you. My husband's pulling up outside right now."

"Meet me, Arlene."

"Corey . . ." Buddy was getting out of the car.

"Meet me tomorrow."

"Where?"

"Same place."

Buddy was almost at the door. "All right," she agreed, her palms perspiring. "One o'clock."

Buddy opened the door, glancing at her curiously.

"I'm sorry," she said, "this is JUstice 8-, not 7-."

"I'll be waiting for you, honey," Corey said, and she could hear the grin in his voice.

"That's all right. No trouble at all." She put the phone down quickly, fearing in her panic that Buddy might yank it out of her hands and hear Corey's voice. "Hi," she said, wiping her hands on her dress.

"Wrong number?"

"Yes. Sometimes it's hard to convince people that they simply dialed wrong."

"Mmmm. That Edwards guy show up today?" he asked, intent on her expression.

"I thought I saw him once. But I couldn't be sure."

"He'll get tired, go away. What's for supper?"

"I haven't had a chance to start anything yet."

"Why not?"

"Well, to tell the truth, I was reading and I forgot what time it was."

"I called you," he said quietly.

"Oh?"

"Didn't get an answer."

"I was probably visiting Agnes."

"That queer?" he said, his face betraying the disgust he felt at the idea.

"I don't know about that," she said, keeping her voice even, "but she was sick today . . . stayed home from work. So I helped her out a little."

Buddy shrugged. "Anyway, I'm starved. Let's go across the street and have some shrimp or something."

"I can cook. It won't take long," she said, knowing his mood often became surly when he felt forced into taking her out to eat.

"No time. Bumped into Hoskins at the office. We're goin' over there and kill some time."

"Tonight?"

"Why not?" he said quickly.

"No reason. I didn't know, that's all."

"That's what I called to tell you."

"I'll be ready in a minute."

"What's the matter with that?" pointing at her dress.

"I'd rather wear something fresh. Please."

"Just don't be long."

They walked across Military Highway to the seafood restaurant, sitting at a booth from which they could watch the road, the stream of traffic that filled it at that hour.

Afterward, they went to the Hoskins' trailer, gratefully sitting outside under the tattered awning. It was so much better than inside, where there was little room, and the kids were continually getting underfoot.

Gladys huffed out of her chair and went inside to fix the beer, declining Arlene's offer of help. "Jus' take a min, honey. Sit down and enjoy yourself."

"Well, Hank, how are things at the Post Office?" Buddy asked, settling into the comfortable chair Gladys vacated.

"Same. Busy. But it always is," Hoskins said with a seriousness he reserved for important statements. "People don't realize how busy the U.S. Mail Service is, Buddy. How many millions of letters and cards and all class mail there really is. Big job."

"Yeah. All we think about is the letters *we* send, and why they don't get there a day earlier, huh?"

"That's right."

Arlene knew his job must be dull, yet maybe he had the right idea. After twenty years or so, a pension . . . plus all the usual Civil Service benefits in the meantime.

What would Buddy have when *he* was ready to retire? She'd asked herself many times . . . asked *him* too, but he seldom cared to talk about it.

'Don't worry your head about it. I'll take care of it when the time comes,' he would say, and change the subject. But he was almost forty, and the 'time' was approaching rapidly. She decided she'd have to speak to him about it again, even if it got unpleasant. He had to start some kind of plan, insurance program or *something* while he still had income to devote to it.

For his own good.

Gladys came back with four cold glasses of beer, drinking her own thirstily. She and Arlene went through the usual amenities regarding how hot it had been, and what was new, and why don't you ever come see me in the daytime, we're both here alone, and that's a pretty dress, Arlene.

The men were talking quietly, and Arlene saw that Buddy was intent on Hoskins' words. When Gladys went inside again to see why one of the kids was crying, Arlene listened.

". . . can't make 'em do anything they don't *want* to. At least, usually. You understand, I ain't what you'd call an expert, Buddy. I mean, I don't get much time to practice, but I think you get someone just right, the right kind of subject, and you can make 'em do anything you want."

Hypnotism again, Arlene thought, wishing they'd drop it, talk about something else. She didn't know why Buddy was apparently so fascinated with the subject. Things seldom took his interest so completely.

"If a guy hypnotized a girl, say," Buddy asked, "could he get her to shack up with him?"

Obviously, they weren't aware of Arlene listening.

"Well . . . I dunno, really." Hoskins laughed weakly. "I never had a chance to try it out."

"But could he?"

"I dunno, Buddy."

"What do you think? Based on the experiences you've had, what you've read."

"Probably," Hoskins admitted.

"That'd be something, huh?"

"Yeah."

"Just go around, hypnotizin' all the good-lookin' chicks. Man, you could kill yourself in a week, tryin' not to let any good ones get away."

The two men laughed together in their enjoyment of the vision, as Gladys came outside again.

"Durn kids, one's always gotta play with somethin' one of the others has. Be the death of me yet." She eased into the chair beside Arlene. "How's your beer?"

"Fine."

"Got plenty more."

"No thanks. Not right now."

"Henry? Buddy? More beer?"

"I will," Buddy said, handing her his empty glass, slapping Arlene playfully on the thigh. "Say, Hank, you want to give Arlene a whirl tonight? I reckon she's feeling more like it than she did the other time." His hand was on her shoulder, and he squeezed it painfully, the pressure ordering her to agree.

"Like to . . . if she's willing."

"She is . . . aren't you?" Smiling down at her, his expression making it clear what would happen to her if she refused again.

"I don't mind," Arlene told Henry. At least, it'll avoid a fight, she thought. And certainly no harm can come of it . . . if he's careful.

The preparations were made, and Arlene stretched out on one of the lounges that had been fixed horizontally, closing her eyes, sensing the group clustered about her, the darkened trailer park surrounding them, hearing the murmur of trucks whizzing by on the highway.

Hoskins began talking to her, quietly, his voice an even monotone, repeating over and over again suggestive words like sleep and rest and relax and eyelids heavy and more . . . many more.

Arlene ignored him for the most part, thinking instead of Agnes and the afternoon . . . of Corey . . .

Damn. Almost forgot. Got to meet him tomorrow. And tell him never to call again. For *any* reason. That was a close one today. What if Buddy had been home and answered it. Even if it *had* been a wrong number, it would have been enough to arouse *his* suspicions.

Hoskins voice droned on, and she realized her eyelids *were* getting heavier, she was relaxing. He was counting numbers, first one way, then back again, and she found a curious fascination in this, found herself listening for the next number, not trying to outthink him, just waiting for him to tell her what the number would be.

Arlene heard Buddy whisper 'He's gettin' her,' to Gladys, and a warning bell flashed through her mind.

What if he *is?* What if he *does* put me under, then starts asking questions?

Prompted by Buddy.

Suspicious Buddy, who might wonder about the time she spent with Agnes today. Or what had really kept her out late Tuesday night.

Would she answer questions like that, if Hoskins had her hypnotized?

She didn't know. And in that lack of knowledge, lay fear. She fought the crushing heaviness of his words, resisted him almost desperately, until she was sure that her mind was alert again. Then she simply lay there, her eyes closed, listening to what he said, but mocking it in her mind, not taking him seriously, until finally, he gave up.

"Guess it won't work tonight, Buddy."

"Why not?"

Arlene opened her eyes slowly. "It sure was restful."

"Can't always put 'em under first time," Hoskins said. "I had her in what you'd call a light trance. Sometimes, a person's got to go through those before they can be hypnotized."

"You mean, she was resisting?"

"No. Not really. Just, some people go under easier than others, that's all."

"Oh. Well, how'd it feel, Arlene?"

"Real good," she told him, hoping he wouldn't get wise to her subterfuge.

"Maybe next time she'd go under, Hank?" he asked, never taking his eyes from her.

"Maybe. Hard to say."

"Well . . . We'll see."

The rest of the evening passed without incident. After the Hoskins children were in bed, the adults moved inside and played poker.

For chips.

Hoskins apologized when he ruled out actual money right at the start. "Hate to say it, but we lose a buck an' it hurts. Hope you don't mind."

"Not a bit," Arlene said, wishing Hoskins would stop watching her so closely. She felt as though he wanted to say something to her, but didn't know how. Wanted to say something privately.

At eleven, they called it a night.

"Some poker game," Buddy said as they walked back to their trailer. "Chips!"

"Well, I don't blame them. They don't make as much money as we do, and they have four more mouths to feed besides."

"Even so, hell, poker's just for old ladies, 'less you got some money on it."

Arlene didn't answer, sensing he was looking for an excuse to fight with her.

An excuse to fight, and then make up.

In bed.

"Don't you think so?" he challenged.

"I'd have to agree, Buddy."

"You don't *have* to."

"I didn't mean it that way."

"Well, what way did you? You agree or not?"

"I *do.* I agree."

"Better to watch TV than play poker when there isn't any dough on the line."

"You're right."

"What was the matter tonight, anyway?"

"What do you mean?"

"You didn't get hypnotized . . ."

"I guess it was like he said. I wasn't ready. I tried, but it just didn't work."

"We'll try again."

"Sure," she said, preceding him inside. "Want some coffee?"

"All right."

He turned on the television, adjusting it while she fixed their coffee, then patted the couch beside him as she put his cup on the table.

"I'm kind of sleepy," she told him. "Been thinking I'd just go to bed."

"What'd *you* do to get tired?"

"Nothing special."

"What's this movie, anyway?"

"Let me look." Arlene flipped through the TV Guide, told him the title.

"Looks good. Stay up and watch it with me."

"I'm really bushed, honey. You watch it if you want to."

"Okay."

He gave his attention to the unfolding plot on the screen.

Someone had told her once that television reminded him of Cyclops . . . a one-eyed monster.

But she was thankful for it then. Buddy would stay up watching it, they wouldn't argue . . . and she wouldn't have to feign a passion she didn't feel.

In the bedroom she undressed, then turned out the light. Before getting into bed, she peered out the side window. There was a light on in the bedroom that Agnes and Francie shared. Arlene wondered what they were doing.

Were they reaching for the heights, straining for that delicious summit?

While she went thankfully to bed alone, remembering . . .

Arlene frowned, closing her eyes. I shouldn't think things like that, she told herself. I shouldn't . . . yet I can't help it. In her mind she pictured the two women, what they were doing, and her body began its familiar tingling.

What was that old joke?

There must be something the *three* of us can do?

Arlene smiled at the thought, chuckling to herself, burying her face in the pillow so that Buddy wouldn't hear her.

She imagined herself walking out into the living room, wearing only a flimsy nightgown. 'Excuse me, dear' she would say, 'but I'm sleeping next door tonight. The three of us have something to do.'

Lord, the look that would cross his face.

Then he'd probably kill me, she admitted soberly. It surely wouldn't be a game to him.

If he ever found out about today . . .

The thought frightened her. He'd consider himself cuckolded, just as if it had been a man, and Arlene knew whom he'd take it out on.

Whose back would be a flaming, angry red.

Whose body would be punched and bruised.

No, it wasn't a game. Not a bit. And neither was this business with Corey.

What's come over me, she thought. For years, nothing. Then, all of a sudden . . .

Is there something wrong with me, she asked the dark room? Is there?

The only answer was the sound of a headache powder commercial on the Late Movie.

Chapter Seven

Corey called again the next morning, sober now, wanting to drive out and meet her near the park.

"But why?"

"See you that much sooner. Please, baby. I'm anxious."

Arlene hesitated, wishing she had the strength to tell him no, tell him they mustn't see each other again. But the memory of the times with him was too good, the excitement she felt when they were together too strong.

"I guess it'd be all right. You can wait at the place where you let me out."

"Great. Make it as soon as you can."

She smiled at his obvious desire to be with her. It was nice to be that necessary to someone. "All right, Corey."

She dressed carefully for their date, repressing the occasional twinges of guilt that flashed through her, the worries at thoughts of what Buddy would do if he ever found out.

He hadn't mentioned where they might go, but she hoped it wouldn't be just to a movie or the beach. There must be some place to go in the afternoon around here, she told herself. And if there was, Corey should know about it.

She selected powder blue bra and panties, stockings with a bluish hue, held in place by wide, frilly blue garters. Her dress was navy blue, with a scooped-out neckline that revealed the tops of her creamy breasts.

When she was ready, she knew she looked good, and was proud. It had been so long since she'd felt it worthwhile to dress 'special' for anyone, so long since she had felt her efforts would be appreciated.

At the appointed time, she left her trailer, walking rapidly through the park, past the grocery store, and along the highway, feeling the excitement start building when she spotted Corey's car a block ahead, parked on the shoulder. He was standing beside it in his whites, and waved when he caught sight of her. Hopping quickly into the car, he backed it up until it was beside Arlene.

"Hi, honey. You sure look wonderful."

"Thank you." Arlene got in and slammed the door.

Corey put the Merc in gear, started slowly up the road. "Where would you like to go?"

"No preference."

"I . . . I'd like to talk to you . . . somewhere."

She sensed the seriousness in his voice and glanced at him questioningly. "Okay."

Corey shrugged a bit, his eyes avoiding hers. "Do you think . . . I mean, would a . . . a motel be all right?" He looked at her then, his face reflecting his fear of being rebuffed.

"I guess so." Arlene's sense of excitement grew. "Just so it's not near here."

"I noticed one place . . . out near the beach . . ."

Arlene nodded, and Corey increased the speed of the car as he headed for the motel.

She'd never been to a motel before, not like this, not to be together with a lover, and wondered if it was taking a chance.

Yet weren't they taking a chance every time they saw each other, every time they were together, regardless of where?

The answer was obvious.

In a few minutes, they pulled into an older motel on the fringe of the populous beach area. The place needed a coat of paint, and weeds grew in the driveway area. When the car stopped, an elderly man came out of a door marked "Office" in a hand-painted sign.

"Any vacancies?" Corey asked, and Arlene heard the nervousness in his voice.

"Yep," the man said, eyeing them steadily. "Gonna stay long?"

"Don't know yet," Corey said. "Just overnight, probably."

The old man nodded, his rheumy eyes on Arlene knowingly. She felt suddenly cheap, tawdry, wishing they hadn't come here.

The old man spit beside the car. "Wanna register?"

Corey went inside while Arlene waited in the car. Though the place was obviously deserted, she felt that eyes were watching her from behind every window, and looked about fearfully, as though Buddy might come driving in behind them.

She slouched down in the seat, as though resting. Corey came back with the key and parked the car in front of their unit.

Inside, she looked about with depression. There was a double bed, that looked lumpy, even though it had been freshly made. A chair and lamp stood in one corner of the small room, a dresser in the other. A door led to a small bathroom, and in the rear window, an air conditioner pumped cool air into the room with a noisy obviousness.

Corey shut the blinds of the windows. "It's not much, is it?"

"Well, it *is* a place to talk," she answered, sitting in the chair. "And it's cool."

"Yeah." He sat on the bed uncomfortably. "Hard to talk to you when you're sitting way over there."

Arlene smiled. "Something tells me it isn't 'talking' you have in mind."

"Oh, yes," he protested quickly. "But it's . . . personal talk, if you know what I mean."

"All right," she said, getting up and crossing to the bed. She stood before the sailor and his hands caught the back of her legs strongly, pulling her body forward until she toppled on top of him while his lips opened hers with an urgency he couldn't control. "My goodness," she said, laughing.

"You drive me crazy," he said tensely, rolling her over until she lay on her back, staring up at him, at the cracked, peeling ceiling of the room.

"Let's not wrinkle my dress," she said quietly.

"Want to take it off?" His words were eager.

"I'd better," Arlene stood up, unfastening her dress, wishing she'd worn a slip.

Corey's eyes were riveted on her as she opened her dress, exposing her lightly clad body to his eyes. "Oh, honey," he said, worshipfully.

Arlene walked toward him again, leaning against him, pushing him back on the bed until their bodies were pressed tightly together. Corey's hands were all over her, touching, caressing with a wildness that she knew would soon be out of control.

She sat up on the bed, reaching for the pack of cigarettes he had placed on the shabby night-table. "What was it you wanted to talk about?" she asked, deliberately teasing him.

"Can't it wait?" His hands touched her thighs, then her breasts, his lips against the soft skin, inhaling her scent. "For a little while?"

Arlene stroked his head while she smoked, proud of her body, proud of the reaction, the need of this man. It made her feel as though life had regained an importance lost years before, as she herself had.

"I guess it can wait," she told him, almost whispering. "It's up to you."

His hands mashed her breasts, tugging at one bra cup until he had lowered it enough to release one breast, as he reached behind her to unfasten the garment. In a moment, it was free, and he pulled it off with haste, falling upon her exposed nudity with a sound that was almost a whimper.

Arlene lay quietly under his onslaught, controlling her own passion, letting it build slowly, watching it objectively as it began welling within her.

"I love you," he said, raising his lips for a moment, looking at her with a wonderment that pleased her.

Arlene tousled his hair playfully. "I really believe you mean that, Corey."

"I do."

"I was afraid I might just be another . . . girl."

"Never!"

It was fire she was playing with, and she knew it. But it added the excitement she wanted, lifted everything they did above the plane of animal emotion, excused it even.

"You love me," she said, "although you know there's no future for us."

"That's part of what I wanted to talk about," he said. "I want you to marry me."

Arlene smiled gently at him. "You know I'm married."

"Get a divorce," he said, going on hurriedly as though afraid he would forget something unless he hurried. "You don't love him, he doesn't love you, doesn't appreciate you, he *can't!* Not the way I do. Arlene, we could be so happy together, just you an' me, and hours and hours to make love and be happy. Please say you will, please, baby."

"You're sweet . . . it's not that easy."

"Why? You don't love him do you?"

"No. Not the way you mean."

"That's the only way there *is.*"

"That's the best way," she corrected. "But after you live with someone for awhile, there's more."

"I don't believe it. If it isn't like this, it isn't worth anything at all."

Arlene pulled his head down until it rested on her naked breast. "Besides, darling, my husband wouldn't ever let me get a divorce. He'd beat me to death first. He's a very jealous man."

"You could just leave him. Just pack up some day and leave a note or something. He couldn't find you."

Oh, no, she thought, and John Edwards' face loomed before her eyes, as a chill of fright went through her. She hugged Corey closer to her. "Yes, he could," she said. "If he wanted to badly enough."

"Well, look, think about it, will you?"

"Sure." A thought crossed her mind. "You're not saying this, asking me this, because you feel you *have* to, are you?"

"No," he said, his face bewildered.

"Sorry. I thought maybe you felt guilty . . . or something."

"Uh uh."

"Okay. Kiss me."

"Yes," he said and bent his face forward until their mouths pressed together as though molded.

Nothing mattered then, not the old motel, the rheumy-eyed keeper, the shabby furniture. The only important thing was the need, the contact, the togetherness they would soon share.

Corey was more sure of himself than he had been before, and she enjoyed his preliminaries even more. His touch was more positive, he knew better what he wanted and how to obtain it. She closed her eyes, relishing the saturation of love that he was giving her.

She felt no inhibition, no awareness of anything but the fierce pleasure of the moment. Every touch of his hands sent a message of delight that was transmitted throughout her entire body. She responded to his tantalizing love play until they both were quivering with their need of one another, of completion.

Corey didn't make her wait long, couldn't himself delay the fruition of their love any more.

She wanted to yell with the great joy of the moment, wanted the whole world to know the way she felt, even though she realized no one would ever know, only she and Corey.

When it happened, she did yell, unable to restrain herself, so tumultuous was the descent from that height, so pounding and pulsating and driving was the relief, the release, the wonderful, wonderful peace that came over her, flooding over her, washing her in its magnificence.

She knew nothing could top it, ever.

Match it? Perhaps. But never could it be any better, any more complete or satisfying.

She cradled Corey close to her, reluctant to let go of him for a minute, anxious to grab every golden second of this feeling that she could.

After a long while, they lay apart, holding hands, their faces beaming at each other in the memory of what they had shared. No words were necessary, no words were spoken for a long moment.

They had a perfect understanding, and needed no more.

When he let her out near the trailer park, she still glowed from the afternoon, still felt warm and cherished and alive. They knew without saying it that they would be together again . . . and soon.

It was enough.

Arlene watched him drive away, then walked slowly back to the park, wishing she could have stretched the afternoon into an eternity of love.

She knew her thoughts weren't practical, but her mind bolted at practical thoughts. After what had happened, it would take a long time to return to the mundane, the sensible.

It took only as long as the time to walk from the highway to the road opposite Henry Hoskins' trailer.

"Hey!" he said as she started by, and Arlene walked on, hoping he would think she hadn't heard him. He and Gladys were the last two people in the world she cared to be near at that moment.

"Hey, Arlene," he said, louder, his voice a command forcing her to stop, turn back, and smile.

"Hello."

"Come here."

"I've got to get home, Hank."

"Buddy ain't there, is he?"

"No."

"Then c'mere a minute."

Arlene could think of no way she could politely refuse, so she walked over to the small fence that surrounded his yard. "What is it?"

"How ya been?" he asked, the start of a smirk on his face, and she was suddenly frightened. It was late in the afternoon, Buddy would be getting home soon, and all she wanted to do was go home. She wished she'd taken the other road in, but it was too late.

"All right. Where's Gladys?"

"She 'n the kids went shoppin' . . . up the road."

"Oh. Well . . ."

"Just a minute." Hoskins laughed, a bit nervously. "Where'd ya go this afternoon?"

"Why?"

"Just curious."

She knew he was baiting her, stalling deliberately, but she didn't want to push him, afraid of what he might say.

"Went to a movie."

"Alone?"

"Of course."

"Funny."

"What?"

"Woulda swore I saw you get into a car with a sailor." He had been looking down at his feet, and now looked up at her, his head cocked to one side, his teeth showing where he grinned.

"Must have been a mistake." But a cold, clammy fear was spreading through her.

"Don't think so," he said, still grinning. "Saw you walk by the store, an' thought I'd see where you was goin,' you know, jus' for the helluvit. Saw ya walk down the road, sailor waved at you, then away y'all went."

So he'd seen . . . now what? He wasn't bringing it up just to help pass the day. Of that much she was sure.

"What do you want, Henry?"

"Call me Hank."

"All right, Hank. What is it you want?"

"Who was this guy, Arlene?"

"Just a friend."

"Buddy know about him?" he asked slyly, grinning even more at her obvious discomfort.

"What do you want?" she repeated, acknowledging nothing.

"I wouldn't want you to get in trouble with Buddy. Nooosirree, I sure wouldn't want that."

"So?"

"I'd be the last one in the world to tell him, less'n I didn't like you. Lucky for you, I do like you. Think you're one helluva fine girl."

Arlene waited, watching the man lick his lips before he spoke again, hating him, the narrow meanness of him.

"You know what I think," he said, "I don't think you were trying to be hypnotized last night at all. I think you were fightin' it, that's what I think."

"Isn't that a bit off the subject?"

"No. 'Cause that's all I want, really, Arlene. I think you'd be a good subject. I wanna hypnotize you sometime, all the way, an' see what happens."

Arlene could imagine what might happen if he succeeded in what he wanted, could imagine herself in a trance, with Hoskins' hands all over her, handling her. He looked slimy enough to do something like that, she thought, and more. God knows how *much* more!

"Why don't we all get together tonight, then? Buddy and I can come over here, or . . ."

Hoskins laughed loudly, interrupting her, then coughing suddenly, trying to stop laughing and coughing. Finally, he became quiet, his eyes staring at her like little buttons. "You act like you don't get the point, baby. But I know you do."

"Point?"

"I wanna hypnotize you all right . . . but alone. Just you and me, Arlene, all by ourselves."

"Oh. I guess I should've known."

"It's a small price to pay, I'd say. Wouldn't you? I hear Buddy gets really upset sometimes at you. Gladys tells me he even hits you when he's mad."

Arlene wondered where Gladys had picked up that information, not recalling anytime she had confided in the woman. But in a trailer park, things got around. It couldn't be helped with everyone living in such proximity.

"All right, Hen . . . Hank. There was nothing important about my meeting that sailor, but Buddy *is* suspicious, so I'd rather he didn't hear about it. It would just upset him without any cause, and there's no need of that. He's had heart trouble before, as I believe you know."

"So we have a deal?"

He was so anxious, she thought. So anxious, and already it was as though his bony hands were handling her, his thin lips kissing her and all she could think of was the stains on his teeth and the surety that he would have body odor.

"I guess so."

"When?"

"You seem to be running this show."

"That's right. Just remember that, and there won't be any problems, hear?"

"I hear." Her exterior was a cold, bitter shell, while inside the frightening thought of being under his power was building into a panic.

"We'll make it Monday. I reckon Buddy'll be home this weekend, won't he?"

"That's right."

"Monday it is, then. I'll stay home from work, get rid of Gladys and the kids somehow, then I'll be over. And you be there," he said, and the threat was in his voice.

"I'll be there." Where would I go, she thought? There was no place, no escape. If she did, he'd tell Buddy . . . and she didn't have to wonder what Buddy would do. Her body ached just thinking about it.

"Jus' wear some kind of robe," he said softly. "Clothes make it hard sometimes to really relax and be hypnotized."

Arlene nodded. "Is that all?"

"For now," he said, dismissing her with a jerk of his head, his beady eyes following her as she walked down the road, the spring missing from her walk, her shoulders drooping where before they had been thrown back with the joy of living.

Arlene wondered if she could kill someone. The punishment wouldn't matter, didn't enter into her thoughts. Only the question about the actual killing, taking someone's life and snuffing it out until it was finished, ended, through.

Never to breath again, or talk or walk or grin salaciously, with a face of evil desire, repressed lust.

She walked on, her eyes downcast, until she was almost in her own yard, looking up at the trailer unconsciously . . .

. . . and freezing at the sight of John Edwards sitting on the step that led inside, leaning against the door, his legs extended straight out, grinning at her shocked surprise.

"Hi," he said, not moving.

"Get away from here," her voice on the edge of frightened insanity, knowing she couldn't stand much more, not that day or any other.

Edwards laughed as though she had said something tremendously funny, a laugh that continued with a hint of madness.

"Leave me *alone,* John."

He shook his head, smiling at her. “Some day I will. After we take care of that business.”

Arlene wanted to turn and run away, but was afraid to make any movement that would make him get up. She was trembling with fear, and knew he could see it, knew her body jerked with the tenseness and fright and weakness that coursed through her.

Thankfully, she heard Agnes and Francie drive up next door. They couldn’t see her, but they were close.

If she screamed . . .

Edwards must have read her mind. “You’ll make yourself look awfully silly.”

“I doubt that. Just leave, John. I won’t call the police. Just go away and don’t come back.”

He made a sudden move in her direction, and Arlene stepped back so suddenly she fell, struggling to her feet in panic to find him still sitting on the step, laughing so hard that tears came to his eyes. He took off his horn-rimmed glasses, wiping his eyes with the back of his hand, laughing more uncontrollably whenever he glanced over at her.

When he finally stopped laughing, she asked him: “Are you going to leave me alone?”

He shook his head slowly, grinning at her.

Arlene turned abruptly and ran to Agnes’ trailer, pounding on the door, glancing back as though he would be coming after her at any moment.

Agnes opened the door, showing her surprise as Arlene pushed past her, inside.

“Lock the door, Agnes.”

“Wha . . . ? Sure.”

“There’s a man over there that won’t leave. I want to call the police.”

“You want me to go over an’ talk to him?”

“No. Please.” She picked up the phone, dialed the operator, and was connected with the police department. They took her complaint, and she waited impatiently, watching the window, until the patrol car pulled up in front of her trailer.

One of the policemen got out, looking around with a puzzled expression, and Arlene knew Edwards had gone, probably as soon as she herself left.

She went outside, told the policemen her story. Some prowler, she said. Never saw him before, she started to say, then remembered the previous trip she and Buddy had made to the station, and told them the truth.

"Did he hurt you?"

"No."

"Touch you."

"No. You don't understand . . ."

"Just a minute." The officer reviewed what she had said. "What did he say when you came home tonight?"

"Well, I told him to get out."

"And?"

"He laughed."

"Did he threaten you?"

Arlene blushed. "He did . . . in the past. He made reference to it. Called it 'the business' we had to take care of."

"You say he's threatened to kill you?"

"Yes."

"Do you have any witnesses?"

"No." She thought, here we go again.

The policemen looked around, one of them even going off into the woods, but coming back to report no sign of anyone. They left, telling her to be sure to call if the man came again, or hurt her in any way.

Arlene went inside, locking all the doors and windows carefully, feeling depressed and frightened, knowing Edwards would be back, if not tonight, then tomorrow, or the day after . . . and he'd keep coming back until he did what he wanted to do.

Something told her she wouldn't be able to prevent it, that some day he was going to make good his threat. Self-pity mingled with her fear and she laid on the couch, crying until she could cry no more.

Dusk had descended on the park, and still Buddy did not come home. Arlene watched from the kitchen windows, waiting for his car to pull in. She hadn't started supper, realizing after her cry that he would be late.

At seven-ten, Buddy called.

He'd be late, he told her, special sales problem came up, had to meet with some people, didn't know how late he'd be.

"Don't wait supper for me."

"I wish you'd called earlier."

"Well, hell, I couldn't, Arlene. We've been through this business before, that's sales work, can't be helped."

"That's not what I meant." She told him about John Edwards, and the police.

"That sonofabitch is gettin' on my nerves," Buddy said.

"Mine too. I'm a nervous wreck."

"Well, don't worry. He probably won't bother ya any more, now that he sees you mean business."

"I think he's a little crazy, Buddy. I don't imagine my calling the police did anything but make him laugh at me."

"Well, look, we'll talk about it when I get home. I've got a client waiting, okay? Just keep your doors locked, and you'll be okay."

He hung up before she could say anything, and Arlene wondered if she was making a mountain out of the proverbial molehill. Yet Edwards had made it quite clear what he intended doing to her . . . and he wouldn't keep hanging around unless he meant it.

Would he?

She didn't know. All she was sure of right then was that she didn't want to stay alone in that trailer, didn't want to be shut up with her imagination, her thoughts of Edwards and Hoskins and Monday.

She locked her trailer and went next door, expecting a hand to reach out and grab her any moment. But she arrived there without incident, accepting Francie's invitation to come inside. Agnes was taking a bath.

"Come on in," she told Arlene. "Tell me what happened."

Arlene sat down, while Francie leaned against the door, and told the two women what the police had said, then that Buddy was going to be late and she didn't want to stay alone.

"We're about to have supper," Agnes said. "How's about eating with us . . . if you're hungry?"

"Sure. You could eat a little, huh?" Francie said eagerly.

"Well . . . maybe. But not much."

"I'll put on another plate," Francie said and went back into the kitchen.

Agnes soaped her breasts, running the cloth over them languorously, her eyes steady on Arlene's face. "That's a terrible thing to have to think about."

Arlene nodded. The steamy warmth of the bathroom was reassuring, as though it shut out the night and the terrors it held. She saw Agnes smile at her gently, and in the remembrance of what they had shared together, she smiled back, knowing she would be protected as long as she stayed there.

"Don't worry," Agnes said. "Everything'll work out all right."

"I hope so. But sometimes you wonder how it ever could."

Agnes nodded. "How about doing my back?"

"Okay." Arlene knelt beside the tub, taking the soaped cloth and scrubbing the woman's back thoroughly. When she was almost through, she became aware of Francie standing in the doorway, watching her expressionlessly.

"Kind of doing my job, isn't she, Agnes?"

"Now don't be jealous," Agnes said sharply. "And for God's sake don't pout."

"I'm not," the girl said with an obvious effort. "I was just wondering if she'd do *my* back, after supper."

"Why don't you ask her?"

Arlene smiled up at Francie, not wanting to have the girl angry at her for any reason. "I'd love to."

Francie hesitated, then returned the smile, stretching slowly, thrusting her shoulders back until her full breasts strained against her thin blouse as though they might burst right through. "I'd like that. Supper's ready," she said, and left.

Agnes got out of the tub and Arlene helped her dry off, enjoying the touch of the woman, feeling herself curiously stimulated at the thought of Francie nude in the bathtub later.

They ate a simple meal, Arlene eating little, so full was she of conflicting feelings and tensions.

Afterward they had coffee in the living room, stacking the dishes, and Arlene became aware of both Agnes and Francie studying her carefully when they thought she was unaware.

Shortly, Francie started her bath, going into the bedroom to undress, leaving the door open so that Arlene caught an occasional glimpse of white flesh, pastel underthings.

Agnes had started washing the dishes, and Arlene offered her help as Francie went into the bathroom.

"I can manage. Why don't you do her back, like you said? If you don't mind?"

"I don't. Happy to."

"I'll be through here in a few minutes."

Arlene went into the bathroom. Francie was almost submerged in a full tub of water, the top foamy with bubble bath.

"Ready for your back?"

"Sure." Francie bent over, exposing a shiny area of smooth skin, and Arlene washed her as thoroughly as she had Agnes. When she was done, Francie straightened up so that her breasts were above the water. Arlene looked at the girl's body with fascination. She had never seen breasts as large, nor as perfectly formed.

Francie was like a Greek goddess, her complexion perfect, her body amazing.

It was a body you read about, a body that publicity agents tried to ascribe to Hollywood stars and starlets . . . but one that you seldom believe could exist.

Arlene thought, if a woman had her choice, this is the body she would choose.

Francie handed her the wash cloth and Arlene washed her back. The girl purred with pleasure under Arlene's ministrations.

"Oh, that feels good," she murmured.

"I guess that does it," Arlene said after a while.

Francie smiled knowingly at her. "Thanks."

Arlene rejoined Agnes, who was wiping the last few dishes. Agnes watched Arlene's face closely, then grinned.

"Quite a body."

"You're a mind reader."

Agnes shook her head. "That had to be what you were thinking . . . if you're living. And," she said, lowering her voice to a whisper, "I know you're living."

Arlene blushed delicately. "I can't argue with you, can I?"

"Not a bit."

When Francie had dressed and joined them, Arlene took her bath, and when Agnes offered to return her earlier favor, she was pleased, relishing the woman's hands on her back, relaxing as she always did under Agnes' touch.

Then she checked to see if Buddy was home yet, but there was no sign of him, or the car.

Arlene and Agnes went back into the living room. Suddenly, a knock sounded on the door. Arlene ran her fingers through her hair as Agnes opened the door.

"Is my wife in there?" It was Buddy's voice, filled with anger and hatred.

"Yes. Will you come in?"

"No. Just tell her to come out."

"I'm right here, Buddy," she told him, going to the door. "When did you get home?"

"Just now." His eyes swept the interior of the trailer suspiciously. "Figured I'd find you over here." His distaste was evident.

"John Edwards was here. The girls were good enough to let me stay until you . . ."

"It doesn't matter. Come home."

He turned abruptly and walked back to their trailer. Arlene shrugged toward Agnes.

"Sorry. He's not always so rude."

"That's all right." Agnes' lips were set in a tight, grim line. "I hope he simmers down . . . for your sake."

"I imagine he will . . . in awhile. He always gets mad if he gets home and I'm not there, wagging my tail like a little dog."

Agnes smiled at the analogy.

"I'd better get on," Arlene said, then added softly: "Thanks. For everything."

"Anytime."

Arlene took the dreadful steps back to her trailer, knowing there would be a scene, hating it, wondering if he'd heard anything, seen anything.

I wouldn't be surprised if he was out there listening all the time, she thought, and wished she could faint dead away at the implication of it.

Buddy was waiting inside the front door, his right hand a fist that he smacked loudly into his left. "Well, that's something to find when a man gets home from work, all right."

"What are you talking about?"

"You. You can't stay away from those queers, can you?"

Arlene ignored him, trying to walk past him, but he blocked her way.

"I want some answers from you."

"Like what?"

"Don't get smart."

"Just leave me alone, Buddy, please. I don't want any trouble with you tonight. You've been drinking."

"So what?"

"So don't say anything you'll regret."

"Boy! Have you got nerve! What do ya *do* over there all the time anyway? Exactly what *do you do?"*

"Buddy . . ."

His hand flashed out, striking her cheek, almost knocking her off balance. Arlene held the spot where it pained her, fighting a desire to cry out, refusing to give him that much satisfaction.

"I want some answers, and you're going to give 'em to me. Right now. I heard the goddamdest runnin' around and scramblin' when I knocked. Now I wanna know what the hell you were doing, that you had to run around like that?"

"*I* wasn't doing anything. I imagine you heard Francie running into the bathroom. She wasn't wearing much."

"Why not."

"Buddy, I didn't ask her why. I was a guest there. What she wants to wear with just women around is her own business."

"That's no answer." His face was becoming redder every moment, as though filling up with some poison.

"It's the *truth,"* she said, lying partially. "What more do you want, for goodness sake?"

There was a long pause while he looked at her, his lip curling slowly into a sneer. His hands dropped to his belt. "I guess I'll have to beat it outa you."

"Don't you dare!"

He had unfastened his belt, now drew it off swiftly. He wrapped half of it around his hand while she watched with a dread fascination, knowing there was no way for her to escape whatever vengeance he demanded. "Are you going to take a lickin' like you deserve or are you gonna fight me?"

"If you beat me, I'll leave you, Buddy. That's a promise."

"I'll teach you," he said, advancing on her slowly, backing her into a corner of the room. "Never thought I'd see the day I had me a queer wife, but by God, I'll beat the queerness out of you, if it takes me the rest of my life."

"Stop, Buddy!" she said, feeling the panic rise as he glared at her, realizing for the first time that he was capable of killing her, right then.

She waited, and the belt bit into her flesh.

Suddenly, she saw him clutching his breast, his face a fierce blood-red, his mouth gasping at the air as though he wanted to say something and couldn't, wanted to breathe . . . and couldn't.

It has to be his heart, she thought. Serves him right, damn him.

But she couldn't just lie there, watching him die. As he collapsed on the floor, Arlene called for an ambulance, then with a haste born of desperation, took the belt from his clenched fist, running into the bedroom and changing her dress hurriedly, so that when the ambulance arrived with a low growl of its siren, it's lights glowing, flashing in the night, they found only a man crumpled on the floor, the distraught wife beside him.

Hastily, the attendants applied emergency aid, then took Buddy to their waiting machine.

Arlene accompanied him on the swift ride to the hospital, her emotions torn, not wanting it to end this way.

Let him live, she prayed. Tomorrow, I'll leave him, I swear, but don't free me *this* way. Everyone has a right to live. And even when she moved, and the tender parts of her body sent their reminder of the beating Buddy had been administering, she maintained her prayer.

Not *this* way.

I have the courage to leave him now. So let me do *that.* Let me prove I have the courage.

This makes it too easy, she thought.

After a few busy, whirling minutes at the hospital, Buddy was out of her hands, and being cared for by the competent medical crew.

I hope competent, she thought. I have to trust, though. I certainly can't tell if someone knows what they're doing in a hospital. You hear stories about negligence, carelessness . . . and there must be a lot of it.

Just as there was in any business.

But in medicine, lives depended on it.

In business, it was only money.

The doctor came out soon, taking her into a quiet, unoccupied room.

"How is he?" she asked.

"Hard to tell. It's a bad attack, Mrs. Ford. I won't try to fool you about that. Very bad."

"I was afraid of it. He kept overdoing."

"He's had these before?"

"Slight only. He never *would* admit it was his heart. Even when a doctor told him. Guess he was afraid it was a sign of middle age."

The doctor shook his head. "Too bad."

"What can I do?"

"Nothing we can do but wait, Mrs. Ford. He's in a coma now."

"God."

"Best thing for you to do is go home and try to rest. I'll give you some pills."

"But . . ."

"I'll be right here with him. If there's any change, I'll call you. But believe me, rest is the best thing for you. You may be in for some hard days."

"If you say so."

"If there's anything to be done, we can do it. That's why we're here."

Arlene nodded slowly. "All right. I guess I'd just get in the way."

The doctor smiled without denying her assumption. He went with her to find a taxi, handing her three small tablets. "One should be enough. If it's not, take two. Take the third one only if it's absolutely necessary. It'd make you groggy all day tomorrow."

"All right, Doctor. And you'll be sure to call me if anything happens?"

"Yes. I promise."

She rode back home in the taxi, thinking how strange it was that everything could change so rapidly. How long had it been since she and Agnes and Francie had been . . . together? Not long. Not much over an hour, and look what had happened, look at the differentness of the entire world.

Yet the people they passed on the street didn't seem affected.

Humanity was supposedly so close knit, so interdependent, yet her husband could He near death in a hospital, which made everything in her life different . . . and none of them knew.

Or cared, really.

And if he died . . .

Arlene shook her head, not wishing to think about that. He wouldn't die, not Buddy. Maybe this would scare him enough so that he'd take care of himself more.

It was a cinch she herself wasn't going to stick around and do it for him.

I'll see him through this, she thought, then that's the end, brother, *finis*.

Our marriage is a far cry from what I want for the rest of my life.

She paid the cab driver, and let herself into the trailer. In the bedroom as she undressed and put on a robe, she found the belt where she'd thrown it earlier.

An anger came over her. SOB, she thought. It didn't matter *what* a person did . . . or was suspected of . . . nothing gave another person the right to beat someone, treat one so savagely.

Wasn't this world supposed to be filled with understanding, love for mankind, togetherness?

Well, where the hell is it, she thought, when a husband can take a belt to his wife? Or better yet, when he feels he has a *right* to do it?

Where's the great Golden Rule that all the churches preach, and the hypocrites re-preach most loudly to anyone that'll listen?

Then her thoughts took another road, and she wondered IF . . .

IF something happens to Buddy, or even IF it doesn't with any finality . . .

IF Corey was the answer.

Funny I should think of him now, she told herself. The afternoon in the motel seemed far away, like some misty dream that will never happen, but might . . .

But if I'm going to leave Buddy . . . which I am . . . I'll need help. Money. Friends.

As though brought by thought-waves, Agnes and Francie arrived at that moment, their faces and words compassionate.

Arlene told them what had happened, leaving nothing out as their eyes grew wide with shock.

"I hate to say it, but it served him right," Agnes said. "I wish you'd just left and come over to our place . . . or better still, never gone in the first place."

"You never know what's going to happen," Arlene said. "I knew we'd have a fight, but usually it's just words, cussin', like that."

"You want to stay with us tonight?"

"I'd love to . . . but I've got to stay here. The doctor said he'd call me if there was any change."

"I'll stay with you," Agnes said. "Francie doesn't mind sleeping alone."

"Once in awhile," Francie amended, then seemed to regret her remark, which could have sounded too flippant for the mood.

But Arlene was aware of nothing except Agnes' offer, and the knowledge that the woman's company was exactly what she needed at that moment.

Francie went home, offering any aid she might be able to give, at any time. Then Agnes fixed a stiff drink for her, which Arlene drank quickly, swallowing one of the pills the doctor had given her.

"I imagine I'll poop out in a hurry," she said.

"Don't worry about it. I'll put you to bed if you do. *And* I'll answer the phone, too, so don't worry about not hearing it."

"Wonderful. You're awfully nice to me."

"I just hope that . . ." she paused a moment, then continued: "I hope I'm not to blame for this."

"How in the world could you be?"

"Well, it was his suspicions that started it. And I'm more or less to blame for what went on over there tonight."

"That has nothing to do with it, Agnes, for goodness sake. It doesn't matter *what* went on or what he suspected. It was the beating he was giving me that made his heart act up. Nothing else. If he hadn't done that, then nothing would have happened."

"I see your point. I'm . . . glad you feel that way."

"Well, I do."

In a few more minutes, Arlene's head was whirling, her eyes seeing things dimly, and she had difficulty keeping them open. Agnes helped her into bed, sitting on the edge of it, rubbing her hand over Arlene's forehead, until she knew she was falling into a deep slumber induced by the pill.

"You be sure 'n wake me, if the doc' calls," she mumbled, and smiled at Agnes' immediate reassurance that she would.

"I'll sleep on the couch, right near the phone, honey," she heard Agnes say. "Everything's going to be all right."

There was so much to think about, Arlene wished she had the strength to stay awake longer, but the pill and the drink, the things she'd done all day, combined against her, until she gave up and accepted the inevitability of the unknowing blackness that enveloped her.

Chapter Eight

The effects of the pill were still evident when Arlene awoke, and for a moment, she didn't recall the events of the previous night.

When the memory flooded over her consciousness, she cringed involuntarily, shaking her head with the terror of it, biting her lip with remembered agony.

God, she thought, what will today hold?

Agnes?

"Agnes?" she called, answered immediately by the woman from the front of the trailer.

"You ready for coffee?"

"Yes. Thank you."

Arlene slipped out of bed, drawing on her housecoat. A steaming cup of black coffee was ready for her when she walked forward, smiling hesitantly at the woman.

"No calls," Agnes said. Arlene nodded.

"Thanks for staying. I'm still a bit drugged."

"Powerful stuff in that pill?"

"Must have been." She sipped at the coffee, bringing the hot liquid into her mouth in small portions, relishing the feel of it traveling down into her stomach.

Why can't this be like any other Saturday, she asked herself? Drink my coffee and go on about the usual business . . . Buddy all right . . . maybe on the road somewhere, but all right . . . no problems, at least *real* ones? No worries. Dread of calling the hospital to find out how he was, frightened that something may have happened and they couldn't call her, the phone out of order temporarily, or something . . .

While Agnes fixed her second cup, Arlene dialed the hospital, getting Buddy's doctor on the phone.

"He's the same, Mrs. Ford," the doctor told her patiently, his voice kind.

"Still in a coma?"

"That's right."

"He hasn't come out of it at all?"

"Not yet. It's hard to predict in cases like this. We're still doing all we can. You have to believe that."

"I do."

"I'm staying right here," he said. "If there's any change, I'll let you know immediately."

"Thank you," Arlene said, wanting to keep talking to him, hear the reassuring voice of the man, even if the words themselves held no promise. But she knew anything else would be extraneous.

"The same, huh?" Agnes asked when she hung up.

Arlene nodded. "I feel so damned helpless . . . as though there was something I could *do, should* do as a wife, regardless of how I feel about that particular category."

"There's nothing. Until his condition changes, one way or the other. If he's in a coma, he wouldn't know you were there, anyway, if that's what you're thinking."

"Maybe I should be . . . when he comes out of it."

Agnes shrugged. "You'd probably just be in the way, honey. When they want you there, they'll let you know."

"That's what he said. I guess he means it."

"Of course he does. Look, I'm gonna go on back home. If you need me for anything, holler. But I've got some stuff I've *got* to do . . . and probably you do, too."

"Yes. Although it doesn't seem very important right now."

"No. Just keep busy, 'Lene."

Agnes opened the door, stepping down to the protruding metal stair, turning back to smile at Arlene . . .

. . . as her foot flew out from under her, she fell, too quickly to yell, and landed on the step, her back and her head knocking against it, all in an instant. She lay on the patio, moaning, as Arlene hurried to her, almost falling herself on the step, seeing the thick coating of grease on it. She bent over Agnes, holding her head up and away from the concrete.

"Are you all right?"

Agnes groaned painfully. "I think so. Gave myself one helluva crack on my back and head." She started to get up, but Arlene held her down.

"Do you think you should move?"

"Wanna find out if anything's broken . . ." The woman came to a sitting position slowly, feeling herself gingerly as Arlene watched with dread that she might be seriously hurt. In a moment, Agnes stood up, leaning on Arlene for support.

Satisfied that she was only bruised up, Agnes laughed. "That's what you call a graceful exit."

"It was supposed to be me."

"Meaning what?"

Arlene pointed to the grease on the step. "That was deliberate."

"Why the hell . . . ?"

"Some people are depraved."

"I know damn well they are!" Agnes straightened up a bit more, grimaced. "Well, thank God I don't have anything broken. What is it they say . . . watch that first step, it's a killer?"

"Something like that."

"Well, take care. I'll see ya later."

"Let me help you home."

"I'm all right, honey. I think," she added emphatically.

Arlene watched her leave, then took the morning newspaper that was lying on the patio and wiped the grease thoroughly from the step.

There was no question in her mind who had done it . . . and why. Part of an endless campaign, she thought. And nothing I can do about it, nothing.

The first thought she'd had had been to call the police. But her previous experiences showed her how useless it would be.

'Can you prove who did it?' they would ask . . . and of course she couldn't, couldn't prove anything, no matter how strongly she knew it in her own mind, how *sure* she was.

So there was nothing to do but wipe it up, hope Agnes was all right, and watch herself whenever she came out of the trailer. Her eyes searched the area, expecting to find Edwards standing somewhere, laughing at her . . . but she saw nothing. Heck, he was probably miles away by now, planning to come back tonight, or tomorrow night, and add something else to his harassment of her.

The phone rang as she went back inside and she hurried to it, fearing bad news from the hospital.

"Hello?"

"Corey. Can you talk?"

"Yes." The relief poured through her. Quickly, she told him what had happened to Buddy. He listened, then:

"I want to see you, honey. Is there any way?"

"Oh, baby, I don't know. I've got to stay home, near the phone, in case they need me." She wanted to be with him, wanted to feel again the delicious forgetfulness that being with him inspired. When they were together, that's all there was, at least for the moment. It was a good feeling. But how?

"Hey?"

"I'm here."

"The reason I called . . . I'm shipping out this evening. Probably for about a month."

The words were like painful needles pricking her.

"Oh, Corey . . ."

"I know. I feel like jumping ship."

"You mustn't do that."

"Is-n't there *any*place? Could I come to your trailer?"

"No," she said quickly, then thought of it. Why not? She could hear the phone, and . . . "Listen. In back of the park, there's a pretty thick woods."

"I'm with you."

"We could meet there, for awhile."

"When?"

"The sooner the better," she said, dropping any pretext of coyness. It was too important, too urgent for that.

"Eleven?"

"Good. I'll wait until then, then walk out back. You be right in line with my trailer." She described where she meant. Then began the long waiting until he would get there from town, until they could be together again, if only briefly.

She opened all the windows in the trailer, turned off the fan, confident that the ringing phone would carry a good distance in the quiet of the summer morning.

Then she waited again, drinking coffee to help kill the time, watching the hands of the dock creeping infinitesimally closer to the hour of eleven.

She wondered if it were proper, to meet a lover while her husband lay gravely ill. Maybe not, she told herself. Maybe it violates every moral code in the book, but I know what I need, I know the feeling while I'm with Corey, and I *need* it today, before he goes away. And certainly if she were to be condemned morally, then it was already an accomplished fact.

But who decides what's right, she asked? Who decides that something's a sin, lumping things into general categories, without regard for personalities, circumstances? Why is a person's life anyone's else's business but his own? Why do some people make careers out of interfering with things that don't personally concern them? Or shouldn't?

Why?

Eleven o'clock came eventually. Arlene stepped outside the trailer, hesitating, her eyes sweeping the woods as she thought that Edwards might be there, even though her hunch was that he would come back only at night.

There was no sign of movement for a moment, then she perceived a flash of white in the trees, knew it was Corey, and walked slowly toward him, through the clearing then into the fringe of the woods, surprised at how rapidly it became dense except for a narrow footpath undoubtedly worn by children playing there.

"Hey," Corey said, stepping from behind a tree, startling her only for a moment.

Arlene rushed to him, gratefully feeling his arms close around her protectively.

"I think I've found us a place," he whispered.

"Good." She held his hand, following him through a tangle of brush and trees, coming in a moment to a tiny grove where the trees arched closely over, their branches meshing until they all but shut out the day.

The spot was densely surrounded on three sides, almost as though it were a small house of Nature. The ground there was clear but for a soft carpet of pine needles . . . and over these Corey had placed the blanket from his car.

Inside, Arlene felt safe and secure, completely shut off from the other world. She could see the trailer vaguely, and was sure she could hear the phone if it rang. And if anyone came to see her, she could see that too.

"It's wonderful," she said, smiling tenderly at him.

"Just made for us, honey," he told her, and kissed her gently.

"This is probably wrong, Corey. But I wanted so to see you. Especially with all that's happened."

"It must have been rough for you."

Arlene nodded, leaning on an elbow, looking down into his face. He put his arm around her, pulling her closer until she lay against him, her eyes closed, her nostrils filled with the scent of pine. A cool breeze played over them, and the branches stirred softly.

"It's wonderful here. So peaceful," she said. "I just wish it could be this way, always."

"Some day," he said, his voice choking with emotion. "Maybe we'd better not talk about it today, though."

"Maybe not. All I know is I'm happy to be with you for awhile, and I think the Navy's got a lot of nerve, sending you away from me for a month."

"You say the word and I'll stay."

"No. Much as I might want it, darling, it isn't to be. Maybe, when you get back, things will be better."

"Meaning."

"I'm going to leave Buddy, as soon as he's well. Then we'll talk about . . . us."

"Oh, you're sweet." His lips brushed her forehead, then met hers, his mouth warm and eager. Arlene responded, pressing against him tightly, wanting to shut out everything but the moment.

Corey rolled over until she was lying on her back, his hand bunching her full breast through her dress, his eyes filled with wonder and love. It was a look Arlene had seldom seen, and she interpreted it correctly, her heart filling with love for him.

He looked at her as though she were everything in the world that mattered, everything that had any value . . . as though he would do anything for her, protect her from everything . . . and meant it.

"I love you," she said, hearing him repeat it, cherishing the words.

"I never knew there could be anyone like you," he said. "You go through life thinking something like this is just in books. Then it happens, and you still can't believe it's real."

"I know."

"But everyone doesn't find someone . . . like we did. Or they find 'em too late. What happens then?"

Arlene shook her head. "I've always heard that each person has a perfect mate somewhere. Only most people never find them, or as you said, find them too late. That must be tragic."

"It *is*."

"Well, honey, we found each other and that's something."

"Everything," he amended soberly, leaning to kiss her again. "It's everything in the world."

His fingers traced the buttons of her dress. "Do you mind?"

"No. I want you to."

Slowly, he unfastened them, pushing the fabric open, baring her shoulders. "I just think of you and I start trembling," he said. "I don't even have to be near you." His lips caressed her skin, moving slowly over the exposed areas. In a moment, he reached behind her back and she raised up to help him, enjoying the removal of the garment, the caresses that followed it. His hands bunching her breasts as he pressed his face between them.

Arlene held his head against her body, her eyes staring at the overhanging boughs, hearing the whisper of the breeze as it rippled through them, as though murmuring a love song to accompany their love.

There wasn't another sound anywhere, only the breathing of Corey as his passion mounted rapidly. It was reflected in his touch, his kisses, his hands as he became a bit rougher, more insistent.

Arlene responded willingly, sensing her own drive toward the peak they would find. For long moments, she could think only of him and the wonderful joy of their closeness, nothing else.

It was as though nothing else existed, anywhere, and the dim sounds of the other world came to her so faintly that they were meaningless, easily shut out.

Now she twisted as he touched her, pushing against him, lost to all but the desire that was building, building, building with his every caress.

It didn't take long.

They reached a peak, together, and as rapidly were back in the woods, with only the memory of the journey, the rapid flight to perfect happiness.

She opened her eyes and found him watching her, a grin of joy splitting his face, mixed with the disbelief that anything, anyone could be so fantastically well-matched . . . and knew that her own expression was the same.

It seemed as though only the briefest of moments passed before he had to leave.

"I hate to go."

"I know. But maybe it'll pass quickly."

"It'll feel like forever."

"A day's like forever . . . now."

"I love you, Arlene. So much."

"I love *you.* I never knew it could be like this, Corey, believe me. I never dreamed."

"Me, too." He got up slowly. "Want me to wait 'til you're home?"

"You go ahead. I want to just lie here a minute and enjoy this feeling."

"Okay." He grinned again. "Think of me."

"Nothing else."

"Bye."

She watched him walk away through the woods, frowning at the thought of not having him near for the next month. It was almost too much to bear, yet there was no choice. Funny, how soon you can get attached to someone, need them. It didn't take long, didn't take very many sharings before it happened.

Arlene pulled her dress together until it covered her body, not bothering to fasten her clothes, so satiated with love that nothing mattered but the recollection of the last few moments.

Being with Corey made her feel whole, complete, for the first time in her life, and she wondered how she'd ever existed before, ever thought she was really happy.

Strange, how you could delude yourself, convince yourself that you were doing all right, that life was fine, and you couldn't ask much more of it than what you had.

Then you met someone like Corey . . . the name didn't matter. For her it was Corey, for others it could be any name.

And the whole world turned upside down, you realized what you had been missing, and your every thought was directed at getting more and more of this thing that had suddenly swept into your life, almost unannounced, certainly unbid, and now a part of every breath you took.

Arlene breathed deeply of the pine-scent, listening to the stirring of the branches, her eyes shut peacefully.

There was the snap of a twig, and she felt her heart sing, knowing Corey had come back, opening her eyes to see his face again . . . and found herself looking into Edwards' burning eyes.

Her hand flew to her mouth, suppressing the scream that gurgled there, her teeth biting hard on her knuckles.

Edwards was kneeling at the entrance to the grove, his mouth in a malicious sneer, his eyes bright behind his glasses as he watched the expression of horror and revulsion that swept her face.

"Surprised?"

"Get out of here."

Edwards only response was to move in closer. Arlene pushed herself back, away from him, her dress falling open. She grabbed it together quickly, frightened at the way his eyes had glanced down at her exposed body, frightened of the thoughts that she knew were racing through his mind.

"John, please leave me alone," she said, trying to be moderate, reason with him.

"After."

"Don't start that again."

"Looks like you were gettin' ready for me," he told her, grinning hugely, inching even closer to her.

"No."

His hands indicated her attire wordlessly.

"I was just cooling off."

"With the sailor?" he asked mischievously.

Arlene's heart sank like lead. Where had he been, what had he heard? "What sailor?"

"Don't pull that crap on me," Edwards said angrily. "I saw ya. I was watchin' you, all the time, I saw what you did with him, and that's what I want you to do with me. That's all." He waited expectantly, as though she would see the reason in his desire, and acquiesce gracefully, since it was such a logical thing to ask.

Arlene wondered if there was another way to get his mind off her body, her flesh. "You wouldn't want me *now,* would you?"

"Why not?"

"After . . . what just happened?"

Edwards shrugged. "No difference to me. First, second, third, fourth . . . all the same."

Arlene couldn't believe he meant it, but he didn't act as though there were anything at all strange about his statement. She was revolted at the thought, her mind near panic at the closeness of him, while she fought to keep a level head, get out of this as best as she could.

She was afraid that screaming would just set him off, be the thing that would light the fuse of his insanity. And screaming wouldn't prove much anyway, no matter what happened. She didn't want to be found in the woods, under any circumstances, didn't want to have to explain why she was there, with whom . . .

"You ready?" he asked quietly.

Arlene shook her head vehemently.

Edwards grinned at her, his hands hesitating. Then one arm flashed and his palm slapped her viciously against the side of the head, knocking her back.

Again her dress flew open, and she grabbed it together, unmindful of the stinging pain.

"You ready now?" he asked, his voice still under control. "It isn't as though I'm askin' anything you haven't done before . . . with plenty of guys, I think."

Arlene gritted her teeth. I If did, she thought, if I did what he wanted, would that be the end of it? Would he leave me alone? The very idea was repulsive, yet . . .

Edwards moved quickly, grabbing her arm, yanking her close to him. She fought against him, but his grip on her arm was like iron. She forgot about the dress, the unfastened bra, anything but getting away from him, running back to the trailer and locking the door. She wished she'd done as Corey suggested, and gone back to the trailer before he'd left . . . but then there'd been no thought of Edwards, nothing but the peacefulness and the need to enjoy every moment she could in that grove that had now turned into a pit of Hell, as Edwards handled her breasts with one hand, his other pinioning her hands and wrists against the ground, finally putting his knees on her hands, hurting them with an excruciating pain, while his hands went over her body as she twisted in vain attempts to get away from him.

Her flesh crawled at his touch, and when he tried to kiss her, she turned her head violently from side to side, tears stinging her eyes, then she held her head still, unmoving as his mouth covered hers. It was as though her immobility was the catalyst that set him for the explosion, for his efforts redoubled, his strength became even greater, and his knees pressing her hands against the pine-covered earth hurt until she thought her wrists would break. She could only twist her body unsuccessfully. Arlene was powerless against him, knowing even then that she would be unable to stop him, unable to escape from him until he'd had his way with her, hoping only that he wasn't serious about killing her. She closed her eyes again as he ripped her last garment off, then pushed her back, her shoulders hitting the bare ground that was exposed from their struggles, her skin mashing against the tiny stones, the buried roots, trying to shut her mind to what he was going to do, and suddenly, without warning, what he was doing, hurting from his handling, suffering his close embrace unmoving, as though in passive resistance lay her only hope, fighting for breath as his paunchy body swarmed over hers, as though he would envelop her and snuff her out, hide her under his flesh and make her disappear as though from under a magician's cape, the hoarse breathing grating in her ears, in and out, panting, the sound of teeth gritting with demanding desire until the end came and he wordlessly got up, while she watched him with a hatred, a horror, a still-terror like she'd never known, realizing only that she was alive, and wondering what would happen now.

Edwards peered down at her, his mouth grim and tight, his eyes darting madly over the length of her body. Then he laughed, the sound of it exploding through the quiet woods, startling her.

"That's all I want," he said, then kicked her, his foot catching her side viciously, doubling her up with the pain as he walked quickly away, soon lost to sight in the thickness of the woods.

Arlene lay there a long time, wanting to cry but unable to bring forth any tears. The stillness descended again, surrounding her, wiping out all but the consciousness of the pain where he had kicked her, the nasty unclean feeling that his attack had left with her, contrasting so with the moments after Corey.

She shuddered, biting her lip. Tears finally dimmed her eyes, and she pillowed her head in her arm, letting the racking sobs of unhappiness, distaste, guilt take over her body.

When she was done, she dressed slowly, discarding the ripped panties under a low-hanging bush, then carefully made her way back to the trailer, entering it as a refuge that no longer had much value.

The damage was done. There would be no more hiding.

She showered, fingering the darkening bruise on her side gingerly. The bastard! But she was rid of him, the price had been paid, and now she could forget him, forget his threats that had now been fulfilled, and go back to some semblance of normality.

Or could she?

She doubted it seriously.

Arlene napped on the couch near the phone, awakening in the late afternoon, sweaty and hot to hear it ringing insistently in her ear. She picked it up groggily, her senses alert as soon as she heard the doctor's voice.

"Can you come right over?"

"What is it?"

"Can you come?"

"Yes."

"Good. You'd better hurry, Mrs. Ford."

"But . . . is he worse?"

"Yes, I'm afraid so."

Arlene dialed hastily, ordered a cab, and combed her hair hurriedly. She felt a premonition, a cold hand upon her, and knew the cab would be faster than driving, she drove so seldom.

The taxi came almost immediately, and Arlene lay back against the seat on the trip, hoping and praying that the doctor was wrong, that Buddy wasn't really worse at all.

But she knew doctors were seldom wrong about things like that.

He met her at the hospital entrance, taking her arm wordlessly as they walked inside. The doctor led her to a small room off the lobby, closing the door.

"Doctor?"

"Mrs. Ford . . . we did all we could."

It took a moment for the words to sink in.

"All? You mean . . . he's dead?"

The doctor nodded, his face showing the sympathy he felt for her. "Yes. Right after I called you. He never came out of the coma, never felt anything."

Arlene shook her head. "But . . . he *can't* be."

The doctor waited, not saying anything as Arlene's mind slowly accepted the fact that Buddy was indeed dead . . . gone . . . dead . . .

"Dead," she said aloud to no one in particular. "It . . . just doesn't seem possible."

Just yesterday he was alive, living, breathing. She didn't want it this way. Freedom she wanted, but not like this, not at the sacrifice of a life, regardless of the reasons for it.

Death was so final, so complete.

When you were dead, that was the end.

There was no more.

Heaven?

Maybe, she thought. Maybe when *I* die, I'll find there is one and that'll be the biggest surprise I *ever* had. But she couldn't believe it, hadn't ever been able to, ever since she was old enough to question what older people told her as fact.

"Can I see him?"

"If you like."

He was staring at her curiously, as though he expected something, and Arlene knew she should cry, have hysterics, break down. But she was emotionally drained, and the only feeling she had was one of deep depression and sadness.

The doctor led her to Buddy's room, motioning a nurse out, leaving her alone after asking her if she'd be all right.

Arlene walked to the bed. Buddy looked as though he were sleeping. So natural, his eyes closed, hands crossed on his chest.

"Buddy?" she said, almost expecting him to open his eyes, answer her. She felt an urge to shake him, wake him up, prove the doctor was mistaken. She even reached tentatively toward him, but withdrew her hand quickly, knowing it was useless, senseless, an impulse.

She stared down at her husband.

"I'm sorry, Buddy," she said. "I never wanted it this way, you have to believe that. No matter what problems we ever had, I never wanted it to be like this. We all try to find happiness in our own ways, I guess. Maybe I was wrong, I don't know. But living's the important thing, and I never would have denied you that, had I had a choice. Honest"

She stopped, hoping no one had overheard, thinking it might sound silly, talking to a body that life had fled.

Arlene reached out, brushed her hand through his thinning hair tenderly. Always so worried about getting older, weren't you? No more, my husband, no more.

Finally she turned and left the room. The doctor was waiting outside.

"Are you all right, Mrs. Ford?"

"Yes, I think so. What do I do now, Doctor?"

"Today, nothing. If you'll give me the name of a funeral director I'll have him make arrangments and contact you."

"I don't know one."

"Then I'll take care of it. You go home, or else to some friend's house. Try to relax, not worry too much. There'll be a shock to this. It hasn't come yet, but it will. I'll give you some medicine."

Arlene waited until the doctor returned. "Take one of these every four hours. And be with someone, understand. Don't be alone."

Arlene nodded. "Thank you. I . . . I know you did . . . what you could."

"Yes, we did. I'm sorry."

She walked outside, breathing the fresh air that was such a change from the antiseptic smell of the hospital corridors.

Dusk had descended, and everything was wrapped in its murkiness.

Off to the west, the sky held only traces of a red sunset as the night swiftly obliterated the day.

Arlene got in a taxicab. “Take me home, please.”

“Sure, miss. Where’s that?”

She realized she hadn’t told the driver, and quickly gave the address.

Behind her, she left her dead husband, a death that was still so new as to be unbelievable in its finality.

Ahead of her, she knew not what.

Chapter Nine

The shock came as she returned to the trailer, letting herself back into the world of the familiar. Everything was so much the same there, despite what had happened.

Buddy’s things were in evidence, things he would never again use, or need.

But the traces of his being remained, as though he would come at any time, pick them up, use them.

It was so *final.*

If one thought stayed with her, it was this. The finality. The end, finish. Nothing else.

She knew that some day it would happen to her, too, and the idea frightened her. To never know another morning, another laugh, another joy. Or even fear, panic. Wasn’t it better to have *those* . . . than nothing?

To have no awareness of consciousness.

Dead.

Agnes spent the night with her. Few words passed between them, or were necessary. Arlene felt better in having someone there, helping to erase the terrible aloneness that death had left in its wake.

Someone moving around, breathing.

Someone *there.*

The pills put her into a dreamless sleep but she awakened the next morning with an immediate recollection, a sudden stinging need to cry that she fulfilled with her face buried in the pillow.

Francie came over soon, and throughout the day, she and Agnes were always there, at least one of them, doing what they could to help keep Arlene from dwelling too long on Buddy's passing.

They were there during the crucial period of the first adjustment, and Arlene realized now how much they meant.

A staid, calm man named Wilson came from the funeral director's organization shortly after noon. With the help of Agnes, they made arrangements for the funeral to be held Monday, settled on the price she wanted to pay, what extras she did or didn't want.

Agnes was practical in the matter of the coffin, and they decided on a cheaper one than that which the man first suggested.

"I want to do right, Arlene, but I think saving the four hundred dollars is important too. He didn't have any great amount of insurance."

Arlene agreed. The cost, even then, would run to almost eight hundred dollars. "Just so it's proper."

The balance of the day after Wilson departed dragged slowly by. There was the wait now. The wait for the funeral, for the burial, for the grim finality, after which there would be the future to think about.

In the evening, they drove to town and viewed Buddy's body at rest in a small side-room at the funeral home.

He looked the same as he had at the hospital . . . life-like, as though he might awaken any moment.

Arlene, peering down at him for a long moment thought of the good times they'd had, and knew she'd miss him.

There were bad times too. No argument there. But it hadn't been all shadow, and in the sadness of death, one usually thought of the good things.

Human nature. Think good thoughts.

She didn't cry. There were no tears left.

The service Monday was short, followed by the trip to the cemetery.

Another brief service followed there, and then the casket was lowered into the grave, the first symbolic shovel of earth heaped on it.

Arlene left then with Agnes and Francie. The Cadillac limousine that was included in the price she paid for the funeral took them back to the trailer park, back to the world that had little awareness of Buddy, alive or dead.

As they drove in, children played in the narrow streets, people hung out washing, sat in their yards reading, walked to the store . . . the same world, nothing changed, except one member of it would not be seen again.

And what little impact it made, actually.

Arlene thought with amazement, even if I were torn apart with suffering, how many would know or care?

Deaths affected only the family.

There was no wide-spread mourning when a member of the human race passed on. But there couldn't be really, she thought. We'd do nothing but mourn all the time.

What a life *that* would be!

In the trailer, the traces of him were still there, untouched. She knew she'd have to do something about them soon, but not then, not right then.

She wanted only to rest, have a drink, adjust.

Be alone.

Agnes and Francie had to go to work after lunch, and she watched them leave with a thankful heart for the trouble they had put themselves to, helping her during the most difficult time.

But it was good to be alone again.

Arlene mixed a martini, toasted the empty trailer. Well, you wanted to be alone, kid. You're really *alone* now.

Chapter Ten

Arlene was on her second martini when the knock sounded on the door.

She opened it to find Henry Hoskins standing there, grinning slightly, nodding to her as she peered out at him questioningly.

"Well?" he said.

"Well what?"

"You gonna ask me in?"

"All right." She stood back, letting him enter, then turned to face him. "What is it, Hank?"

"You're not wearin' a robe . . ."

Arlene stared at him uncomprehendingly . . . then it dawned on her, the threat, the promise, the assignation. Surely, he couldn't be . . . but with Hoskins it was possible.

"Hank, I buried Buddy this morning."

"I know. Sorry to hear it."

Arlene waited. The man made no move, standing in the middle of the living room, his hands clasping each other nervously.

"I have a lot of things to do," she said.

"Rather make it another day?"

"What?"

"Look, I know you been tore up, an' all, but we made a deal, remember?" His face reflected his fear that the bargain was not to be kept.

Arlene looked at him with horror. What sort of man *was* this? How callous, how . . . she realized she was looking at human garbage, walking, talking garbage, and it nauseated her. "You'd better leave," she said, pointing to the door.

Hoskins' eyes roamed over her, filling with the beginnings of frustrated rage.

"You promised!"

"The circumstances have changed, wouldn't you say?"

"I stayed outa work."

"You knew Buddy was dead."

"I figger a promise is a promise," he maintained stubbornly, and Arlene found herself treating him as she would a little child. His date with her had obviously become a fixation, and nothing was going to dissuade him from it.

She wondered what sort of code a man had who told himself a promise was a promise, even when blackmail had been used to extract it, force it from her.

"Listen, Hank. It's not a promise that I intend to keep. Now I'm willing to forget it if you are."

He shook his head slowly.

"You have no *choice!*" she said, starting to lose her temper at his stupidity, the natural distaste she felt for him.

Hoskins moved swiftly beside her, his bony hands reaching for her breasts, intent on proving her wrong.

Arlene slapped his face with all the strength she could muster, and he staggered back, holding himself, his eyes surprised. “Get out. I’m not going to say it again. If you don’t leave right now, I’ll call the police and have you locked up.”

“But you promised,” he said again, as though that were everything, nothing else was necessary or worthy of consideration.

Arlene said nothing, waiting for his next move. She saw his eyes sweep her body again, covetously, knew his thoughts.

“I’ll get even with you for this,” he threatened, but Arlene could think of nothing he could do to hurt her now. He could tell the world about Corey, and there was no one whose disapproval would bother her in the least.

Hoskins apparently sensed this, realized that he held no power over her any longer. The defeat showed in his face as he turned bitterly and left, slamming the door shut with all the fury of a man who could find no other way to express it.

Arlene locked the door behind him, sinking into the couch with the unreality of his visit overwhelming her. He must be crazy, she thought. The whole business was like a bad dream, and she knew no one would ever believe that he had actually come and tried to make her keep such a bargain.

She shook her head. Of all days. Martini, where are you?

She mixed a large supply of the cocktails, ‘before I get too tiddly’ she told herself, and sat down to get seriously drunk.

There were hours ahead before Agnes and Francie would return from work, hours of no company, no one to talk to . . . unless she picked someone like Hoskins, and it wasn’t companionship that *he* wanted.

It made her flesh crawl just to think about letting him hypnotize her, get her in his power, knowing what he would do to her once he did.

It might not be anything but handling her . . . but even that was a creepy thing for her to visualize.

Forget him, she told herself. He’s gone, he knows its useless, he won’t come back.

She drank two martinis rapidly, wanting to reach the glow, the happy, in-between stage where nothing really mattered, nothing was very important, everything took on a happier hue.

She reached it quickly, then nursed her third drink . . . fourth really . . . maintaining the feeling, not wanting to get sloppy, just keep the pleasant edge.

She didn't really know what she would do now. Work, of course. But where? And the insurance. She didn't know exactly how much life insurance her husband had left her, how much of a cushion to help her readjust to making her own living again.

She recalled times they'd talked about it, in the beginning of their marriage, even times when she'd discouraged the purchase of more insurance because they needed the money that would go to payments for the more urgent business of day-to-day living.

Make a mental note, she told herself. Call the insurance man tomorrow, find out, get settled.

And pick up his things. It won't help to have them around, reminding me. Won't prove anything.

She thought of people who *did* keep reminders around, pipes, clothes, uncompleted hobby projects. It didn't seem healthy, somehow.

Even if you loved someone with all your heart and soul, why give yourself that little sting every day, why?

The place for the dead was in your memory, in pictures, in occasional conversation . . . but not everywhere you turned, not the reminders of the everyday, not that.

Not for me, anyway.

She realized she was getting a bit beyond the in-between stage, getting unsteady, and knew if she had to talk aloud, her tongue would be fuzzy, her words poorly formed.

Drunk.

So what, she thought? So I'm drunk. I guess I've got the right. I can do anything I want to, now. Go anywhere, anytime. Buy anything. And get drunk, if I choose.

Someone rattled the door, and she cheered up even more. The women were finally home from work, she wouldn't be alone any more. Giggling slightly, she made her way to the door, unlocked it, then made her way back to the couch, staggering slightly.

"C'min," she called.

The door opened, and a cold shock of sobriety hit her. "Leave me alone," she hissed.

John Edwards smiled at her, closing the door and locking it again. "Hi baby."

"You got what you wanted," she said, wishing she were more sober. He swam a little bit when she tried to focus her eyes on him.

"I want more."

"No."

"Ha!" He moved closer to her, and Arlene cringed back in the couch as far as she could go. "You loved it and you know it. Women like a man 'at treats 'em rough."

"You're wrong."

He sat beside her on the couch, stretching his legs out in front of him. "What are you drinkin'?"

"You really make yourself at home, don't you?"

Edwards nodded. "Unnerstan' your husband died."

"How did you know that?"

"One of your neighbors told me. Shame. You'll be needin' a man around the house now."

"Not you!"

"Why not? I'm good in bed, I'll keep ya in line. You were going to marry me once, remember?"

"I'll never forget it."

He reached out, placing his hand on her knee, holding it with a strong grip, hurting her. "It'll be just like ol' times. Now I've laid ya, you won't have any fear on that score."

Arlene was sobering rapidly. The fear she had of this man was intense, yet she tried not to show it, sensing that any display of hostility might set him off, erase the apparent good mood he was in.

Maybe, she told herself, maybe if I don't alarm him I can get him to go away for awhile. Then I can pack, leave, something, anything.

"Well, I'd have to think it over, John."

"Nothing to think about."

"I've got so many things to straighten out, take care of, now that Buddy's dead . . ."

"I'll do 'em for you."

She shook her head. "I think it's better if I do."

"That's the kind of decision you won't have to make anymore, Arlene." His meaning was clear, and it angered her. "That's what you need a man for, make decisions, take ya when you get sexy, buy ya things." He squeezed her knee even harder, and she couldn't repress a grimace. "That husband o' yours musta handled you like you was a china doll or somethin'. You get used to a real man's way, you'll like it." His hand moved swiftly under her skirt, and she pushed it away impulsively, unthinking.

Edwards' face flushed. "Don't you ever do that again."

"Listen, John . . ."

"Shut up! I'll do the talkin' around here. When I want to touch you someplace, handle you someplace, squeeze ya, love ya . . . you'll do it, hear? And that's that. That's the way it's going to be."

He waited, expecting an argument, seemingly disappointed when she said nothing. "Stand up."

"Why?"

"Because I told you to," he said loudly, shouting, the sudden change startling her. "Do it."

Arlene stood before him, wondering what he had in mind, how she could get rid of him, get help.

"All right," he said.

"Why did you make me stand up?"

"Because I wanted to. The sooner you get to doing what I say without wondering WHY, the better off you'll be." He wandered to the pitcher of martinis, poured himself one. "Not bad. Where's your glass?"

"I've had enough."

"Dammit," he said, keeping his voice low with an effort, "I asked you a question."

"Over there."

"Get it."

Arlene started for the glass when the phone rang. She stopped, looking first toward the phone, then to Edwards.

"Who is it?"

"I don't know. A couple of people said they'd call, see if I was all right."

"Better answer it then. But be quick, an' tell 'em you're fine, no problems, understand?"

"Yes."

The phone rang for the fourth time and she picked it up quickly, frightened that the calling party would hang up.

"Hello."

"Hi honey." It was Corey. "Can you talk?"

"Yes," she said, not hiding her surprise. "How are you?" Wondering why he was calling, how . . .

"We're not gonna ship out 'til Wednesday now, honey. Maybe we can get togeth . . . . . ."

"I'm just fine," she said, interrupting him. "Everything's all right."

"That's good," he said, and she heard the question in his voice as he wondered what she was getting at. "Your husband there?"

"No. Not now, like I say everything's fine and I'm doing okay. There's no need for you to come over." She prayed silently that he would get a hint, somehow. Edwards was watching her closely, and she sensed that he was becoming impatient.

"I don't get it, honey. Maybe I'd better hang up and call again later, huh?"

"No," she said quickly, panic building in her breast. "It was a lovely funeral. I'm sorry you couldn't be there."

Edwards gestured at her to hang up.

"What?" Corey asked, utterly confused.

Arlene knew that she wasn't getting through to him, that what might be her last chance to obtain help was slipping away with every passing second. In desperation, she realized she had to gamble everything on the next instant. "Corey . . . HELP, FOR GOD'S SAKE HE . . ."

Edwards yanked the receiver away from her, smashing it down on the cradle, turning to her with rage shaking him. His mouth trembled, his eyes blinked crazily.

Arlene backed away from him.

"I wanna marry you, and you call for help, huh? Well, there's ways of fixin' smart dames like you." He grabbed at her dress, catching a handful of fabric in his fist, tearing it savagely.

Arlene tried to run past him, but he brought his fist down on her shoulders, knocking her to the floor, falling on her instantly, his hands ripping her clothes away in a frenzy.

He talked to himself as he tore her clothes off, repulsing any effort she made to free herself, to kick him, bite him. It was as though he was a machine, doing a job, and nothing could interfere with it.

Arlene opened her mouth to scream, but he took a handful of her torn slip and jammed it into her mouth, gagging her, holding it in there until she thought she couldn't get another breath.

Where is Corey, she thought wildly? Did he understand? Why doesn't he come? Quickly?

She knew she would faint soon since there was a limit to what a person could stand, could keep within themselves, and knew she could kill him, if only there were a way, something she could get to and use against him. There wasn't a court in the land that wouldn't say she was justified.

But what was there?

"Arlene?" It was Corey's voice, shouting at the door. She tried to answer him, but the torn slip was still in her mouth. Edwards gave no indication he had even heard Corey's voice, but kept intently after his objective.

Corey pounded on the door, and she heard the sound of other voices outside, calling to her.

She whimpered, tried to get the slip out of her mouth, but Edwards kept her from it easily. Suddenly, he eased up a bit, and Arlene seized that moment to pull her knees back, jamming them against him with all the strength she could muster. While he was momentarily off balance, she lunged at the door, her finger flicking it unlocked just as he caught her with a rage-filled surge, babbling incoherently, as the door flew open and Corey came in with two policemen, the bulk of them suddenly filling the room wonderfully. They tackled Edwards instantly, pulling him away from her, but not before he had lashed out at her with his foot. He fought them with energy inspired by madness, until one of the cops tapped him on the head with a blackjack, and Edwards slumped to the floor without another word.

Arlene took the housecoat that Corey brought her, pulling it around her bruised body gratefully, still wanting to scream, even though the terror was over, her body jerking with her attempt to keep from it, until the crying overcame her, and she put her head against Corey's chest until she was rid of it.

She told the policemen what had happened, remembering to mention the help she had sought earlier, but been unable to get.

"From what I saw, miss, they'll put him away for a long time," one of the cops told her.

"I hope so. I've been in terror for a long time."

They took Edwards away then, loading his unconscious, bulk into a prisoner's van they had summoned.

Arlene watched them drive away with a great sense of relief and salvation.

Then she fainted.

When she came to, she had been undressed and tucked into her bed. Corey was sitting beside her, holding her hand, and the first thing she saw was his concerned expression.

"Guess it was too much for me."

"That wouldn't surprise anyone."

"I'm so glad you called . . ." her voice started to break, and she stopped, controlling herself.

"Me, too. God, when I think what might have happened if I hadn't." He shook his head, understanding the closeness of the terror that had been averted. "A woman came over a little while ago from next door. Agnes, I think her name was." Arlene nodded. "When I told her I'd stay with you for a while, she said just call her when you need her."

"Good. She's a good friend."

"She said . . . she told me, your husband . . ."

"Yes."

"Oh baby, what a nightmare you've had since I saw you last."

"It's been terrible, Corey. But I think it's all right now."

"I'm gonna *make* it right."

"You're sweet."

"You *will* marry me now, won't you?"

Arlene smiled gently. "I think so, Corey. Yes . . . I think so."

"I love you so, darling."

"I love you, too, Corey. But I need a little time to think about the future. I'm so confused and mixed up right now."

"I'm sorry. I guess it's too soon to talk about anything like that, huh?"

She nodded, appreciating his understanding. "Too soon. Everything's happened so fast, so violently. I'm not sure I fully realize, emotionally, all that *has* happened, Corey. You can just digest so much at a time."

They spent the evening together, saying little. It was enough to hold hands, to know that they loved one another, and that the multitude of nightmarish happenings was past.

LOVE CAMP ON WHEELS

Tom Harland

1

A the highway, big diesel trucks headed south to Los Angeles and, below the outskirts of San Marco, the trailer park drowsed in the sweltering smell of the river, surrounding sycamores and water seeping in semistagnation through irrigation canals. Television sounds murmured down the rows of lights. At a big fifty-footer, a squeal of laughter came from a patio party and, in the dimness of the trailer that came with his job as manager of the park, Stan Barton wiped lipstick from his mouth and got a cold can of beer out of the built-in refrigerator.

He punched a couple of holes in the top. Foam bubbled, glittering wetly and, at the back of the trailer, in the sleeping area, Mae wriggled smooth bare shoulders to get out of her bra. A random reflection of light from the park slitted through drawn Venetian blinds and slanted across her sleek tan. Stan sensed her eyes probing toward him through the shadows.

She spoke his name and he grunted.

"No beer for me, hon."

"Okay."

"I never drink beer, Stan."

"Sure," he told her. "I know that."

"When I drink, I stick to bourbon."

"I remember."

"Not scotch, Hon. Just good old bourbon."

"Damn it, Mae. I heard you the first time."

"All right," Mae said. "Don't be mad."

"I'm not."

He gulped beer. Mae nagged constantly at their mutual memories but no use blowing his stack. Anyway, letting Mae ramble along about her unchanging drinking habits was a whole lot easier than having her needle him with questions about Linda Terry. Stan wiped his mouth with the back of his hand and, after a moment's silence, Mae began humming softly to herself.

The sound was part of the nagging pattern. She had always murmured snatches of melody when she stripped for him and, standing moodily in the dark, staring out through the trailer window to watch a loaded station wagon make the turn at the entrance to the park, Stan wondered if Mae went into her humming act for her new husband. Or maybe fatso and his moneybags got a different treatment. Some day, Stan thought, he and butterball Larry Higgler would have to get together and swap scientific information about Mae. Not that they had a chance of solving her bedroom impulses. Probably it would take more than one high-priced headshrinker to figure out how Mae got her kicks. To Stan she was still just the stacked bundle of sex who had married him and then divorced him—a dumb-sounding blonde with the thirty-six, twenty-three, thirty-six measurements and a stainless steel mind.

He drank more beer and Mae kept on humming. But even as he listened to her, Stan could not keep Linda out of his mind. The calm cool—yet not detached—way she had last looked at him baffled him. She was harder to figure than any woman he had known and Stan damned the trailer park business and the oddballs who infested it. Maybe he was turning into a queer cat himself, with a lesbian for a boss and letting himself become involved with a married woman like Linda Terry. He lit a cigarette and started loosening ice cubes in the sink.

Be smart, he told himself harshly. At thirty-two, he was no starry-eyed kid and, at eight hundred dollars a month, he had everything to lose and a big fat dirty nothing to gain by bucking up against Meg Taylor.

Meg owned the trailer park. She signed his paycheck every two weeks and any strange ideas she had were none of his business. If she wanted to move her latest go-go girl and her husband into the park rent-free, it was her privilege. What went on between Meg and Linda was a private arrangement. If Ben Terry stood still for the setup, why should Stan worry about Ben's wife? His job was to follow orders. If Meg wanted Linda and Ben to get special consideration, that was good enough and so, Stan thought grimly, to hell with Mrs. Ben Terry. She was just one more blue-eyed, dark-haired promise of trouble with her look of inscrutable helplessness. Lovely and trapped females were an all-American product like hardtop convertibles.

And their price came just as high.

Stan reached for the fifth of bourbon. All women had one thing to offer and he sure as hell was not going to let a swivel-hipped tease like Linda derail his gravy train. He unscrewed the cap. The bottle glittered. Whiskey brimmed and slopped over the rim of the shot glass.

"Mae," he called.

"Yes, hon?"

"Water?"

"No—" She barely paused in her humming. "Just ice."

Her voice blurred, muting to a little warm throaty crooning and, without trying to see her, Stan could visualize her stretched lazily on the bed. From the sound, he could imagine her exact state of readiness for him. He turned to her at last and the headlights of a car maneuvering in the park threw dim reflections through the trailer. Mae's blonde hair shimmered in the faint glow and her eyes were fixed on him as he neared the bed.

She touched her lips with the tip of her tongue.

"Honey."

"What is it now?"

"I'll have my drink later."

"It won't be good after the ice melts."

"I don't care."

The headlights of the car outside flicked out but Stan could still see her on the bed as if he had cat eyes. Her invitation hit his senses and memory supplied him with an image of her the darkness concealed. Her subtle perfume wove into his veins, stirring his hungers and, after putting their drinks aside, he made ready to join her.

When he came down to her, she snuggled close to him and wound her arms around his neck.

"Like me?"

"You know the answer to that."

"Remember our marriage?"

"What part?"

"You used to say I was delicious."

"You still are."

"Really, hon?"

"Yes," Stan said softly. "Really."

He kissed her and buried his face in the softness of her flesh. As his lips caressed her face and body the thought flashed through his mind that the best way to forget one woman was to make love to another. A demanding beat began to pound in his blood. *To hell with you, Mrs. Ben Terry,* was his last thought of Linda. Then nothing existed for him but Mae and the hammering pulse of their essential oneness. He had married her once—she had never let him forget it and perhaps she was right. Maybe marriage was forever as the preachers and the faithful said. . . .

He grew aware of her sudden resistance.

"Wait," she told him.

"What's wrong?"

"Nothing."

She moved away from him, rolled to the edge of the bed, reached for her drink. She sat up, a dark silhouette in the dimness of the trailer. Stan knew a familiar anger—she had been like this during their marriage, often denying him at the crucial threshold of passion. But the denial was never permanent—and it always had a reason. Stan waited.

And while he waited, the thought of Linda Terry returned like the answer to any question at all.

Not an answer he would have chosen, but that seemed to have chosen him. Had he become the kind of man who could get involved with Linda's kind of woman?

Their whole relationship was imminent, a dangerous possibility, not a thing that had happened. His thoughts recreated the instant when they had met, many weeks before.

Stan had told himself when he first took the job with Meg Taylor that he was making one hell of a good adjustment. The supervisory job he had had before, the job that had vanished, had been only a way station on the road to something better. Meg was a damned good businesswoman, in addition to other things. If he stuck it with Meg, he could still reach the big success in life that he had expected as a kid.

Then one day Ben and Linda Terry had driven into the park.

With the godlike detachment of the success he was still sure to achieve, Stan had entertained himself by studying the odd-looking pair.

Ben Terry seemed satisfied with himself, a fact to marvel at in itself. Ben looked about fifty. He was dirty, fat, powerful and at ease. An itinerant worker, Ben seemed to have no inkling of his own lowliness. He had a trailer, a shirt and pants, a woman—as far as Ben was concerned, these made him a king.

The woman knew better. She was half Ben's age, maybe younger. But she wore defeat like a Spanish shawl. Her gaze had stayed on Stan while arrangements were made for trailer space, but only from under half-lowered lids. He had had the damnedest feeling that she had wanted to tell him about herself.

It took me by surprise, he thought she wanted to tell him. *They forgot to explain when I was a kid that this is a rough world. By the time I caught on, everyone else was way ahead in the game. Do you play the game too, Stan?*

What she had said aloud, when arrangements were completed, was, "Where does the trash go?" The words were a question, not a statement—yet he had an eerie feeling that she was somehow telling a lie. He had wanted to challenge her, demand to know why she was interested in trash.

He had answered, "There's a big burning basket. You'll see it in the morning."

The fat husband grunted. The slim wife, shoulders bowed in the narrow shift she wore, said, "Thanks, Mr. Barton." She turned to the fat man. "Is there anything else I ought to ask about, Ben?"

"Ask has he got any tools to fix a window. You wanted your stuck window fixed."

"Oh, that can wait," Linda said. "It's not important." The words came out like a jeer at herself. Somewhere along the way, she had stopped insisting on anything that she wanted or needed—why?

She followed Stan outside, as though nervously unable to terminate the conversation with simple poise. "We don't ask much," she explained. "We're easy to please." Then, her gaze suddenly and disconcertingly direct, she commented, "It's been parks and camps from one end to the other. But you're the first—"

"First what?"

She made a gesture with her hands that meant, *Forget it. . . .*

"Say it," he ordered.

She was used to obeying, he guessed, to bowing to a show of force. And what did you have when a woman obeyed you—because others had trained her to do so? She looked at him once more in that half-shrewd, half-frightened way, her face uselessly beautiful, her pride nonexistent. She said, "Most people that work in trailer parks are sort of pushy. I get the feeling you've been to school a lot. I admire that."

Then she turned away. They had said nothing personal, nothing memorable—but he could not forget. Ten years ago he would never have noticed whether or not a woman like Linda was pretty. He would have been above a girl who could marry a Ben Terry.

He would not have noticed Linda except as a face in a crowd.

He was still above Linda Terry. But he had taken a downward look. And Linda had taken an upward one. They had faced each other across an invisible barrier compounded of luck. Stan meant to stay on his own side of the barrier.

His ex-wife, Mae, no matter what else she was, was no loser . . .

Now Mae sipped her bourbon. "I wasn't going to come over here, Stan."

"No?"

"I happened to stop at the park office earlier—and saw something," Mae went on. "Usually I just come over to your trailer and wait for you but Sonny and Birdie were around here hosing down the shuffleboard court and that scrunty pair always gives me the creeps. He's got eyes like a rat and she isn't much better. You ought to fire them."

"Meg likes them."

"She would."

Mae took another sip of her drink, put her glass once more on the small night table beside the bed, lay down and snuggled up to him again. Her breath smelled faintly of whiskey as she muttered that Sonny and Birdie deserved to be married to each other. Stan still waited, lying motionless beside her. He knew Sonny and Birdie were not what Mae wanted to talk about.

At last Mae mentioned Meg and Linda.

"I saw them in the office," she said.

"Doing what?"

Mae giggled. "I'll let you guess. But I'm glad I ran into them."

"Why?"

"I'm curious about the women Meg picks."

"Okay," Stan grunted. "So you saw Linda."

"She looks like a gypsy."

"Does she?"

Stan tried to cut the conversation short right there by kissing Mae. He did not want to be reminded of Linda.

Mae pulled her mouth away. "She's too thin to be pretty, Stan."

"All right."

"I wonder why Meg went for her?"

"Damn it," Stan said. "Ask Meg."

He rolled over on his back and stared up into the hot darkness of the trailer. Outside, a car passed—its sound receded toward the far end of the park while Mae kept on talking about Meg and Linda.

"I guess they call it love."

"Sure," Stan said slowly. "I guess they do."

"And her husband must know all about it. The way Meg talked about Linda, they must have been seeing each other for at least a month now. You heard Meg, Stan. She moved them out of that other trailer park across town and brought them over here. They don't pay rent, I've heard—and probably she's paying all the rest of their bills too." Mae paused for a moment. Finally she asked, "Stan, what kind of man would let his wife do what Linda is doing?"

"You saw him, Mae."

"He looked just like anybody else."

"Maybe he is."

Stan felt himself sweating, probably not altogether from the heat. Damn it, he did not want to think about Meg or Ben any more than about Linda. To hell with them all—especially her. Nobody just met a woman and said hello and got it right between the eyes. That kind of crap was all in the mind. He had about sold himself on the idea that what he felt for Linda was some kind of juvenile reversion when Mae suddenly made one of her shrewd shots in the dark.

"Stan," she said softly. "You'd better be careful."

"About what?"

"About getting involved with Meg's woman."

"Linda?"

"Yes, hon," Mae whispered. "And don't sound so startled. Remember, Stan? Way back when we were married you told me

I had the hard instincts of a professional whore. Maybe you were right, darling—at least I have a sixth sense about you."

"You're crazy."

"Am I?"

"Yes—this time you are."

He turned to her and his kiss smothered her further efforts to speak. He used his arms and hands to crush and coax the resistance from her. He felt as if he had to prove something to himself and maybe he did.

"Mae," he whispered.

"Let me go."

"No," he said. "Not this time."

His arms tightened and gradually she melted. Once more her arms twined about his neck and she moved to meet him.

"Stan," she murmured.

"Go on," he muttered. "Say it."

"You're a big homely bastard."

"Are you sorry you walked out on me?"

"Sometimes, hon."

"Like now?"

"Yes," she murmured. "Like now."

She shivered and became his fully—as she often had been. Long moments came when he knew that nothing existed for her save their union—when she had no other husband and worried about no other woman for him.

They had always, he remembered, had the knack of possessing each other, knowing each other fully at these intimate times, no matter what happened during the periods between.

"Stan," she gasped.

By way of answer he kissed her.

"Never stop loving me."

Her words wormed through what he felt for her—they made him think and wonder, though he had wanted to do neither. He was disturbed. What did she mean by love? When she had left him he had thought he knew the answer. He had pigeonholed her in his mind as a woman who considered love a commodity—something that, if not actually for sale, was to be traded for security, more economic safety than he could provide . . .

And once more, even as he held Mae in his arms, even as each of them rediscovered mutual fulfillment, a vision of Linda—her eyes silent, trapped and questioning—intruded upon his awareness.

He was dimly alarmed at finding himself thinking of one woman while making love to another—was he losing touch with reality? He tried to shut his mind to Linda Terry and could not.

There had been a search for security also behind her silently questioning gaze.

Once his instinct would have been to protect, to reassure. He had enjoyed being kind. Big Stan Barton to the rescue, had been the cry. Sometimes it was his team that needed him. He had been a football hero.

Years ago, while he was still in school, the girls had cried on his shoulder in trouble real or contrived. Faith in himself had made him a multimillionaire. He could give away worlds and systems, have more left to draw from.

These days he was poorer, afraid to give away a downward look.

2

The valley was wide, flat and sheltered from the Pacific by the mountains. The land was some of the richest in California. Where the river spilled into the ocean were artichoke farms but farther inland lettuce was the big crop.

Under a blazing summer sun, work gangs of sweating Mexican braceros thinned down endless rows with short-handled hoes. Day and night, big diesel and electric rigs pumped irrigation water into muddy ditches. Huge field machines mechanized a dozen complicated operations so that they could be performed simultaneously—these very machines had automated Stan Barton into the trailer park business and out of seven years of seniority with a local lettuce shipping corporation.

Stan still remembered the morning his boss had called him in for the bad news.

"We're shutting down all our packing sheds, Stan."

"No more hand labor?"

"That's right. No more picking and hauling and stripping and icing. Methods are changing here just as they are everywhere else. These new machines not only do the whole operation but lower costs and increase efficiency. From now on the stuff will be processed in one continuous mechanical handling and go right from the fields to the railroad and trucking lines."

"A lot of people will lose their jobs."

"Sure, Stan. But it's happening all over."

"That's not much help."

"No, I guess not. But we'll retrain as many employees as we can."

"But not packing shed bosses?"

"No, Stan. Not packing shed bosses: To retrain you we'd have to demote you and you wouldn't be happy."

And that had been it. A machine had taken his job and he had started cashing unemployment checks. Some of the old gang had gone back to field work. A few of the younger kids with suitable educations moved past the old-timers into the company's retraining program. At thirty, Stan had found himself both over the age limit and with an educational background not suited to company policies.

For a little while, he had tried selling used cars but had soon found out that peddling jalopies was not a business to be learned in a day, a week or a few months. His sales had been too far and few between and, one Saturday, he had faced another lost-job interview.

"I'm sorry, Stan."

"Don't worry, Al. I understand."

Al, who ran the used-car agency, was his friend but friendship had its limitations.

"It just isn't your racket."

"Sure, Al. I found that out."

They had smoked a cigarette. A little later, at a bar across the street, they had had a few rounds of beer. Finally Al had mentioned Mae.

"Maybe she could help you, Stan."

"No, thanks."

"You two were married once."

"Sure, Al. We were young—she was a doll and I was a football hero. Once upon a time things like that cut a lot of ice but ice grows cold to live on. When big money didn't follow the glory, Mae decided she had made a mistake. Probably she was right.

At least, she married a load of dough when she married Larry Biggler."

"Well, Stan, I still see Mae—she drives over from Monterey every week or so and, even if I am getting my nose out of joint by talking to you about her, I want to tell you it never hurts to use old contacts. Larry Biggler swings a lot of weight all over the Coast. Probably Mae can get him to do pretty much what she wants him to and, in a situation like this, he might be able to do you some good. You're a good man, just temporarily misplaced. Larry might know just the spot that's waiting for you."

"He might."

"But you still don't want his help?"

"No, Al. I don't."

"You're crazy."

"Okay, Al. Maybe I am."

Stan had stalled the discussion at that point but a week later Al had phoned Stan the tip that had gotten Stan the manager's job at the trailer park.

"This is a break for you, Stan."

"Sure, Al. I know."

"I gave you my recommendation."

"Thanks, Al."

"Just treat Meg right and she'll treat you right."

Al had added that Meg Taylor was a lesbian but that she was also a beautiful natural redhead and not inhibited by her tastes in business deals. At thirty-five, she looked twenty-five. She did not consider herself in competition with men—what she offered women was all woman, without taint of perverted masculinity. Her hair was burnished copper. Her legs were long and slender. She wore high high heels and flesh-colored nylons and sheath dresses and her hips were full and wide—a woman's hips. She was slim and her bosom looked inviting. She had seemed anything but a deviate to Stan at their first meeting.

"So you're Stan," she had said, studying him.

"That's right."

"Al said you were big."

Her odd, almond eyes had looked right at him, without reserve but also without giving him a sense of intrusion. Later, after discussing his previous job experience and showing him around the trailer park, Meg had crossed her legs, smoked a cigarette and talked frankly about herself.

"Do you know about me, Stan?"

"Only what Al told me."

"Are you surprised?"

"A little."

"Did you expect a flat chest and a butch cut?"

"Maybe."

He kept his answers short and straightforward—and had found that he liked her. She seemed to like him. They had had a couple of drinks and Meg had gone over the ground rules of the park. With an average of a hundred trailers constantly in the park, the business grossed between thirty-five hundred and four thousand dollars a month. Space rent, depending on the size of the trailer, varied from thirty to forty-five dollars a month and the vacancy rate depended on making and keeping the park attractive to permanent tenants. Any brawls, fights or noisy drunks cut into immediate profits and lowered her chances to up the property in value and make a long term capital gain.

"You see what I mean, Stan?"

He nodded. "I understand."

"Then you'll realize I'm not worried about trailer park experience," Meg explained. "I have an accounting firm to do my books and take care of my other investments. Sonny and Birdie Shedley have been here for two years. He does the yard work and the heavy cleaning. Birdie works on the registration desk. Any other seasonal help is easy enough to hire but I need a man who can take charge and see that the park is run quietly and efficiently." She had paused briefly to tell him why the man she had just fired had not been able to fill the bill—he had intruded on the privacy of some of the paying customers. "But," Meg had finished slowly, "I think you can handle the job, Stan."

"I'll do my best."

They had agreed on terms and, from that first day, Stan had had no complaints. Meg paid well. She trusted him. Outside of suggesting he keep Sonny and Birdie on the payroll, Meg had let Stan run the place as he wanted. She was not afraid to put money into improvements. A good idea got a fast go sign from Meg. She was loyal, honest and direct in business and soon let him know there was a place for him in her future expansion plans. From a beginning five hundred a month, his salary had risen steadily to eight hundred and, until Meg had moved Ben and Linda Terry into the trailer park, Stan had figured he had the world by the tail.

He still tried to figure things so.

Linda Terry had to be just a slut.

Figure it out. She was married and making out with Meg at the same time. A man would have to be out of his mind to take a second look at her. Talk about damaged goods. Mae was right too. Linda was not especially pretty and even if she had been, he was no dewy eyed kid. The world was full of willing women and he no longer expected a ticket to cloud nine.

Anyway, he had a job to do. There were rents to be collected and squabbles to be settled. A new unit Meg was building needed almost constant supervision.

Following Mae's last visit, Stan let Sonny do any work that had to be done around the Terry trailer but on the following Wednesday, during Sonny's night off, Linda came down to the office to say that a fuse had blown in her trailer.

"I hate to bother you," she said.

"That's all right."

He got a box of fuses while Linda told him Ben was up in town. He got Maggie Adams, a fat little woman who paid her rent by filling in for Birdie, to come to the desk to tend to the telephone.

At the door, on his way out, Stan brushed against Linda and she looked up at him.

"I'm sorry to trouble you like this."

"I'm here to keep things running."

He tried a grin and talked about the weather and the heat but by the time they got to her trailer his tensions were in full swing. His throat felt tight, his legs rubbery. While he was fumbling for the trailer's fuse box in the dark, Linda pressed close to him.

"Right there," she said.

"Okay."

Stan got the fuse in. Lights came on and he turned. His back was against the rim of the trailer sink and he looked down at Linda. Her dark hair was brushed damply away from her cheeks and he remembered Mae's telling him Linda looked like a gypsy. All right, she looked like a gypsy. He blinked against a strange illusion that he was seeing all of her at once and intimately. Not only the full curve of her mouth, the clean lines of her cheeks and nose and the throb of a pulse at her throat but all of her—even beyond what was covered by the flimsy summer dress she wore. He had a sudden awareness of her whole personality with all its problems and complexes and deep within her he once more sensed a call for help. He was afraid to move and light in the trailer blurred. A hard twist of tension spiraled down into the pit of his stomach.

Suddenly Linda shivered too.

"Stan—"

"Huh?"

"You've been avoiding me."

"Yes." He nodded numbly. "I guess I have."

A moment passed and he knew as surely as if she had told him that she had deliberately blown the fuse. His hand rose to touch her face.

Bitch, he thought bitterly.

Suddenly she shook her head, jerked back from his hand.

"No," she said. "Don't."

"Didn't you want me here?"

"Yes," she whispered. "But I was wrong." Her voice trembled and she clenched her hand. "Please," she said harshly. "Go away, Stan. You'd better hurry and get out of here."

3

"Darling," Meg said.

Linda turned on the king-sized bed. She said nothing.

"Do you like it at the trailer park?"

"Yes." Linda nodded. "Ben and I are all settled."

"How are you getting along with Stan?"

"Just fine."

"He told me he had to fix a fuse for you the other night."

"That's right, Meg. He did."

Linda stretched on the soft mattress. Red-shaded light darkened to soft crimson shadows at the far corners of the room but at the edge of the bed, where Meg sat smoking, it glinted hotly in her thick red hair and gleamed on her smooth bare shoulders. In the confines of the apartment the warm night air held the fragrance of dusting powder and eau de cologne.

Linda tried to force herself to stop thinking about Stan.

She moistened her lips and turned her head toward the window. Outside, across the street in the San Marco city park, an old humpbacked Sicilian was playing an Italian melody on his accordion. The familiar sound rose and fell against the light hum of night traffic but all that really mattered to Linda was that Meg should not continue to talk about Stan. She waited, listening to the music, attempting to erase all memory of Stan by conjuring up an image of the old Italian as she had sometimes seen him during previous visits to Meg's town apartment.

When Meg said nothing for a while, the little hurt of tension left Linda's throat and she relaxed. She looked up at Meg and Meg reached out a warm hand and softly stroked Linda's sleek waist.

"It's nice here too, Meg," Linda murmured.

"Then leave Ben and come to stay for good."

"I can't."

"Why not?"

"Please, Meg. I just can't."

Linda shut her eyes and tried not to listen to Meg. Talking about Ben or to Ben never got her anywhere. Her thoughts about Ben revolved in endless circles and no amount of inward searching could ever touch the beginning again or take her back home to the wind and dust of the Sacramento rice fields or that sun-blasted Ishi courthouse wedding. Being young and leaning on Ben's being older and presumably wiser than she was something she no longer could believe. Nor would arguments ever make him let her go. His wife was his to own. With a shiver, Linda opened her eyes.

Meg put out her cigarette and looked down.

"Darling, Linda," she whispered.

"That sounds nice."

"You're beautiful."

"No, please. Don't say that."

"Does it scare you?"

"Yes," Linda said softly. "I guess it does."

She held her breath against the teasing, tantalizing motion of Meg's moving hand and knew a small throbbing sense of guilt.

She wanted to tell Meg to stop but then her memory washed back all the trailer camps and farms and ranches and harvests and threshing crews and sweltering nights and roadhouses and beer brawls she had lived through. She remembered Ben in his sick, stumbling drunks and she remembered his sweat and pawing and the bruises on her mouth from being hit.

Ugly years came back, cramped and dirty and lonely and all men blurred into Ben, pinching and hurting and clumsy. From the first night she had met Meg, Meg had been sweet and clean and gentle. Her money had bought Ben's drinks and, once he figured out what Meg wanted meant no work for him and free rent, drinking credit and loans that never had to be repaid, he made everything easy and convenient.

"Linda," he had said. "Be nice to Meg."

"Do you know what she is?"

"I know."

"And you don't care?"

Linda remembered Ben's lifting a drink. He had not answered her and to this night she did not know just how he felt. But he stayed out of her bed. Maybe he had that arrangement, too, with Meg and suddenly Linda did not care. Being warm and petted and loved had a goodness that did not need explaining. A hot, melting sensation made her feel weak. Breath quickened in her throat. She shut her mind to Stan. He was like Ben and the others. Men had only hurt her.

"Meg?"

"Yes, darling."

"Remember that first night we were together?"

"I'll never forget."

Linda murmured, "Neither will I."

Her voice trembled and she stirred under Meg's touch. She still was in touch with reality. She heard, from outside, the sounds of traffic, the distant shunting of a freight at the depot and on the sidewalk footsteps crossed cement. The music had stopped. From down below, on the first floor of the building, came the faint, muffled sound of a door slamming. A swift hot pulse began to pound in Linda's ears. She felt boneless and limp and sleek and reveling in luxury as she raised her hands to caress her own breasts.

"You little witch," Meg murmured.

She stretched out beside Linda. Warmth crushed to warmth. Red hair fell in a silken shower and Meg pressed her lips to Linda's. Meg's hand came up to cup Linda's breast. Slim delicate fingers caressed and squeezed and Linda moaned softly.

"Not too hard, Meg."

"Hurt?"

"A little."

"Want me to stop?"

"No," Linda said shamelessly. "Don't stop."

She closed her eyes and hugged Meg but turned her head away. Meg suddenly released her, pulled away.

"Okay," she said.

"What's the matter?"

"Just go to hell, baby."

"But why?"

"I'm tired of fighting for it."

Meg rolled away from Linda and started to get up. She crouched and small burning flecks of light pinpointed angrily in her eyes.

Her voice was thin and hard. "I fall in love with the damnedest people."

"Don't say that, Meg."

"Shall I take you home?"

"No, Meg."

"Then you want to stay?"

"Yes," Linda whispered. "I want to stay."

She swallowed and stared at Meg. Blood beat in her throat and her thinking became nakedly sensual. Maybe, she thought miserably, once you started, you could never stop. Perhaps Meg had more of a hold on her than the horrible alternative of Ben. Her mind blurred to flesh and its wants—to pleasurable satiation as opposed to loneliness and pain.

"Meg," she murmured brokenly.

"Have you changed your mind?"

"Yes," Linda whispered. "I want you."

"Are you going to turn away again?"

"No," Linda promised abjectly.

Her lips quivered. She reached up tentatively to stroke Meg and suddenly the last shred of Linda's pride crumbled.

"Meg," she pleaded.

"What, baby?"

"Love me."

"Say please."

"All right, Meg. Please—"

She nearly choked on the begging words—then she was past thinking. A helpless need to be cherished blurred her vision. She wanted to be held and hugged and kissed. As Meg came back to her, Linda's voice blurred to sobs but she could not control the violent responses that sent tremor after tremor rippling down into a vortex of molten heat. She hugged Meg helplessly and gritted her teeth. Darkness entered her eyes but, even in the final explosive release, she found a lonely emptiness.

She remembered, moments later, how she had felt walking with Stan and her reaction in the trailer when he almost touched her. Now that Meg had finished with her, she felt free to think of Stan—in fact, something forced her to remember Stan.

She looked up at Meg out of a deep and tired and exhausted well of shame.

Meg murmured, "You were wonderful."

"I'm glad, Meg."

"But are you happy, darling?"

"Yes," Linda lied. "I'm happy, Meg."

The lie was not a difficult one for Linda—the words "happy" and "happiness" had curious connotations for her. She had been almost twenty before she learned, literally, their real meaning. Before that, she had assumed they referred to surrender, abnegation of rights, passive acceptance of indignity great or small.

Once she had had parents—what had become of them she no longer knew. Later she had been a ward of the state. There had been a series of foster homes and foster parents, some tolerable, some just plain nuts. The nuttiest had been the Haleys. They had also been the most conscientious.

When Linda had been ten, Sophie Haley, a disappointed actress, had insisted that Linda learn and recite long monologues from Shakespeare by heart. In the house where Linda had stayed before, she had been given to understand that in fair exchange for the family's hospitality, she was to do all the cleaning. She had assumed that learning that junk by heart was a similar payment.

"Of course not," Sophie Haley had stated indignantly, when Linda sought to establish the contract. "I don't ask you to learn for my sake, but for your own. I don't want you to recite like a parrot, I want you to be happy to recite. Now are you happy, Linda?"

"I'm happy." Linda had yielded, privately thinking that it sure was hell to be happy—and when she was grown up and free, she would never have to be happy again.

4

Heat was the norm in the valley. Even when the rains came they brought no really cold weather. Winters were short, wet, sloppy and river-fogged. Then the hills baked again to a parched brown and the thermometer hovered steadily around or over the hundred mark.

By July the sizzling cement road past the trailer camp was too hot to touch. Midday traffic broiled in the sun. Ice cream drive-ins and orange juice stands stayed open late but work in the lettuce and vegetable fields and at the railroad sidings never stopped. Under a glare of lights, loading went on all night, bringing a summer rush, too, to the trailer park.

Heavy equipment operators and skilled field labor moved up from the Imperial Valley. There was a steady business in overnight tourists and, in addition, during the first blistering week of the month, Stan worked and sweated right along with his hired crew to connect the hookups to the new units.

Late one Wednesday afternoon, the gang finished ditching in all the lateral sewer lines. Stan and the contractor went over changes Stan wanted to make in some of the plans until dark. Later, after checking at the office with Birdie to see that everything was going all right, Stan took a shower, changed clothes and drove to town to eat. He stopped at a bar for a cold beer and, on his way back to the park, he spotted Linda waiting for a bus at the stop in front of the movie theater.

Stan put his foot on the brake but before he pulled his blue Ford convertible over to the curb to give her a ride, he hesitated. Nobody had to go looking for trouble. That was for sure and, any way the cookie crumbled, Linda stood to do him no good. At the very least, the odds were stacked against him, considering her relationships with Ben and Meg. Either he got a not too bright husband on his back or he took a big chance of lousing up a good job.

Stan told himself grimly to be smart. He had a good, profitable arrangement and his life to run. After scratching around where the scratching was thin, he intended to keep things as they were. During the two weeks since he had visited her trailer to fix her blown-for-the-occasion fuse, he had been wise enough to keep his distance. A casual good morning or a few words about the weather had been all the contact he had had with her. And there would be no profit in abandoning that routine now.

He was about to drive on past her when he realized Linda had already recognized his white-topped blue convertible. And suddenly he was angry at himself.

To hell with dodging and ducking around a corner. So she looked like a gypsy and might have some weird ideas about what made some things go—but he was not a kid and she had no hex on him. Let her wiggle that fanny. She was just another woman. She had nothing he had not seen before and anyway, since they both lived at the park, he could not go on avoiding her forever. Sooner or later, he might just as well weed out the nutty idea that she was something special.

But when he stopped and she got in beside him, arranged her skirt over her nylon-sleek knees, sat primly with her purse in her lap and looked at him, his chest tightened.

"Almost missed you," he said.

"Did you?"

She kept staring at him and Stan's grin grew stiff. But he told himself he would be damned if he would turn his head. Let her look. Then, for what seemed to be a long time, he could think of nothing to say and felt idiotic.

Finally she thanked him for stopping.

"No trouble," he told her. "I'm headed home anyway."

"You're sure?"

She had the damnedest way of asking questions, Stan thought, and not only out loud. She paused and he felt her eyes waiting again and, though he still avoided looking at her, Stan was barely conscious of the night people on the street. A gang of T-shirted teenagers scuffled across the sidewalk to the theater box office. A girl squealed and voices and sounds blurred to the hot hum of night traffic and Stan's anger at himself grew.

He eased the car into the fast traffic lane.

"Busy night," he managed.

"I guess it's like this all summer."

"That's right," Stan nodded.

He tailed a cut-down hotrod full of kids until it lost him. He and Linda discussed the heat. They agreed the rare cool nights were pleasant and, Stan thought, he was really pitching a great line. It had just the right touch of nothing. He and Linda Terry were just a pair of trailer park neighbors heading for home.

At a red light Stan fished in his shirt pocket for cigarettes. He offered her one.

"Thanks." She turned a little and her skirt rustled. He thumbed his lighter and she leaned toward him and tilted up her face. The light of the flame glowed in her eyes and glistened on her lips. She inhaled. When the light changed and Stan had the car in motion again, she put her head back and seemed to close her eyes.

"This is nice," she murmured at last.

"Just riding?"

"Yes," she said softly. "Just riding."

Her eyes stayed shut. She pulled so hard on her cigarette that its tip glowed hot. After several long moments, she turned to glance at him.

"Tell me something," she said.

"What do you want to know?"

"Don't you like to have the top down?"

"Sometimes," Stan said. "Why?"

"Nothing really. I just wondered."

He doubted the question represented what she really wondered about. She leaned back again. A wisp of hair got caught by the airstream and vibrated against her smooth cheek. She tucked it back into place.

Stan asked if she had gone to the movie alone.

She took a deep breath and frowned.

"Yes," she said at last.

"Where's Ben?"

"I don't know," Linda answered slowly. "He and Sonny went somewhere together."

"I didn't know they were buddies."

"Didn't you?"

Linda finished her cigarette without saying more. Stan had the cynical notion that, just to wind up his questions logically he ought to ask how she happened to be missing a night with Meg. Then, just as quickly, he dropped the idea. Where Linda crawled into bed was a big fat nothing to him and, changing the subject, he started talking about the construction job at the park and how late they had finished work.

"So I came to town to eat."

"Lucky for me."

"You might have picked up a ride anyway."

"But not with you."

Her head turned toward him again. A moment of silence crept by. Again Stan could feel her eyes waiting, asking, but he kept watching the road and let her remark pass unanswered. Maybe it meant something, maybe it did not but, in either case, her luck and his did not add up to the same thing. Finally, easing back to safer ground again, he continued talking about getting the new park units into operation.

"Right now," he said, "time is money."

"But you like that kind of work."

"I guess you're right," Stan admitted.

He grinned and told her he had a strong back. For a moment he thought back to many hot summers in the packing sheds before the sorting and grading became mechanized. He told her about them and next about how he had goofed in the used-car business. While he talked he tried to figure out what there was about her that kept getting to him.

Maybe, he thought, it had something to do with glands or chemicals because she was sure as hell not the greatest looker he had ever seen. If she were to oppose Mae in a beauty contest, Mae would likely win on a voice vote. On the other hand, Mae had been catty when she had said that Linda was too thin to be pretty.

Slim was a better word because, where it counted, Linda had all she needed. Her legs were long, straight and, from what he could tell, well formed. And, while her breasts were not big league, neither were they insignificant.

Appraising her in such terms, Stan began to feel hot and bothered again. He wet his lips and glued his gaze to the road. He told himself to stop acting as if he had rocks for brains. Of all the women in the world he did not need, Linda was number one. Maybe, he thought, he was just being sandbagged with the old stolen-fruit routine. He doubted that she would taste any sweeter for being stolen from a couple of oddballs like Meg and Ben—but when she mentioned a cool drink as they turned into the trailer park, he decided to go for the long ball.

Her voice held a warm, throbbing huskiness and Stan figured that patting her fanny was the best way to get the magic out of the moonlight. He parked and walked her under the patio awning and to the door of her dark trailer. As if accidentally he brushed against her and touched his hand to her leg.

"Sorry," he said.

"Are you?" Linda whispered bitterly.

She whirled to look up at him. Her eyes flashed and in the shadowy reflections her face showed anger. From another trailer came a muted spatter of canned television laughter. Near the laundry rooms someone walked behind a bobbing flashlight. In the darkness under her own sheltering awning, Linda stood taut with her slim back to the trailer. Her breasts heaved.

She spat out angrily, "No—you're not sorry."

"You could be wrong."

"Not about this."

Her mouth trembled.

"Nobody has to tell me." Her voice retained an edge of harsh mockery. "You've got it all worked out. I'm a no-good bitch—and please don't make it worse by trying to tell me I don't know what I'm talking about. I've been in and out of every migratory camp in California and, believe me, there are no dirty words I haven't heard or any dirty names some man hasn't called me. So don't be backward. Go right ahead and tell me I'm a whore and a cheap little chippy and a pig and a queer and round-heeled. Who the hell do I think I am to get proud because you want to cop a feel?"

"Listen," Stan tried to say, "I—"

"Oh, hell," Linda interrupted. "Don't apologize. I've been pawed before. Go ahead and get your hands up under my dress. Nobody else was ever shy about trying to get a little but maybe I've been had too many times to interest you." She paused and stared. "Well—don't be afraid to ask. Do you want it or don't you?"

Her lips stayed parted. Moisture glistened on the dark curve of her mouth and Stan breathed heat and closeness and warm woman-fragrance. He moved to a pounding beat that wavered between anger and small, licking explosions of flame. His hands lifted to her arms. He shoved her to the side of the trailer and her head went way back so that he could look down into the front of her dress.

"Go on," she spat. "Look."

"Shut up," Stan said.

"Shall I take my bra off?"

"Damn it," Stan told her again. "Shut up."

"Go ahead," she said. "Kiss me."

Her eyes half closed. A tremor rippled through her. She swallowed and suddenly her arms flew up to twine around his neck.

"Stan," she murmured.

Her breath was hot and moist against his mouth. She tightened her arms, pulled his lips to her and made a small straining moan in her throat.

"Stan—"

Her body molded to his—her firm breasts crushed against his chest. Her mouth moved hungrily under his.

A car passed them slowly. Its headlights flickered through a shifting procession of shadows and, for a silently explosive moment, spotlighted Stan and Linda in a clinging kiss. Gears rasped as the car completed its turn and somewhere somebody laughed. Stan was jolted back to awareness of where he was and what he was doing. Anger and alarm raced through him like heat lightning and he jerked his mouth away from Linda's.

He blinked against the sting of perspiration. The night stopped spinning. As if he had been down in a deep well, he sucked fresh air into his lungs. Although he knew only a few minutes had passed since he and Linda had stopped, it seemed a thousand years had passed. He stood stripped of sense and reason.

He reached behind his neck to grasp Linda's wrists. Her hands were locked in a surprisingly strong grip.

Muscles set hard across his shoulders as he strove to break free without hurting her. He thought numbly, *I ought to have my head examined . . . talk about picking them . . .*

He shoved her away from him and she stumbled a little and sagged against the trailer.

"Stan," she gasped.

"No, thanks," he said harshly. "No sale."

He turned to stride away, wondering who had seen them in that brief spotlight. He hoped it had been one of the transient park visitors. If the passing motorist had been one of the regulars, the story could be all over the park by morning.

5

In midafternoon, the next day, Ben Terry came down to where the new trailer spaces were being laid out. He crossed an open utility ditch and stood off to one side while a big, lumbering, dirt-caked diesel roared and lurched into position to pour ready-mixed concrete. Working in the glare of the blazing sun, a gang sweated and manhandled the metal trough to the first of the patio slab forms.

The foreman yelled and motioned with his hands to get the angle he wanted and, right then, during the brief lull in sound before the pouring started, Ben walked over to Stan. He nodded and, with a paunchy grunt, hitched at his khakis.

"Howdy, Stan."

"Hi, Ben."

"Pretty warm, ain't it?"

"It's warm all right," Stan agreed.

He waited, his gaze slanted guardedly at Ben. His evening before with Linda was vivid in his mind and he wondered what Ben had heard and what the fat man wanted to do about it. He did not think Ben had come to look over the job—Ben was the type to do his kibitzing at a bar over a cold beer. Besides, for a split second, Stan thought he saw something hard and thin and calculating in Ben's eyes.

Stan decided to hold tight. Again Ben cursed the heat. He breathed heavily and mopped his forehead, twisted to shove his handkerchief back into his hip pocket. Khaki fabric stretched and strained. Around Ben's middle, a roll of fat bulged over his belt and, at his unbuttoned shirt collar, thick black tufts of chest hair matted damply. Perspiration soaked his armpits. Moisture gleamed in the wet creases of his beefy neck and Stan found himself wondering what about Ben had ever seemed attractive enough to Linda to make her marry him.

Or did they just plain deserve each other? She sure as hell worked both sides of the street. Probably she had done about everything there was to do with other men, too.

Still, Ben was a homely bastard. His teeth were stained and broken. His mouth and nose were too big and his squinty eyes too small. His coarse gray-black hair was still thick but there were bags under his eyes and his skin was fleshy and porous. He had to be more than twenty years older than Linda. His jowls were beginning to sag but, in spite of the potbelly and all the extra lard, he might not be nearly as soft as he looked.

His bones were big and, with powerful shoulders, he was built to carry weight. Chances were, he could manage to do a lot of dirty fighting too. But, even conceding that under all his blubber he packed a big slug of solid muscle, he seemed hardly the kind of hot-shot lover to end up with a sultry babe like Linda.

But, of course, it was perfectly possible that Ben had hidden talents. Although Stan's mind did not conjure up a pretty picture, Ben might be a real dreamboat between the sheets. The idea was hard to square with the Linda-and-Meg equation—but all things considered, when it came to a pair like Ben and Linda, no set of answers was likely ever to come out exactly even.

Machinery rumbled. The gang had started pouring concrete. Ben seemed as good at stalling as Stan and finally Stan decided it was his move. He fished cigarettes out of his shirt pocket, walked slowly away from the noise to the shade of some sycamores. Ben followed him. Stan turned to face the fat man.

"Well, Ben—don't see you down this way very much."

"No," Ben answered slowly. "That's right Stan. I guess you don't." He paused to reach down and pluck a blade of grass. Rolling the slender green thoughtfully between his blunt thumb and stubby forefinger, he continued in the same slow drawl: "Of course, I got to figuring it would only be neighborly for me to take the time to thank you."

"Thank me?"

"That's right."

"For what?"

"Why, for last night, Stan." Ben nodded. "Linda was mighty obliged to you for riding her home from the movie. Ain't everybody so accommodating." Ben paused to shift his boots in the dry dust. He glanced up for an instant. Hard pinpoints of light gleamed between his slitted eyelids. He blinked and licked his lips, then went back to studying his blade of grass. "We talked about it when I got home," he continued. "Linda told me you were real nice about picking her up."

"I was glad to do it," Stan said carefully.

"Sure you were."

Ben looked up again and Stan started to sweat under his shirt. Damn the fat bastard anyway. He obviously knew something—but how much? Stan's anger mounted but most of it was directed at himself. Nobody, he told himself bitterly, had put a monkey on his back. He had sure as hell had his chance to stay in the clear. Last night, he could have let Linda go right on standing there on the curb in front of the movie theater. Let the bus company earn a few dimes should have been his fadeout and exit thought.

And even after he had picked her up, he had had no federal instructions to walk her to her door. All he had needed to do at that point was to stop long enough at her trailer to let her out. Nothing else. Probably, in her round-heeled career, she had hit the road plenty of times a lot farther from home than those few steps.

The odds were that she had expected him to take her anywhere but home. He had nobody to blame for having been caught with her but himself. No guns had been rammed in his back. He might as well admit the simple truth—he had been curious about her and not satisfied until he had pushed his luck too far.

Okay, so now he knew. A ride home could ring the bell. Or just breathe on her but, he thought angrily, at his age, he should have been able to read the signs without having to handle the merchandise. After all, part of his job was to handle the dynamite potential of a trailer park, where opportunity and availability were hardly ever very far apart. If some willing doll had it up for grabs, she always managed to make the arrangements—he had simply blundered blindly into a completely unnecessary situation and one he would have condemned anywhere on the park property.

There was a grapevine of information that never failed and on many occasions he himself had suggested a rubber-tired solution to situations similar to the one that now existed between himself and Ben. Somebody simply hitched up and trailed his rig and his wife to another park—but in this particular instance no simple answers could apply. Neither he nor Ben were ready to leave.

Just what did Ben know? Stan asked a few careful questions about Linda. How did she feel today? Did she like living in the park? Ben gave him noncommittal answers that told him nothing he really wanted to know. Maybe Ben had nothing to tell him—then again, perhaps the fat man knew he had Stan in a corner as long as nothing broke out into the open.

Stan turned away from the man and had to squint to shut out a brilliant glare of the sun that flashed off the windshield of the cement truck. The driver held the door out and leaned out of the cab to back around to a new position. Heat waves rose from the diesel's exhaust. A sledge started driving a form-bracing stake into the ground and Stan found the rhythmic pound of the hammer matching his thoughts.

Keep fooling around with a walking, talking, hip-swinging bundle of dynamite like Linda and he would not just have Ben nosing around. Before the dust really got stirred up, he would have Meg on his neck too—and when it came to worrying about Ben or Meg, Meg came first.

Abruptly Ben said, "By the way, I sure do hope we don't have no trouble around here."

He squinted at Stan.

"What are you getting at, Ben?"

"I think you know, Stan." Ben nodded slowly. "I'm sure you do."

Stan had a jolting image of himself, engulfed in a quagmire so profound that it included the enmity of Ben Terry. Ben Terry should have been a stranger to him. They should have lived in different worlds.

Where the hell had he lost the way, taken the downward turn?

Was it all the fault of automation?

He knew better than that. There had to have been a flaw in him from the start, a proclivity for failure.

Maybe that was what Linda had recognized in him. Maybe from the first the barrier between her bad luck and Stan's good luck had been flimsier than he knew. But Linda had known.

6

Later that same night, in the hot bedroom of the apartment behind the trailer park office, Birdie Shedley sat on the edge of the bed wearing only her flesh-colored nylon panties and matching bra. She pushed her fingers up into her short mousy hair, then brought her hands down slowly over her small high breasts and her boy-slender hips. At last, with a thoughtful expression, she began rubbing her thighs.

She knew Sonny was really mad. Nobody had to put it on television when he got hot under the collar. Birdie frowned and listened to the angry slamming sounds from the kitchen.

She took a deep breath and half closed her eyes. Big, she thought—the big know-it-all man—but, if he had so many brains, why hadn't he told Stan some of the things he had been telling her? Damn it, asking for an extra day off needed no act of Congress. Anybody with an ounce of good sense should have been able to get a yes answer out of Stan. So Stan had been in a bad mood about something when Sonny had gone over to talk to him. It should have made no difference. Stan was still a nice big easy-going guy. Just tell him that any work that got missed would be picked up later during the off hours. A nitwit would be able to be honest about a promise like that but not Sonny.

Hell, no. He had to go at everything with a chip on his shoulder. Maybe little men hated the world and all the big men in it—not that some did not deserve being hated. Ben Terry, for example. Him and his fat hands. No matter how she tried to keep out of his way, he always managed to touch her. Birdie shivered. Ben gave her the creeps but now Sonny had an idea that something Ben had told him could help Sonny get Stan's job. A fat chance Sonny had. He was all talk. All mouth but he was mean too. If anybody knew him, she did. When he hit her, he meant to hurt. Probably putting bruises on her made him feel like he weighed two hundred and stood six feet tall instead of being five-seven and a hundred and thirty-five—but what he did to her did not change him. He might be tough and strong and wiry but he was still little. And he was little all over—inside and out. Birdie blinked. Maybe knowing his smallness was what made him touchy.

Much would have been possible had Sonny been more of a man. He dreamed and schemed and plotted to take away Stan Barton's job. A bigger man would have dreamed of taking over Meg Taylor's trailer park. Most of the time nothing came of dreams and plans. But no one charged you extra for the large ones.

Her brain was not a giant thing, but it served her size of ambition. She daydreamed lazily over the things she knew about Meg Taylor that could do Meg harm. That was one advantage of Birdie's job—she got to know a lot about people. She had vague ideas of some day using the knowledge.

People came and went, leaving mysteries behind them. A few months ago, for instance, there had been those girls named Clark who hardly ever came out of their place by daylight. Meg visited them at night—and what went on? Birdie never had a chance to find out. One day a man drove in, asking questions that might have fit the Clark girls—and the next morning they were gone.

There were kids running away from their folks and husbands running from wives and wives running from home towns. Most thought they were different from anyone else. Most were scared. Meg knew they were scared. If only there were some way of scaring Meg—

It was nice to think about, anyway. There was only one person whom Birdie did not dream of hurting.

Her thoughts drifted back to Stan. He treated her nice. Maybe she did do the scrubbing and cleaning but he never got smart and he was big too. She wondered what being married to Stan would be like. Her being tiny would be all right—a man didn't mind a small woman. Thinking about Stan in such terms made the breath thicken in her throat and warmth flow through her. When she heard Sonny coming, she stopped thinking about Stan and put a meek expression on her face.

"Feel better, Sonny?" she asked softly.

"Oh, hell, Birdie, stop whining at me."

"I just asked."

"Then stop asking."

"Well, gee," Birdie objected. "I'm not the one who wouldn't give you an extra day off. You don't have to get mad at me."

"Just keep it up," he warned.

"But, Sonny, I only—"

"Damn it," he yelled. "Shut up."

His close-set eyes narrowed and his face gleamed with perspiration. With a quick jerky motion, he raised a half-smoked cigarette to his lips, took a deep drag. Birdie watched his nicotine-stained, hurtful fingers with guarded fascination, then studied the shadows that smoking sucked into hollows of his cheeks. From the hard way he looked at her, Birdie thought she had said one word too many. She held her breath and got ready to flinch but finally Sonny shrugged and relaxed. He exhaled and then, turning, squashing the butt out in the ashtray on the dresser, he bent and stripped out of his sweaty T-shirt. White motion fluttered. He walked toward the closet. The T-shirt dropped over the back of a chair and, with his back to her, his hands went down to his belt.

He asked over his shoulder, "Maggie on the desk again?"

"Yes."

"Isn't that getting to be a habit?"

"She's got a deal with Meg. Besides, she offers to do it."

"Sure," Sonny muttered. "She would. Nosy old bitch. Gives her a chance to see who comes in and who goes out. She can sit there on her fat can and get a cheap thrill thinking about what goes on around here." He paused and got out of his pants. Birdie's mouth felt dry. She could almost feel the next question coming.

He asked it. "Was Maggie on the desk last night too?"

"Part of the time."

"Around ten?"

"I guess so."

"You guess? What the hell does that mean? Either she was or she wasn't."

"Well," Birdie said slowly. "I was in and out." She looked down for an instant and warmth mounted in her again as she thought back.

About ten last night she had gone to the laundry rooms to turn off a faucet somebody had left running. Her immediate surroundings blurred at the memory of how she had seen Stan and Linda. Once more she felt the swift surge of satisfaction she had felt last night when Stan had pushed Linda away and, without a word or backward glance, had walked back to his car.

Hoarding what she had seen, she got hold of herself. To hell with Sonny. He took everything. No matter what she got, he took it but there was one thing he could not do. He could not get into her mind and tell what she was thinking.

She looked up, shrugged. "Yes, come to think about it, Maggie was on the desk about that time last night."

"Where were you?"

"Me?"

"Who do you think I mean?"

"Golly," Birdie said. "Am I that important?"

"Yes," Sonny said.

"Well—I was probably back here."

"Probably."

"All right," Birdie went on quickly. "Don't look at me like that. I'm just trying to get it all straight in my head. You know how hard it is to work around the park and to try to keep house too. I had a million things to do."

She tipped her head to one side. After thinking a moment, she told him she remembered she had been doing wash in the sink. Her voice picked up strength. Nobody in the whole wide world could tell what she was thinking—and keeping Stan's secret safe for him made her feel oddly powerful.

Even later, when Sonny got ready to make love to her and talked dirty to her, she felt all right inside.

"Sonny," she whispered, as if it might do some good, "don't hurt me."

"I'll do whatever I want."

She turned her head on the pillow to avoid his beery breath. His fingers picked and pawed. His hands clutched at her flesh, squeezed.

"Sonny," she whispered again. "You're hurting me."

He snorted. "What have you got to hurt? Other women look like women."

"I can't help how I look."

He mumbled wordlessly, his lips trailing wetly down her neck. His fingers hurt her and his teeth hurt her. She twisted and squirmed and, because he always thought that meant she liked what he was doing, his lips came back up to her face.

"Love me, baby?"

"Yes," she lied. "I love you."

"Say it again."

"I love you, Sonny."

"All the way?"

"Yes, Sonny. All the way."

"Any time?"

"Sonny," she said. "You know—"

But he wanted her to say it his way, so it sounded as if he owned her and, because she knew how mean he got when she crossed him, she used his words. They ached in her throat. Any time he wanted her, he could have her. What she had belonged to him. If he told her to get down on her knees, she would get down on her knees. If he told her to crawl, she would crawl. Any way he wanted her, she was his. Her voice trembled. His hands ran over her stomach and his kiss mashed and ground against her mouth.

Everything was hurt and pain. That was what he wanted and what he told her women wanted. Even his voice saying her name grew harsh and hammering and suddenly she lost herself in his overwhelming toughness. A molten heat made her feel weak and helpless.

"Sonny—"

"Relax a little."

"I'm trying, Sonny."

Birdie caught her breath in the breathless room. Sonny's tangled sandy hair was matted to his sweaty forehead. Thin lines of moisture glinted on his face as he swallowed and licked his lips.

She slipped her hands over his shoulders to stroke his back and tried to remember the waiting ache that had been one of the reasons she had married Sonny. But he kept talking to her. Once again he told her she was too thin. Words came out of him, rising and falling, reminding her of everything she did not have—and finally reminding her also of the fact that he had never satisfied the ache she had hoped he would cure.

"She's got it," he said finally.

"Who?"

"Don't be dumb. You know. That Linda Terry."

Birdie almost laughed. Two things kept her silent—fear that he would hurt her more and envy of Linda because Stan had kissed her last night. What would Linda want with someone like Sonny when she had her sights lined on Stan? Let Sonny talk—maybe he was talking just to make her mad—but he still did not know what she did. If Sonny talked all night, he would not be any closer to knowing what was in her mind. Unless she told, nobody would ever know. Not one single solitary person in the whole wide world. A secret just had to be kept. She looked right up at Sonny. It made her feel good to have something he could not take away from her. She kept her eyes wide open until she heard him start whispering about how sooner or later, if Ben had it right, he and Ben were going to catch Stan fooling around with Linda.

"Just wait," he said.

"For what, Sonny?"

"For me to get Stan's job. Meg'll fire him."

Birdie suddenly got scared. Probably she ought to tell Sonny about what she had seen. Her nerves wavered. If he ever found out she had kept it from him, he would really explode. But if she did tell, she knew she would not get any thanks. As likely as not, she would get swatted for lying to him in the first place.

Birdie breathed deeply. Once more she thought of Stan. Big, she thought. Stan was a lot of man—more than either Ben or Sonny. And Stan had broken away and left Linda last night—probably neither Ben nor Sonny would ever catch him near her again.

Birdie's speculations about Stan suddenly included Mae. The fact that his ex-wife kept on coming back the way Mae did had to prove something. It meant she missed being with him. Certainly with her looks and her shape Mae would not have to beg anybody to take her—Birdie experienced a fierce burst of satisfaction at the fact that Stan had divorced Mae. That had to mean something too—perhaps Stan was still looking for the right girl.

A flutter of hope raced through Birdie. Maybe knowing something about Stan that he did not know she knew would not hurt her own future. Maybe she could talk to him. They might become friends—perhaps more. Her mind started pretending and her image of Stan suddenly translated itself into passion.

"Darling," she said suddenly.

"Take it easy."

"Just hold me," she begged Sonny. "Hold me tight."

She hugged him against an ache of longing that seemed to fill all of her. She pressed her cheek to the damp pillow and time flowed in ever widening rhythmic cycles. Her lips trembled on the verge of a cry and she clenched her teeth against pain as Sonny dug his fingers into her flesh.

She thought about Stan and pretended. . . .

7

In the park's recreation room television was on constantly. Facilities were also provided for card players and on Friday nights, Meg arranged some kind of special entertainment for the tenants. Twice a month she sprang for live Western music and a professional square-dance caller.

On all communal nights Stan made it a practice to keep hard liquor outside in the individual trailers. At least having to trot back to his home base to get a shot, a drinker got some exercise along with his alcohol. In any case, troublemakers were rare and, with Birdie and Sonny on hand to help him out, Stan almost always managed to keep order and to have a good time too.

Every so often, Mae dropped by to dance. Sometimes she even brought old tubby Larry around to complete the evening with her ex. And because Stan was pretty sure nobody had ever had any idea of what Mae considered to be logical behavior he always gave Larry a firm handshake and a straight-faced greeting. Then he usually shuffled Larry off on Meg.

"They can talk about money," Mae said on this particular night.

"While we dance?"

"That's right, hon."

"Easy," Stan said.

"In what way?"

"You'd better not use that term around Larry."

"He wouldn't notice, hon."

"Don't be too sure."

"Oh, hon—I know him."

She moved close against him and studied his reaction, laughing up into his face. Her hips shifted in time to the calypso record. He danced her to the edge of the crowded floor, watching the colored Japanese lanterns raise coppery glints in Mae's golden blonde hair, put a wicked shine to her eyes.

"Well?" she murmured.

"Lay off tonight," Stan said.

"How do you know what I'm thinking?"

"I don't—but I know the ideas you give me."

"Don't tease me, hon."

"I'm not teasing you. What you really think at any time is anybody's guess."

"But not how I feel about you."

"How do you feel about me?"

"Sometimes—" Mae pouted—"you get me all mixed up." Her long thick lashes fluttered and, turning her head for an instant, she flicked a swift glance over to where Larry was standing with Meg beside the refreshment table. Then, looking back up at Stan, Mae wrinkled her nose. "I don't understand, for example, why you couldn't have Larry's money."

"There must be a reason," Stan said dryly.

"What's the reason?"

"Well, for one thing Larry'd probably hate to part with it. It's brought him so many things. Including you."

"To hell with him."

"A husband has his rights, Mae."

"You didn't stand up too hard for yours."

"What's that supposed to mean?"

"Take a guess."

Stan frowned. Another couple bumped them. Across the room, a woman giggled loudly. Voices blended into the calypso beat. A little gust of warm wind brought the smell of heat and dust and night in through an open window and Mae took a deep breath.

"Hon," she said softly.

"What now?"

"I wish we were married again."

"What makes you think it would work this time?"

"One thing—you're the only man I ever really loved."

"And you've just found out? I'm flattered."

"Stop it, Stan. You know that when we were married, even if we did fight and yell at each other, we had a lot of fun too."

"So?"

"Things aren't that way between Larry and me—and please don't tell me I've got his money to keep me warm. You were wrong when you said his money bought me."

"Isn't money the reason you married him?"

"Yes—but I get all creepy with his hands and when he wants to breathe all over me and have me tell him how he feels." She paused, added: "Know something? The minute I get through dancing with you, he'll want to know what you said and what I said."

"Everybody gets curious now and then."

"Not like Larry."

Mae continued talking about the days when she and Stan had been married. Her voice grew warm and husky, her eyes heavy with thought. The music stopped and abruptly, for no reason Stan could understand, her expression became bitter.

He followed her gaze and saw Linda and Ben Terry talking to Meg and to Larry.

"Look at her," Mae murmured silkily. She canted her head appraisingly. "Not bad tonight either, that Linda Terry. Orange would look like hell on me but with that black gypsy hair brushed up like that, she gets away with it."

Mae stood still while the crowd moved around them, heading back to where the coffee and soft drinks were being served. Stan could feel her itemizing her assessment of Linda. Mae's staring check list started at Linda's high heels and slim ankles, followed the curve of her legs, lingered with a catty caress on slender hips and finally rested on the swell of Linda's breasts. Finally Mae moved toward the group and Stan followed.

"I'm curious about her," Mae said.

"What else do you want to know after that inventory you just took?"

"There're things about her you can't see."

"Such as?"

"You know—like what she does with Meg."

"Sorry," Stan answered. "I can't help you there."

"I know—you don't have to glower at me. But I'd like to talk to her ugly husband."

"For Pete's sake, why?"

"He might tell me something interesting."

"I doubt it," Stan said.

"Honey," Mae murmured. "Don't underestimate me."

She gave him a swift smile and, a few minutes later, after they joined the group at the refreshment table, Stan was not surprised when Mae had the next dance with Ben. As Ben took her in his arms Mae looked up at him with a wide-eyed invitation that caused Stan to smile. Ben might be in for some surprises tonight. In fact, he already seemed astonished.

Stan took Linda out on the floor. Two could play Mae's game, he thought—perhaps even four.

He was surprised at how lightly Linda fitted into his arms. He barely felt she was there—yet she made him more sharply aware of herself than Mae had with her sensuous approach.

"You dance as if you liked it," he said.

"Sometimes I do. Right now I'm not sure."

She looked up at him, her eyes guarded. None of the emotion she had shown at their last meeting was there. It was as if she had drawn an invisible blind between herself and him. She followed his lead easily on the jammed floor, her body barely touching his.

Stan said, "Ben had a talk with me."

"I know."

"He thanked me for bringing you home."

"He told me."

"You two must have had quite a discussion." Stan's eyes narrowed but he forced a grin. "I guess when you told Ben how that ride home ended he nearly died laughing."

"I only told him you brought me home."

"Then you left out the best part."

"I had to tell him that much. He would have found out anyway and you don't know Ben." Linda fell silent. She turned briefly to glance toward Meg and Larry. Finally, lifting her gaze to meet his again, she said, "What's the difference? No matter what I told you now—you wouldn't believe me."

"You may be right," Stan said. Without understanding why, he wanted to hurt her.

"Then let's not talk."

She had a right to be silent and Stan said nothing. He breathed the clean fragrance of her hair and the scent she wore. Warmth mounted to his chest. His hand felt the movement of back muscles and he tried not to remember the clinging heat, the sweet begging taste of her mouth. He lost track of the music and had to steady her to keep from stepping on her foot.

He muttered an apology to which she made no answer. He tried to look at her and hate her.

Certainly he had no reason to like her. Whatever she had told Ben of their last meeting, Stan suspected that warning other men away from Linda was an old story to Ben. She had a way of communicating her hungers—whatever these were—and Stan had no doubt other men besides himself had responded to them.

Still, unlike Mae, she did not seem to be up for grabs to the highest bidder or, with Meg on her string, she would not have made a play for him.

A faint alarm rang through him—had he been foolish to dance with her at all? If Meg warned him away from her tomorrow, that would be it.

He glanced down at Linda. Her face was averted. He studied the soft curl of hair over her ear. The ear itself was delicate and made for all the things he would not and could not say to it. Rhinestones flashed and glittered in her earrings and he watched the play of light on her high-boned cheek.

Abruptly she turned to look at him and once more her guard was down. Liquid lights played in her eyes and her lips parted. He saw the white, even gleam of her teeth, the moist tip of her tongue. There was hunger in her look again and her hand pressed lightly against his shoulder. In a startled instant he realized she was ready to take up, right in the middle of the dance floor and with both Meg and her husband probably watching, where they had left off the last time.

Eternity was in her eyes—not just this moment. Whatever she had been to others, in the past, what she offered him now was more than a one-night stand—but what alarmed him most was his own reaction. In that moment he was ready to buy all she offered—the whole package.

He reminded himself that she was bad luck—but the reminder had no meaning. The barrier between them was gone.

They were making contact. Nothing else seemed to matter. Perhaps later he would be sorry. Although he doubted it. More likely, later he would be too wise to be sorry.

The music and the voices around him grew remote in his ears. His arm around her tightened as he drew her against him. His face bent down to hers and savagely he thought to hell with Meg and Ben, both . . . and his alarm died. Nothing mattered but this moment.

A fractional instant before his mouth met hers, she turned her face away.

"Stan, we'd better stop."

"Why?"

"I can't dance. It's too crowded—"

The spell was broken—he returned to reality. "Okay." He nodded stiffly. "Anything you want."

"Don't hate me," she whispered.

"Hate you?"

"Yes—we—you could get in trouble—"

He stared at her and she looked right back at him. She was, of course, so right that the thought of what he had nearly done put a hard lump into his throat. Her eyes seemed to get bigger and bigger under his gaze and color seemed to drain out of her cheeks. Her lips moved as if she wanted to add something to what she said but she made no sound. Time locked to a standstill between them and he had the crazy feeling of being alone with her.

A hand grabbed at his arm and the room jolted back into focus. Mae and Ben stood beside Stan, wanting to change partners.

"Come on, Stan," Mae said.

"Sure." He nodded numbly.

"Ben wants his wife back."

Stan nodded again. "Okay."

Ben's fat flabby face glistened with a damp sheen of perspiration. He grunted and got hold of Linda. As Linda and Ben moved away, Mae whirled into Stan's arms.

"All right, hon," she said. "Keep away from that damned gypsy."

"I just danced with her."

"I saw you and dancing wasn't what you had uppermost in your mind. Don't go prowling for what you don't need. Save it for me. I'll come back over on the weekend and hum you a song." She paused, added: "And be careful too. Both Ben and Meg have the evil eye on you."

"I'm not worried."

"You should be."

"Why?"

"A man should worry about his bread and butter."

She pressed against him but he scarcely noticed. He could not rid himself of the feel of Linda in his arms or of the memory of the moment when he had been ready to throw away everything he owned for her. Unease rode him now—would Linda eventually destroy him? Perhaps they would wind up ruining one another, he and Linda.

When the music stopped and he and Mae started to walk back to the table, Mae shot a cautious little glance at Stan.

"Oh, oh," she said.

"What's wrong now?"

"Fat daddy has got that certain green-eyed look."

She let go of Stan's hand. When they reached Larry, Mae looked up at him and smiled sweetly.

"Something the matter, Larry?"

"No," he said. He stared stonily at Stan and then turned to look at Mae again. "I just think we'd better leave."

"All right," Mae purred. "Anything you want, darling."

8

"You humiliated me," Larry said.

"Oh, hell."

"Stop swearing."

"All right." Mae sighed.

She stretched under the sheet and stared resignedly at her husband. Larry padded soundlessly over to sit on the edge of her twin bed.

The springs squashed down under his naked weight. Mae saw the soft light put shadows in the creases of fat on his body. The flesh sagged on his hairless chest and, under his several chins, shaving pimples reddened to an angry rash.

Mae expected him to reach up and start picking at his skin. He was forever pinching and squeezing at its imperfections but for once he kept his fingers away from his face. He simply sat there breathing hard, with his mouth open, his stomach bulging.

It was too bad, Mae thought gloomily, that he did not just stick to eating and let her alone. Half the time he was just a mouth that worked for a stomach—but he was at his worst without clothes.

Mae had never forgotten her honeymoon. That first night in a plush Las Vegas resort motel had been awkward for both of them and for Mae something particularly ugly and all but ridiculous.

Larry had had his hands all over her. Of course she had been pawed plenty of times. That part was nothing new. Far back in junior high school, she had learned to protect herself in the clinches—but that kind of kid necking and petting—and what she had known with Stan—were a lot different from the way Larry handled her.

Mae closed her eyes. To hell with it. Everything cost something. Nothing bought nothing. Let him have his kicks—it was all in a night's work. With a little shiver she felt him lift the sheet from her legs. His hand was moist, creeping. Her stomach muscles tensed and her skin crawled. She flinched as his fingers worked up.

He squeezed and pinched and, finally, said again, "You humiliated me."

"We went over that."

"But I felt awful."

"Just because I danced with Stan?"

Larry said, "Not just because you danced with him but the way you danced with him."

"I danced with Ben too."

"Not that way."

"What way?"

"I don't have to describe it. Anyway, just words wouldn't do it justice. You'd have been arrested at any decent restaurant."

"You're being silly," Mae said.

"I don't think so."

Larry kept stroking and fondling her. His fingers were soft, fat. The sheet slid to the floor. The bed made muted, protesting sounds as Larry's unwieldy weight sprawled hot and sticky beside her. He covered her with moist kisses. She forced herself not to push him away.

"Go ahead," she said. "Have a ball."

"You don't care one way or another, do you?"

"No," she lied.

"That's the way you are."

"Yes," she said. "I guess so."

"Maybe that's why I love you so much."

"Maybe."

Mae shut her eyes. Nothing bought nothing, she told herself once more. But if Larry got a lift out of her pretended indifference he had bought something with his money—and his pawing of her was a little worse than nothing. She waited with clenched fists. To take her mind from him she forced herself to remember the first time she had proven to herself that sex was worth money.

She was sixteen and living with her older sister, Marilyn, and Marilyn's small husband, Eddie Tucker.

Eddie had a one-track mind.

"Listen, Mae," he always started.

"Get out of my bedroom."

"I just want to talk to you, Mae."

"Not again?"

"It wouldn't hurt you. I'd be careful."

"Forget it."

"Couldn't you use some spending money?"

"Sure, Eddie. I already told you."

"Five hundred dollars?"

"That's right."

"Just for one time?"

"That's right, Eddie. Just for one time."

"Why, you grabby little witch, I ought to slap you. The five C's sure as hell wouldn't be buying anything you haven't been throwing at me ever since we took you in. Damn it all, Mae, I'm feeding you and giving you a place to live. What do you think an accountant makes anyway? I'm not made out of gold and don't give me that crap about the insurance your father left. There wasn't much left after the bills and expenses were paid and you know Marilyn blew the rest on that bird-brained Hawaiian tour she took. Now all she wants to do is to look at her slides and complain she doesn't belong in a place like this."

"Don't tell me your troubles, Eddie."

"No, I guess I shouldn't. All you care about is you."

"That's right."

"My God, Mae, what kind of minds do you and your sister have? Half the time, she won't even give me a look and you're even worse. All you think about is money. Maybe you ought to hitch yourself to a cash register and stop pretending you're not for sale."

"I'm not pretending."

"Five hundred dollars is crazy."

"Then don't buy."

"They don't even get that price in the city."

"Too bad."

"But you don't care?"

"Not unless you've got five hundred dollars."

One crazy night while Marilyn was at the movies he came sneaking to her bed.

"Mae," he said thickly.

"Have you got the money?"

"No."

"Then get out of here."

"Not this time."

He clamped his hand over her mouth before she could scream or twist away. His scrawny strength surprised her. She bit and clawed and drew blood.

"Mae," he panted.

"Let me go."

"No. Be still. I won't hurt you. I promise."

"Go to hell."

His begging mouth hurt her—later she decided that beggars liked to hurt. She fooled him into thinking he had won. A soft whimper coaxed him into momentarily relaxing his hold on her. Her swift, explosive kick almost paralyzed him.

"Now get out and stay out," she told him.

"I can't move. I'm hurt."

He doubled up in anguish, lying on the floor. At last he crawled out on his hands and knees but Mae had made a lasting impression on him. Eddie never tried to get rough with her again.

During the next days, weeks, months he grew insulting and told her as often as he could that the day would never come when he would pay her a thin dime.

"Just keep it."

"I am."

"It's all the same. One woman is just like the next."

"Suit yourself, Eddie."

"Don't worry, Mae. I will."

Over and over, month in and month out—but he never stopped looking.

By the time she was in her last year of high school she was an obsession with him. And before Stan came along finally to marry her, Eddie changed his tune.

"Okay," he said one day.

"You really want it?"

"Yes."

"The price is still the same, Eddie."

"I know that."

"But you've got the money?"

"Yes, you little louse, I've got it."

"Five hundred?"

"Yes," Eddie had gritted. "Five hundred. . . ."

Mae opened her eyes. Instead of Eddie's bony hands and thin body, she felt Larry's lard crowding. The present came back into focus and she realized dimly that Eddie had taught her something she should have kept in mind.

In one night she had learned to hate Eddie.

"Larry," she gasped. "Stop it."

"Why?"

"Just stop it."

"You didn't say that a minute ago."

"I'm saying it now. Stop what you're doing—before it's too late."

Before I learn to hate you too . . .

She did not say the last because she knew that Larry would not have understood—any more than Eddie had. Just as Eddie after that long-ago night, Larry still had ideas. He panted and leaned over her.

"Mae, I wish you'd be nice."

"I'm trying," she told him bitterly.

He missed her point.

"You could try acting as if you were at least thinking about me," Larry complained. "We're married. You're my wife but sometimes you lie there and look as if you were thinking about somebody else. It makes me feel I'm married to a whore."

"Don't say that."

"Well," Larry insisted. "It's true. All you wanted was money."

"You ought to be ashamed."

"For using that word? Money?"

"Yes," Mae said. "For using that word."

"I don't suppose you ever sold yourself."

"Damn you," Mae said. "Shut up."

Larry stared hard at her and Mae wondered if that night with Eddie still showed. Her other nights with Larry should have been different—after all, she had married Larry. She had given him more than Eddie ever got. All Eddie had gotten from her was that one night.

Larry's eyes roved over her, examining, appraising—not caressing. Nor did his voice hold tenderness when he spoke her name.

She looked at him without answering.

"You're pretty." He spoke as if he were stating a fact, not paying her a compliment.

He waited and watched. Then he pinched her, evidently just to see if she would try to stop him. She made no move. Deliberately hurting her, not even pretending to be making love to her was a new tactic for him but, curiously, she was not afraid. She had never been afraid of Eddie or any other man.

Neither she nor Larry had exactly gone into their marriage with stars in their eyes, she thought. In her way she understood him. After all the work and years of investments and hard-headed real estate deals, he would have few illusions. Money was a medium of exchange—something whose value he knew. A dollar bought so much at any given time—prices fluctuated and she knew he had never expected her to come cheap. Her price with him had started all the way up at the top.

With marriage.

Looking at him now, trying to analyze his reasons for having given her a small hurt by pinching her, she could almost follow his logic. As long as he got what he had paid for, Larry did not balk at the cost. Tonight she had offered him nothing more than the cold fact of her marriage to him and both his mention of money and his pinch had been to remind her of the fact that he had a substantial investment in her.

He had, of course, she knew, been careful about that investment as about all others. If he had not had her tailed from the very beginning and stacked up a file of evidence about where her trips to see Stan had ended, she might have tried to get a nice fat settlement and walked out on him just like she had once walked out on Stan. He had never used the evidence except to tell her—as matter-of-factly as he had tonight told her she was pretty—that he had it in a safe place, just in case either she or Stan ever decided to get badly out of line. He had no wish, he had told her, to wake up murdered some morning or to be made to look like a fat fool in divorce court. He was sorry she was still seeing Stan and felt jealousy, but it was better she should be betraying him with her former husband than someone else. After all, he had a pretty good idea of why she had left Stan to marry him.

Money—though he had not used the word then.

On the way home tonight, Mae had deliberately built up Larry's ego by complaining to him about Stan and that Terry woman. She had all but let him understand she was dropping Stan altogether. If he had believed her, he could hardly have been more wrong.

Her mouth tightened. Before she let Stan get any real ideas about that gypsy slut, there would be trouble. A warning to Meg might run Linda's little red wagon off the track. Mae let her breath out slowly. One way or the other it would turn out all right. She would see to that.

As her mouth softened, Larry leaned down to kiss her again. This time she made no protest, though she still was not afraid of him. Her thoughts shifted mercurially from Stan back to Larry—if he hurt her again, she would simply hurt him back.

But now she let him kiss her.

"A penny for your thoughts," he whispered.

"I was thinking about us."

"Honest?"

"Yes," Mae lied. "Honest."

She knew he did not believe her—and the fact that he did not was some repayment for that pinch.

9

The new trailer sites were all finished. Before the end of July Stan had rented the last one out to a good-looking young married couple. They were both just kids—neither looked more than twenty-two or three—but the boy was already a wheel. His firm had sent him out from Los Angeles to supervise a new automatic computing machine the lettuce shippers were installing.

"Everything is electronics now," the kid said.

Stan nodded.

"It's all progress."

"Sure," Stan said softly.

"You people here ought to know," the boy went on. "Right now, with the braceros posing the problem of increased labor costs, modernization is especially important to the industry. Our machine will provide continuous statistical estimates for planting and harvesting. Sales futures and area shipping requirements will be automatically available. Besides keeping separate totals for all of the individual growers, having our equipment do billing and filing will allow management to eliminate a large part of their present office help."

"So who needs people?"

"I don't look at it that way."

"Oh?" Stan said.

The boy shrugged. "Times change. So do jobs and, in a great many cases, a machine like the one I'm putting into operation here not only does the work of a number of employees quickly and without mistakes but, in the long run, it actually lowers the final cost of the product to the consumer."

"But how much lettuce does that machine buy?"

"That's a pretty tired question," the boy said.

"Okay—It still needs an answer. If a machine only lengthens the line at the unemployment check window, it can't be all good."

"That's an oversimplification."

"Maybe, but some people are being hurt."

"I'm afraid that is inevitable," the kid said.

"A word like that buys no groceries."

"I know it doesn't," the kid admitted. "On the other hand, people get hurt in traffic accidents too and cars used to frighten horses. I'm just a technical expert. My job is machines and electronics. So far as the rest of it goes, there must be a solution. A lot of people have learned to duck cars and today even horses ride automobiles."

The kid was bright, all right.

Stan grinned. He changed the subject and talked about what there was to do and see in the area. Arguments were easier to answer than problems were to solve. The kid would have a number of both on his hands before he was through living. And he was right in a sense—every change pulled the rug out from under somebody. The kid had mentioned cars—certainly, after the coming of the automobile, a lot of blacksmiths and buggy-whip makers must have had a rough row to hoe. Maybe the basic problem of life stayed pretty much the same—and perhaps the people who had to face them did also.

Stan knew he was thinking like a bargain basement philosopher. The fact that history and people who made it repeated themselves was not worth a hoot in hell when a man was pounding pavements, looking for a job. For the rest of the day the job he had drove him. With Sonny cutting right out at five-thirty he even put in overtime.

That night, after a late dinner in town, Stan only wanted to relax before hitting the sack when Birdie Shedley came to his trailer.

"Gee," she complained, "it sure is hot."

"Well," Stan said, "it's good for lettuce."

"Big deal."

Birdie flopped down at one end of Stan's bunk and fanned herself with her hand. Her narrow bare shoulders gleamed under the thin straps of a yellow cotton sundress. She stretched her tanned legs straight out before her either for Stan or herself to admire. Stan was curious about what she wanted—she seemed to have something besides her job at the park on her mind.

He brought her a beer and she thanked him.

"Everything helps," she said.

"I guess so."

"But nylon panties get hot."

"Oh?"

"Some women just don't bother."

Birdie looked up, her eyes animalistically calculating. Sipping his beer, watching her shift position slightly and throw back her shoulders to emphasize her small bosom, Stan grew wary. He gave her a cigarette and held a match. When she leaned to the light, he saw she wore no bra. Stan went back to his beer and nodded in the direction of the office.

"Anything wrong?"

"No," Birdie said. "I just came over to talk."

"Sonny still in town?"

"Yes." Birdie shrugged. "Him and that Ben Terry. Maggie's looking out for the desk, so I came here." Birdie looked long and steadily at Stan.

"Maggie says women used to be different."

"She ought to know."

"Well," Birdie continued, "I don't believe her. Maybe they never used to talk about what they did or did not do but being picky about words and calling legs limbs and stuff like that wouldn't make me stop thinking." She paused again and Stan could almost feel her trying to decide if he minded her having dropped in and the way she was talking. Abruptly she shrugged. "Anyway—" she sighed—"I get sick of being alone and looking at television. Every time I see another Western I feel like I'm going to scream and those doctor shows give me the creeps. Half the time I get to thinking I'm getting something wrong with me but I get just as sick of listening to Maggie. Sonny says she only likes to take over the desks so she can see who comes in and who goes out but generally it is just the same old parade around here. Of course," Birdie added slowly, "Meg came down again."

"I must have missed her," Stan said.

"Don't worry. Meg didn't come down to see you."

"Oh?"

"No," Birdie said. "Meg came to get Linda."

"Did she?"

"Doesn't she always?"

"I don't know."

"Well," Birdie said. "I do."

She drank beer, studied the can thoughtfully. Finally she turned, reached around to put the can on the window ledge behind her. The twisting movement tightened her thin dress and made it abundantly clear she wore nothing under the dress. A simple male response breathed across his mind, was gone. Of all the thin women in the world, Birdie was the one he needed the least. He began to consider how to get rid of her. He had a feeling she had not said everything she had come to say.

"Well," she remarked finally. "It takes all kinds."

"I guess so, Birdie." He had not the foggiest idea of what she was talking about.

"What do you suppose it is like?"

"What is what like?"

"You know," Birdie said. "What they do. Meg and Linda."

"I wouldn't know," Stan said.

"But you must have thought about it."

"Why?"

"Well," Birdie began, "Because you—" She let her voice trail away to silence. Then, as if she had changed her mind about what she had been going to say, she continued musingly: "Even if you never thought about them, it's different with me. I mean I can't help wondering what kind of a charge they get—it seems funny to imagine two women making love." Birdie smoothed her dress down over her thighs. "Probably it's none of my business what Linda lets Meg do to her but, when Sonny and I first came here to work, Meg got her hands on me a couple of times. Gee, I was so dumb that I just thought it was accidental. Of course, Meg had a college girl around then and by the time that broke up, I had sense enough to know what Meg wanted."

"So?"

"Well," Birdie said quickly, "so naturally, I—" She giggled again. "Now you're trying to embarrass me."

"Why do you say that, Birdie?"

"Because," she said sulkily. "You made it sound like you think I thought I wanted to—" Her voice trailed away again. For a moment, regarding him suspiciously, her eyes took on a hot glitter. Then, still moving her hands slowly along her thighs, she said seriously, "I've never for a moment thought I'd like it like that."

"Like what?"

"You know, Stan. With a woman."

"Okay," he said.

"Don't you believe me?"

"Why shouldn't I?"

"Men are for women and women are for men." Birdie looked steadily at him while she twisted around once more to pick up her unfinished beer. This time, maybe because he knew what to look for or because he had finished his beer on top of several drinks he had had earlier, she looked more of a woman to him.

Her expression altered subtly, told him she knew she had made some sort of impression on him.

He went to the refrigerator for another cold can.

When he came back, Birdie said, "Anyway, that's how I feel."

"How, Birdie?"

"Just like I said."

"A woman should be satisfied with a man?"

"That's right."

"You're a smart girl," Stan said slowly.

"Don't make fun of me."

"Believe me," Stan said. "I'm not."

He lit another pair of cigarettes, handed her one. All the while her eyes were wide on him. They were somehow as naked as she was under that dress and for some reason she was getting to him. He could not figure out why or how. Maybe, he thought bitterly, he needed an antidote to both Mae and Linda—Birdie was certainly different from both. But trouble was still trouble. A roll with her would really put him behind the eightball. But even as he was picking around for tactful words in which to tell Birdie to pack up her little kit bag and get going, he still wanted her.

But he knew that beyond this moment she meant less than nothing to him. So to hell with it, he told himself.

"Gee," she sighed.

"Still hot?"

"I'll say," Birdie said. She loaded her voice with double meaning.

Stan stood up. He decided to be brutal. "Maybe you'd better get out of here, Birdie."

He knew instantly she was not going to obey. She curled around to lie on his bed, staring up at him. Next she squirmed the dress straps down over her shoulders. She twisted and fumbled with hooks and, before Stan could do anything to stop her, slid her arms free and stripped down to her waist.

"Stan," she whispered.

"Birdie," he almost shouted.

His voice rasped harshly but Birdie simply went on staring at him, as if hypnotized. Then she began to talk in breathless fits and starts about what she had wanted from Sonny and what he did to her. She kept licking her lips as she spoke. Her bitterness turned to pleading. She promised him anything and when he tried to talk sense to her, she only shook her head.

"Damn it, Birdie. We can't. Not here."

"I just told you—"

"But Maggie knows you're over here."

"To hell with her."

Birdie twisted out of her dress. Stan leaned down, grabbed her wrists. He tried to pull her up. She continued to twist and writhe and made up for her lack of weight by furious activity.

"Stop being crazy," he told her.

"I'm not—"

She exploded from the bed, coming at him so suddenly he had to let go of her wrists to catch her. As soon as he released them, her arms whipped around his neck and her mouth found his. There was a supple strength to her. Trying to pry her loose was like trying to dislodge a leech—she writhed to keep him from solidly gripping her; and, writhing, she felt boneless. But she was not without flesh and warmth, Stan found, and she was again more woman than he had expected.

The discovery jolted him—as did the realization that, with the light on in the trailer, any passerby could see in right through the screen door.

"Birdie," he hissed. "Let go."

"No—"

She was determined. He could not release himself without hurting her.

"Wait," Stan said harshly. "Listen to me."

He finally got through to her. She quieted. Reaching around, he broke her grip on his neck and she sagged back to the bed. He found the light switch and plunged the trailer into darkness. All he needed to add to his troubles was an addition to what he suspected was his growing reputation as Don Juan of the trailers. He took a deep breath and told Birdie to get her dress back on.

"And hurry," he said.

"But I just told you. I'll do anything."

"Birdie," Stan said. "Get out of here."

"Do you know what I'm offering you?"

"Yes, dammit, I know."

"Isn't it good enough?"

"Just get out."

"Why? You'll never get it from her."

"Whom?"

Stan held his breath. Time itself seemed to wait in the naked heat. Perspiration glittered on Birdie's upper lip and she swallowed. The small motion at her throat triggered Stan's return to reality. He grew aware once more of the run of time, other movements and stirrings in the park. A car passed. Highway traffic murmured faintly. A big bumbling insect fluttered and batted against the screen door.

Looking hard at Birdie, Stan repeated numbly, "Whom did you mean?"

"Linda."

"What about her?"

"You made a pass at her."

"You're crazy, Birdie."

"No, I'm not. I saw you."

Stan grunted. "When?"

"The night you brought her home from the movies—at least that's where she told me she was going. I was over there by the laundry."

"So you walked down to have a look?"

"Yes," Birdie said.

"Have you told anybody?"

"No," Birdie whispered. "Not yet."

10

During the long, long irrigated summer no rain had fallen in the valley. Week after week, month after month, the sky had been hot and cloudless until the river had become weedy and dry under its willows, cottonwoods and sycamores. Even its occasional underground seeps never flowed far enough to wet the heat-blasted gravel banks but now and then at the deep bend behind the trailer park there was a shaded rock pool.

Stan had installed a shaft through the bottom of the pool to tap a permanent vein of underground water and hooked up a small electric pump that fed into a permanent sprinkling system. When the pool filled, he drew additional water from it, pumping it through a screen. To make sure the job was done right, he had assigned himself the job of keeping the screen clear and one night Linda surprised him at it.

"Hello," she said softly.

She had come up soundlessly behind him. Her voice was warm and throbbing. Stan stared up from where he knelt. A drumbeat of what he always felt for her started in his blood and he fought it. Making each movement deliberate, he put his Stillson wrench aside and, wiping his hands dry on a rag, stood up to face her.

"I guess I'm the last person you expected to see," she told him.

"I wasn't expecting anyone."

He studied her in the fading twilight—she stood slim and brown-legged in sandals. A hot breath of wind fluttered her denim skirt and at the open collar of her white blouse her throat made a dark, supple column. *Gypsy,* he thought—Mae had been right. Her black hair was brushed back severely—yet there was an untamed quality about it—and even in her motionless pose. He could not see her eyes but in the starlight her full sensual lips parted in something that was not a smile but an invitation.

Stan's chest tightened and he looked away. On the ground, where he had let it fall, lay a crumpled white rag. Another breath of wind stirred the leaves and once more fluttered Linda's skirt against her legs. A chorus of frogs croaked and on the far side of the pool and up in the trees a squirrel chattered.

When he looked back at her, Linda had not changed position.

"I hope you don't mind my coming," she said finally.

"It's a free country."

"Do you want me to go away?"

He did and yet did not. The simplest answer to his problem with her would be for Ben Terry to pack his wife in his trailer and pull out—take her far away. Stan put in a moment of wishful thinking, then came back to his immediacies.

A slow anger built in him as he realized why Linda had chosen this particular night to look him up. Meg had told him earlier in the day that she was leaving for San Francisco on business and would be gone the rest of the week, maybe longer. On top of that he knew, as did nearly everybody else in the park, that Ben had gone off on one of his binges. Ten chances to one, the way Ben stayed drunk once he got started, he would not be around for days.

Little Linda had nothing but time on her hands, Stan thought grimly. No wonder she had tailed him down to the pool—after the way he had reacted to her at the dance, she probably figured he was always good for a laugh.

"Go or stay," he said. "Suit yourself."

"Then I'll stay."

"Okay."

"Unless you think I'll contaminate you."

"I'll be all right," Stan said.

"Will you?" Her voice dripped sarcasm but in the very next instant, she raised her hands in a little apologetic gesture. "I'm sorry." She studied him for a moment, finally walked over to the box that covered the pump controls and sat down.

He asked, "Are you lonesome with Meg away and Ben off on a bat?"

She sighed. "I guess."

He listened to the night sounds—crickets, the occasional rustle of wind, the distant hum of traffic, a dog barking somewhere—and tried to tell himself that Linda was bargain-basement goods. She did not even have the guts or spirit to come after him openly—or arrange to meet him somewhere in town at some time when her absence might inconvenience either Ben or Meg—she had to sneak up on him when chance circumstances made it safe for her to cheat. Except for that brief moment on the dance floor when she had offered him everything, she had never shown herself to him as anything but a coward.

"Is that so bad—being lonely?" she asked. "I was—and I saw you come here to work on the pump." She paused. "I guess you're still mad about Ben."

"Ben's the one who ought to be mad."

Linda nodded. "I guess you're right." She watched him fish out a pack of cigarettes, shake one loose. She accepted one and he gave her a light. She said slowly, "Ben often doesn't act or feel the way he ought to. Mostly it isn't a question of why he gets mad—just when. But I told you the truth at the dance. No matter what Ben hinted, he was only guessing. Nobody knows anything more than that you brought me home from the movie."

"A few people do," Stan said.

"Who?"

"Whoever was driving the car whose lights nailed us, for one. Birdie, for another."

When he had finished telling her about Birdie's having been at the laundry, Linda's expression grew strange. Finally she shrugged.

"Then we're all even," she said slowly.

"Who?"

"The three of us."

"How do you figure that?"

"It's very simple. Late last Saturday night I saw Birdie coming out of your trailer."

"Were you spying on me?"

"No—I wanted to see you. Instead, I saw her."

She waited and Stan wondered if she felt she had scored some kind of a tit-for-tat victory. He felt things closing in on him when he remembered what finally had happened that night with Birdie. He kept his face carefully composed.

"So you saw Birdie. What did you think?"

"It doesn't matter, Stan. You don't have to worry."

Hell, no. But Birdie had finally got to him that night. She might have come to his trailer for any reason at all as far as Linda knew—but she had come to be loved and in the end she had had her way.

Partly he had given in to her to keep her from talking about Linda—but partly his response had been to Birdie herself. Her words, voice, and lips had pleaded and coaxed him and her seal-like slimness had clung to him with a hunger not to be denied.

She at no point met his standards of loveliness—but there had been a kind of beauty in her savage need. To this he had responded and his ultimate union with her had become something he would remember—perhaps in some recesses of his mind even treasure. His pleasure had come from her fulfillment rather than his own.

Later she had said, "I knew it could be like this."

And at the end, just before Linda had seen her leave the trailer, Birdie had promised almost pathetically, "I'll see you again, Stan."

"Sure." He had tried to give her lying assurance.

"But I better get out of here now."

"I guess so, Birdie."

"That's right."

Just the memory of her leaving brought back the relief he had felt that night. Now he forced himself to stop thinking about Birdie. No more of her—once had been enough. Maybe more than enough, since Linda probably suspected the worst.

There was no way for Linda to know how it really had been between Birdie and himself so, Stan thought, to hell with her. He owed her no explanations. Let her balance things out and call the accounts even. She was hardly a woman who could be nominated Virgin Of The Month. Maybe once a day—say around ten o'clock on a slow morning—she might collect a few votes.

"You'll miss Meg till she gets back, won't you?" he asked.

"You didn't have to say that." Linda's voice was low. Her mouth trembled but her eyes did not waver. Her shoulders went back a little but in a moment her posture broke. She made a tiny gesture of defeat. "All right," she said slowly.

"What does that mean?"

"Simply that I know your mind is made up about me," Linda answered swiftly. She caught her breath—her next words were hard and vicious. "But don't think I'm asking for sympathy or for an apology. Make your thoughts as ugly and dirty as you like. If you want me to, I'll even admit I'm a slut."

"I didn't ask you to say that."

"But a slut is what you think I am. Give me credit for a little intelligence. I'm over twenty-one and I know what I'm doing. What you meant by that remark you just made about Meg was that I go to bed with her. All right, it's true. Is that enough—or do you want me to go into details for you?" Tears glittered wetly on her lashes but when he moved closer to her to put his hands on her shoulders, she threw her head back to look up at him mockingly. "Be careful—I might be catching."

Stan said, "Shut up."

She was hurt and, oddly, he felt the pain. His eyes stung—hers still mocked him.

His hands tightened. "Linda, we'll go some place tonight."

"Will we?"

Her eyes widened. For a moment she looked almost frightened. Then she shook her head and tried to pull away but Stan would not let her go.

"I'll head for town in about an hour," he said.

"So?"

"Be ready."

"No," she said. "Forget it."

"I'll pick you up around where the construction trucks have been coming through the back gate."

"Don't hold your breath," she whispered.

"Why?"

"Because I won't be there."

She looked away.

He felt total bleakness. At their first meeting, he had felt he was looking down at her from some too-near, though loftier, plateau. . . . and that she was looking upward at him.

Now he was the one to do the beseeching. . . . to look up. Somewhere their paths had crossed and, inexplicably, she was operating at a higher level, he at a lower one.

"You'd better show up," he stated warrningly.

She laughed sadly, mocking them both.

11

But she was there, waiting in the darkness at the side of the rutted dirt road. She wore the same clinging sheath she had had on at the recreation hall dance. Warm color hugged her slender hips even in the bland glare of his headlights. She got into the car without speaking, pulled shut the door and, without looking at Stan, leaned against the back rest and shut her eyes.

"You look lovely," he offered.

"Looks aren't everything. Are they?"

"They help."

"Maybe you like your whores well dressed."

Her voice was bitter but when he glanced at her in sudden anger he saw a stubborn glitter in her eyes.

He said nothing.

After a moment's silence she said contritely, "Forget what I said. I'm sorry."

"Never mind."

"But I am sorry." Her voice shook. "Forgive me?"

"It's not that important."

"Then why not say you do?"

Again he caught that desperate waiting, searching in her eyes that had troubled him at their first meeting, when she and Ben had signed into the park. He was tired, tonight, of reminding himself that solving her problems—and he knew them better now than he had then—was none of his business. She sat half-turned to face him, slender ankles crossed, skirt tight above nyloned knees and, whatever she was to Meg and Ben, to him she was all woman. And probably a whore—so that her crack about his liking his whores well dressed might not have been too far off the mark.

Granting that what he felt for her was liking.

"Okay," he said slowly.

"Then I'm forgiven?"

"Why not?"

He drove slowly through the heat of the summer night, aware of the scent of dust and live oak and the occasional pungently offensive odor of stagnant irrigation water, and tried to analyze what he really felt for her. He was doing tonight exactly what he had promised himself he would not do. Why? In a sense, beyond her attractions as a woman, she appealed to his ego. When a woman asked questions, a man liked to have the answers. But did he have the answers to the complex riddle Linda posed? Mae had been—and still was—puzzle enough for him, yet nowhere in Mae's life was there a complication such as Meg had given Linda.

In the last analysis, he decided, she attracted him simply as a woman. Perversely, the fact that he felt she was in trouble added to her allure. Sardonically he reflected that what was true of Linda had in a sense been equally so of Cleopatra, Helen of

Troy and other great sexpots of history—their personal problems had drawn men as an open flame drew moths. But once he was consumed by the flames Linda kindled—would anyone remember Stan Barton as they did Marc Antony and Caesar?

He grinned sourly into the night. He was letting this thing run away with him. Even back in school he had recognized that Antony and Caesar were dead and—at least not for him—all history had never brought either of them to life again. He had never been much of a scholar and if he were to tell Linda what he had just been thinking of, she would probably jump right out of the car and run away screaming—something she probably would do if he parked on a lonely road and made love to her right now.

Maybe that was the answer.

Stan pulled off the road and the convertible lurched in a rut. He braked to a stop and turned to her.

"Okay," he said. "Where to?"

"You choose."

"How about a place where we can drink?"

"All right," she nodded.

"And dance?"

"Is that what you want to do tonight?"

"I'm open to suggestions."

"And I'm just asking."

She paused, her face canted impishly—but her expression was forced, neither natural nor convincing. There was too much sadness, perhaps real tragedy in her, to permit simple humor and Stan knew he was getting the needle. And yet he knew she was unsure of him also.

After a moment her eyes left his and it was as if contact between them were broken. They shared nothing but their surroundings—the hum of traffic and the glare of headlights flicking by, punctuating brief instants of emptiness. Her gaze remained lowered to the purse clutched in her lap and Stan thought, all right, you smart chick—keep asking but don't be surprised at the answers.

"I did have something else in mind," he said.

"Oh?"

"You must have guessed."

"Why do you say that?" she asked slowly.

"I just had a hunch."

"About what?"

"About you and me," Stan said.

He took out and tore open a pack of cigarettes. While he was lighting one for her and one for himself, she turned away from him and raised her eyes to stare straight ahead through the windshield. She did not look at him as she accepted the lit cigarette, put it to her lips and took a deep pull.

Some element of fear communicated itself from her to him and abruptly he felt disgusted with what he had been about to do. If it were true he liked his whores well dressed, it was also true he did not like them frightened.

He asked, "Remember what you asked me about the convertible top—the night I brought you home from the movie?"

"What was that?" She puffed furiously on the cigarette and her voice trembled.

"You wondered if I ever put it down."

"I remember," she nodded.

"Want it down now?"

He put what he hoped was a reassuring smile into his voice and she turned again to look at him.

"Yes," she whispered. "I'd like that."

He lowered the top, put the car in motion, not as puzzled by her fright as he once might have been. In some ways, he decided, she was more like a kid than a tramp—besides, she had expressed something close to what he himself felt.

In his own way and for his own reasons he, too, felt frightened by what was happening between them.

He remembered that there was one of Mae's silk head ties in the glove compartment. He took it out, gave it to Linda and she smiled her thanks. With the car's top down, even the small hot wind created by his slow driving through traffic had begun to disarray her hair.

This time an honest humor came into her voice as she asked, "Do you always carry spare head ties?"

"Not always."

"Only for special guests?"

"That's right."

"But this one even has a familiar scent."

"It does?"

"Yes," she said sweetly. "Mae's."

But she was not angry—nor did she have a right to be. Actually she seemed to take the fact that he had given her something of Mae's as a sign of acceptance. She moved to sit closer to him and, in answer to his random questions about her earlier life, talked softly about growing up in the wide, flat Sacramento River rice country.

Stan pulled up at a motel that had dining and dancing facilities. He found them a booth, ordered drinks and Linda continued reminiscing, until Stan excused himself to go to the desk.

When he came back, he found her eyes again bitterly questioning.

"So here we are," she said softly.

"We don't have to stay."

"No? Didn't you just make arrangements for an overnight cabin?"

He shrugged, "Whether we use it or not is still up to you."

Linda leaned back in the upholstered booth and stared silently at her drink. Again she accepted a cigarette but this time she smoked more calmly than when she had expected him to make a pass at her in the car. She seemed to have accepted his suggestion that the decision was up to her.

Presently he asked, "Are you in love with Ben?"

She shook her head.

"Meg?"

She sat perfectly motionless, watching the smoke spiral upward from the tip of her cigarette. Finally she raised her eyes to his.

"This is funny."

"How do you figure?"

"Because you don't even like me."

"Are you sure?"

"Pretty sure."

She reached to jab her cigarette out in the ashtray in nervous little stabs and, in that instant, with that odd out-of-focus feeling she often gave him, Stan realized she was right. Liking was not what he had for her. Desire—yes. But even that was different from any want he had known for a woman before. It was as if what he really wanted was to penetrate her wrongness and set it right—repair and correct her as he might some delicate and damaged machinery, though she was certainly no machine and probably not delicate. Her type homesteaded bar stools, though she had not quite yet reached that final stage. She was still putting out her bait close to home, where she could retrieve it and run to Ben's dubious protection.

Or, more lately, Meg's.

She had not answered his question about Meg. He asked it again.

Once more she failed to answer him directly. Staring straight at him, she said, "That's one thing about Meg. She does like me."

"I asked about you. Are you in love with her?"

This time she shook her head. "No comment."

One thing was sure, he thought—she was certainly not being propositioned for the first time. Nobody had to tell her the score. She had guessed about the cabin as soon as he had visited the motel desk, though he had made his arrangements well out of her earshot. He had not even intended to tell her about them unless things had worked out that way. But she had not needed a handy little printed set of instructions to tell her what was up.

If she wanted to be hard to get, he could go along with that too.

"Let's have another drink," he suggested, "while you make up your mind about tonight."

"Just one?" she asked mockingly.

"What do you want me to do—order it by the case?"

"So I'm still the boss?"

"That's right."

"And you don't care one way or the other what I decide?"

"I didn't say that."

"Then what did you mean? Did you expect me to clap hands and say, 'Goody, I've got a place to sleep tonight—and not alone, either?' Did you expect me to say in so many words I'd just love to go to bed with you?"

Stan said, "I haven't yet asked you to do anything. I didn't even tell you about the cabin—so far you've done all the talking and guessing. But since you're making a point of what I expect of you, would it make any difference to you whether I expected it or any other guy? Or a girl for that matter."

Stan had pitched his voice low. Now he reached for his drink. *Okay, baby,* he thought angrily, *you're being so smart—go ahead and field that one . . .*

Linda lost her sneering look. She studied him carefully now. Stan turned to watch the couples milling around the dance floor. A teen couple was doing the twist with an air of almost painful concentration. Music jingle-jangled. At the edge of the floor, bringing a tray of drinks from the bar, a cocktail waitress wriggled between the crowded tables. She shifted her hips as expertly as a football player doing some broken-field running. But sight of her brought Stan's attention back to Linda.

"Well?" he asked finally.

"Well what?"

"You didn't say. Would it matter who asked you—me or some other guy?"

"You asked more than that."

"Forget the rest."

Her eyes seemed to soften. Suddenly she did not look hard or cheap or so sure of getting all wrong answers from life and Stan abruptly was not so sure of his definitions either.

She became beautiful for him right then. Maybe not movie or television or magazine cover beautiful but lovely with something unguarded and untouched shining in her dark eyes. But the expression vanished and she was quietly apprehensive again.

She made an apologetic gesture.

"Sometimes I get bitchy," she said slowly. "All the words come out wrong." She stared down at the table and, fiddling nervously with her drink, whispered, "I wish I never had to say anything or hear anything ugly for the rest of my life." Her eyes came up. "But wishing is for kids and anyway there isn't anything that is really perfect, is there?"

"I'm not sure, Linda."

"I am," she said softly.

12

Stan had rented cabin seventeen. He found it in a corner of the motel lot right at the edge of a river inlet. The bedroom window faced out on a faint shimmer of shore lights glittering across the dark water and, in their pale rippling reflection, Stan and Linda smoked and had another round of drinks.

"Don't turn the light on," she said, moving at last away from him.

"All right."

"After all," she added. "I've had experience. I know my way in any bedroom."

"You didn't have to say that, Linda."

She was silent for several long moments before she whispered, "I'm sorry."

A faint blend of music and voices came from the direction of the bar and cocktail lounge. From the next cabin came the muted thump of a door slamming but for Stan the only real sounds were those made by Linda moving about the dark cabin. He listened intently, trying to interpret them, and from their faintness he thought she must be at the far end of the room when suddenly she spoke beside him.

"Stan, unzip me."

He found her form in the dimness. He fumbled at her back until he found the zipper. He pulled down, the fabric parted and he breathed clean woman smell. She moved away from him again and this time he tried to follow her with his eyes as well as his ears. She grew partly visible to him in the pale glow of the mirror, loosening her dark hair. It spilled down her back and Stan's heart began to slug. His face grew warm.

"Linda—"

"No," she said abruptly. "Stay where you are."

"But I—"

"No," she whispered again. "Wait."

She was movement in the night. He wanted to see her but she still would not let him turn on a light. He ached to touch her but she told him to keep his distance. She left the mirror's faint, reflected glow and he lost even the sound of her in the dark recesses of the room.

Then, suddenly and without warning so that he almost jumped, he felt her hands on him. He reached for her and found warm, soft nakedness.

He drew her to him and kissed her.

Later, on the bed, Stan remembered her hands—during and after that kiss. They had been incredibly light and expert—wherever they had touched him, their caress still seemed to linger. Even holding her to him, he could barely see her in the dim reflection of river lights, but touching her had told him what he needed to know. Her lips had imparted to his all the wanting he had ever felt for any woman.

"Linda—"

"Wait," she whispered. "Tell me something first."

"All right. What?"

"Am I pretty?"

"You're beautiful."

"Right now? You can't really see me."

"I don't need eyes to see you when we're like this. You're beautiful."

And in a way, he was glad of the darkness—she became something new to him in the intimate night, something no man had seen or touched because he had not. The concept was illogical and unreal, but it was thus that he wanted her. In the more lucid part of his brain, he knew that no darkness could wash out what she had been and done, but at least one of his senses was sharing her with no one and his other senses found perfection.

He was lost in his need of her when suddenly her hands ceased their caressing and he felt her grow tense.

"Damn it," she said helplessly.

"What's the matter?"

"This is no good for us."

"Don't say that."

"Why not? It's true." She took a deep breath. Then, softly, she added, "I didn't want this to happen, Stan."

"Didn't you?"

He tried to keep the irony from his voice but could not. Who in hell did she think she was kidding? He had not slugged her or gotten her drunk to bring her here. Everything had been strictly regulation—getting him into bed with her had probably been her idea from the moment they first met and he had recognized the mute question in her eyes. He continued caressing her, literally feeling his way in the physical dark—but sensing, too, that he had to break through into some mental or emotional midnight where her innermost secrets lurked.

Some of those she, herself, probably only partially understood.

"All right," she whispered. "Have it your way."

"How's that?"

"You want what any man wants."

"And if I wanted more, would you have it to give?"

"Oh, hell," she broke in acidly. "You don't even think I have as much to give as most women. You and I both know you think I've been used too often. Here I am in bed. Isn't that evidence enough? Nobody pushed me down—isn't that what you think, word for word?"

"Almost," he said carefully. "It's not all I have in mind, though."

"What else could there be? I'm a slut and a tramp and I can prove it. A woman grows up learning all the man-happy rules that go with the double standard and I can probably show you a few things you've never even thought of."

"Just be yourself," he said. "Be exactly what you are. Show me what you feel like showing—throw out the rest."

"You don't think I'm a slut and a tramp?"

"Yes," he said honestly. "You probably are. But those are just words we learn from the things we do. Before you were either of those, you were just Linda. You've never stopped being you."

He kissed her and she barely responded. But she relaxed again and after a long moment whispered his name.

"Yes?" he asked.

Her voice seemed to come from her thoughts, from far away. "Who was Linda, Stan?"

"That's something I don't know. I hope to meet her tonight."

"So do I. Is that why we came here—to find Linda?"

"Sure."

Once more, he bent down to kiss her and again she barely responded.

Finally she said, still in that faraway voice, "Suppose Linda doesn't live here any more? I've tried to go back, Stan, back to before I married Ben—before a lot of things happened. I've tried to find who I used to be. I couldn't go back. I couldn't remember—" Her voice caught on a sob.

"I'll help you," he said.

He tried and knew she tried also. He kissed her and now she gave him all she had. Their hands explored and implored—but at the ultimate instant she tensed and denied him again.

"Just go on," she said through clenched teeth. "Make me. Others have."

He shook his head. "I'm not others."

She clung to him then, fiercely, but there was no softness or tenderness to her touch. She strained and shuddered. She said his name in a little thin whisper.

"What is the matter?"

"I'm sorry—but I can't."

"All right—so you can't." He did his best to keep frustration and anger out of his voice. "I told you—just be yourself."

"That's right." She laughed suddenly. "Why should I apologize?"

"I said forget it."

"Then to hell with it."

"All right," Stan nodded.

Suddenly, mockingly, she asked, "Where's Linda?"

"You're Linda. You can't help being you."

"So get me another drink, will you?"

"And a cigarette?"

"Yes." Her tone mocked him. "And a cigarette." Her eyes narrowed and glinted angrily but she waited, motionless. Then, after he had given her a cigarette and drink, she sipped and smoked sullenly and started to tell him about her having been seduced while she was still in high school.

"But I was old enough," she said.

"You don't have to tell me."

"But I want to, Stan. My very first real love was this engineering student who was working that summer with a county surveying crew. Maybe his education had something to do with how I felt. He knew so many things and he told me I was beautiful. Nobody had ever said anything like that to me before. Besides, he had been to Europe. So in the evenings, I'd sneak off down to the creek behind our place and he would tell me about places like Paris and Rome and the Riviera and we swam in the nude. Now isn't that a romantic picture? Me and my long legs and skinny with practically no build and old lover boy over six feet and just having himself a great time. After all, like I said, he had an education and whatever he wanted to do must be all right, I figured. Anyway, I had nothing but stars in my eyes and my heart was all pitty-pat." Linda paused. Her voice shook. "But I believed him and so I didn't even mind being hurt. He loved me and you know about love, Stan. That always makes everything all right."

"Nobody knows about love," Stan said slowly.

"Oh, but I do and I want to tell you. At least, you ought to know the end. I mean, it was so neat and trite and complete and financial. Because, when the surveying party he was with got ready to move on and I saw him the last time; he gave me a twenty-dollar bill. Imagine, Stan? A whole twenty-dollar bill. Wasn't that a nice thing to do for a ragged, ravished little kid? Even the words have a certain poetic rhythm." Linda took a long drag on her cigarette. Then she shrugged. "All right," she said, "I didn't mean to start telling you the story of my life. Anyway, for all I know, I might have had a break. Earn while you learn. How does that sound?"

"It sounds like hell."

"Yes," Linda nodded slowly. "I guess it does. But, Stan, have you ever noticed how being good or bad is not so much what you do or don't do but more what you talk or don't talk about. Maybe you can tell me a different kind of love story—one that doesn't involve money."

He shook his head. "Most love stories involve money one way or another. Maybe it makes some difference how it comes into the picture, but money in itself doesn't have to spoil anything."

"You mean if a thing is spoiled, it's bad to start with. Like between you and me."

"There hasn't been anything yet between you and me. Anyway, nothing much."

"That's right," she said. "There hasn't. I talk too much sometimes."

"Like now?"

"That's right," she whispered. "Like now."

She crushed out her cigarette, finished her drink and stretched out on the bed once more, her hands to his shoulders. She looked up at him and her eyes grew heavy and hot again as they had that night at the dance when he had thought he had seen eternity in them. He went down to her and a shiver went through her when he touched her. She returned his kiss passionately but in the next instant, she was whispering against his mouth about Meg.

"She loves me, Stan."

"Didn't you just say you talked too much?"

"But don't you want to know, Stan?"

"Know what?"

"About me and Meg?"

"Only how you feel about her."

"I just told you. She loves me."

"And that's all there is to it—just her side?"

"That's my side, too."

Stan both understood and did not. He raised his head and looked down at her, studying her face as much as he could in the near darkness. Her expression told him nothing but from her sudden stillness, he got the impression that she was more scared than she wanted to admit. Of what—her involvement with Meg or her being here with him? He could not even guess. She might simply be teasing him, giving him a bad time because she herself had been hurt. But when he tried to retaliate by suggesting that they have a therapeutic talk over another drink, Linda shut her eyes and clung to him.

"No," she whispered. "Stay right here."

"Is that what you really want?"

"Yes."

"You're sure?"

"Yes. I'm sure."

She lay very still in his arms and instinctively he cradled and caressed her as if she were a child needing reassurance. Once more he had the feeling that the real darkness surrounding her was not the physical one in the room but some never-ending night that emanated from within her to conceal her from realities as most people knew them.

The woman in her seemed strangely distant until suddenly she whispered, "Stan, remember? You told me I was beautiful."

"That's right."

"Tell me again."

She waited and he bent down and breathed the words to her parted lips. For moments afterward, almost as if she were fighting not only what he was trying to make her feel but herself, she lay still and rigid. But, gradually, she started to yield. A soft murmur began in her throat. She began to stroke his back and her mouth fastened to his with unfeigned hunger.

Then, she wrenched her lips away.

"Stan! This is crazy."

"Why?"

"Because it can't be any good."

"Why don't we wait and see?"

"All right."

"Just hold me."

"I am."

"And—give me time."

"Don't worry," he said. "I will."

His mouth went down to hers gently. It moved from her lips to other parts of her—the woman in her was back and he did not mean to let her escape again to her private darkness. His blood pounded with the night's long denial and she grew supple and passionate in his arms.

Once, when she moaned, he asked, "Am I hurting you?"

"No—but I'm scared."

"Of what?"

"Of you—of this. I don't want to like it."

"That doesn't make sense."

"No." She shivered. "I guess it doesn't."

She closed her eyes. Her lips were warm and soft under his and they trailed fire. Her arms tightened around him but once more, she asked him to wait.

"No," he said. "Not any more."

"Please, Stan," she whispered.

She struggled, then stopped and waited rigidly—and he knew she once more had him licked. He could force her as others had done and she would not resist him. But to do so would put him in a class with those others and there he did not want to be. It would also end things between them.

Neither of them spoke. He held still until she reached for him again.

Her breath caught and they became a living, writhing tangle of oneness beyond the individuality of either. It was as if, together, they were seeking something neither could find alone—until suddenly—shockingly—their union grew real.

Linda tensed, relaxed and tensed again. She clung to him as if in anguish and slowly, some deep source of strength was released in her. Her transition was as elemental as earth—as the sea and its tides. Her hands moved over him, caressingly, holding him to her with a force beyond physical strength—he sensed this embrace was forever. He would still feel it and be bound to her by it long after this night was over and they had parted.

"Stan," she whispered.

"I know."

What did he know? Whatever it was, she knew it too, without further question.

His breath burned raw in his throat. She twisted and moaned as if he had plunged a knife into her heart. Her breath sucked in sharply and he knew a brief wonder—did she feel as lost in him as he did in her. It was as if he and she had assumed a third identity belonging to neither of them—he sensed her fighting this submersion of self and he held her hard and close. Something she was trying to say suddenly smothered and muffled against his chest. She gave up trying to escape. Her hot breath fanned his neck and, when her mouth came back to his, he knew it did so from a need beyond her self. Her lips writhed and clung, sweet and fragrant and his thinking funneled down to an infinite reach of distance. From here to that infinity, she belonged to him.

When the moment hit, she sobbed once. Her arms clamped and locked about him. Warmth encompassed them, rose and subsided.

She murmured softly and a long time elapsed before she slowly, reluctantly, released him. Her eyes opened languorously and she wet her lips with her tongue.

He waited.

"Stan," she said shakily, at last.

"What, Linda?"

"I'm scared."

"Because it was like that?"

"Yes," she whispered. "Because it was like that."

13

Linda took off her high heels and slipped quietly into the trailer. She closed the door softly behind her. For a moment, she waited and listened. When, at last, she turned to go through the tiny kitchen area to the sleeping compartment, a hulking shadow moved in the light reflected from outside the trailer and Linda came to a dead stop. Her eyes widened and she clenched her hands helplessly.

"Ben," she whispered.

"Welcome home."

He grunted and came toward her.

"Hell," he said, with a heavy slurring sarcasm that warned Linda he had been drinking steadily but was not drunk. "Don't just stand there looking so damned surprised to see me awake and waiting. After all, it's only two-thirty in the morning."

"Ben," Linda said again numbly.

"Go on, you bitch. Tell some lies."

"But, Ben," Linda tried again. "Let—"

Her voice faltered and broke. Her mouth and throat were dry. A sinking panic hollowed out the pit of her stomach and her heart pounded against her ribs. Terror plucked at her nerves and a burst of heat mounted to her face. Tears stung her eyes. Her whole body went weak and she flinched but, before she could turn her head to avoid the blow, Ben slapped his hand across her mouth.

"Come here," he rumbled.

"No, Ben. Please, don't."

Linda blinked and her words blurred to a shivering, pleading moan but he hit her again. She sagged, lost her balance and went to her knees. Pain cut the inside of her mouth and she wanted to crumple down and huddle on the floor but Ben got his fist in her hair. He clenched his fingers and pulled her head up and back so he could lean down and stare into her eyes.

"You were with Stan," he said thickly.

"Ben! You're hurting me."

"Shut up," he said viciously. "And don't try to lie to me either. Sonny spotted you sneaking out the back way. He came to town and fetched me back here to wait for you. I saw you coming in with that big, smart bastard and I saw him kissing you good night. And now, by hell, I'm going to teach you something."

"No," Linda whispered. "No."

She tried to squirm away from him but, with his huge fist knotted in her hair, he kept her down on her knees. His eyes squinted, small and fierce. A fleck of spittle frothed at the corner of his loose mouth as he called her a string of dirty names. Afterward, in the tiny bed area, in the glare of the night-light he ripped and tore the dress from her. He stripped her roughly.

"Don't, Ben," she begged.

"Didn't I tell you to shut up?"

Color left her face. She huddled on the bed and tried to cover her breasts with crossed arms. His hands reached down to force her arms to her sides and he brought his face close to hers. He smelled of beer and stale tobacco.

"Okay," he grunted. "Now tell me."

"What, Ben?"

"About Stan."

"No," she whispered. "Please."

"Did you let him do this?"

"Don't," she moaned. "You're hurting me."

"Then answer me."

His mouth moved wetly to hers and she shivered with disgust. His strength crushed her resistance and she shuddered and closed her eyes but his voice kept right on asking.

"Tell me," he said.

"I can't."

"The hell you can't."

His fingers gouged her flesh and, at last, dug from her the admission he wanted.

"You let him take you to bed?"

"Ben," she moaned. "I just told you."

"But say it again."

Her voice tightened and her throat rasped but Ben wanted it all. He got his mouth right down to hers. His eyes gleamed hard and small. She felt suffocated by his breath and her words seemed to shatter and go to pieces as she said them.

But behind the broken words, her memory was vivid and glowing . . .

Linda, you were wonderful . . .

No, don't say that . . .

Why not?

Because it makes being here be like buying a ticket to some kind of a peep show or a movie. Even a ride on a roller coaster can be wonderful . . .

Damn it, Linda, stop it . . .

Why?

Because I didn't mean it like that . . .

Didn't you?

She remembered the angry taste of asking him the question and the glow of two cigarettes in the dark, the smell of sedge grass, brackish water and tide flats and the breath of wind stirring the drapes. She had been bitter to keep from crying. A two-hour romance in a ten-dollar motel was just a cut above being a common whore. To put it in words had been to change it from something perfect, pure and eternal to something cheap and shoddy. When she had finally been unable to hoard the moment that had been beautiful, she had gotten up, reached for her clothes and told Stan to take her home.

Please, Stan . . .

Wait, Linda. Look at me.

What for?

Because I want to talk to you . . .

There isn't anything to talk about . . .

You could be wrong . . .

No, Stan . . .

Then, this was nothing?

He had paused and waited but she had simply kept her head down so he would not see the tears glittering in her eyes. Then, later, all that long way back home to the trailer park, she had stayed on her own side of the seat and said very little. But just before they had reached the park, Stan had put his hand on her thigh.

Linda, listen. . . .

To what?

I want to talk about us . . .

Stan, there isn't anything to say . . .

I think there is . . .

We had a good time—let it go at that . . .

Is that the way you feel?

Yes . . .

I don't believe you . . .

You'd better. Look at me. I've made a mess out of my life. I'm a loser, a bad luck charm. And it's not just Ben or Meg either. Even when I was just a kid, things were never right for me. So, be smart. Forget the whole thing—if you don't want to do it for yourself, do it for me. I'm all right now. Meg is good to me and I'm tired of ugliness and bitterness and being poor and living in places where people have nothing. Don't feel sorry for me either. I know where I am with Meg and, anyway, when it's all said and done, maybe that's the kind of woman I am . . .

I don't believe that . . .

There's a lot you don't know . . .

About what?

About me and Meg . . .

Linda had stopped and lapsed into silence. She had huddled miserably in her corner of the car seat. Then, at the park, with the dark trailers sleep-quiet, she had stared up at Stan and in that last moment suddenly, helplessly, she had gone into his arms. With a kind of savage, straining fury, she had hugged and kissed him.

Linda, listen to me . . .

No, damn it—no . . .

She had thrust him away, grabbed her purse and gotten out of the convertible. A moment later, she had slipped into her dark trailer . . .

"All right," Ben puffed wetly. "Be still."

"No, Ben. Please."

"If you liked it from Stan, you'll like it from me," he said thickly.

His breath grunted and, turning her head helplessly from side to side on the pillow, she fought being choked by the rancid odor of sweat and beer.

"Wait," she whispered. "You're hurting me."

"Maybe you need to be hurt."

He kissed her and hurt her with his teeth. Ben's hands gouged and massaged and the big ugliness of him sickened her but she managed to lie still.

"That's better," Ben muttered.

She struggled to breathe and hated him but suddenly, she gave in completely. She did not even try to turn her face away from him. Why bother? Nothing she could do would stop him and he had not beaten her as much as he might. Maybe she was being lucky. It could be a whole lot worse. Anyway, why pretend? He was part of her life. Nobody had to tell her he was never going to free her. He was her husband and a husband had his rights. How many times had she heard him say so? Her thinking stopped there.

She held her breath. Ben kept right on hurting her. His bare arms and shoulders and the heavy sagging of his chest shifted in slick shadows. Light glittered on his sweaty face. His weight flattened and pinned her.

Go ahead, she thought dully. *You've got your rights. Take them. Do anything . . .*

Ben's big clumsy hands worked, pinched, pawed and clamped. Blunt fingers splayed and hooked into her flesh.

Later, he told her about how he and Sonny were going to get Stan to hell and gone out of the park.

"You'll see," he grunted.

"See what?"

"I'll be manager here myself."

"How?"

"You just wait for Meg to tie the can to that big punk."

"Because of me?"

"Yes," Ben said heavily. "Because of you."

He stopped talking and Linda closed her burning eyes and gritted her teeth. Damn him. She did not want to feel anything, but mental agony tore at her. She blamed herself for adding to Stan's problems—and promised herself that, no matter what she had to do, she would not let Ben do anything to hurt Stan.

14

Stan hated to have to be tough about the rent but the park was meant to be a profit-making enterprise. Upkeep and overhead went on every day and keeping collections up to date made the difference between red ink and black. But on that following Monday night, checking the delinquent list with the tired-looking blonde at the counter, he wished to hell there was an easier way of going about it.

"Listen, Madge," he said. "You'll soon be three months behind."

Madge Olson nodded. "I know."

"Didn't Hank go back to work last week?"

"Yes."

"Well, then?"

Stan waited and looked down at the delinquent list. Names, figures and penciled notations blurred. He felt beat with talking and listening. For a moment while he waited for Madge to get her story going, he took a quick breather, glancing around the office.

At the entrance, a big moth batted clumsily against the double screen doors. Off to one side, clustered around the soft drink machine, Madge's two little girls and a bare-footed, tow-headed boy who had walked over with them argued about how to spend the dime he held clenched in his grubby hand. Their voices bickered back and forth. The TV was tuned to a quiz show. Somebody had just won a jackpot and, near the cash register, perched so she gave the effect of overflowing her stool, Maggie nodded with an expression of satisfaction and fanned herself with a folded newspaper.

Outside, headlights flickered. A car headed out through the gate and, about the same time, two cigar-smoking poker players in shirt sleeves came in. They nodded and headed for the recreation room and their nightly card game.

Stan brought his attention back to what Madge had to say.

"We've had a lot of hard luck."

"But you bought a new car."

"I know," Madge went on with a hunted expression on her worried face. "Hank figured the deal was too good to miss." She paused as if she knew that did not make much sense. Her fingers picked nervously at her hair. In a pathetic rush, she said, "If you'll just let us have a little more time we'll start catching up by paying something on account this pay day."

"Friday?"

She nodded.

"For sure?"

"Yes—I promise."

Stan knew her word was good. Even if Hank could not be trusted to give you the right time, Madge was okay and Stan wrote Friday's date down beside her name. After she had gathered the kids and gone, Stan put the delinquent sheet away and, glancing over at Maggie, lit a cigarette and inhaled gratefully.

"There ain't no reason for them to be behind," Maggie said.

"I guess not."

"You know what a cab driver makes?"

"Sure," Stan said. "Plenty."

"But they'll never have a dime the way Hank spends it."

"Maybe not."

Stan waited a second. To hell with Madge and Hank. Beyond collecting their rent, he did not give a damn one way or the other how they budgeted their money. It was none of Maggie's business either and Stan toyed with the notion of getting her nose off the trail by asking when Birdie and Sonny intended to get back from the shopping center. Stan dropped the idea when Maggie launched into her standard lecture on no-good husbands and how things had changed since she was a girl. To shut out the sound of her voice, he leaned over the counter and started balancing the day's accounts.

All the while, trying to concentrate on his work over the sound of Maggie's voice and the murmur of noise from the recreation room, in the back of Stan's mind was a vision of Linda and the problem of what he was going to do about her. He had not been able to see her or to talk to her after bringing her home from their motel tryst. He knew from the grapevine that Ben had been at the trailer waiting for her. Maybe she had been able to brazen things out. So far, Stan had heard nothing to the contrary but if Ben had gotten the truth out of Linda, the question might not be what to do about Linda but rather what Ben was going to do about him.

Well, he could handle that fat slob.

And Linda?

Stan tried to think but, outside of knowing from park gossip that she had been over to the laundry room and had seemed to be all right, he had nothing to go on. Maybe that was best. Probably, he thought savagely, a one-night stand just put another notch in her garter belt but that kind of bitter cynicism did nothing to combat the mounting heat the mere thought of her sent through him.

He remembered her voice, warm and husky, murmuring against his lips. The clinging touch of her hands—the memory of the ultimate embrace he knew he never could escape—these were sheer torture. His recollections of the night blurred to a flooding warmth and he had to fight to get hold of himself. To hell with Linda. She had Ben and Meg and, as Mae had said, she was a crazy gypsy bitch and deep trouble. She had even asked him to forget her. Why not add up the experience it had taken to make her so good in bed and start figuring how much time she had spent learning the trade. She had bragged of that, too. He waited for the muscles in his stomach to relax and saw Maggie look at him curiously.

"Are you all right?" she asked.

"I'm okay."

"There are a lot of bugs going around."

"Don't worry about me, Maggie."

"The doctors find something new all the time."

"I guess so."

"If you feel bad, be careful."

"I'm okay," Stan said again.

He looked down at his balance sheet once more. Next, his attention was diverted by a brief flurry of complaints. A fat woman named Keedley wanted something done about her neighbor's men friends.

"It's a disgrace," she grumbled.

"I'll check into it," Stan promised.

"You'll need an adding machine."

"We'll see," Stan murmured soothingly.

"Her husband is working over in Fresno."

"I know."

"She ought to be ashamed."

Stan promised again to check what was going on.

"I can't sleep. I hear them all night."

The fat woman wet her lips and took a deep breath but before she could get going again another woman came in to report a plugged drain in the washroom.

"It ought to be fixed tonight," she said.

"I'll take care of it," Stan told her.

He also promised to have the ruts in the road in front of number twenty-nine fixed, to do something about the dust from the playground, to replace a broken overhead light and to make sure the kids stopped playing around the incinerator. After the rush had subsided he went back to his balance sheet and, a few moments later, after counting and recounting the cash in the cash register, he came up thirty dollars short.

"Maggie," he said.

Maggie listened but she did not understand how any money could be missing. There had been no cash transactions since she had taken over from Sonny, so she could not have made a mistake handling the money. Her eyes became guarded. No, she had not actually checked the register. She had simply accepted Sonny's cash count and, after carefully going over his figures again, Stan, soothed her down. He was willing to bet she had not tapped the till but he was not so sure about Sonny. Before going out to work on the drain and head home for a shower, Stan told Maggie that he wanted to talk to Sonny when Sonny got back from town.

"Ask him to drop over to my trailer, Maggie."

"Shall I tell him about the money?"

"No," Stan said. "Let me worry about that."

He shrugged as if it had no real importance and went out. He unplugged the drain, checked a few other complaints and, an hour and a half later was in his own trailer. When Sonny finally slouched in, Stan made no bones.

"Sonny," he said bluntly. "The cash is short."

"So?"

"What the hell does that mean, Sonny?"

"I borrowed the dough."

"Borrowed?"

"Sure," Sonny said easily. "That's all."

He shrugged and stood his ground, cocky in khaki pants and an open-necked white sport shirt. Shadows made his skinny face cadaverous and his cigarette bounced as he inhaled. When Stan started to give him hell and told him he knew damn well that nobody borrowed money from the till without permission, Sonny shrugged again.

"Listen," he said at last. "I'm on your side."

"My side?"

"Sure," Sonny began. "Ben says—"

"What's Ben got to do with this?"

"Well," Sonny smirked. "You went out with his wife the other night and Ben and I figured—"

Sonny paused and grinned.

"That I wouldn't want any more trouble?"

Sonny nodded. "Something like that."

Stan lunged, collared Sonny, spun him to the patio, whirled him around and slammed him against the side of the trailer. He had instantly made up his mind that there would be no deal with Sonny.

"Listen," he gritted.

"Wait, Stan. For Pete's sake, take it easy."

Sonny's eyes bugged. He gulped and swallowed. His scrawny throat worked. Sweat glistened on his face. He sucked air and listened while Stan told him to get the money back where he had got it. No more nonsense about borrowing.

"Do you understand that, Sonny?"

"Sure, Stan. Sure."

Sonny's head bobbed up and down.

"Don't forget."

"I won't, Stan."

"I'm still the boss around here."

There was a pause.

"Okay. I know that, Stan."

"All right then, you little bastard—don't ever forget that either."

"All right, I got it."

"Then get over there and straighten the cash out."

"Sure, I'm going."

Sonny took a deep breath and shook himself as Stan let him go. He edged out toward the path to the road but paused and turned back. His eyes slitted and burned narrow.

"Stan," he called back.

"What now?"

"I guess I had you wrong."

Stan nodded. "I guess you did."

"Well," Sonny finished softly. "Don't worry. I never make the same mistake twice."

15

Linda forced her legs to relax. She took a deep breath and leaned back in the custom-upholstered Cadillac convertible. Tears clouded her vision and, for a moment, looking down from the secluded bluff where Meg had parked, Linda saw the velvety glitter of the town below melt into a twinkling network of merging lights. When Meg turned to her and caressed her thigh gently, Linda shivered.

"Meg—"

"I only want to talk."

"It's no use. I told you that."

"Please, Linda. Give me a chance."

"Then don't touch me there."

"Why not, darling?"

"Just don't."

Linda swallowed and trembled. Meg's hand slowly continued its tender, stroking motion. Linda watched it with a kind of hypnotized fascination. Meg's slim soft fingers made her feel weak. She lifted her head and leaned against the seat's backrest until she could look up at the star-studded sky. A loose wisp of black hair blew softly against her cheek and Meg moved closer. Linda felt a tremor ripple through her.

"Meg," she said helplessly.

"What, baby?"

"Who am I?"

"Don't you know?"

"No," Linda whispered.

"Don't be afraid of what we are."

"I'm not. I just don't know."

Linda caught her breath and, for a moment, turning her head, she looked right into Meg's eyes. A burning magnetic shock hit her. A desire to surrender washed through her and she felt drawn to the soft, warm, red waiting of Meg's parted lips. Small, fierce tremors made her feel limp and boneless. Then, fighting against the weakening forces that flooded through her, Linda stared up at the sky again.

"Damn it," she said bitterly.

"Then you are afraid?"

"Maybe I am."

Meg drew back a little but the warmth of her hand kept rubbing and petting and Linda did not have the strength to do anything about it. She felt listless, defenseless. She wanted tenderness. She knew an all but irresistible longing to give in, to stop battling against what Meg wanted her to do. Maybe what she was, was not important. After all, there were billions of people on earth, so what happened to her was just a drop in the bucket. There was no use getting overdramatic about herself. But the memory of her night with Stan kept coming back.

She remembered liquid fire and a sweet burning ache. She remembered tender hurt, kisses with a goal and purpose beyond anything she alone could feel—something that required two persons merging into one being that could not exist save for those two people alone. She could never be with anyone what she had become with Stan—nor could he experience with anyone else what he had shared with her.

She remembered the swollen cut inside her bruised mouth and black finger marks pinched on her breasts by Ben later that same night. She remembered Ben's wet, panting kisses, his wallowing heaviness and tensed all over again. Even her nausea came back and so did the harsh, blunt, brutal truth. Ben had his rights. She was his wife. Why not face it? No matter what she did, he had his claim on her. Even if she ran away with Stan, every day would be just twenty-four long hours of waiting for Ben to come to get her.

Too, she had no reason to think that Stan would want a permanent attachment to grow out of his having shared a motel room with her for a couple of hours. She had been in enough beds to know that all men came fully equipped with a built-in double standard. And even having things work out as perfectly as they had with Stan did not change the fact that she had been what was generally known as easy.

A good woman simply did not go to bed with a man because that was the thing she most wanted to do in the whole world. Not in the good old U.S.A. American women were supposed to come hermetically and antiseptically sealed in cellophane and already mounted on a fresh wholesome split-level pedestal. Then, as if inhibitions were turned on and off at the flick of a switch, they were expected to bring to their husbands all the know-how of a street walker.

But, Linda thought miserably, she was not being fair. Even if Stan wanted to continue with her, he could not overlook Meg. Nobody could. Linda had crossed a line and lived in two worlds.

Meg leaned toward her again.

"Darling—"

"Please, Meg."

"Please, what?"

"Don't call me that."

"But, Linda, you look so hurt."

"I can't help it."

"But I can," Meg said softly.

She pressed close to Linda. Her touch was soft, warm and beguiling. Linda made a protest and Meg drew away again. She turned to face forward on the seat and, with a small shaky motion, opened her purse and tore the wrapper off of a package of cigarettes.

"Here," she said. "Take one."

"All right."

Linda waited. Meg's lighter flickered in the warm wind. They smoked and Meg brought a bottle out of the glove compartment. Linda drank with a kind of stubborn hopelessness. Why fight, she thought numbly as Meg continued to work on weakening her defenses.

"You know how I feel about you," Meg said.

"But we weren't going to talk about that."

"Then we can be just friends."

"Can we, Meg?"

"Why not? I only want you to be happy."

"Your way?"

"Not unless that is what you want, too."

Meg turned away and inhaled smoke. Her eyes returned to Linda. They stared at each other and the night was still on the deserted bluff and the world seemed far away. At last, Meg again moved toward Linda. Another moment passed and, slowly, Meg passed the tip of her tongue over her lips. Finally, almost as if she had to force herself to do it, Meg leaned away from Linda again. She shrugged.

"Linda, be sensible."

"About what?"

"About everything, baby."

Meg made a gesture of patience. Carefully, her voice avoiding bitterness or recriminations, she began to talk about Stan. Little by little, she brought out that she knew about Linda's motel tryst with Stan. And, listening to her, Linda suddenly came abruptly up against the numbing realization that money could buy anything.

Not just some things but anything.

Meg knew all the secrets about who got kissed and loved, in whose bed and how long it took. Her money owned Stan and Maggie. It had bought Sonny, Ben and Birdie and what had happened to Birdie that night she was at Stan's trailer. All the little, hot squirming, wriggling, intimate details grew naked in the calm and cool and controlled and unemotional sound of Meg's voice.

"I hate having to say these things," she said.

"Do you?"

"Please," Meg coaxed. "Don't make it any harder for us, Linda. I'm just honestly trying to show you that it's foolish for you to let yourself be hurt over Stan. At least, by now you ought to know that it can't be serious with him. He has Mae and—"

"And Birdie?"

"Don't be angry. I had to tell you that."

"But how did you get her to talk about it?"

"That was easy, darling."

"Easy?"

Meg murmured, "Everybody has a price. Besides," she added softly, "from the very first, Birdie always was curious."

"About what?"

"About our kind of love."

"So you—"

"Please, darling," Meg broke in swiftly. "Don't be silly. Birdie leaves me cold—for one thing, she's too willing. Anyway, bribing her was both simple and cheap. A lot of money, you know, is a relative term and Birdie's ambitions are small. Of course, at the same time, a little teasing made dealing with her easier." Meg paused and looked at Linda with renewed speculation. After a moment she asked, "Are you jealous, Linda?"

"Of somebody like Birdie?"

Meg persisted, "Are you?"

"I don't know," Linda said at last. "I don't know."

She closed her eyes and thought about Birdie and Meg but nothing really made sense. What Meg and Birdie did was not important to her. Being parked alone with Meg meant nothing either but suddenly, with a kind of other-world craziness and a little hopelessly, Linda thought that maybe Meg was right about her.

So why fight it?

Just be what Meg wanted. One way or the other she would win anyway. As Meg had said, everybody had a price. Not even if the best things in life were free and low-grade commodities such as peace, comfort, luxury and security had to be bought. You did not have to be poor and in debt to breathe air, walk in the woods, look at the sky, wade in a river or stand in the sun. And even the kind of love that Meg offered could be made beautiful and almost respectable with money.

Meg moved closer to her again.

"Linda," she whispered.

"Look at me, darling."

Meg paused and her hand moved down to Linda's thigh again. Linda felt oddly detached from what was happening to her. She stirred and her tensions relaxed. She turned her cheek against the seat back and the lights of the town below seemed to be on another planet.

The softness of Meg's breasts crushed against her.

"Darling," Meg said shakily.

"No, Meg. Please."

"But you don't really want me to stop."

Meg's lips parted. Her eyes grew heavy. Linda shivered. Her stomach muscles tightened and small, delicious explosions coursed through her.

"Wait," she begged suddenly.

"Why, Linda?"

"Because I need to think, Meg. I—"

Her breath smothered. Meg kissed her mouth and suddenly Linda forgot everything but the feel of Meg. Her fingers curved and slid over the smooth satin texture of Meg's skin but even as she felt on fire inside, she got her mouth away from Meg's.

"No—" Linda shuddered—"I won't."

"Won't what, darling?"

"You know."

Linda caught her breath. Then Meg was kissing her again and to escape the widening whirlpool of emotion took more strength than Linda commanded—she couldn't stop what Meg was doing to her. Linda turned to Meg, whose voice, muffled and muted, murmured, "I love you."

"No, damn it. I don't want this."

"But you do," Meg whispered. "You do, darling."

16

"Stan," Mae crooned. "I've missed you lately."

"Like this?"

"Yes, hon," Mae hummed. "Like this." She stirred and looked up at him. Her hands trembled and stroked his bare shoulders. She murmured. "I need you."

"I'm flattered."

Mae pouted. "Don't talk like that." After a moment's silence she asked, "Stan, what's the matter?"

"Nothing," he lied and kissed the tip of her nose.

But he was bothered by memory of Birdie and the way he had had to get rid of her earlier in the evening. Probably, he thought, he should have put a little frosting on the cake but, with Mae due to arrive almost any minute, he had had neither the time nor the patience to string the argument out.

"Birdie," he had said. "I'm busy."

"Too busy for me?"

"I didn't say it like that."

"But that's what you meant."

"All right, have it your way. That was what I meant."

Stan remembered Birdie, skinny in shorts, almost flat under her halter, bare legged and with flip-flopping sandals—and her eyes suddenly slitted and vicious.

"Damn you to hell," she had stormed.

"Listen, Birdie, I—"

"Can that."

"Okay, Birdie. No argument."

"But you still want me to leave?"

"That's right."

"You didn't say that the other night."

"That was a mistake."

"Mistake?"

Birdie's voice had shrilled and, when Stan had tried to tell her he was sorry, she had started cursing him in short blunt words. She described with spitting ugliness the night when she had been good enough to be in his bed.

"I didn't hear you complain."

"Birdie, for Pete's sake, that's over."

"Over?"

"I said I was sorry."

But admitting that he was sorry had been wrong. Maybe, since he had only wanted to get rid of her, there had been no right thing to say. Anyway, she had sputtered, seethed and called him a big no-good bastard and told him to go straight to hell. Then, in a last hot-eyed burst of fury, she had warned him that, before things were over, he would really be sorry.

Thinking over Birdie's threat, Stan found the nagging murmur of Mae's voice grated on his nerves.

"Hon," she whispered. "Are you sure there is nothing wrong?"

"I just told you I was."

"Yes," Mae murmured, "I know but—"

Her voice faded. Stan kissed her mouth, face and neck and got the right things said. She sulked but gradually her eyes grew heavy-lidded. She returned his caresses with languorous deliberation.

"Like me?"

"You know all the tricks."

"That's no answer, Stan."

"Isn't it?"

He kissed her to stop her from saying more. Her arms twined around his neck and all of her yielded, surrendered utterly.

"Hold me, darling—"

Her voice grew thin and eager, and the humming began in her throat. Her fingers locked at the nape of his neck. She pulled his face to hers.

"Stan," she whispered against his lips.

"What is it?"

"You belong to me—remember."

"Don't say that, Mae."

"It's true."

"Not now. It can't be."

"I love you," she insisted.

Nobody knew about love was what he had told Linda but this much Stan knew—Mae did not love him. With her, love was a thing that began and ended with herself. Probably he had always known how she felt but the fact that she was merely using him no longer mattered. He found time to wonder at the change in himself even as he made love to Mae—had his night with Linda changed him? A gypsy, Mae had called her with jealous apprehension. Had she been more correct than either of them had guessed? Had Linda actually worked some occult magic over him?

Mae said abruptly, "Something's the matter—you're not with it, lover—" and even in passion her eyes narrowed in angry speculation.

He almost laughed out loud. Mae's all-inclusive world was always militantly alert—in it love and war existed side by side. Many of the things he had never understood about her thought processes were suddenly clear to him. He had a new insight—a new detachment toward her—and it was possibly this factor that alerted him.

Normally, when he was with her, he would have remained oblivious to an earthquake. Now he grew aware of another presence in the trailer.

"Listen," he whispered tensely.

"To what?"

"Wait—"

Stan covered Mae's mouth with his hand. Tension froze him into immobility and surprise sent a plummeting emptiness through him—for the moment neither his brain nor his senses worked. Cautiously, without conscious volition, he turned.

Larry stood in the trailer's doorway.

"I've had you watched before," Larry said. His lips barely moved. His fat mouth glittered wetly. His eyes were hot with anger, yet hard with thought. He looked dangerous. "This time," he finished slowly, "I thought I'd come see for myself."

Her eyes huge in her suddenly white face, Mae crawled trembling to her knees. She crouched so, pulling at the bedsheet to cover herself.

"Larry—"

"Bitch."

"No, please—"

"Whore." The big man spoke without emphasis, using his words descriptively rather than as epithets.

Mae's voice broke. With the sheet clutched to her naked, heaving breasts, she simply stared. Hard, bluish glint of gunsteel glittered menacingly in Larry's fat fist and Stan tasted fear. His guts tightened in anticipation—he wondered if Larry was going to squeeze the trigger of the tiny automatic.

"Listen, Larry," he said warily. "If you knew all the time—"

"Shut up."

"Why the gun now?"

"Goddamn it, Stan, shut up."

The gun moved but the hot, thoughtful anger in Larry's eyes turned to sick staring misery. The thought came to Stan that the difference between life and death was always as close as the next car on the highway—or an unlucky break—and it must have occurred to Larry too. If he squeezed that trigger, the result would be murder—not an accident—and he was not prepared for that.

He spoke to Stan. "The gun is for you—only if you try to start anything. I need self-defense to get away with killing you." He turned to his wife. "I was right here, Mae, all the time."

"No, Larry."

"I watched."

Mae cringed, saying nothing.

"And I saw you."

Larry moved to the bed, began slapping Mae's face from side to side methodically. He was almost crying as he explained he had waited too long to do what he should have done in the beginning. Finally he pulled the sheet away from Mae and told her to get her clothes on.

"You're still my wife, Mae," he said heavily. "Unless you want to change that."

"I—don't. You know I don't, Larry."

"Then do as I tell you."

Stan started to breathe again. He knew that, this time, when Mae left his trailer she would not be coming back. Her eyes were withdrawn when she looked at Stan and he knew that in her stainless-steel mind wheels were turning. Her kind of love could be worked out in decimal points and she would not push her luck or risk losing her bank account. Probably too, she had known a moment before Larry had made his presence known that she had already lost Stan—as Stan himself had guessed it.

Larry made no objection as Stan left the trailer. Outside, to his surprise, he saw a prowl car. Birdie, her thin face vindictive, was talking to one of the officers and pointing to Stan's trailer.

Stan remembered Birdie's threats of vengeance as he walked to the prowler.

"There's no trouble here," he told the cop.

"The lady here called us."

"She made a mistake."

"You're sure?"

"Yes," Stan nodded slowly. "I'm sure."

The prowler pulled away, leaving Stan with Birdie. She looked at him for a moment, then turned and ran to her quarters behind the park office.

17

"Damn it, Stan," Meg said angrily.

"I told you I was sorry about last night."

"That's fine. Suppose Larry had used his gun?"

"He didn't make his money shooting people. He's not dumb. He just wasn't sure about me."

"But the police were down here."

Stan said, "That was Birdie's idea."

He had an empty feeling in his gut, as if he were waiting for the axe to fall. Meg was, at this moment, unpredictable—the park represented much of what she lived by. He could not tell for sure whether she was really on the warpath, but he had the sensation that his trailer was suddenly too small. Slanting in through the venetian blinds, the glare of the morning sun put hard pinpoints of light into Meg's eyes.

Stan thought numbly that even before she had arrived to start giving him hell for what had happened with Mae and Larry, he had known there were going to be repercussions. To begin with, after Larry and Mae had gone, Linda had slipped over long enough to warn him that Sonny and Ben intended to see that Meg used the brawl as an excuse to fire him. The idea made sense. They could draw straws for his job—he had everything in the park except his personal life running so smoothly a dummy could handle things.

But whether Meg needed an excuse or not might no longer matter. She had getting rid of him in her eyes—probably because of Linda—and so, Stan thought, eight hundred dollars a month and the best job he had ever had was on the verge of going down the drain. Sickness churned in his stomach. Sweat burned the palms of his hands, raw from his latest tussle with the water system. But abruptly, instead of giving him the business before really lowering the boom, Meg started discussing his relationship with Linda in almost normal terms.

"You seem to know a lot about it," he said, bristling slightly. "Did Linda tell you?"

Meg shook her head. "She didn't have to. I keep an eye on what goes on in the park. You've played around with Birdie too. If Sonny should get jealous, he could be dangerous."

Stan neither admitted nor denied anything.

Meg leaned back in her seat and made an impatient gesture with her hand. She went on, her voice hard and even as she told him Birdie was oversexed and curious in all directions as well as frustrated in her marriage to Sonny. Finally Meg began to suggest that the situation with Birdie and Sonny made it all but impossible to keep Stan on any longer as park manager—but she still shied away from actually handing him his walking papers. Indecision flickered in her eyes. Finally she put a new needle into him by telling him that Mae had also telephoned to warn her to be careful about letting Linda become involved with Stan.

"Did you know that?" Meg prodded.

"No," Stan admitted. "I didn't."

"But you don't sound surprised."

"Nothing about Mae could ever surprise me, Meg."

"Didn't you once trust her?"

"No," Stan said softly. "Not Mae."

He kept his voice flat. Mae no longer had any hold on him. He kept his attention on the strange, calculating waiting in Meg's eyes. At last Meg seemed to come to a decision. She took a deep breath and asked him if he would mind her discussing frankly her own relationship with Linda.

Stan said, "Why should I mind if you don't?"

Meg said simply, "I love her."

She paused. Stan's noncommittal nod seemed to give her some sort of bitter amusement. She crossed her slender legs, foraged in her purse for cigarettes and said she hoped he understood what she meant.

"I think I do."

"Think?"

Meg raised her eyebrows and once more seemed wryly amused. She let him give her a light, inhaled and shook her head.

"No," she said at last.

She paused and Stan watched her warily.

"No what, Meg?" he asked.

"You can't understand."

"About you and Linda?"

"Yes."

She studied him silently. Under her outward calm, he realized, she hated him. But her voice was perfectly steady when she told him next that she had talked things over with Linda before coming over to see him.

"I brought her home just after midnight last night. I understand she saw you after that."

"Did she say she did?"

"Yes, she told me."

Meg's eyes contracted and for once she could not hide their slitted fury. She compressed her lips, then pulled herself together.

She said carefully, "I should tell you this if you don't already know it—I've been in business too long to let personal feelings interfere with the good management of my investments. Do you follow me, Stan?"

"Maybe."

"You've made money for me," she said.

"I know."

His annoyance was beginning to rise to the surface. Until now he had been too concerned about the possible loss of his job to be aware of his deep-down irritation with Meg's cat-and-mouse tactics. If she meant to tie the can to him, she did not have to beat around the bush. All she had to do was hand him his walking papers and tell him to get going. He sure as hell had no way to stop her from doing that. There was no need for her to stick her fingers into his personal affairs.

"Stan, I have a proposition for you."

"All right."

"But first," Meg said. "You're through here."

"Fired?"

"Not fired, Stan. Just through."

"Because Linda came to see me last night?"

Her eyes did not waver and she did not change expression as she outlined what she had in mind for him. He was to take over the supervision and eventual management of a new trailer park that was to be built on a beach property Meg owned south of Los Angeles. The deal had been in the works for weeks. He was to receive a fifty-dollar a week raise and a working share of the business as a bonus for completing construction of the new park and putting the operation into the black. If he accepted the offer, he was to leave for the new location immediately.

"Well, Stan?"

She stared at him and he knew that what she was offering him was a trade—he was to give up Linda for a brighter future. Breath thickened in Stan's throat.

"Meg," he said finally. "Do I have to give you an answer right now?"

"Yes," she nodded. "Right now."

18

Late that evening, after dark, Stan was packing his clothes when he heard a slow, hesitant clicking of high heels outside his trailer. Stan took a look out through the screen door. Under the shadow of the awning, slim in black capri pants and a white blouse, Linda looked up at him.

"Stan?"

"What are you doing over here?"

"I had to come."

She made a helpless pleading gesture and suddenly Stan saw her too clearly—not only as she was, but as she had felt in his arms and as she had made him feel. His eyes stung with a kind of inward vision and understanding and suddenly he knew that both Meg and Mae had been wrong about her. She looked more like a kid than she did like a gypsy—or a consort for a lesbian.

"Please let me talk to you," she murmured.

"Linda, I—"

His chest tightened and he tried to fight this effect she had on him. It was unreal and unrealistic—he tried to force his attention away from her, to his actual surroundings. Out in front of the trailer, two boys on bicycles whistled and pumped by in the passing glare of a pair of headlights. He forced his eyes to follow them into the darkness. Somewhere a car horn blasted and he turned toward the sound. His eyes searched among the rows of trailers for familiar distractions and he made himself listen to the faint indistinct murmuring of distant television. Somewhere at the back of the park, someone was hammering but Stan's attention really never left Linda.

At last he looked back at her, opened the door and gestured her in.

"It's your funeral."

"How do you mean that, Stan?"

"Figure it out. It's pretty simple."

"Simple?"

"Okay. Do you think Ben would want you here?"

"No."

"Or Meg?"

"No."

"And this trailer park has eyes."

"Yes," Linda nodded. "I know."

But she came into the trailer anyway. Her body brushed against him as she entered and he breathed in her clean fragrance. Memory writhed within him—it was impossible for him to be near her without wanting her. Thinking of the deal he had made with Meg, he almost hated Linda for having come to him tonight.

They had nothing. They could never have anything. Neither of them was cut out for an existence independent from others.

From people like Meg.

Besides, Linda had a husband and a taste that could again take her way out to left field. Call it every nice polite name in the book and it still came out to make her different from other women—but even as he tried to talk sense to himself and remind himself that he owed her nothing, his want of her remained.

"Stan," she said. "Do you know why I'm here?"

"I asked you why you came," he reminded her.

"Please, Stan. I couldn't just let you go." She hesitated, then told him that she had learned from Meg where he was going and why. "I wanted you to tell me if what she said was true."

"It's true," he said bluntly.

"You're leaving tonight?"

"Yes—tonight."

He looked right at her and, even as their stares locked, he wanted to hate her. He wanted to hammer on the table and shout that he did not want her or need her clinging to him for strength he did not have.

"Damn it," he gritted. "Listen to me."

His eyes bored into her and she cringed. He had a fleeting thought that maybe Mae had been right from the start. Maybe Linda was too thin and maybe she did look like a gypsy and act like one. A kind of brutishness in him suddenly made him want to batter to death anything good she might think of him and he of her. He heard his voice—like that of a stranger's—telling her she was no good and how he had everything to lose and nothing to gain by having anything to do with her or even talking to her. His voice rode roughshod over her faint protests—he did his best to make the memory of anything they had shared seem ugly. He wanted it to be ugly for himself as well as for her. He wanted to forget her forever.

But gradually his manufactured rage turned to frustration. His words grew empty, meaningless. His fury trailed away to nothing and in the end he tried to brush aside his relationship to her as if it no longer mattered—as if it simply had died.

Linda shook her head. "No," she whispered. "I don't believe that."

"Can't you stand the truth?"

He tried once more and with detailed harshness beat down the memory of that night with her at the motel. Only it did not work. As he went into specifics, he kept looking at her and feeling he could never stop.

At last he grabbed Linda by her bare arms. His fingers tightened and he pulled her to where their eyes were only inches apart.

"Linda," he said.

She whispered, "Let me go."

"To hell with that. Just tell me something."

"What?"

"Why did you really come here tonight?"

"Just to say goodby."

"You're lying."

He brought her even closer. She tried to break free but he drew her against him. Her breasts crushed against his chest and suddenly her arms were around his neck.

"Oh, Stan," she moaned.

"Then this is what you wanted?"

"No—"

"You're lying," Stan told her again.

His voice shook. He knew a savage impulse to push her away but all at once her upturned face seemed clean and proud—and once more he felt as he had that night at the motel that no man had ever known her before as he did. Her eyes had an infinite liquid depth they probably had held for no other man—and certainly never for Meg.

"Linda," he asked, "do you love me?"

"Don't make me answer that, Stan."

"Why not?"

"Please," she begged. "Just don't."

He kissed her and her arms tightened and her lips parted against his. She was warm and giving and fierce and hard all at the same time. When he finally released her lips to ask her again if she loved him, she shook her head helplessly.

"All right—I love you."

"And you'd do anything for me?"

"Yes," she whispered.

"Right now?"

"If that's what you want."

"But I haven't said I love you."

"I know."

"But you'd still do whatever I asked?"

"Yes."

"Anything?"

"Yes," she whispered. "Anything."

Her voice was blurred and, in that instant, from the tortured expression in her eyes, he knew she too had made a bargain with Meg. No wonder Meg had been so uncomfortable and indecisive. She had not been able to fire him outright because Linda had traded herself for his new job.

The realization shocked Stan and with it he had the thought that he could still let the deal stand. All he needed to do was to keep his guesses and his questions to himself. Just pack up and get out and forget this woman who would be anything for him and do anything—and had proved it in a way he would never have asked her to.

While Stan was still staring rigidly at Linda, trying to digest what had really happened, Ben came over to start yelling for Linda to come out and get home. His loud abusive voice reached the patio and switched to a string of curses. Then he began pounding the side of Stan's trailer.

Linda jerked and tried to push herself free—and suddenly Stan knew that all deals were off.

"Look at me," he heard himself saying.

"It's no use."

"But I love you."

"I'm no good, Stan."

"I don't believe that."

"I'd ruin your life."

"I don't believe that either."

Stan waited. Outside, Ben slammed both fists against the door. Screen ripped and he roared for Linda to come out and, with a little shudder, she sucked her breath in sharply.

"He'll kill us, Stan."

"Let me worry about that."

"But Ben is not your problem."

"You're wrong," Stan said softly. "He is now."

19

South of town the valley gradually spread to grazed land and scattered cattle ranches. In the distance the highway climbed through foothills to crest the steep mountains and curve down on the other side to the coast. Where the water warmed to surfing and palm-studded beach resorts, below Los Angeles, Stan had the new trailer park filled to capacity for the start of its first full season.

He padded across the bedroom of the manager's apartment and, leaning down before he got into bed with Linda, he kissed her mouth tenderly.

"Well?" he whispered.

"What is it, darling?"

"Did you like your wedding day?"

"I had to wait more than a year."

"But you're an honest woman now."

Stan kissed her again. He reached out to switch off the light.

"Stan, will being married make things different for us?"

"I hope not," he said softly.

His hands caressed her bare shoulders and, as he moved down beside her, she turned into the circle of his arms. Warmth built between them and Stan thought back briefly to the time when they had not been married and the problems they had licked. Ben had turned out to be all bluff, fat mouth and empty threats and, in the end, once Linda started getting her divorce, he had taken his rig and headed back up into the northern California rice country.

Meg had made Sonny manager at the park Stan had left and maybe, for those first bitter weeks alternatingly storming and sulking about Linda, Meg might have consoled herself with Birdie. At least, before Mae and Larry had come out with the news that they were finally producing an heir to his money, Mae had dropped a hint that Birdie had been keeping Meg's bed warm—in any case, Meg had finally rehired Stan.

Perhaps the new blonde Meg had brought back from a trip to Hollywood made the difference. Or, more probably, besides realizing Linda had never really been for her anyway, Meg knew grudges paid no dividends on her investments.

But when Stan remembered how he had almost failed Linda and failed himself, he knew fear did not have to be the numbed terror that Linda had known for life. It could be a small moment of darkness presaging the loss of a job, a dread of walking the streets and not knowing where to turn for your next meal. And the thing to fear most was fear.

"Linda," he murmured.
"I love you, Stan."
"You always say that."
"It's always true."
"Honest?"
"Yes, darling. Honest."
"Then maybe we ought to do something about it."
"I think so too," Linda purred.
"Right now?"
"Yes," she whispered. "Right now."

THE END

Also from STARK HOUSE PRESS:

A Trio of Beacon Books

Marijuana Girl/Call South 3300: Ask for Molly!/The Sex Cure

ISBN: 978-1-94450-89-2

$19.95 Kindle Edition: $5.99

A Beatnik Trio

Like Crazy, Man/The Far-Out Ones/Beat Girl

ISBN: 978-1-951473-13-6

$19.95 Kindle Edition: $5.99

Ingram Content Group UK Ltd.
Milton Keynes UK
UKHW020757280423
420934UK00016B/592